IN THE BLOOD

IN THE BLOOD

A novel

by

Dave Hoing & Roger Hileman

www.penmorepress.com

ISBN-13: 978-1-950586-45-5(Paperback)
ISBN 13:-978-1-950586-44-8(e-book)

BISAC Subject Headings:
FICTION / Historical / Post World War II
FICTION / Literary
FICTION / Music / Jazz
FICTION / Romance/ Historical

Cover Illustration by Christine Horner

Dave Hoing's photo by Diane House
Roger Hileman's photo by Eric Corbin

Address all correspondence to:

Penmore Press LLC
920 N Javelina Pl
Tucson AZ 85748

ACKNOWLEDGMENTS

The authors would like to thank the following people for their editorial and proofreading assistance: Carol Kean, Nora Meierotto, Jim Musser, Karen Nortman, and Bob Schott.

Reviews

Just spent most of the day finishing it because I couldn't put it down. I think it's wonderful.

—Karen Nortman, author of *Time Travel Trailer*

Here there be magic. Even though it's gritty historical fiction, *In the Blood* is a 20th century fairy tale. Hoing and Hileman have a rare gift of taking an improbable premise and stripping us of our disbelief. Their prose leaves no choice, lest we miss out on a great story.

—Carol Kean, reviewer for *Perihelion* and *Steemit*

This book is about music, it's about cultural shifts, and it's about life. *In the Blood* is smartly written, with every musical term and description spot-on.

—Diane Thayer, music educator

In the Blood is a tour de force....

—Donald Schneider, *Midwest Book Reviews*

PART ONE

WHITE BIRD

Chapter 1

K.C. BROWN WAITED IN the wings and practiced the fingerings for "Ko-Ko" on her alto sax. Her clothes and underwear stuck to her like cellophane. Naturally the night of her audition would be the hottest one of the summer, but that was okay. Jazz was supposed to be played hot.

The club, the New Orleans—or Narlins, as everyone called it—had been built before the turn of the century as a vaudeville house. The tiny auditorium smelled like reefer smoke. Drums, an upright piano, and a standup bass had been placed on the stage, although no one was at them.

It was Sunday, and the club was closed. Only two people had come to try out so far, but it was early. Jazz musicians showed up when they showed up. A single light bulb dangled above the stage as the other hopeful, a Negro teenager, was attempting what might once have been "Bird Gets the Worm." He put his soul into it, but the number's lightning tempo was way beyond his abilities. Who would choose such a difficult number for an audition?

K.C. told herself she wasn't nervous, as she sucked on her reed and twisted the mouthpiece back and forth to produce just the right angle for her embouchure. Her life didn't depend on this gig. Nothing depended on it. She had a job, a fiancé, and an apartment of her own. Most girls would be happy with that. And she was, but nothing fulfilled her like music.

Closing her eyes, she calmed herself as she usually did, by imagining her brother Kenny's voice. Kenny had died in the war. *You can do it, Squirt*, he said.

She peeked out from behind the curtain at the judges. In the periphery of the light, two colored men in black suits sat on the same side of a small table across the dance floor. The fat one on the right sported wire-framed glasses, a Cab Calloway mustache, and slicked down hair. An intimidating scowl indicated he was unimpressed.

The second man appeared equally underwhelmed and equally intimidating. Still, K.C. knew it was the fat one she'd have to win over. White or black, all bosses had that same *I-own-you* look.

The teenager finished playing. He gazed at the two men. The two men glared back. "You ain't gonna say nothing?" the boy asked.

Apparently they weren't.

A few awkward moments of silence later he slouched off the stage, brushing K.C. as he passed. If he noticed she was white, he didn't react. He was so distraught he probably didn't notice her at all.

Sucking in a breath of courage, she stepped out from behind the curtain, holding her instrument like a cross to ward off evil. The men were whispering between themselves and shaking their heads. They ignored her.

K.C. cleared her throat.

Boss-man looked up. "Oh, *hell*, no," he said. "Prom's over on the west side, Shirley Temple. Get on back there, and maybe they'll let you march in the halftime show come fall."

She could sense other people in the gloom at the back of the room. Probably the musicians in the band—the ones she hoped to be playing alongside after tonight. "I'm twenty-two," she said.

"My ass. This look like the country club to you?"

Even in the murky light it was obvious there was something wrong with the second man's fingers, some kind of deformity. "Paper said you were looking for an alto sax player," K.C. said.

"Yeah, well, I don't see one up there," Boss-man said.

"Didn't say they couldn't be white, or a girl."

"I'm saying so now. Even if you're good, which you're not, why should we hire a white girl who probably learned her shit from a better black player, when we could hire the better black player?"

"My brother Kenny taught me. He was Charlie Parker good."

He and Badfingers exchanged a look of amusement. "So what I'm hearing is, you're not even the best in your family. Should've been him I'm telling no to. He too scared to come?"

"Can't. North Africa, forty-three."

He paused, like he was going to offer the same old clichéd words of condolence everyone else did, but instead he said, "My people cleaned toilets in the war. What kind of reed you got? Like you'd know the difference."

"A Rico. So you going to let me try out, or what? Me and that boy are the only ones here."

"Plenty of horns in this town."

"Can they take the changes in 'Ko-Ko'?"

Boss-man laughed, a sound like a sputtering engine. "'Take the changes'? Ain't it somethin' how dat white girl do talk jive? What I mean is, the young lady is impressive in her ability to express herself in the appropriate vernacular. Your brother teach you that, too? Go on, you're wasting my time. Spits'd be rolling in his grave, and he's not even dead."

Badfingers leaned toward the fat man. "Nobody can replace Spits, Dwayne, but she must have some kind of balls just coming here tonight. Let's see what she's got."

K.C. took a step forward. "I don't need balls, I got *this*," she said, thrusting her sax toward them.

Tell you what, little White Bird," Boss-man—Dwayne—said. "I'm gonna bring the fellas up here for your number. All you got to do is keep up."

"I play along with my records all the time."

"Ooo-*wee*, you play along with *records*? Guess we ought to sign you up right now."

"Really?"

"This is *live* music, doll-face, and that's a whole different breed of cat."

Four men appeared out of the darkness and climbed the stairs to the stage. The one with the trumpet was handsome, but she didn't like the way he looked at her. Not a leer, more of a stink-eye. As they took their places at the instruments, Badfingers introduced them. "Catfish is the eighty-eighter, Leon's the screamer, Syd's the hide man, and Thump's got the doghouse. I'm Freddie. I'm the boneman, but I ain't playing tonight. This here's Dwayne. What's your name, White Bird?"

"K.C. Brown."

"Kasey?" Dwayne snorted. "You ought to be carrying a tennis racket, not a horn."

"K like in Kansas. C like in City."

Catfish tinkled a few measures of "One-O'Clock Jump" with his right hand. Count Basie? Was he being sarcastic, or just loosening his fingers? He winked at her, but it didn't seem flirtatious.

"Let's get this over with," Dwayne said. "All you kids ever want to play is bop. 'Ko-Ko' it is, boys. Key of B flat minor. You know where B flat is, Little Orphan Annie?"

"My name is *K.C.*" Annoyed, she pressed the octave key and blew him the highest damn B flat in the sax's register and held the note until her lungs gave out.

Atta girl, Squirt.

"Well, you got the pipes," Dwayne said, "but do you have the chops?"

He'd barely spoken the last word when she launched into the intro to "Ko-Ko." Her nervousness disappeared as she let the music carry her. Leon hopped in on trumpet without hesitation, playing in unison an octave up, matching her note-for-note. Next he was supposed to riff alone, but the rest of the band came in instead, skipping the remaining bars of the front, running once through the head and then going straight to the bridge.

That's where they lost K.C. She knew the entire number, but her mind blanked with the unexpected change. That wasn't how the record went. She could see the triumphant twinkle in the musicians' eyes as she struggled to remember her part. They were playing so fast, so confidently, that by the time she found her place in one section, they were on to another. After a few failed attempts, she lowered her sax.

The band continued without her. Leon's trumpet was a battered old thing that blew notes so pure the angels must weep. Syd and Thump pulsed rhythm like sweaty love. Taking the changes, Catfish became a four-handed demon.

When they finished, K.C. gazed helplessly at Dwayne and Freddie.

"Got to fly real fast just to stand still with us, White Bird," Dwayne said.

"They jumped ahead in the piece," K.C. said. "I wasn't ready."

"This is *jazz*, K.C.," Freddie said. "You can't not be ready."

"I can play," she pleaded.

"Not with us," Dwayne said.

She wasn't going to cry, she *wasn't*.

Freddie approached the foot of the stage. He offered her a business card.

She glanced at his fingers as he withdrew his hand. It looked like every one of them except his thumbs had been crushed or wrenched sideways at the first joint. She wondered if there'd been an accident, or he'd been born that way.

The card was simple, black ink on white card stock, with little curlicues highlighting the letters and phone number.

F. D. Ross
DWAYNE HITE PRESENTS
THE BLUENOTES
Swinging the 40s
Venues large or small
WA4-3232

"Forget your records," he said. He sounded almost kind. "That little bit you did? You got something. But it ain't enough to love the music. If it's just gonna be a hobby, might as well put down your horn and go work at the five and dime. You gotta bleed it. And just so you know, next time, if there is a next time, we don't do bop. Think Duke, not Dizzie or Yardbird."

Chapter 2

EVERYONE HAD GONE HOME but Catfish and Freddie. Freddie sat at the same table he'd been at all night, smoking a reefer while 'Fish woodshedded at the piano on stage. Freddie admired the man's talent, even more his stamina. He seemed immune to fatigue. He'd play till 5:00 a.m., go to work slaughtering hogs at 6:00, and be back at Narlins by 7:00 the next night. That left maybe three hours for eating, sleeping, and making little catfishes. He and his wife Janae had five kids, a couple of them under four.

Freddie mopped the back of his neck with a handkerchief. Damn Iowa summers. Damn Iowa weather, period. Only decent times of the year were late spring and early fall. He drew in a mouthful of smoke, watching as his misshapen fingers pulled the joint back. Thirty-one years later, they still pained him. He used to be able to play piano like 'Fish, better, only it was Scott Joplin rag at the Narlins, the colored couples on the dance floor two-stepping that rhythm and the whites trying not to hurt themselves.

He'd never forget his father Lewis's look of horror when he saw Freddie's newly mangled hands.

Daddy, they used a hammer.

Catfish was diddling Euday Bowman's "Twelfth Street Rag." "Hey, Boneman," he said, "you gonna sit there sucking weed all night? Get your ass up here and give me some slide or go the hell home."

To what? he thought. "Man, I hate that song."

"I'll play something else." 'Fish started in on Goodman's "Whistle Blues."

"'Bone's in my locker upstairs. Too lazy to go get it." Once he'd lost the dexterity of his fingers, trombone was the only instrument left to him.

Shay walked out on him a week ago. Probably staying with her mama Nelly. The two didn't get on well, though, so she'd come back. She always did, but the house was hollow without her. Even their cat, Washington, moped.

Freddie was in no hurry to leave. He loved Narlins, the closeness, the dark, the stink. It was like walking back in time. Not that those times were ever that great. They just happened to be *then*, and then was always better than now. Almost always.

'Fish was right. It was late. He crushed the joint on the top of his shoe, stuffed the remainder in his jacket pocket, and stood up. "How do you get away with staying out all night?"

"Nothing to get away with. Janae likes to sleep alone." 'Fish broke into a grin so wide his teeth reflected the single bulb's glare. "Don't mean she gets outta bed when I do come home."

Freddie put on his white Fedora and pulled the brim down. "You sure all them youngsters are yours? I stop by your place twice a week when you're at work."

"Always thought a couple of them looked odd. I just figured they took after her side."

Freddie smiled. "Heading out. Pick up the tempo, man. Maybe we ain't Bird, but 'Whistle Blues'? Damn."

****

If a colored man felt like fighting, all he had to do was walk into Curtis's Garden. It was the least seedy of Waterton's roadhouses, and it did not cater to Negroes. Like everyone else, the owner hired black bands to entertain his white customers, but just try getting a drink between sets. Going in any other time was asking for trouble. Freddie had ended up on his face in the gravel parking lot more than once.

Shay was gone again, and Freddie was in a foul mood. He slowed down as he approached the Garden, thought about stopping, and didn't. Fifteen years ago he'd have vented his frustrations with a good rumble, but fifteen years ago he wasn't fifty. Nowadays the rest of his bones ached near as bad as his fingers, and his body was so worn down he had to rest up after sleeping.

Instead, he drove around with his windows down, hoping the stars and the cooler air would calm him. July nights were steamy, but nothing like the blast furnace of July days. Although he wasn't a cabbie anymore, he still loved driving. It made him feel powerful and free, like he could go anywhere and do anything. His black '40 Ford's rounded fenders made it look like an upside-down bathtub. Maybe not the prettiest design, but the car handled well. The heater took up most of the middle of the dash. The speedometer was a narrow slit with the numbers in a straight line. Sometimes he had trouble reading them in the day, but they lit up when his headlights were on—not that he'd ever paid much attention to the speed limit anyway. The odometer showed over 190,000 miles. The Bluenotes usually rode to out-of-town gigs in an old school bus now, but he'd put plenty of miles on the Ford back when everyone had to find their own way.

Even the stars were ugly tonight. The constellations filtered through the miasma pumped out by the west-side factories. Freddie pulled to the curb in front of the Diminished Fifth, a dilapidated jazz bar on East Sixth and Franklin, not too far from his house in Smoky Row.

It was always the same thing. *Why don't you make more money? Least the taxi was steady work. Who you screwing now? I know you're screwing somebody. I hate this town. We gonna be treated like niggers anyway, might as well take me to Chicago.*

In view of her former line of work, accusing anyone else of screwing around was funny, in a sad sort of way.

Freddie didn't understand the attraction of Chicago. He doubted she'd ever been there. She was from Spring Valley, Mississippi, a village so small that the sign saying you're entering Spring Valley and the one saying you're leaving it was the same sign. If he was going to move to a big city, it would be New Orleans or Kansas City, where the jazz was hot, or New York, where it was burning down the town. Chicago had the scene, too, but he just didn't like it there. Same heat as Iowa in summer, only worse, with its thousands of miles of asphalt drawing in the sun and spitting out fire. Same cold in winter, too, and a couple million more maniacs who didn't know how to drive on snow.

Truth was, backwards as Waterton was, Freddie liked it here. Forty-five, fifty thousand people, enough size to keep them from getting bored, not enough to swallow them whole. The white folks here didn't like blacks any more than they did in Biloxi or Selma, but most were too stupid even to be good racists.

Freddie opened his car door. Stench from the Diminished Fifth spilled out onto the sidewalk, weed and tobacco smoke, vomit and beer. Leon was probably inside drinking. Maybe Syd was with him, even though he never touched booze or drugs. He was a straight arrow who preferred to spend most of his free time with his wife Marlye and son Nat. Thump would be scoring horse in the back, or over at Pamela's Triangle Club, a strip joint better known as Grits 'n' Tits.

He peered through the screen door and saw Screech and Ironhead, two semi-permanent members of the Bluenotes. They couldn't always be counted on to rehearse, but they showed up for gigs. That was a problem when there were new charts, but somehow Dwayne made it work.

The usual stale music blared from the jukebox, because no self-respecting live band would book the place. God only knew why real musicians wasted their nights at this hole.

Yet here he was. Maybe it was the greasy ambience. His wife had left. Yeah, so? At the Fifth he could hear a hundred stories that made his life seem blessed. Sometimes he needed to know he wasn't feeding from the bottom of the trough.

Ain't coming back this time, she'd said, same as always, and then whack, a palm upside his ear, and she was out the door. He'd never raised his hand to a woman, but that didn't stop Shay from slapping him when she had a mind to. Never hard, though sometimes he caught a fingernail. No nookie, no cooking, the temper of a rabid coon, and still he missed her.

Hell of it was, he couldn't even remember what he'd done this time.

He caught sight of Leon at the bar, smiling and using his looks to impress some woman. Screamers always got the chicks, although Leon was more about the set-up than the follow-through. All he wanted was the attention. He was married, after all.

Freddie intended to drink one beer and leave, but didn't even do that. Reefer relaxed him better and eased his body's pain. He could blow weed at home without enduring that hideous jukebox.

Anyway, Washington would be hungry.

****

He stretched out naked on the bed and puffed on a joint. A fan on the chair next to him was on high, but all it did was buffet him with hot air. His back stuck to the mattress and his thighs to each other.

He turned on the shadeless floor lamp, the bedroom's only light.

Washington perched next to him and licked her paws. She had the most interesting coloring, dark gray on top with vertical tan stripes down her back and neck, light gray on the bottom with dark stripes circling each of her legs, and a speckled belly. Shay had insisted on naming her Washington. He had no idea why. Washington didn't look very presidential to him. When he reached up to stroke her whiskers, she hissed and batted at his hand.

Even the cat was mad at him. He pushed her onto the floor and sat on the edge of the bed to look through the *Record*. Three weeks in, the Berlin blockade was still big news. The son of one of Waterton's councilmen was involved with the airlift. More about Tito's break with Stalin, and the implications for the rest of Europe. Freddie didn't know who Tito was. Locally, Waterton was getting a professional basketball team, slated to begin play in the '49-'50 season with the new National Basketball Association. Negotiations at Roth's were breaking down, and a strike seemed inevitable. Catfish and Leon worked there.

Scary to think how many kids 'Fish would have if he was home more than three hours a day.

Freddie smoked the joint down to the nub and dropped the remainder in the ashtray. One time he'd dozed off with a roach in his hand. It had fallen to the floor and singed a small spot in the carpet. Shay had carried on like he'd burned down the house. She forbade him to patch the hole, as a constant reminder of his slovenly ways.

It did teach him to be more careful.

Washington mewed and pounced on something under the bed, a spider or one of those creepy centipede-y things. Or maybe it was just a thread blown around by the fan. Never could tell what would capture that cat's interest.

Freddie tossed the paper down and turned to his side, letting the hot air wash over his face like a healing balm.

Chapter 3

TONIGHT K.C. AND HER fiancé Jack Schoonover were going to see *Abbott and Costello Meet Frankenstein* at the Waterton Theater, but today she was serving Green Rivers and ice cream sundaes behind the soda fountain at Dale's Grocery. Jack was one of two assistant managers. Everybody knew they were an item, so, for propriety's sake, whenever they worked together Dale scheduled her there, where she'd be under Austin Tyler's supervision.

A Negro boy approached her. K.C. knew most of her customers, but this kid wasn't familiar. He was small, his head not reaching the counter. "Chocolate malt with three scoops," he said. "And not two. I know how to count."

He showed her a dime, of which he seemed quite proud.

Three scoops were fifteen cents, and Austin didn't like coloreds in the store anyway. "Where's your mama?" K.C. asked.

"Outside. She gimme this for sweeping the kitchen floor."

This look like the country club, Shirley Temple?

K.C. was still angry about the old switcheroo the band had pulled on her last night. Fat boss-man Dwayne was the specific target of her ire, but at the moment all Negroes were being torched by the fallout. "Nickel a scoop," she said.

The kid put the dime on the counter. Apparently he could add one and one and one and come up with three, but not multiply three times five.

"Hey," Austin said. He was just over in produce, and must have overheard the conversation. He glared at her as if saying *What do you think you're doing?*

"Three scoops is fifteen cents," K.C. said to the boy. "That's ten. I can give you two."

She immediately regretted her harshness when his eyes went all watery. It wasn't the kid's fault Dwayne was a jerk. She started to make the sundae, but Austin stepped in after the second scoop. "You gonna pay the extra nickel?"

"He's just a little boy," she said.

"I don't care if he's the king of Africa. Fifteen cents or two scoops. Dump it in a Dixie Cup and get his black ass out of here."

K.C. took a nickel from her apron, a tip left to her by her last customer, a boy named Davy who happened to be over the moon for her, and set it next to the dime. "Happy?"

Austin answered by going back to primping the lettuce.

K.C. gave the kid his three scoops, then added the milk and malt powder. Now more disgusted with Austin than Dwayne, she put a fourth scoop in a separate cup and whispered, "This is for your mama."

"Thank you, ma'am!"

The kid scooted out of the store before Austin saw that he had two cups. When he was gone K.C. pocketed her nickel and rang up a dime in the register.

Ma'am. Well, she probably did look old to him.

****

"Ch-Ch-Ch-Ch-Chick," Lou Costello rasped for about the millionth time. Every time he was scared he stuttered the name of Bud Abbot's character in the movie. *Ch-Ch-Ch-Ch-Chick.* K.C. hated it. She didn't find Abbot and Costello funny, and monster movies were just dumb. But Jack liked them, and she loved Jack. Besides, the theater was air-cooled.

When they went out they always sat in the back corner where he could put his arm around her without other people seeing. If the place was nearly empty, like tonight, they might neck. Who cared what was on the screen then?

Still, *Easter Parade* was over at the Paramount, just released last week. Irving Berlin's music was too tame, but she was a sucker for sappy love stories, and that Fred Astaire could really dance.

"Having fun, Kase?" Jack said, nuzzling her ear. As Dwayne had surmised, her name really was Kasey, but she spelled it K.C., Kansas City Brown, a good jazz name. He'd also been right about her age. She'd just turned nineteen two weeks before.

Although Jack hadn't formally asked her to marry him yet, it was a given. He was already talking about a house, kids, and a teaching job after college. A few times she'd managed to sneak him past the landlord, Mr. Somers, to spend the night in her apartment. She was excited about their future, but, man, could Bird take those changes!

That little bit you did, you got something....

Bela Lugosi's casket opened with a creak. Predictably, Costello sputtered "Ch-Ch-Ch-Ch-Chick." K.C. pretended to laugh. Jack "accidentally" brushed her breast. The casket lid closed before Abbott saw Dracula, and once again Costello looked the fool.

Sigh.

****

The next morning Jack twiddled his thumbs in the back row where the trombone section sat during the school year. He'd rather be making out in K.C.'s apartment, especially since she hadn't been in the mood to invite him over last night. "Why not play music people *like*?" he said. "You know me, I got nothing against Negroes, but who listens to jazz?"

"I do," she said.

More than a year after graduation, K.C. still used the West High School band room to practice her sax. It was the only place she could go where the noise wouldn't bother anyone. Her apartment walls were too thin, and she wasn't welcome in her parents' home these days. Mr. Pierson thought highly of her from her three years as section leader and president of the West band. Since it was summer and there weren't any other rehearsals, he'd let her in every Saturday she wasn't working, and most Monday, Tuesday, and Thursday nights for a couple of hours after supper. He encouraged her—keeping his own phonograph here for her to play along with—but had quit trying to coach her technique. What he liked and what she played were different things. Besides, as he'd admitted early in her junior year, "You surpass me."

The school board forbade her to bring anyone with her when she was in the building after hours, but Mr. Pierson didn't object on the few occasions Jack tagged along. He was right next door in the music office working on next fall's marching band drills in case Jack got frisky.

K.C. sat on the piano bench and assembled her sax. Piano was the only instrument she'd ever been formally trained on. She'd taken lessons since she was four, years spent learning not only notes but the keys, time signatures, chord progressions, structures, and theory. And everyone told her she had that natural knack that couldn't be taught by anybody.

"I'm not saying I don't like your playing," Jack said, "but would a little Eddy Arnold hurt you once in a while?"

K.C. strapped the sax around her neck and started pounding the piano's keys, exaggerating the country rhythm to everybody's—every-*white*-body's—favorite song this summer, "Bouquet of Roses." She didn't sing often or particularly well, but she didn't care. When she finished the intro and came to the verse, she warbled in a purposely obnoxious twang. "I'm sendin' you a big bouquet of ro-woe-woe-woe-ses...'"

Jack, oblivious to her sarcasm, perked up. "Yeah, like that."

"You can't be serious," she said. "How does that even compare to this?"

She picked up her sax and blew through "Ko-Ko" the way she'd intended to the other night at Narlins. She stuck every note. When she finished she was exhausted.

You gotta bleed it.

Jack looked at her with genuine perplexity. "Well, it's really fast."

Chapter 4

JAN GARBER AND HIS band performed at Waterton's Electrical Park Ballroom in the third week of July. He wasn't big time like Goodman, but his too-sweet dance music was popular on ballroom circuits throughout the Midwest. The *Record* had run full-page ads two Sundays in a row. Local bands never even got a mention unless it was for charity.

The Bluenotes played Electrical Park three or four times a year. The admission policy wasn't as restrictive as Curtis's Gardens, but by tradition and preference the audiences here were still mostly white. Freddie and Dwayne sat at the back, near the exit. Glasses low on his nose, Dwayne took notes, always looking for lines to borrow for his own charts. He had the best ear in the business. Garber's band was playing "Stars Fell on Alabama" while two or three dozen couples slow-danced in the sawdust.

"Man," Dwayne said, "time somebody retired that number."

"Horns could be tighter," Freddie said. "None of them are good as Spits."

"Nobody is." Dwayne set his pencil down. "Bass line's for shit. This whole damn chart's right out of the Fake Book."

Freddie called his attention to the couples. "Notice anything about them?"

"I don't know, Boneman, the way they're moving, looks like they're in pain."

"That's just how white folks dance. What I mean is, they're old. Ain't one of them under fifty."

"Neither are you."

Freddie fumbled to light a cigarette, tobacco this time. Electrical Park was air-cooled, but somehow he'd worked up a sweat just sitting around. Maybe he had a fever. "Swing's running on fumes, Dwayne. It's boppers and crooners now."

"We got Ironhead."

"That's the good news. The bad news is that we got Ironhead."

"You saying we ought to hire us a Sinatra? Hell, Leon had to play that slow, his lips'd fall off his face."

Freddie took a drag and smiled. "I like swing, too, but that white girl got it right."

"White girl?"

"Horn player that tried to do Bird at Narlins. That's what kids want."

"Can't dance to that shit."

Freddie nodded toward the white people on the floor. "Like them?"

"It does hurt to watch," Dwayne admitted.

****

Tim Piper was the manager of Electrical Park. He stopped by Freddie and Dwayne's table between sets. He smiled when he noticed Dwayne taking notes. "Lifting lines again?"

"Nothing to lift so far," Dwayne said. "What do we owe the honor?"

"Still looking for an alto sax?"

"Bet you're gonna tell me where I can find one."

Piper smiled. The fluorescent lighting made his skin look paler than it already was. He said Garber's manager knew a talent agent in Des Moines who represented a horn man that might be interested in playing with the Bluenotes.

"You know a guy who knows a guy who knows a guy?" Freddie said.

"The kid did a set with Satchmo once."

"Isn't that sweet," Dwayne said. He took off his glasses, breathed on the lenses, and cleaned them with his sleeve. "Breathing Satchmo's air doesn't make him a player."

"From what I hear, this kid is."

"He got a name?"

Piper handed Dwayne a scrap of paper.

Dwayne snickered. "Darwin Kieffer? *Darwin*?"

Piper shrugged. "Maybe he's got a jazzy nickname, like Catfish and Thump."

"If he's so good," Freddie said, "why would he come here? Kansas City's not much farther from Des Moines than Waterton."

"You need a horn man or not? Call the number."

"What's in it for you?" Dwayne said. "Finder's fee?"

Piper shook his head. "Half your usual rate next time you play here."

"You don't pay shit now."

"How else could I afford Garber?"

"Yeah, that's what I thought." Dwayne shoved the paper back at him. "The hell with that. Your boy Darwin's ever in town, tell him to try out same as everyone else, and you're still paying our price."

****

There'd been rain earlier, finally breaking the heat spell. It was still misting, just heavy enough to need the wipers, but not enough to keep the rubber from squeaking across the glass. Dwayne didn't drive, so Freddie dropped him off at his house on Oneida Street.

Kid who jammed with Satchmo. Right. They sat through Garber's sugar water for *that*?

One thing, with all those old white folks, Electrical Park shows got over early. It wasn't 10:30 yet. He decided to swing by Narlins. Screech and Ironhead were scheduled. Screech was guitar first and then trumpet, good but never ambitious enough to explore better options. Ironhead played tenor sax by trade but sang when doing gigs with Screech, and sometimes with the Bluenotes. He had a voice that drew the ladies and a personality that drove them away.

When Freddie arrived the parking lot was almost empty. A few people were drinking at the bar, but no one was dancing because no band was playing. The owner was a wiry black woman whose father had wanted a boy. Her real name was Rufus, but she went by Ruthie. Her husband, Big Daddy Johnston, had died three years back, leaving Narlins to her.

Freddie found her sitting alone at a table doing the books. "Where is everyone?"

"Ironhead didn't show, and Screech wouldn't play without him. You look like hell."

"Feeling my age." A young white couple was sitting near the edge of the dance floor, the boy looking perturbed, the girl sad. Both had beer bottles. "They old enough to be in here?"

Ruthie glanced at them and shrugged. "What do I care? I'm losing my ass. City takes away my liquor license, so what?"

Syd's drums and 'Fish's piano were permanent fixtures on the stage. Whoever was performing on a given night was free to use them. Freddie pointed toward the piano. "Mind?"

"Nothing but gravity holding your ass to that chair."

Freddie climbed the steps and sat at the old upright. It was bigger than the Baldwin Acrosonic his mother Beatrice had left him, but just as beat up, its wood scraped and dented, its ivory mostly gone. His hands hovered over the keys. His fingers had been twisted in different directions, making it difficult for him to play anything but chord clusters. His thumbs were undamaged, though, and if he bent his wrists at just the right angle he could sometimes compensate enough to play slow tunes. That eliminated the rapid syncopation of the ragtime he'd loved as a kid.

He pressed the keys to approximate "'Michael, Row the Boat Ashore.'" His finger joints screamed at the smallest pressure. Even at a glacial pace, he flubbed several notes. Shay loved this old spiritual, one of the few things that could calm her angry soul. But she was gone, and his hands were broken. He decided to sing. His voice lacked Ironhead's alluring gruffness, but he could hold his own.

"Michael, row the boat ashore, hallelujah...."

The few people present groaned. People came to Narlins for jazz, not old Negro spirituals. Freddie didn't care. He played, and missed notes, and sang.

"Michael, row the boat ashore, hallelu-u-u-jah...."

He heard agitated whispers from the white couple just below the stage, then footsteps approaching. He kept going, thinking *Shay*, thinking, *This ain't 1917*, thinking, *Daddy, they used a hammer.*

"There you'll hear the trumpet sound, hallelujah...."

Someone touched his shoulder. "Mr. Ross?"

A girl's voice.

Freddie glanced up. White girl, brown hair, maybe five-five, a little too thin. Still had her bottle of beer, not a drop missing from it. He pushed her hand away. "The hell?"

"Sorry about your fingers," she said.

"Ain't your business to be sorry," he said. "Do I know you?"

"K.C.," she said. "I was hoping you'd be here tonight."

"Huh?"

"White Bird."

Her. Claimed she was twenty-two. She'd go to jail, she got caught drinking in here. Her boyfriend, too. Or would, if he wasn't already storming out of the building. "He don't look too happy," Freddie said.

"That's Jack," she said. "He was mad I made him come. He'll get over it."

She took a sip of beer, and made a face.

"Put that shit down," Freddie said, "before Ruthie calls the cops. Carrying around a Schlitz don't make you grown up."

She set the bottle on top of the piano. "I don't like it anyway."

"What do you want?"

"You need an alto sax."

"That's Dwayne's job. I'm just the boneman."

"You have a business card."

"For bookings. Don't mean I do the hiring."

"You said I've got something."

Freddie turned back to the piano keys. "You're the one thinks noodling along with records makes you a player. That don't cut it. You got to play live with other musicians, make us feel what you feel, trade fours, give and take. If you don't know what we're thinking before we think it, then you ain't fit to be on stage with us."

"I can do that."

"You learned all that in what, a couple of days?"

"I've been practicing."

"Jesus Christ." Freddie switched to a different number. "Amazing grace," he sang, "how sweet the sound, that saved a wretch like me."

The girl touched his shoulder again. "Teach me."

"Get your hand off me. You trying to get me lynched?" She stepped back and stared at him so hopefully that he dropped his eyes. He balled his deformed hands into something like fists and pounded the keys. "It look like I can play horn?"

"Hey, Freddie," Ruthie called from her table, "Miss Snowflake giving you trouble?"

"She was just leaving."

"Call Dwayne," the girl pleaded. "Give me another chance."

"Why's a white chick wanna jam with a colored band?"

"Black players are the best."

"You planning on turning black anytime soon?" Freddie stood up and headed toward the stairs.

Without asking permission, K.C. took his place at the piano. She played her own version of "Amazing Grace," a slow, heartbreaking version that made Freddie pause. The notes flowed and weaved and, in their quiet power, expanded to fill the entire room. He listened, a little choked up, until she finished, remembering how Mama used to play it. This kid did it better, from a place in her soul that other people never reached. "Holy shit, girl, where's that coming from?"

"Inside me. Piano and sax. Just give me a chance."

That broke Freddie's rapturous mood, which annoyed

him. "You was doing good till you started talking again."

"What am I supposed to do?"

"Stick to what you know. Playing ivories like that, you could make real money entertaining rich white folks. The Bluenotes is just a down and dirty swing band for down and dirty people. What you want is crazy."

"Is not."

"You got a union card?"

"Do I need one?"

"Ain't getting anywhere otherwise."

"Where do I get one?"

"Easiest way's through Dwayne, and you know how that's gonna go."

"I'm good enough. I know I am."

She wouldn't give up. Freddie tried a different tack. He jabbed a bent finger at her. "I don't care if the sun shines out your ass, girl, you ever thought what it'd *mean* to play with us?"

"What do you mean, 'what would it mean'?"

"White don't like black, and they don't like anyone who does. Know what else? Black don't like white all that much, neither. You play with us, your own people gonna call you a nigger-loving whore. *My* people gonna call you a nigger-loving whore. So. You a nigger-loving whore?"

"Stop saying that."

"Don't like my language, little White Bird? Going on the road with us old cats ain't like charm school. We sweat and stink. We drink beer till we're stupid. Thump shoots horse and we all blow weed. Well, except Syd. We piss against the wall, if we can make it that far. We fart and then laugh about it like schoolboys. Think 'nigger-loving whore' is bad? You oughta hear us when we really get on about women. We go into *detail*. See what I'm saying?"

"You talk dirty—so? I know all the words."

She was still looking at him like this thing was possible.

"Don't give me that face," he said. "Then there's sleeping. No decent hotel'll take us, so we usually got to stay in places no self-respecting roaches and rats go. Restaurants make us eat in the kitchen. You ready for that?"

She looked at her feet. "I don't care, long as I can play."

Freddie sighed. "Dwayne says no, and you wanna come back less than a week later and try again? Nobody gets good that fast. A year ain't enough. Two, maybe. But now? No way."

"You'll have a new horn man by then."

"We better. There's other bands."

The girl—White Bird—K.C.—looked like he'd just cut into her chest and eaten her heart. Like he'd shit on her dream. Which he had.

"I want to play with the Bluenotes," she said.

"Now you're just being stubborn. Anyway, Bird is bop. We play swing."

"Swing is okay."

"Dwayne's a genius, maybe Syd, but the rest of us ain't all that special. So what is it? 'Cause we're the only ones put a ad in the paper?"

"That, too."

"Uh-huh." His trousers were loose at the waist. He pulled them up. Couldn't seem to keep on the weight lately. "Your boyfriend take off?"

"He's waiting in the lot."

"I'll walk you out." Freddie led her down the stairs, across the dance floor, and past Ruthie, who glanced up with a raised eyebrow. They paused near the exit. "Start with licks from tunes you know, mess around with them. Memorize a bunch, so they're ready when you need them. Learn to play this lick against that line. This note off that one. Can't do that with records."

"How can I learn all that if I don't have a band to practice with?"

Freddie shrugged. "Hell of a thing, ain't it? Start your own."

"With who?" She looked like she was drowning in air. "Mr. Ross, I work in a *grocery store*."

Chapter 5

THE MIST HAD INCREASED to a heavy drizzle. Jack was waiting in the lot in his shiny red 1947 Dodge pickup truck. His father had bought it for him to commute over to Iowa State Teachers College, where he was in his sophomore year. He wanted to teach high school economics.

K.C. slid in next to him and slammed the door.

"I take it he said no," Jack said.

"Shut up."

"What did you expect?"

"Shut up."

Jack turned on the wipers and shifted into first. As he pulled out onto the street, K.C. slumped down on the seat.

"Well, *I* know you're good enough."

You don't know your butt from a hole in the ground, she thought. He'd played violin in high school orchestra, but never made it to first chair.

She didn't answer him, and they rode in silence until they'd crossed the Fourth Street Bridge over the Oak River to the west side.

"Can you sneak me into your place tonight? I know how to cheer you up."

K.C. glared at him. Boys in general, and Jack in particular, could be intensely stupid. *Yeah, my life just went to hell, and you're going to make it all better by screwing me.* "Shut up," she said.

Jack sighed. "I didn't mean *that*. I thought we could listen to *Ozzie and Harriet*."

He turned on Park Street and again onto Wellington. Her apartment was in Wellington Court, a complex that sounded a lot fancier than it was. He stopped in front of her building and leaned over to peck her on the cheek. "I work at nine tomorrow, so you're at the soda fountain again. Take your break with me?"

K.C. snatched her purse from the floor and got out. She lifted her face to the mist. What she needed was a good thunderstorm, lots of thunder, lightning, and wind. Jack looked at her, waiting for an answer.

"Why not," she said, and closed the door.

****

K.C. didn't have any female friends—male, either, for that matter—so when she needed a shoulder, she usually turned to the younger of her two older sisters, Krissy. It was nearing midnight. She stood at the pay phone at the end of the hallway, debating if it was too late to call. Krissy worked six to four as a secretary at the Iowa Cream Separator Company, so she'd have to be up by 4:30 to bathe, do her hair, and put on her makeup. K.C. got as far as putting the nickel in and dialing the first three numbers before hanging up and hitting the coin return. She retrieved the nickel and checked her mailbox—empty, as usual—before trudging up three flights of stairs to apartment 4B.

The key was worn nearly smooth and often stuck in the lock. Mr. Somers had promised to make her a new one, but, then, he'd promised to fix the dripping faucet, too. The apartment was cheap, but it was furnished. It even had a refrigerator. K.C. wiggled the key until she heard the click. Her apartment was a dump, its floorboards warping, its patchy wallpaper painted over with a color that might once have been brown. She'd just washed her sheets, so the place smelled of Dreft. They were hanging up to dry over her kitchen chairs.

K.C. took off her shoes and left them next to the door. Despite the cool air outside, it was hot and clammy inside. She opened the only window in her apartment.

A car drove by, its headlights reflecting off the wet pavement. The drizzle was now a light rain. She loved the sound of rain almost as much as she loved music.

She took the pins out of her hair and went into the bathroom. At least her apartment had one. Some places shared a single toilet between all of the residents. She couldn't imagine how disgusting that must be.

We piss against the wall, if we can make it that far.

When she finished in the bathroom, K.C. walked the four steps to her bedroom to change. She kept a framed picture of Kenny on her dresser. He was so handsome in his Army uniform, not smiling at the camera, to make himself look tougher. She loved looking at him, even when it made her sad. He was still her brother, though, so she lay his picture face down when she changed clothes or had Jack over. There were some things brothers just weren't meant to see.

She wore boy's pajamas, like she had as a kid. She stripped down to her panties and put the top on first. It had a red plaid design like a lumberjack's shirt, only made of cotton. K.C. never understood why men's clothes had their buttons on the wrong side. Did the sexes really need to be opposite even in that?

Next she pulled on the bottoms, lifting them slowly to enjoy the smooth feel of the fabric against her legs. No matter how bad her mood, getting into her jammies always felt sensual. They gave her the same pleasant shiver she got when she first eased into a bathtub of hot water. The little slit in front of the bottoms was funny, though. When she was little she used to reach inside and stick her thumb out as if it was a boy's thingy—which was the only term she had for it then.

Must be weird to be a guy.

The thought brought a momentary smile, a reprieve in an otherwise crappy day. She sat on the bed. Her sax was in its case on her dresser, and there went her smile. She figured she wouldn't need it tonight, and she didn't.

We play swing.

Okay. She was fond enough of Duke Ellington, her favorite of his being "I Got it Bad (And That Ain't Good)." "It Don't Mean a Thing If It Ain't Got That Swing" was catchy, too. She reached over and took out the sax, leaving the reed in the case. The instrument was always clean, the brass spotless and shiny. Popping the pads, she did the fingerings for "I Got It Bad." It wasn't as challenging as Charlie Parker's riffs, but she still got goose bumps as she imagined the orchestra coming up around her.

This was what she wanted. This was her dream.

You got to play live with other musicians.

K.C. stopped her imaginary concert. Most of her old high school bandmates had scattered to various colleges, or gotten jobs, or married, or gotten jobs *and* married. Anyway, they didn't understand Negro music. They were fantastic with "Begin the Beguine" or "Stardust," but, then, Porter and Carmichael were white.

You got a union card?

That had to be bullshit. Kenny had never had one, and he'd done shows all over town.

K.C. sighed. Nobody understood her desire to play with a colored band. Sometimes not even her. Certainly Jack didn't, and—other than herself—he was the least prejudiced person she knew.

Jack.

Jack, Jack, Jack. He represented every girl's dream: a house, a family, a dog in the yard. While he taught economics, she could acquiesce to her parents' wishes and go to business school to become a secretary like Krissy. Or she could just stay home, make babies, and vacuum her floors with the latest Hoover.

Yet would the housewife gig really be so bad? It had worked out all right for all the other girls she knew.

And she was positive she loved Jack.

"'That's the story of, that's the glory of love.'" She didn't know why the Goodman tune suddenly popped into her head. That song always made her sad.

K.C. put the sax away and fell back on the bed. Sticking her thumb out through the slit in her pajama bottoms, she thought, Peek-a-boo, little thingy.

Chapter 6

FOR YEARS FREDDIE HAD made ends meet by driving a taxi, but too many speeding tickets, illegal lane changes, and run red lights cost him his job. A small savings account left to him by his father hadn't lasted long. At least his parents' house in Smoky Row—his house now—was free and clear, but he still needed money for food, utilities, gas, car tune-ups, property taxes, and reefer.

Luckily, Dwayne was good to him. Too good. Even when the Bluenotes weren't getting gigs, like now, he kept Freddie on the payroll. Said the booking agent got paid no matter what. Well, Freddie did have the business cards, but he suspected Dwayne's generosity was more a result of friendship and charity.

But then, he could afford to be generous. Dwayne wasn't nationally famous, but he'd been publishing his scores around the Midwest for years, and every time someone bought his sheet music or a band played one of his charts, he got royalties.

Freddie rummaged through his old monitor-top fridge for something to eat. The appliance was an original 1927 model. Aside from an occasional leak, it was good as new. He found some ham slices, cheese, and Miracle Whip. Using week-old bread, he made himself a sandwich, then went to sit in his rocker.

His mother had passed away in '37, two years before his father. Her old Baldwin piano stood against the west wall where it had always been, a shrine to the woman who'd sparked his interest in music. He wouldn't insult her memory by playing it with his disfigured hands. When the urge came over him, like tonight, he used the upright at Narlins. Even so, he asked Dwayne over every few months to tune it for him.

Washington hopped onto his lap, snatched a piece of ham, and scurried into the bedroom. He'd have to clean her cat box today. When its smell was strong enough for him to notice, it had to be bad.

He considered turning on the radio. Some days early in the morning or late at night he could pick up a Chicago station that played jazz. Usually it was white jazz like Shaw, Goodman, or Beneke, but music was music.

Instead, he finished his sandwich and nodded off, thinking about that poor white girl who wanted to be black.

****

He woke to someone pounding on his door and calling his name. The sound startled him, and he nearly bolted from his chair. "The hell?" he cried. "Hold on."

Harold "Toad" McLemore, Thump's brother, was on the porch, jittery and wired like he was dancing in fire. "Fuck, man," he said, "ya gotta come."

"What's going on?"

"Thump."

"Shit, he O.D. again?"

"It's bad, man—foaming spit out his nose and mouth. His

whole body's jerking."

"Where is he?"

"Over at Dwayne's."

"Anybody call a ambulance?"

"Dwayne said get you. You got a car."

Freddie was dressed only in his underwear and a T-shirt. He pulled on a pair of jeans and grabbed his keys. "What time is it?"

"Hell, man, I dunno. Noon?"

They rushed down the steps and jumped into Freddie's Ford. "How long he been down?"

Toad stared at him wildly. "What's it matter?—just *go*."

Freddie started the car and backed out, then slammed the gas and sped toward Oneida Street. He was nearly out of gas, but all he could think was *Thump, you stupid nigger,* and *Goddamn, Dwayne, you better not've been letting him shoot horse at your place.*

****

Freddie had known Thump for two years before learning his real name was Earl McLemore. Thump wasn't many heartbeats from death when Dwayne and Toad loaded him into the backseat. His left arm was pocked with needle marks, from above the crook of his elbow down. Dwayne got in front next to Freddie, while Toad sat in back holding Thump's head. Straight, Thump played as good a doghouse as anyone in town. High, he didn't know a standup bass from a fencepost. He was a lost soul that everyone seemed to love. No one knew if he'd lost himself before the heroin or because of it.

The only hospital on the east side was Allen, a couple of miles down the road.

Dwayne was sweating something fierce, so much his

lenses steamed up. Thump was worse. His throat made gurgling sounds.

Freddie blew through three lights, praying his gas would hold out, and that the cops were anywhere else. It did, and they were, and with his gauge below empty, he whipped into the lot next to the Allen emergency room.

He and Toad lugged Thump into the hospital. He was still breathing when the orderlies brought a stretcher for him. They wheeled him to the back, with Toad right behind.

Freddie hadn't put on shoes when he'd left home. The nurses wouldn't let him go in any farther in bare feet, so he went back outside to his car, where he kept old boots that he used when fishing.

Dwayne had moved to the grassy area that surrounded the parking lot on three sides. He leaned against a wellmanicured tree and pounded his fist into his palm.

Freddie joined him, grateful for the shade and a nice breeze. "You ain't going in?"

Dwayne just looked at him. Freddie had never seen his friend so shook up. His barrel chest heaved and his little mustache twitched. He clenched his jaw like his head was about to explode.

Dwayne, always in control, was not in control now. He sank to his knees beneath the tree.

"Now ain't the time," Freddie said, "but we're gonna need to talk about this."

****

Several hours later Freddie was in the waiting room with Toad when the doctor gave them the news: Thump was going to live. Freddie rushed out to tell Dwayne, who'd been too distraught to go into the hospital when Thump's survival was in doubt.

By then, half the jazz musicians in Waterton had gathered in the parking lot. Even Catfish and Leon got the word somehow, and left Roth's early. There were a lot of glum faces, and a lot of angry ones.

Freddie whistled to get their attention. "Thump's okay," he said, and the cheering began. The crowd had brought beer, to either celebrate or mourn. They opened the bottles like beer was champagne.

What had started as a deathwatch turned into a party, so, naturally, somebody called the police. When the squad car rolled up, most of the crowd scattered, leaving only the core group of the band behind.

"We got crows on the lawn," the officer said. He leaned on the hood of his car with his hand on his gun. "You boys having fun?"

"We ain't breaking no laws," Leon said.

"Bet I can find one." The cop looked at a beer bottle that had been dropped on the grass. "For instance."

"That ain't ours," Catfish said.

"Right."

Freddie had been in jail before, more than once. Since no day was a good one to get arrested, he stepped forward to make peace. He motioned toward the hospital and explained, more or less, about Thump, without mentioning the overdose. "He's gonna make it. We're just happy."

"Go be happy somewhere else."

"Yes, sir," Freddie said, but before he could be happy somewhere else he had to get gas. He had a five-gallon gas can in his trunk, but, of course, when he needed it, it was empty. Dwayne, Syd, and Leon went inside to wait until Thump was well enough to see them. Freddie and Catfish walked four blocks to the nearest filling station.

"Thump's not always gonna be this lucky," 'Fish said.

"I don't know," Freddie said. His feet chafed against the boot leather. "Maybe the best thing for him's just to give it up."

"We can't lose another player, Boneman. Spits was bad enough."

"More important things than the Bluenotes."

"Like what?"

****

Freddie had bruises on both arms, probably from Thump's thrashing about. He'd driven the others home, then returned to Allen.

A tube pumped oxygen down Thump's throat. Tape held a needle in place in the back of his left hand. It attached to a tube that led to an IV bag that dripped clear fluid.

"Hell of a time finding a decent vein," the doctor had said earlier. "Hasn't seemed to be a problem for him, though."

Thump had his usual two-day stubble. His skin, normally darker than Freddie's, appeared almost pale. He was breathing easy, though. His eyes were half open.

"Goddamn Negro," Freddie said.

Thump shifted his gaze a fraction of an inch. "Boneman?" The tube in his throat garbled his speech. The effort made him wince.

"Yeah. You gotta stop this shit."

"Why?"

"Look at you."

"Nothing to see here, folks, move along."

Freddie smiled. "Horse is gonna kill you someday."

Thump closed his eyes. "When was I ever alive? Go on home, 'Bone. I'm tired."

Chapter 7

DALE'S GROCERY WAS a family business that had been on West Third since the early 1900s. It was located in a transitional neighborhood between the nice homes to the west and the shabby ones to the east, just over the river. Rumor was that A&P was trying to buy out some of the small grocers in Waterton, including Dale's, and relocate them to a supermarket on the edge of town where they could build a big parking lot. But the current owner, Dale Rodgers III, was holding out.

K.C. didn't care one way or the other. She hoped to be long gone from the retail business by then.

She hadn't had a customer at the soda fountain all morning, so Austin sent her to face the shelves. It was her least favorite job, more tedious even than stocking. To make matters worse, Davy, the kid who had a crush on her, was hanging around pestering her. He couldn't be more than eleven.

"I smoke cigarettes," he said. "Luckies."

"That's stupid," K.C. said, pulling cans of tomatoes to the edge to make the shelves look both attractive and full.

"I've been with girls. You know, *with*."

"Good for you."

"Do you have a boyfriend?"

"You know I do."

"Bet I can guess your bra size."

K.C. took a deep breath. *You oughta hear us when we really get on about women.* She looked up and down the aisle to make sure no one else could overhear, then took a step toward Davy and whispered, "If you ever mention my boobs again, Jack will take you out back and beat the shit out of you. He's just over at the meat counter. Got that?"

Davy broke into a wide grin. "You said *boobs*. Swell!" With that he ran out of the store, announcing to the world in a loud voice, "K.C. said *boobs*, K.C. said *boobs*."

****

"Kase, did you really say *boobs*?" Jack asked in the break room.

"I was having a come-to-Jesus talk with him. He wanted to guess my bra size."

Jack smiled. "I could have told him that."

"You do, and you'll never see them again."

"That'd put the kibosh on kids then, eh?"

K.C. took a swallow of 7-Up and didn't answer. House, children, dog. Dictaphones, typewriters, and frisky bosses. Comfort. Security. Love. Happy parents.

She stared at Jack so intently he started to squirm. He had so many good qualities, but there was one thing that bothered her about him, and it wasn't even his fault. He missed the war by a day, turning 18 on September 3, 1945. He could have enlisted at 17, but couldn't be drafted until he was 18. He didn't enlist. Then President Truman declared VJ Day on September 2, and Jack was off the hook. He still had to register for the draft, but was never called, and probably never would be.

Her brother didn't miss the war. Kenny didn't wait to be drafted, enlisting in '41. He was brave. He was the best. He volunteered for every dangerous mission. He died. He never got to have a wife, or a house, or children, or a dog. Worse, all of his music died with him—all, except what was left inside K.C.

She felt so small-minded for her resentment toward Jack, but what could she do? *Maybe we should break up.* "Maybe..." she said, but didn't finish.

Jack must have thought she was answering his question about not having kids. "See you tonight?" he said.

"I got nothing else to do."

****

"Everything's wonderful, Kasey," her sister Krissy said on the phone. "Ben, Micah. Wouldn't trade my life for anything."

Krissy pronounced her name Kasey, one word, rather than K.C., two words, accent slightly on the second. So did their parents. And Mr. Pierson. At least they didn't call her Kase, like Jack did.

"I'm glad it works for you," K.C. said, "but I've got other things I want to do."

Their older sister, Kathryn "don't call me Kathy" Bolton, had opened a dance studio in St. Louis, so K.C.'s artistic dream wasn't unprecedented in the family. She'd likely be sympathetic, but long-distance calls were too expensive.

"Maybe if you'd stuck with piano.... Even so, music? You know what the folks think about Kathryn, and she isn't even involved with Negroes."

"That's not their business. I don't live with them anymore."

43

"Neither do I, but I can still visit. She can't."

"Won't."

"Either way." After a long pause, Krissy added, "Jack's okay. There are worse things than being married to a teacher. Anyhow, I like him."

"So do I," K.C. said.

"Problem solved."

Just like that. "Okay..."

"Okay, love you. 'Bye."

K.C. replaced the receiver and checked the coin return, just in case.

****

She brought her sax to practice in the band room, but when she got there, she sat down at the piano instead. Much as she loved sax, nothing vented her frustrations like pounding the keys.

Mr. Pierson was surprised, and maybe a little delighted. He was a saxophonist himself, but neither liked nor comprehended the musical direction in which she wanted to go.

When she was still taking lessons K.C.'s piano teacher had marveled at her talent, at one point challenging her to learn Godowsky's *53 Studies on Chopin's Études*. Chopin was difficult enough, but Godowsky? His variations were hard. *Really* hard. Beyond her abilities, beyond any high schooler's. But she had managed to conquer the one she liked best, Opus 10, #3, "Tristesse." It was in E major, four sharps. A lot of musicians she knew preferred flats, but sharps didn't bother her. She could go out to five with no problem. Six or seven took some thinking.

Although she hadn't played it in two years, the piece came back to her quickly.

"Impressive," Mr. Pierson said, "Chopin."

"Godowsky's Chopin. Jeez."

"In all my years, you and your brother have been the most gifted musicians I've ever worked with. So many kids walk away from music after they graduate. I'm so happy you stuck with it. I'm sure Kenneth would have, too."

"Thanks, Mr. Pierson. He planned to."

"You're not in school anymore, knucklehead. Call me Jerry."

"Ever heard of a musicians' union for jazz players?"

"Of course, but it's not just for jazz. Musicians Protective Union, local 137, out of Cedar Rapids."

"Do I really need a card?"

"If you're serious about playing, you will."

"Do you have one?"

"I kept up my dues for years, but I'm not a performing musician anymore, so I eventually let it go."

Making it up as she went, K.C. used a playful glissando to transition out of "Tristesse," modulated to F, added a stride rhythm, and somehow found herself in the middle of Lion Smith's lightning-tempoed "Finger Buster."

"Improvisation," Mr. Pierson said. "I doubt Chopin would approve."

She kept playing as she spoke, never missing a note or skipping a beat. "In bop, an improv solo is called 'taking the changes.'"

He laughed. "I'm old, I'm not dead. I've heard the lingo. This just in: I teach band."

"Sorry."

"You know, Kasey, you're a tremendous saxophonist, better than I ever was. But I wonder if it's your best destiny. If you intend to play it professionally, sax has to be your primary instrument. You aren't a player until it becomes an extension of your body, a third arm, a piece of your soul."

Mr. Ross had told her practically the same thing. Must be something all old people said to discourage young ones from achieving what they wanted.

"It is," she said.

"And yet you're playing piano, when you came to practice sax. What is it about bebop that draws you to it?"

"It's fast and fun."

"Fast and fun won't cut it as a pro. You need to become dedicated to your craft. It has to be something you do because life isn't worth living without it. Something you can't *not* do."

"My parents hate it, so it must be good."

"Are you aspiring to, or rebelling against?"

K.C.'s fingers flew up and down the keys, twisting, bouncing, crossing over each other. She built to a big climax that wasn't in the original, alternating rapid-fire chord clusters between her right and left hand, and ending on an arpeggiated thirteen chord that slashed through the air like a battle scar. When she was finished, she gasped for breath, heart pounding, perspiration flowing.

"Wow," Mr. Pierson said. "Just... wow."

"It's what Kenny wanted," she panted.

****

She got Jack past Mr. Somers again. She suspected the landlord didn't really care what she did, or who she did it with, as long as he had his money every Friday.

They sat on her bed. She turned Kenny's picture down.

Jack wanted to kiss her. She let him.

He wanted to take her clothes off. She let him.

He wanted to take his clothes off. She let him.

Then he wanted the usual preliminaries. She did that.

Always prepared, Jack had been to the drug store. As soon as they lay down he went for the homerun. He was enthusiastic, but needed reassurance that she was enjoying the experience, too. She wasn't, particularly.

"Yes," she said. Some nights were better than others. This wasn't one of them.

At least he rounded the bases quickly. "Bet I can guess your bra size," he puffed.

Chapter 8

FREDDIE HAD BOOKED GIGS in Cedar Rapids and Davenport for the next two weekends, figuring the band would've found a horn man to replace Spits by then. And now Thump was out of commission, too, while they waited for him to recover.

Dwayne had connections, though. As a temporary fix, he lined up an alto sax and standup bass from out of town. Since both played in other bands, they couldn't join the Bluenotes full time, but they were happy enough to make a little scratch filling in when their own groups had open dates. Since they were in Waterton anyway, Dwayne even talked them into rehearsing some of his charts with them at Narlins.

Freddie didn't know the sax man. Calvin Arceneaux was from Omaha, but said he was here visiting relatives. His last name sounded like "arsenal," so he went by Bullet.

Freddie had met the bass man, T.J. Diksha, a few times. He was from Marion, which was right next to Cedar Rapids. When the Bluenotes gigged the Rapids they drank in the same bars as his band.

T.J.'s supplier lived in Waterton, so he came here a

couple of times a month for reefer.

Everyone had been more or less on time for the session, even Ironhead and Screech, a rare thing for them. Dwayne sat at his usual table beyond the dance floor. He'd been an eighty-eighter in the '20s and '30s, but now preferred to listen and write.

He was good at that. With one hearing of a number, Dwayne could chart every note, every chord, every accent, every drumbeat. Most anyone could hear the outer voices, the melody and bass, but Dwayne caught every middle voice like it was playing by itself. Yeah, he lifted riffs from other bands, but who didn't? Unlike others, what he did with them blew away the originals.

Freddie sat with his legs hanging over the edge of the stage and greased his trombone's slide. Syd was already at the drums and Catfish at the piano when T.J. lugged his bass in from the wings. Ironhead's tenor sax hung around his neck like a sack of oats. He looked bored, nothing new for him. Screech was on trumpet tonight. He and Leon ran scales in the back.

Bullet brought a chair up from one of the tables, carrying his alto sax with the other hand. Freddie noticed he was limping bad.

"You aren't gonna sit when you play," Dwayne said.

"We ain't playing, we're practicing. You try standing with these knees." Bullet was wearing bright yellow Bermuda shorts. He pulled up the hem on his left leg up to show white scars crisscrossing from thigh to calf. "Other one looks better, feels worse," he said. "Pissed off husband, two floors up. Had to get away by a fire escape. 'Cept there wasn't a fire escape. So. I stand for gigs, and that's it."

Freddie massaged his fingers and wondered if they'd be straight now if he'd gotten medical attention right away.

"The hell, man," Ironhead said, "one o'clock in the afternoon? I need sleep."

"Only good time you ever have for rehearsing is *never*," Dwayne said, "and that doesn't work for the rest of us. You're here now, so shut up."

Leon and Screech finished their runs and headed up front. Dwayne handed them several charts to distribute on stage. Each chart consisted of six sets of two staves each, one with the melody, the other with chord symbols and slash marks to indicate any special rhythm he wanted.

"What's this?" T.J. said, adjusting his music stand. "'In the *Nude*?'"

"Little something of my own," Dwayne said. "No disrespect to Miller."

"He stole it from Wingy Manone, anyhow."

"What's the T.J. stand for?" Ironhead said.

'The Jenius."

Dwayne chuckled, but Ironhead nodded. He seemed satisfied with the answer.

"Genius starts with a G," Dwayne said.

"My folks always was bad spellers."

Freddie studied the chart for a few moments. Everything made sense, but, then, it would. Dwayne wrote it. He got up and stood next to Bullet's chair to share his stand. At gigs they had specific places, but at rehearsals, when they had them, things were more informal.

"All right," Dwayne said. "Start at section E."

"Hold on," T.J. said. "At the end?"

"Don't matter with old standards," Freddie explained. "We can do those in our sleep. But with new shit, we always go from E on out, then back to A. Knowing the tail makes you feel the front better."

"What do you mean, 'new *shit*'?" Dwayne laughed.

"That makes sense to you all?" Bullet said.

"It will to you, too," Syd said.

They spent a half hour doing the last thirty-two bars, then the middle, then the front. When Dwayne was satisfied they understood his intent, he had them go through it from the beginning. "Okay, Leon," he said, "take the intro with the rhythms, then Screech come in under him on the first chorus. Bullet and Ironhead got the next twelve, then lay out at B. Screech, take a stroll with Syd and T.J. at C. After the shout chorus, wait for my cutoff. No fermata, just watch me."

Dwayne snapped his fingers to get their attention. "Uh-one, uh-three. Uh-one, two, three."

Leon eased into his line, squeezing out notes in a way only Leon could squeeze. Screech added color. Freddie took his pickup, and then the whole band came in swinging. Although everyone knew T.J. from the Cedar Rapids shows, no one but Dwayne had heard Bullet play. Freddie didn't know what to expect, but the man came in smooth, tight as silk with Ironhead.

Ninety seconds in, they all felt it. Even with two new members, first time through a new chart front to back, the band was riding the current together. No one was one, everyone was all, baptized in blessed waters, immersed in the life force called jazz. Once they finished the number, they looked like they'd just witnessed the Rapture.

The feeling was better than any drug, better than sex, better than breathing.

Except to Dwayne. He leaned back and said, "Well, that was for shit."

"God*damn*, man," Screech said, "what d'you want?"

T.J. picked up his bass and headed toward the door. "I'm gone."

"Cool your ass off," Dwayne said. "All right, it wasn't that bad. Little rough at D, is all. 'Fish, maybe just give me the shells there. Bullet, hit the accents a little harder. One more time, and we're back to the standards."

"He always such an asshole?" Bullet whispered to Freddie.

"This is a good day."

****

Freddie didn't go to church when Shay wasn't around to make him—which, lately, was most of the time. Nothing against the Holy Word, it was just that Sunday mornings came so soon after Saturday nights. Even if the Bluenotes didn't have a gig, Freddie and Dwayne were out scoping other bands, or Freddie was woodshedding on the trombone, or socializing, or doing nothing but staying awake. It was hard to change habits, especially when it meant getting up early to go listen to people who couldn't sing. The preaching was fine, the message good, but he always walked out with a headache. In jazz, some notes were sung between a quarter and a halftone flat on purpose, for a certain effect. In church, the congregation sang the hymns every which way, flat or sharp, in quartertones, halftones, whole tones, or no tones, without regard to key, or even an awareness of the melody. The poor souls who could carry a tune only served to call more attention to the wrongness of the rest.

At least that was how it was with the Baptist folks at his church on East Donald Street. Maybe the Lutherans over on West Fourth had choirs of angels.

Freddie sat on the toilet and ran through Dwayne's new chart in his mind. Washington had already battled her own reflection in the mirror over the sink, and was now lying at his feet. Her tail flicked, and she randomly batted at his toes, just to remind him it was her, not that cat in the glass, who was running the joint.

She stared at him, ears slightly back. Her fur twitched, signaling she was about to pounce. Damn thing had clawed her way up his legs so often he had permanent scars. He was naked on the toilet. This was not a good time for her to use him as a climbing post. "You do and I'll twist your head off," he said. "You're faster than me, but I'm still bigger, stronger, and smarter."

Clearly not intimidated, Washington launched herself at him, sinking her claws into his right thigh. To her this was playing. She didn't know she was causing pain. Or maybe she did. She was a cat. Freddie backhanded her, sending her flying, along with scraps of his flesh.

Washington wasn't good at taking hints. She might have attacked again, but a booming voice did what violence couldn't. "Goddammit!" he cried, and the sound frightened her out of the bathroom, fur puffed out, tail jerking into the question mark shape that pissed-off cats got.

Each side of his thigh had four parallel slashes, with the dew claw puncture marks below the cuts. He dabbed at the wounds with toilet paper and sucked in his breath. *Shit, that hurt. Shit. Shit.* Seemed like any time he bled anymore it took forever to stop. Maybe thin blood was one of the signs of old age.

Washington mewed. She was back at the bathroom door, eyes fixed on the mirror, even though she couldn't possibly see herself from that angle.

Cats were too stupid to understand they were looking at themselves in the mirror. Their minds didn't work that way. Freddie wondered how many things humans saw but didn't understand because *their* minds didn't work that way.

Chapter 9

K.C. AND JACK BOTH had the day off. Ever the romantic, Jack wanted to take her fishing. Krissy wanted to take her shopping at Block's Department Store over her lunch hour. K.C. wanted to sit in her apartment and feel sorry for herself.

Self-pity wouldn't get her a gig with the Bluenotes, though, so she agreed to meet her sister downtown just after noon. Shopping was better than fishing, and Krissy didn't ask anything of her other than her company.

K.C. didn't own a car, so she had to walk, take the bus, or bum a ride. The day was sunny and not too hot, and Block's was less than half a mile, so she walked. She paused on the Fourth Street Bridge to watch the Oak River curl southeast. Its waters were slow and, if not spectacular, still pretty, in a peaceful sort of way. Funny how that narrow ribbon of calm was the dividing line between Waterton's caste system, with most well-off white people living on the west side, and the poorest blacks and whites on the east.

Two bridges down, at Sixth Street, a group of kids were playing in the water outside a huge drainage tunnel that emptied into the river. It stretched two miles underground to

In The Blood

Dry Run Creek in Liberty Park. The water in the tunnel was rarely more than ankle-deep. Once, in grade school, her friends had tried to convince her to travel its entire length without so much as a flashlight to guide them. They were boys, of course, who claimed they'd been through it a million times. It wasn't completely dark, they said, because there were three or four places where daylight filtered down from manholes. Despite their taunts, K.C. was always too scared to go with them.

It probably would have been fun, if she'd let herself do it. As she watched the kids splash, she regretted her timidity. On the other hand, her recent willingness to try scary new things with her music hadn't gotten her anywhere, either.

To the northeast, unseen from here but not un-smelled, stood Roth Packing, one of the largest hog kill operations in the nation. The place was a powder keg right now, its workers threatening a strike that could shut down the plant for weeks. Several of K.C.'s high school friends and their fathers worked there. A strike wouldn't affect her, other than raising the price of pork chops and bacon.

To the west, beyond the Mullan Street Bridge, the west-side factories and foundries belched fumes every day of the year except Christmas and the Fourth of July. Today an easterly breeze carried their stink away from her.

A white Harris Dairy truck clattered by. This late in the day it would be empty, its milk delivered to the porches on its route. She didn't turn in time to notice the driver. If it was Wyatt, he would have been at her parents' house by 7:00 this morning.

K.C. looked at the boys by the drainage tunnel one more time. She could hear their laughter. One of them waved in her direction, probably thinking she was someone else.

She proceeded across the bridge without returning his

wave. To her right, the plush Paramount Theater showed serials every Saturday afternoon and the latest Hollywood releases twice a night during the week. Its marquee still advertised *Easter Parade.*

Farther down the street was the Music Shoppe, her home away from home when she was a kid. While waiting for Kenny to pick her up after her piano lessons, she'd pore over the bins of sheet music. As she grew older the store lost its charm. The scores they'd offered no longer challenged her, and mail ordering better stuff through them was expensive. Still brought back nice memories, though.

To her left, Block's was the second tallest building in Waterton, eight stories. Krissy met her at the south entrance. She was dressed in a tan blouse and rust-colored skirt that hung to mid-thigh, with the black dog-leash belt that was just the bee's knees with fashionable ladies. To top it off, she'd gotten a new pair of tortoise shell glasses. Although they were stylish, K.C. was surprised she'd wear them in public. Krissy thought glasses made women look unattractive.

Shopping with Krissy usually meant following her around while she looked at things K.C. couldn't afford. They stopped in several departments, each one staffed by a pleasant sales girl. Eventually they arrived in the lingerie section, which was where Krissy had intended to take her all along. One of the Block's girls greeted them with a cheerful smile. "Hi, Mrs. Whitney. Can I help you find anything today?"

"No, thanks, Julie, we're just looking."

As the girl bounced away, Krissy pulled K.C. toward a rack of fancy negligees. During the war most ladies' undergarments had been made of rayon, but three years out nylon and silk were available again.

Krissy held up a sheer red one against her torso. "Killer-diller duds, eh? Ben's gonna love this."

"You can see right through it," K.C. said.

"Well, *yeah*." Krissy winked at her. "You should get one for your honeymoon."

K.C. didn't tell her the honeymoon had happened long ago and the marriage might not happen at all.

"Let's go try it on," Krissy said.

"I'll wait out here."

"Suit yourself." Krissy disappeared into the fitting room. K.C. could see her feet beneath the door as her dress dropped to the floor and she stepped into the negligee. "Oh, Kasey, you should see this. Ooh."

Ooh. Was that all it took? Was that the secret? Get sexy underwear to make your man happy, and that would make you happy? K.C. could have pleased Jack this morning by going fishing with him. She did please him by seeing *Abbott and Costello* when she would have preferred *Easter Parade*. Those were things that didn't require a negligee, but the principle was the same: do what he wants, and all will be swell.

Krissy had gotten a husband who owned a successful auto body shop, a son, and a nice house by the golf course out of the deal.

K.C. had an apartment, a job at Dale's Grocery, and a savage musical urge that could neither be denied nor satisfied. She checked her watch.

"Dad ought to fire you."

Their father was a middle-level manager at I.C.S.C.—the Iowa Cream Separator Company—where Krissy was a secretary. "He does dock my pay when I'm back late from lunch. Him and Mom would like you to visit."

"Since when?"

"Since always. You wouldn't have to practice that sax so

often."

Why not just amputate my arms? "Kathryn wouldn't have to run her dance studio, but she does."

"They don't approve of that, either."

"But she does it anyway."

The negligee fell, the dress went up, then the door to the fitting room opened. Krissy emerged with the slinky garment folded over her arm. "Honestly," she said, "sometimes I think you only do things to annoy them."

"Annoying them is a bonus," K.C. said.

"You can be such a sourpuss. Do you need a ride?"

"I'll be okay." K.C. touched the material of the negligee. Soft and cool, it probably would feel as good to wear as it would for Jack to take off her. If she'd buy one, that is, which she wouldn't. "This must cost a fortune."

"I've got a Block's Charge-a-Plate."

A husband, a kid, a house, a body shop, and a charge account. The Dream.

Are you aspiring to, or rebelling against?

****

"Dammit, Kase," Jack said. When he didn't want to take the time to drive out of town, he liked to fish under the Eighteenth Street Bridge. Bullheads and crappie were usually decent there.

With a free afternoon and nothing else to do, K.C. had humored him after all, although she hadn't brought a pole. Instead, she lay on her back in the shade of the bridge, popping imaginary pads on an imaginary sax, jamming to an imaginary swing tune. *K.C. and the Bluenotes.* She liked that, although Mr. Ross and Dwayne might have something to say about it.

There was no sound save the movement of the water and the occasional rumble of a car passing over the bridge.

Jack planted a Y-shaped twig in the ground to rest his pole on when he tired of holding it. "Dammit, Kase," he said again, "are you even paying attention?"

"You're fishing. What am I supposed to be paying attention to?"

"You could—I don't know—maybe talk to me."

K.C. fingered the keys for an especially difficult run, lots of accidentals and grace notes. "About what?"

"Please stop doing that. You're here with me now."

K.C. put her hands down, resting her arms across her breasts as if she were in a coffin. She noticed the aging cement on the bottom of the bridge, the rusting metal supports. The Oak River whispered by, *Shhh, shhh....*

"Krissy bought a negligee today. It's really for Ben."

Jack wiggled his line, and his bobber bobbed. "Why would Ben want a negligee?"

Jesus Christ, K.C. thought, rolling to her stomach. She rested her head in the crook of her elbow and watched him. The grass felt cool on her skin. "So he can take it off her, stupid."

Jack smiled. "Oh."

"She wanted me to buy one for our honeymoon."

"Did you?"

She regretted bringing it up. This wasn't a conversation she wanted to have, not now, maybe not ever. "You don't have any trouble taking the clothes I already have off me."

Jack got a nibble, snapped the pole too fast, and lost the fish. He reeled in the line to find a filament of worm guts dangling from the hook. A can of fresh night crawlers, just collected from his parents' yard this morning, was in his tackle box. He pulled one out, a fat wiggler. K.C. could see its sliminess from where she lay. Most girls she knew would be disgusted, but she wasn't. It was just a worm. Now, if it had been a spider...

Jack speared several loops of the worm onto the hook and recast the line. After notching the pole in the Y of the twig, he came to crouch next to her. He didn't say anything.

K.C. heard his breathing over the shushing of the river. She didn't look up, but could sense he was staring at her.

Finally, he said, "Am I such a bad guy?"

He'd removed his shoes and socks when they'd arrived. K.C. gazed at his feet, the fine hair on the top of his toes, the green stains on the bottom. She reached out and squeezed his ankle, reassurance for herself as much as for him. "No," she said, "you're a good guy."

"Then what?"

"Then nothing." His line bobbed weakly, once, twice, followed by a strong jerk that nearly dislodged his pole. "You got a bite."

Jack hurried to the pole, and after a brief struggle, pulled in a nice crappie. "Guess what we're having for supper?" he said, smiling with a look of triumph. Boys were so proud of their fishing prowess, when all it was, really, was luck. Toss a hook into the water and hope a big one happened along.

"You're cooking it," she said.

He would, too, and he'd serve it to her, and it would be delicious, and he would love her with all his naïve heart.

As K.C. got to her feet, she ran through the difficult scale in her mind again. "You ready?" she said.

"I kind of wanted to stay out here with you a little longer."

She brushed grass from the front of her blouse. The breeze was pleasant, the sky as blue as skies ever got. The Oak River's gentle motion lulled her senses.

"Wouldn't you rather stay inside with me?"

Chapter 10

THUMP WASN'T GETTING BETTER. After he threw up everything he'd eaten, the nurses had to feed him through an IV tube. It was late, past visiting hours, but Freddie and Dwayne were still in with him. The lights were low so Thump could sleep. His snoring was loud and erratic.

"Goddam freight train," Dwayne said.

Freddie squinted at the chart at the end of the bed. All he understood were Thump's name, MCLEMORE, EARL PAUL, and the word heroin. The medical terms might as well have been written in Swahili.

Thump groaned, twitched, and resumed snoring. Even asleep, he grimaced like he was in pain. At least the breathing tube was out.

"He shot up over at your place," Freddie said, not a question.

Dwayne took Thump's hand and stared at the floor. "Me and Spits went through this, back in Chicago, in thirty or thirty-one. I didn't think he was gonna make it. I never used, you know, except reefer and a little toot. But Spits, man, he'd try anything he could get into his veins. Dumb shit would've done Drano if he could've fit the crystals into a needle."

Freddie looked out the window, watching the car lights go by on Highway 63, three stories below. The moon was at half of half, whatever that sliver was called.

A sparrow had built her nest in the corner of the windowsill outside. The little ones would be gone by now, but the mama sparrow still roosted there. She took no interest in Freddie, if she noticed him at all. She seemed content in her homemade bowl of security.

Freddie was jealous of her.

He was furious with Dwayne, with Shay, with the pain in his own body, and with his mangled fingers.

He was scared for Thump, and he was nervous about the uncertain future of the Bluenotes without him. The band couldn't afford to lose him, too, not right after Spits. T.J. was good enough, but he wasn't staying. And he wasn't Thump.

"So this one night," Dwayne continued, "sometime during the war, W.C. Handy's in town from New York to listen to one of Satchmo's new charts. I didn't grow up some poor slum nigger, but I never ran with big dogs. Me and Spits are doing the local clubs, hoping somebody's paying attention. Spits comes up with a connection who gets us a meeting with Handy. Hear what I'm saying? *W.C.-fucking-Handy*, and he's gonna talk to us. We know our shit, but Handy?—he *invented* black music. All them twelve-bar phrases? Yeah, that's him."

Freddie tapped on the window. The little sparrow fluttered her feathers but didn't fly away. He knew about Handy. What he didn't know was why Dwayne would let Thump pump poison at his house.

"Well, the night comes, and I'm pacing outside Handy's dressing room backstage. Spits doesn't show. I'm about to drop a load, I'm so frantic, and then the door opens, and there's the man himself. He says, 'You Dwayne Hite?' and I forget all about Spits. Jesus, Freddie, that cat's a genius. He taught me more music in an hour than I knew my whole life before that. I diddle a few of my tunes on the ivories for him, and he likes what he hears. He doesn't say 'I'm gonna make you a star'—nothing like that—but he does give me a name and an address to send my charts to, to get published."

Freddie turned away from the window and sat in the second chair next to Thump's bed. Dwayne was still holding his hand. Since he'd already hinted where this story was leading, Freddie could guess why Spits didn't come that night, but he asked anyway. "Spits was strung out somewhere?"

Dwayne let go of Thump's hand, patted it, and leaned back. "Motherfucker had crawled into a dumpster to die, I think. Cops found him, drove him to a hospital that took colored folks. He was there a week. They lost him three times, but always got him back. After that I knew we had to get out of there, out of Chicago, away from the hard shit. Handy inspired me to a life of music, and Spits drove me away from the center of it."

"Plenty of horse here, too," Freddie said, nodding toward Thump. Freddie had never done anything stronger than weed, and then only because it relieved his joint pain.

"So what you're thinking is," Dwayne said, "'Spits almost dies O.D.ing, yet you let Thump shoot up at your house.'"

"Yeah," Freddie said.

Thump farted, and his stomach gurgled. Dwayne smiled, but it was a sad one. "I wasn't around when Spits did the dope. I'm meeting W.C. Handy, trying to get famous, and he's out trying to kill himself."

"Spits arranged it. Not your fault he didn't come to get famous with you."

"Well, I'm not gonna lose a friend that way. Thump's

gonna do what Thump's gonna do, but if he fucks himself up in my basement, I'm right there to get help."

Thump's gassy emissions were foul enough to make Freddie gag. He fanned the air to clear the stink. "Maybe," he said, "you could stop letting Thump do what he's gonna do, instead of giving him a place to do it."

"I'm not his daddy."

Freddie stood up. "Seems to me you ain't much of a friend, either, if you think giving him a comfortable place to kill himself is helping. Ain't just you. Me and Leon and Catfish, Ironhead, Screech, Syd, we all just stand by. We gotta keep those needles out of his arms, man."

****

Freddie was too exhausted to stay awake, too wired to sleep. He found Catfish at Pamela's Triangle Club—Grits 'n' Tits—drinking beer and watching the spinning tassels. Country music crackled from the ancient loudspeakers. The white boys must've got to the jukebox with their nickels first. Other nights blues or rag won out. Didn't really matter. Only difference between Iowa and Mississippi was that there segregation was the law, here just the custom. Poor whites and poor coloreds sat in equal numbers at separate ends of the stage and shared leers at the girls. There were four strippers a night, one at a time, white, black, and sometimes Mexican. Everybody whistled at the white girls, but only the black cats showed much interest in darker shades.

The girl up now was white, a year or two either side of twenty, and more pretty than not. Swaying in a spotlight, she might've been getting a high colonic, for all the fun she looked like she was having.

'Fish had his belly up to the stage, practically staring up the girl's cootchie. Or would have been, except she had on a little triangular patch of cloth in front held on by a g-string and decorated with glitter. The city would shut the club down if she didn't wear something.

Freddie walked over to him. "'Fish."

"Boneman. What're you doing here?"

"Free country, ain't it?"

"Looking for me?"

"Not really."

'Fish burped. "How's Thump?"

"Same."

"Shit."

"How come you never come see him?"

"Got this thing about dead people."

"Thump ain't dead."

"Sure as I show up, the mean-tempered bastard's gonna die on me. Just up and die right there. He's pissy like that."

Freddie plugged his nose. If the stink of beer and body odor weren't bad enough, the bathroom door was always ajar. The toilet probably hadn't been cleaned since Prohibition, so the whole building smelled like a sewer. The owner, Pam Garson, couldn't afford air-cooling. Even on cooler nights, like now, humidity oozed from the walls, slime from crumbling drywall. As far as class went in Waterton, Narlins was a couple of notches above a cheap whorehouse, the Diminished Fifth a couple notches below. But if a man was sinking down, he'd pass through Hell before he got to Grits 'n' Tits.

Freddie only visited when he was feeling especially blue, thinking the girls might lighten his mood. It rarely worked. "How can you stand this place?"

Catfish held a dollar up for the stripper, but didn't touch her. She snatched the bill and tucked it into the triangular patch. It appeared to be her first of the night. "Any other stupid questions?"

"And your old lady lets you come here?"

'Fish grinned. "Janae don't mind, 'specially on days she ain't interested in the old push-and-pull. Figures if I get it out of my system here, I won't climb all over her when I get home."

"All this skin, don't it just fire your blood more?"

'Fish flexed his bicep. "A beer, a deserted corner, and a strong right hand...."

"Damn, man, I'd never tell anybody if I did that."

"Like you don't."

Pamela, an overweight white woman, approached Freddie. Sweat stains circled her armpits, and grease spotted her blouse, like she'd used it to wipe her mouth after eating. Dirt streaked the folds of her neck. "Gotta buy something if you're gonna watch the girls."

Grits 'n' Tits didn't really serve grits, or any food, other than peanuts and leftover popcorn from the movie theaters. Freddie knew the rules, and Pamela knew he knew. "Nah, I don't want nothing," he said, teasing her.

She didn't like being teased. "Buy or bye-bye. Can't have riffraff coming in to get their jollies for free. I got a business to run."

Freddie laughed. *Lordy, no, Pam, you sure can't let riffraff into a fine establishment like this.* "Coke."

Pamela eyed him suspiciously. "You working for the cops now?"

"Not coke—Coke. Coca Cola."

"Two dollar minimum."

"Two bucks for pop? I can get it for a nickel at a gas station."

"Go to a gas station, then."

Freddie fished two bills from his pocket. "Extra money you make on the pop, buy yourself charm lessons."

Pamela dropped the money into her apron pocket. "Asshole," she said, and left.

"You're one smooth-talking sumbitch," Catfish said. "Shay come back yet?"

"No."

"She gonna?"

"Probably."

"Why's she always leaving?"

"Damned if I know. Looking in on her mama, maybe."

"You getting a little something on the side?"

"Nope."

"Maybe you should."

Freddie raised his voice louder than he intended. "I ain't like that."

"Cool off, Tarzan. I'm just messing with you. You told me she won't do you anymore. I don't get me some two, three times a week, I'd pull my own nuts off."

Freddie chuckled. He'd pay to see that. "Once or twice a *year* would wear me out."

'Fish looked him up and down. "I was you, I'd be the one leaving."

"Hell, no. It's my house."

A young black man shouted a lewd comment to the stripper. One of the whites at the other end took offense. "Don't you go sniffing after that white meat, boy." His friends agreed.

'Fish didn't even raise an eyebrow, but some of the other colored men took the bait. Both sides rose, cursed, and made threats. "They're early tonight," he said, glancing at the clock above the bar.

The stripper never varied her routine. She'd seen it all before, too.

"Maybe we should get out of here," Freddie said.

"Can if you want, but they're just shaking their dicks at each other. Cowboys'll calm down when she goes over there and wiggles for them." 'Fish took a swig of beer. "So, Shay. Say the bitch does come back. Why would you let her?"

"She's the only one the cat likes." Pamela returned with the Coke, practically throwing it at him as she passed. It was warm. "One of these days," Freddie said, "she'll just be there, and we'll both act like she never left. Till she does it again."

"You're a strange dude, Boneman."

The stripper slouched her way to the white end of the bar, where the white boys didn't hesitate to deposit the dollars themselves. Catfish watched her go, obviously appreciating the view.

Chapter 11

HOW FAR ARE YOU willing to go? Kenny asked her.

Her brother had written her at least once a week when he was in the service. K.C. kept every one of his letters, tied in a lace bow in the back of her dresser drawer. She hadn't reread any of them since his death because they made her cry. But even five years later, she still spoke to him in private moments. He answered, too, in the same way God did when people talked to Him. His advice coincided with what she wanted to hear—that, or what she needed to hear, which was not always the same thing.

She lay face down on her bed, eyes closed, listening to distant thunder and feeling the eyes in his photo on her. "Whatever it takes," she said into her pillow.

'Whatever it takes' is a lot. Maybe too much, if you get my drift.

"I made you a promise."

I didn't ask for that, Squirt. You don't owe me anything.

She owed him everything. "What would you do?"

Whatever it takes, he said, and if an imaginary voice could speak with a grin, his did.

"Then shut up. I'm doing it."

K.C. rolled over. Jack had recently gone home. She'd just gotten dressed in her jammies and set Kenny's picture upright. She'd enjoyed it this time, *really* enjoyed it, and that worried her. Everything would be so much clearer if she could just hate the sex, hate Jack, hate any future that didn't include jazz.

But she didn't. There was nothing wrong with Jack. He was smart, dependable, and fair-minded. He adored her and didn't stray. He was usually a capable lover. And, as Krissy always pointed out, he had "prospects," even if those prospects were only teaching economics classes. Most girls would sell their soul for a steady man like him.

Kathryn might understand. She'd opened the dance studio against their parents' wishes. "Not a proper occupation for a lady." A few years before that she'd made them angry by announcing she was joining the Coast Guard's women's reserve force, SPARS, when both they and the WAVES were training at Iowa State Teachers College. She ultimately changed her mind because the Coast Guard moved SPARS training to Florida, but the damage had been done. Dad and Mom wouldn't tolerate the idea of one of their daughters in the military, although it would only have been clerical work here in the States.

Then again, even Kathryn had toed the line in one way. She'd married J.W. and produced grandchildren for them.

And Krissy? She was so annoyingly *content* that K.C. wanted to scream, out of both disdain and envy.

God damn it.

She just wanted to play saxophone. Be the best. In front of audiences who knew what the best was.

It was so simple. She didn't *want* to want anything else.

K.C. got up and went into the bathroom, thinking about Jack as she peed.

Am I such a bad guy?

"Is he such a bad guy?" she asked Kenny, but he was silent this time.

****

Before going to Dale's in the morning, K.C. rounded up the courage to call the phone number on the business card Mr. Ross had given her. She listened to her nickel fall through the slot, then dialed slowly. Half of her hoped he wouldn't answer.

He did.

"F.D. Ross?" she said.

"Yeah, this is Freddie. Who's this?"

"White Bird," she said.

"Motherfuck," he said, and the phone went dead.

Now all of her wished he hadn't answered, because by answering the phone he'd answered her question.

She hung up and headed off toward work. Wherever the thunder had been last night, it hadn't come here. The streets were dry, although the sky was overcast and might still squeeze out some rain.

The way she figured it, Dwayne would never accept her of his own volition, not if she was the second coming of Johnny Hodges. He had it in his head that a white girl couldn't play jazz, so he'd hear mistakes where there weren't any. He'd nitpick and criticize. He'd try to embarrass and intimidate her. He'd invent reasons to deny her.

Freddie Ross had to be the way in. Win him over, and he'd convince Dwayne. Yet the three syllables he'd just spit at her told her what the chances of *that* were.

She could get a list of the Bluenotes' play dates from the local radio station and follow them to each city, each club, each performance. She could pester them until they gave in (never), had her arrested (possibly), or posted lookouts to keep her away altogether (likely).

Maybe she could step down another wrung on the ladder and approach other band members, to influence them into influencing Freddie into influencing Dwayne. That level of subterfuge was confusing even to her, especially since she'd only met them once and didn't know their real names.

Or she could marry Jack, and make everybody happy but one.

How different things might have been if Kenny hadn't allowed patriotism to override his musical ambition...

But no one, not even she, could criticize him for that. Hitler had been a monster.

K.C. crossed at the intersection of Fourth and Wellington. Someone in a Chevy honked and waved as he went by, but she didn't see who. Most of the wives along this stretch had planted little flower gardens in front of their houses, oranges and whites, reds, blues, and yellows. Blossoms were out in all their glory. It was lovely. Bumblebees buzzed from petal to petal, their legs bulging with pollen. Good thing she didn't have allergies.

A squirrel on a bird feeder flicked its tail and chattered angrily at her. "What did I do to you?" she said, then turned left onto Third Street.

And there was Dale's, red brick and black tiles—her life, her career, her best destiny. Jack was working today. So was Austin. Love from one and bigotry from the other. Jack would pinch her butt when no one was looking. Austin would make comments. That little hemorrhoid Davy would probably be in, too, to speculate about her anatomical dimensions.

Through it all, K.C. would be scooping ice cream and mixing cherry Cokes.

In The Blood

She paused in the parking lot. She so, so, *so* badly wanted to say *To hell with it.* But she went in anyway, and smiled at the customers, and greeted her coworkers with a semblance of friendliness.

****

That night a disc jockey at KXM knew the Bluenotes' upcoming schedule, but not the band members' real names. He put her in touch with Tim Piper, the manager at Electrical Park Ballroom. Over the phone, Piper said, "Why are you asking?"

K.C. thought about lying, but decided against it. "I'm trying to get an audition as their new sax player, and I want to talk to all of them to find out what I need to know."

"*Who* you need to know is Dwayne Hite and Freddie Ross."

"I've already met them."

"No luck, huh?"

"I want to meet the other band members."

"Why? You plan to suck your way up the chain of command?"

How far are you willing to go?

"Do you know their names or not?"

"Won't help you any. I tried to interest Dwayne in a boy who played with Louis Armstrong. He wouldn't give him the time of day. He sure as hell isn't going to consider a girl."

K.C. added a quaver to her voice that almost sounded real. "*Please...?*"

"Why the Bluenotes in particular? There are other bands in town."

"I heard they're the best."

"I don't know that I'd say that. Yeah, maybe. Syd's really

good. And Spits, when he was there. Leon was with Lunceford's Orchestra in Europe about ten years ago. You said you met him? Handsome cuss, isn't he?"

She vaguely remembered the trumpet player was good looking, but couldn't recall his face. He was the one who'd given her the stink-eye.

"And Syd played with Coltrane and Terry in the Navy," Piper continued. "Did all the Honolulu clubs. 'Course, that was before they got famous. Won't find a better hide man than him. Seems like every band needs a drummer, so he could play every night of the week if he wanted to."

"He's not exclusive to the Bluenotes?"

"They're not married, they're musicians."

"That's Leon and Syd," she said, trying to get the conversation back on track. "Then there's Catfish and Thump."

Piper sighed. "And Ironhead and Screech. And now two temporary fellas, Bullet and T.J. Got a pencil?"

She did. She pinned the paper against the wall next to the pay phone and held the receiver between her neck and shoulder. "I'm ready."

"Leon Finch. Sydney Clayton. Catfish is Charles Elliot. Thump is Earl McLemore. Ironhead is Byron Granger. Screech is Stephen—with a 'ph'—Granger. They're second cousins, or something like that. Got a place out by Lesterville. They're not very good farmers, but they do have a hog roast every fall that's good, unless you're the hog. No idea who Bullet is. T.J.'s got a strange last name, sounds Indian. Not Apache Indian, Calcutta Indian. Dik—? Diksha. That's it. Don't need to waste your breath with those two, they're not staying. Just the Cedar Rapids gig this weekend, and maybe Davenport next week."

"Why do they need two fill-ins? I thought they only lost

their alto sax."

"Spits, yeah. Thump's in the hospital over at Allen."

"What happened?"

"Heroin."

"Will he be all right?"

"Hell if I know. Not any time soon, I'd guess, since they brought in T.J."

"Do you have addresses? Phone numbers?"

"I'm not their social secretary."

"Okay, thanks." K.C. was about to hang up, but Piper stopped her.

"Word of advice, young lady? The other boys are just employees, even Leon and Syd. You know how Jesus said no one comes to the Father but through Him? Well, no one comes to the Bluenotes but through Dwayne. If you're going to be kissing ass—or other parts—it had better be his. And, as you may already have figured out, Dwayne doesn't like girls. At all."

Chapter 12

THEIR TRANSPORTATION WAS a battered old school bus Dwayne had rescued from the junkyard a few years back and parked in an empty lot on Newton Street. It used to be yellow, but kids had covered it in so much graffiti it was hard to tell what color it was anymore. He put just enough money into it to keep it running for out-of-town gigs, and not one penny more. Although he didn't drive himself, the expense was worth it, because getting all the musicians in one vehicle meant he didn't need to worry who was going to show up for a gig.

Their driver was an almost-blond, almost sixty-year-old woman named Sue Acheson, who'd driven a bus for the Waterton School District before getting a job at the West Side Public Library. Having corralled misbehaving children for twenty-five years, she wouldn't tolerate any nonsense from jazz musicians. One time when Ironhead had made some crude comment to her, she'd stopped the bus right on the highway and marched back to give him hell. She grabbed him by the shirt and got nose-to-nose with him. She told him if he ever said that again she'd kick his nuts so hard they'd fall out his butt. A lifetime of smoking had made her gravelly voice intimidating. Freddie'd been scared of her, and he wasn't even the one being yelled at. After that the band more or less behaved around her.

It was a Friday night. They'd had to wait until Leon and Catfish got off work at Roth's. Both had stayed late, and were tired. They slept most of the way down.

Still, there was plenty of time when the bus pulled off Highway 218 into Cedar Rapids. Sue took side streets to a fairly nice building called the Harlem Ballroom. Freddie had found that amusing when he'd made the booking. Cedar Rapids was a lot bigger city than Waterton, but had a smaller colored population, so almost everyone in the audience would be white. It was if the owners were saying, "Come, all ye of fair complexion, and be thou like the hepcats of New York."

Sue shifted into park. "All right, boys, I'm leaving at twelve-thirty, whether you're on board or not."

The Bluenotes were scheduled to play from 9:00 until midnight. "Hell," Dwayne said, "with all the encores, we won't be out before two."

Sue lit a cigarette and peered over her glasses at him. "You'll be lucky if they stay for the second set."

"You're not coming in?"

She gave him a look. "Byron going to sing like Sinatra?"

"Sinatra's bullshit," Ironhead said, quickly adding, "ma'am."

"Then I'll stay out here and have a snooze."

It was only 7:30. The July sun would be up for another hour and a half. "In the bus?" Freddie said. "You're gonna cook."

"Wouldn't be the first time. I like the heat. Helps me with my tan."

The band had never played the Harlem Ballroom before.

While they unloaded their instruments from the bus, Dwayne went to show the manager their union cards. Nobody got booked anywhere above the level of a dive without them. Even Ruthie at Narlins required cards from bands she didn't know. When Dwayne returned, he led them to a side entrance. The ballroom had a piano, but Syd had to bring his own drums. The earlier act was in a break when the band arrived backstage. Freddie glanced around the curtain at the audience. As expected, they were all white, but, surprisingly, most of them were young—teens and twenties, not at all what he'd expected. The Bluenotes played swing, which appealed to the older set.

"You see that?" he said to Dwayne.

"Uh-oh," Dwayne said.

"Who'd you think would be here?" T.J. said. He was from neighboring Marion, and knew Cedar Rapids well. "It's called Harlem, man. Old white people ain't gonna come to Harlem."

Come, all ye young of fair complexion, and be thou like the hepcats....

Freddie had a flash of K.C., the little White Bird. He hadn't been very nice to her on the phone. Then Syd was lugging in the bass drum and asking for help with the rest.

Catfish perked up. "Is that a baby grand they got out there?" he said. "Ooh-wee, man, that gives me a boner."

Freddie couldn't help looking. 'Fish wasn't really in an agitated state, but Freddie understood his reaction. In 1917, when he'd still had straight fingers, he'd played a baby grand at a gig at Electrical Park. It had been glorious. Scott Joplin had just died, but Freddie had put on such a show he'd thought the great man might climb out of his grave and shake his hand. Ended the night with Joplin's "Solace," a sad and sweet song perfect for mourning the loss of a musical genius.

"It's probably out of tune," T.J. said. "Was last time I was here."

"Well, ain't you the cheerful little bluebird?" 'Fish said.

"You want in tune down here, play the Danceland Ballroom."

Freddie chuckled. The Danceland hired only A-list orchestras. The Bluenotes were somewhat further down the alphabet, although in reputation, not necessarily talent.

"What are we gonna play?" Bullet said.

Dwayne distributed the set list to everyone. "We'll start with my new chart, see how that goes. If they like it, we can stick with the faster stuff."

"There ain't three hours of fast stuff here," Leon said. "Unless you let us do some Bird."

"We don't practice that shit," Dwayne said.

"I know some," T.J. said.

"Me, too," Bullet said.

"All of us do," Freddie said, "but it ain't what we do."

"Might not have a choice," Screech said. "That's what kids want, and kids is what we got tonight."

Syd and Ironhead ended up carrying the drums in by themselves. They put them in the wings while the opening act returned to the stage.

That band was made up of older black men, like themselves.

"The Edgar Robbins Eight," T.J. said. "They stink. Times must be tough if the Harlem would hire them."

"They hired us," Freddie said.

"Uh-oh," T.J. said.

****

The young crowd was in a foul mood when the Bluenotes took the stage. Freddie didn't think the Edgar Robbins Eight stunk, exactly, but they'd never play Beale Street. They made the mistake of playing standards by white orchestras led by Bradley, Beneke, Gray, and Dorsey—the same mistake the Bluenotes planned to make.

"In the Nude" went over well enough. Dwayne had written in just enough hot rhythm to satisfy their urge to sizzle with the music. A few Basie and Ellington tunes kept the rowdies happy for a while, but they grew restless when the band played any tempo below allegro.

They made it through the first set without too much grumbling, but a number of people left. Of the ones who stayed, there were a few smiling faces, couples who wanted to dance slow and play grab-ass and earlobe-bite.

Freddie, Leon, and Catfish sat backstage drinking Cokes while the others went out back to piss. "Never been lynched before," Leon said.

"Ain't them you need to worry about," 'Fish said.

"Wasn't them I was talking about," Leon said, gazing off into space. Freddie followed his eyes, but he wasn't looking at anything.

"Yeah," 'Fish agreed, his face sullen. That was strange, because 'Fish was the kind of cat who took things as they came, never too angry, never too happy. He usually walked away okay.

Neither of them spoke again until Freddie couldn't stand the silence. "How's the eighty-eight? Other than out of tune, I mean."

"Smoothest action I ever felt. Like butter, man. Like velvet."

"Get your boner back?"

'Fish half smiled. "Who's asking?"

Then there was another silence. Dwayne and the others came in from the back. Dwayne looked over his glasses at 'Fish and Leon. "Somebody die?"

"Freddie's gotta find us more gigs," Leon said.

"Like every night," 'Fish said.

"Ain't no way," Freddie said.

"What the hell?" Dwayne said. "Why?"

"Roth's is going on strike August second if we don't get a new contract," Leon said.

"It ain't August yet," Dwayne said.

"No way a contract's happening by then," Leon said. "Roth's is offering nine cents an hour. Won't budge. *Nine cents.*"

Ironhead, Screech, Bullet, and T.J. decided that might be a good time to go back on stage and re-tune. Syd went with them.

"Go to work anyway," Dwayne said. "Management will let you in."

"Ain't no scab, man," Leon said. "My daddy came up from Mississippi for the railroad strike. Look what happened to him."

"That was a long time ago. Things have changed."

"Like what?"

"Got to feed your families," Dwayne said.

'Fish and Leon stood up and turned toward stage. "That's why we need more gigs."

"Hell of a time to tell us," Dwayne said.

"Didn't know till tonight. Workers took a vote."

Dwayne remained seated in the wings as everyone else walked onto the stage. "Could've voted against it," he called.

"We did," Leon said.

"They didn't," 'Fish said.

"They won," Leon said.

Freddie looked out over the crowd as he re-greased his slide. Not many friendly faces. There weren't enough places in Waterton to play every night—not enough anywhere in Iowa. Des Moines, maybe. But they had their own bands. Sue couldn't get off her library job that often to drive them, and no one else had a chauffeur's license. Freddie hadn't renewed his after being fired from his cabbing gig. With his fingers, he wouldn't try to handle a bus anyway.

Spits.

Shay.

Thump.

Now this.

"Screw it," Leon said. "Bullet, you know 'Ko-ko'?"

"Yessir, I do."

"Let's burn this house down."

****

The white kids approved, even though the band ran out of material halfway through the second set. Jazz musicians prided themselves on being able to play anything, but they had to start with *something*, and there were only so many Charlie Parker, Dizzy Gillespie, and Thelonius Monk pieces they knew. After a few numbers, it was just a lick here, a riff there.

The last half of the set turned into an extended jam session, no order, no structure, just a series of melodies, harmonies, and rhythms invented on the spot. Dwayne nearly busted a blood vessel in the wings, but Freddie had to admit he hadn't had this much fun at a gig since—well, ever. At least since 1917. Everyone was breathing hard, sweating, and laughing, and by midnight the Bluenotes got the calls for encores nobody'd expected.

Sue waited for them after all, but she wasn't happy. "Some of us have to work in the morning," she said. The library was open 9:00 till 1:00 on Saturdays.

"Sorry," Freddie said, "but goddamn. Goddamn. You should've heard us. Should've heard the crowd."

"Well, good for you. You smell like water buffaloes. Open the windows on the way home."

"Yeah, so we can jump out," Leon said, and neither he nor Catfish were smiling.

Chapter 13

K.C. WASN'T MAD AT Jack when he wouldn't drive her to Cedar Rapids, because she hadn't expected him to. If they'd gone to see the Bluenotes, they wouldn't have gotten home before two. He had to open at Dale's at 6:45.

Staking out their gigs wasn't the smartest move, anyway, and going to Narlins hadn't gotten her anywhere.

She had a better plan. Although she knew their names, she didn't know their addresses. If they had phones, they'd be listed in the telephone directory. But they probably didn't, since they seemed to conduct their business out of Narlins. However, there was one band member whose whereabouts she knew. He wasn't in Smoky Row, and he was easy to get to without a car.

At West Fourth Street K.C. caught the city bus that would take her across the river to Allen Hospital. On East Fourth it passed the Paramount, Block's, Kresge's, Palace Clothiers, antique shops, bars, banks, and the Strand Theater. The Strand's marquee advertised *Key Largo*, with Bogart's name above the title and Bacall's beneath it. K.C. thought Bogart was a funny-looking man. His head was too big for his body, but he was sexy anyway, with his growly voice and five o-clock shadow. Tough guys appealed to her—a category, alas, that Jack didn't fit into. But he was cuter than Bogart, in a choirboy sort of way.

At Washington Park the bus turned left onto Franklin Street. That's where Waterton started to deteriorate. The east-side businesses within a few blocks of the river were well kept and safe, but the houses in the residential areas beyond downtown grew progressively shabbier. A lot of them must once have been grand, two- and three-story Victorian structures with gabled roofs and fancy window frames. Now most of the paint was gone, the roofs sagged, and the wood was rotting at the corners. The glass in some windows had been replaced with cardboard. The houses looked like they could collapse at any moment.

People still lived in them, though. The weather had turned hot again, and three little black girls sprayed each other with a hose in one of the yards. Didn't seem to bother them that they were poor. K.C. smiled and waved, but they kept playing.

At the stoplight on Mullan an easterly breeze caught the bus's diesel smoke and blew it in through the open windows. K.C. coughed. She hated that smell.

The bus turned right and headed north. Here residential mixed with business. The buildings continued to get worse, the bars seedier, the houses smaller and more dilapidated. Pawn shops started popping up, and greasy cafes, and one out-of-place A&W Root Beer drive-in restaurant.

Then there was Sam's Pet Emporium, which she'd heard sold live monkeys, but in this part of town she'd never be brave enough to investigate.

Somewhere out this direction, in the bowels of Waterton's poverty, was the notorious Pamela's Triangle Club. K.C. knew what kind of entertainment they had there, and she knew what the triangle referred to. She wasn't a prude, but that was disgusting. Worse, a woman ran the place. K.C. had never understood how a female could hire girls to display themselves to horny men, many of whom were probably married. She had no intention of finding out.

If Jack ever went there... well, she'd no longer be so conflicted about him. But, being Jack, he wouldn't.

Past the Emporium, Logan Junior High rose like a castle above peasant surroundings. Then there were a few more houses, another service station, an auto body repair shop, a scrap yard, a used car dealership, yet more houses, and, finally, Allen Hospital.

K.C. put her ticket in her purse for the return trip and got off near the visitor's entrance. The receptionist was a young black woman with glasses and hair that had been straightened on an ironing board. That was how colored girls got the kinks out.

"May I help you?" she said.

"I'm looking for Earl McLemore."

The woman checked her list. "You family?"

A receptionist couldn't be expected to personally know every patient who came in. K.C. smiled. "Just a friend."

"Okay. Three eighty-seven. Follow the blue line past Surgery, turn left at the first hallway, and follow the red line to elevator B."

Several nurses passed her. Two were pushing a stretcher with an old man into Cardiac, one a wheelchair with a gasping pregnant woman. As her crude male high school friends would say, the lady was about to "pop." A doctor hurried behind with a clipboard and a stethoscope.

K.C. found the red line, and then Elevator B. As she waited for the car to come down, she realized she had no idea what she was going to say to Thump.

Turned out she didn't have to say anything to him. His room was just past the third-floor nurses' station. He was asleep, but he wasn't alone. A middle-aged white woman sat next to his bed doing the *Record*'s crossword puzzle. She looked up when K.C. entered.

"Hello," the woman said. "Get the wrong room, dear?"

"This is three eighty-seven? Mr. McLemore?"

"Yup. How do you know him?"

"As Thump?"

The woman smiled. "Not what you call him. Everyone calls him Thump. I meant, who are you?"

"K.C. Brown. I play alto sax."

"Uh-huh. With who?"

"The Bluenotes."

"No, you don't."

"Well, I auditioned for them at Narlins."

"I see. And you're here to see Earl, why?"

"I heard he was in the hospital, and thought I'd look in on him."

"That's sweet." The woman went back to her crossword. "Large artistic work, four letters, second letter p?"

"Opus," K.C. said.

The woman scribbled the word in. "Hey, you're good. Fits with octopus."

"How's he doing?"

"He's farting, so he's not dead. Playing bass isn't the only reason he's called Thump."

K.C. turned her head away to hide her blush. That was information she didn't need. "Maybe I should come back later…?"

"No, dear. Sit down. Where are my manners?" She nodded toward the second chair.

K.C. perched on the edge of the chair, as if preparing to bolt. Maybe she was. She hadn't known what she was going to say to Thump, and she didn't know what to say to this woman.

"Kasey, was it?"

"K.C., like in Kansas City."

"Hi, 'K.C. like in Kansas City,' I'm Sue. Now, why don't you tell me what you really want with Earl."

"Just to talk."

"Your audition didn't go well?"

"How do you know that?"

"He can't help you, honey. Dwayne Hite's the man to see." Sue set the newspaper and pencil on the nightstand next to Thump's bed. "Earl's a junkie. If you want a connection to the Bluenotes, he's not your guy."

"I didn't mean it to sound like I'm using him."

"How could it sound any other way? It's all right, I know a little something about jazz musicians. There's a need. Whatever it takes. Never seen it in a white girl, though."

K.C. recalled her most recent imaginary conversation with Kenny. "I'm going to go now," she said.

"If Dwayne senses you're using Earl to get to him, you'll have no chance."

K.C. felt ashamed. "I've got no chance anyway. I'm sorry."

Sue seemed to take pity on her. She gave K.C. the newspaper and pencil. "Write down your name and number. I'll talk to Thump."

"I don't have my own phone. This is my boyfriend Jack's. Thanks."

As she handed the paper and pencil back, a black teenaged girl poked her head in the room.

"I was hoping you'd come," Sue said. "K.C., this is my

daughter, Emmaline."

"Oh," K.C. whispered, unable to hide her shock. "She's black."

Sue grinned. "You don't have to whisper, dear. She knows she's black."

****

From the window of the bus, K.C. saw a black 1940 Ford pull into the Allen parking lot. A man who looked like Freddie Ross got out. The bus hadn't left yet, and she was tempted to confront him—beg, demand, threaten, promise, grovel, anything—but she'd had enough humiliation for one day.

She rode the bus back as far as the east side of the Fourth Street Bridge. From there she'd walk to her apartment. *Easter Parade* was still at the Paramount. "ENDS FRIDAY," the sign said. A musical love story might be just what she needed, even if it was Irving Berlin. The show didn't start until 7:00, though, and it was only 4:15. Jack was off tonight. Maybe she'd sweet-talk him into taking her. He owed her, after Abbott and Costello.

Sue had introduced herself and her daughter but hadn't explained why they were there. Could she be Thump's *wife*? A white woman and a black man? That didn't play well, not in Biloxi, not in Birmingham, not in Chicago, and not in Waterton.

White or black, married or not, the biology worked the same.

As she stepped onto the bridge she threw a rock into the river, tried to find symbolic significance in the ripples, didn't, and crossed over.

How far *was* she willing to go?

You plan to suck your way up the chain of command?

Jack didn't *demand* suck jobs, but he wasn't shy about asking, and that was okay, because they were a couple. Besides, he reciprocated. But doing it for love and doing it to get a job were different things. She wouldn't go *that* far.

And she wouldn't need to, because she was sure none of the members of the Bluenotes would expect that.

Why wouldn't they? Kenny's voice answered. *You don't know them, Squirt.*

"Shut up, Kenny." He was only supposed to tell her things she wanted to hear. Still, Sue had a black daughter, and they were both in Thump's room. At some point, under some circumstances, Thump had expected *something*. And gotten it.

Chapter 14

AUNTIE AUDREY'S WAS THE only restaurant in Waterton that served authentic Southern food. Freddie hadn't been south of St. Louis since his father Lewis brought the family up from Biloxi during the Illinois Central strike in '09, but he'd never lost his taste for the cuisine. He was meeting Spits for lunch, not on business, just because. Dwayne didn't know, and didn't need to.

Displaced Southerners made pilgrimages from all over the state to worship at the counter of Auntie Audrey. The place wasn't busy yet, but it would be once the church crowd arrived. Freddie'd promised Spits he'd wait for him to order, but the chicken-fried steak and catfish sizzled in back, smelling mighty fine. The family next to him was eating collard greens, hushpuppies, and grits. Couldn't have Southern food without eating grits. Freddie was pretty sure it was a law. The father had gotten himself a mess of crawfish, too, which was a little too Creole for Freddie's tastes, but still made him nostalgic for his childhood, before women, before money, before responsibilities, before any of the cares of the world.

The kids were clamoring for pecan pie.

Pecan pie.

He was about to give in to his stomach when Spits burst through the door, looking like a high-end pimp in a hundred-dollar suit. He had his trademark Scottish tam pulled down over his eyebrows, and flashed the rakish smile that drove the ladies wild. His white spats were long out of style, but somehow he made the look work. Some might think him flamboyant, and they'd be right. "Frederick Douglass Ross," he bellowed. "How you doing, Boneman?"

Freddie rose and shook his hand. "Good, Jesse. You?"

"God*damn*, it smells good in here. What are you having?"

The mother of the family glared at him and covered her youngest child's ears. Spits took his hat off and bowed an apology.

They sat down. "One of everything," Freddie said.

"I was going to offer to buy..."

"*You're* buying? Is Jesus coming tomorrow?"

"I don't know, has He cleared it with Dwayne?"

"Be nice."

Spits winked and hung his tam on the back of his chair. "Nah, Boneman, I'm just feeling generous. Get what you want."

Freddie wasn't going to argue. The menu was a handwritten piece of paper, folded in half, but it might as well have been an engraved tablet of gold. The food was that good. Freddie made his choices, Spits made his, then Freddie went to the counter to order for them both.

When he returned to the table he said, "Haven't heard much about you lately. You playing with anyone?"

"Don't have much fire left. How was your Cedar Rapids gig? Dwayne must've found an alto?"

Freddie put his hands together. "Gig was good. Cat

named Calvin Arcineaux filled in on horn."

"Bullet? I've heard of him. Out of Omaha, or Council Bluffs, or something? He do okay?"

"Yeah, but he won't be staying. You know about Thump?"

"Word gets around." Spits stood up. "I have to micturate, my friend."

"Man, I don't even want to know what that is."

He lowered his voice so the woman next to them wouldn't hear. "Take a piss."

Freddie pointed to the restroom. "Don't let me stop you."

Spits seemed off today. Forced cheerfulness. Evasive. But, then, Freddie hadn't seen him for a while. Dwayne had waited a month to advertise for a replacement, thinking Spits might change his mind. He hadn't. Didn't call, visit, or stop by at Narlins, either. Meanwhile, Dwayne filled in with sidemen as best he could, none of whom could match Spits's style or energy.

Freddie tried not to listen in on the family's conversation. Two more customers came in. Time passed. He checked the clock. Spits must've *really* had to pee. Then Audrey's granddaughter Janeen brought their orders out. "Hey, Freddie," she said. "Separate tickets?"

"One."

"Who's paying?"

"Spits."

"*Spits*? Well, don't that beat all?"

Freddie had ordered pork knuckles, cornbread, poke salad, and of course pecan pie. Audrey didn't serve alcohol, so he'd gotten a large glass of Barq's Root Beer. Spits had two fried chicken wings, turnip greens, and hot tea.

Three minutes later Spits still wasn't back, so Freddie went ahead without him. He wasn't a mixer—he ate one food at a time, always the meat first. He'd gotten almost to the pie when Spits finally reappeared.

"I'm starving," he said, without explaining why he'd been gone so long.

Freddie was afraid he knew. "You didn't get much."

Spits sat down and broke one of the wings into three sections. He ate two of the three, then pushed the third to the edge of the plate. "Is Thump going to die?" he said.

"Docs say not this time, but I don't know. Stupid shit's still in the hospital. Can't keep nothing down."

"T.J. covered, right? He's better than Thump."

"Don't matter if he is or he ain't, 'cause he ain't staying, either. Before you left, everything was fine, now it's all going to shit. Bluenotes can't be down two. And Leon and 'Fish, they're going on strike at Roth's in August, so they need to play *all* the time. I can't get us the gigs, they'll find someone who will."

"I'm not coming back, Boneman. Not as long as Dwayne's there. You know why."

"Yeah." Freddie was quiet for a moment, then chuckled. "This white chick tried out for your spot—eighteen, nineteen years old. Thought she was Charlie Parker. Dwayne called her White Bird."

Spits took a bite of turnip greens. Freddie thought he'd scoff at the idea, but all he said was "She any good?"

"Might be someday."

"Let her play."

"You serious?"

"It'll do Dwayne good to have somebody different hanging around."

"Guess you can't get much different than that."

"White Bird? I like it."

Spits's eyes weren't quite focusing. He was stretching out

his words and sweating more than he should. The day wasn't that hot yet.

"You wouldn't mind a girl taking your place?" Freddie said.

"That's funny." Spits started to sip his tea, but set the cup down and slumped forward, elbows on the table, head in his hands.

"Goddamn it, Jesse, show me," Freddie said. He didn't care if the lady next to them was offended. "Roll up your sleeve."

David Hoing & Roger Hileman

PART TWO:

BLACK CAT

Chapter 15

THE DAVENPORT GIG WAS a disaster. It was at the Cabana Haus on July 31st, two days before the Roth strike. Leon and Catfish were off kilter all night, their minds not on the music. Leon wandered into changes that made no sense, and 'Fish suddenly developed club fingers. Although the Davenport crowd was more to Dwayne's liking than Cedar Rapids'—middle-aged folks who appreciated swing—the Bluenotes finished in silence, no applause, only resentment from an audience who felt they'd been cheated of their dollar admission.

They had.

The manager had to pay Dwayne because of their contract, but he vowed they'd never play the Quad Cities again. Freddie wondered if they'd ever play anywhere again. This kind of thing could follow a band. Everyone had an off night sometimes, but Leon and 'Fish's erratic performances had been contagious. The rest tried to compensate, but gave in to frustration early in the second set and just went through the motions. It was one thing to be bad, another not to care.

Hopefully, Waterton was far enough from Davenport that

they'd be able to redeem themselves with other gigs before word of the "catastrophe at Cabana" reached there. That didn't seem likely. T.J. was done. He'd driven himself to Davenport, and was going home to Marion. Got in his car and left, didn't even say goodbye. Thump was finally out of the hospital, but who knew when—or if—he'd be able to doghouse again. And while Bullet hadn't made noises yet about returning to Omaha, a show like tonight's could hasten his homesickness.

No one spoke as they filed onto the bus. Even Sue was withdrawn. Thump, her former brother-in-law, was recovering at her house. She hadn't especially wanted him there, but she didn't trust him to stay straight alone. Emmaline had given up her Saturday night to look after him while Sue was with the band.

The drive back was three and a half hours of unspoken tension, bumpy roads, and thunder. Rain was coming down hard when the bus pulled into Waterton. Dwayne bummed a lift home from Sue so they could talk about Thump.

As Freddie left the bus, a gust of wind knocked his hat into a puddle. That was how the night had gone. As he stooped to get it, Leon stepped out behind him. They looked at each other for a moment.

"Damn, man," Leon said, rain in his face.

Freddie squeezed his shoulder. "Yeah."

****

He woke Sunday afternoon with Washington on his chest. She batted at his nose and lips. When he opened his eyes she mewed, as if to say *As long as you're awake anyway, you might as well feed me.*

He set her on the bed and stepped around the corner to the bathroom. A little congested, he blew his nose. There was blood on the toilet paper. Not much, but it shouldn't bleed at all. Sometimes the dry air of winter did that, but it wasn't winter, and the air was hell and gone from dry. He got a cotton ball from the medicine cabinet and pushed it up his nostril. After doing his business, he went to the kitchen and opened a can of tuna for the cat. It was her favorite, though it gave her the runs.

The clock said 1:30. He got the Sunday *Record* from the mailbox. The headline, of course, was about Roth's. "ROTH WORKERS TO STRIKE AT 12:01 A.M. MONDAY." That was tomorrow.

He skimmed the story. Like Leon had said, Roth's was offering a nine cent an hour raise. The union wanted twenty-nine. Neither side would budge.

Nobody'd get rich off nine more cents, but the meat packing plant already paid more than most companies around town, so that didn't seem all that unfair to Freddie.

But, then, he didn't have a real job, just what Dwayne paid him, plus a split with the rest of the Bluenotes when they played. *Why don't you make more money*? Shay often nagged, just before she went on strike against *him*. One of her many complaints.

Freddie took the cotton out of his nose. The bleeding had stopped. He got dressed and went out for a walk. He did that a lot, with little else to do during the day. Auntie Audrey's was open. He didn't mind eating there two Sundays in a row. It was a long haul for his old bones, but he wasn't going to waste gas driving.

The late night rain had left puddles everywhere. Clouds were still low and heavy, promising more downbursts. For now it was drizzle, dripping from sagging telephone wires. The west-side factories pumped smoke into the air. The stink combined with the fresh scent of rain and the smell of worms.

A group of boys was playing catch in the field next to the Illinois Central tracks. One of them overthrew another and the baseball rolled all the way to Freddie. Not confident of his arm or his grip, he tossed it underhanded to the nearest kid.

His fingers—hell, all his joints—seemed to ache more when it rained, although his body didn't really need an excuse to hurt anymore. It just did. He wiggled his fingers to limber them up, like he had when he could still play piano. Thinking of those days jolted the memory of "Twelfth Street Rag." He used to love that tune, long and long ago, but no more. Now the thought of it made him cringe. Threatening bad people was a bad idea. The last number he'd played before he'd found out just how bad was "Twelfth Street Rag."

Now, when he had so many other things to worry about, it ran through his head like a broken record. "Goddammit, Freddie," he muttered, "get that shit out of there."

He found his usual bench at a little patch of greenery generously called Jackson Park. The park was nestled between unoccupied houses with overgrown yards. Most had been condemned by the city. The bench was still wet, but he didn't care. He sat with his eyes closed, a moist breeze in his face.

He mentally rolled through some other charts, thought about Shay, and then the strike. Nine cents an hour. Maybe it wasn't fair to the Roth workers. It certainly wasn't fair to Freddie, or to Dwayne, or to Syd, Ironhead, or Screech. Nine cents an hour meant trouble for the Bluenotes. Nobody had said it. Probably nobody would. But with Spits gone, Thump ailing, and Leon and Catfish preoccupied with the strike, Freddie didn't see how the band could go on.

Both had voted against the strike, but they were union

men who'd back the workers. Especially Leon. His daddy had crossed picket lines in the railroad strike of '09, and one night he didn't come home. His body was never found, but no letters from him ever came, either, no phone calls, no indication of what had happened. That taught Leon a lesson he didn't want to learn but couldn't forget.

A robin landed on the sidewalk and snatched a worm that had beached itself there. The bird cocked its head at Freddie, then flew off with its lunch.

It ain't enough to love the music.

You gotta sweat it, you gotta bleed it.

No doubt Leon and 'Fish loved the music. They'd asked him for more gigs, but, after Davenport, Freddie wasn't sure. Roth's trumped jazz.

He sighed, and then the sky opened up with big teardrops of rain. Freddie rose from the bench, his clothes soaked. He'd forgotten his hat. From here Audrey's wasn't far, but there was no reason to hurry now. A person could only get so wet. After that it didn't matter.

When he walked in the door, Audrey's granddaughter Janeen laughed at him. Luckily the church crowd had pretty much cleared out by then. The three remaining customers smiled sympathetically. Audrey came out from the back, took one look, and said, "You ain't sitting that wet butt on any of my chairs."

"Good to see you, too, Auntie."

Audrey wasn't really his aunt, or anybody's, as far as Freddie knew. She turned to the girl. "'Neeners, go get 'bout three clean aprons from the closet." To Freddie she said, "Didn't your mama teach you more sense than to walk in the rain?"

"Wasn't raining when I started out."

"You okay?"

"Compared to what?"

Janeen returned quickly with the aprons. Audrey placed two of them across the seat of the chair and the other over the back. "Now sit. What can I get you?"

Freddie gave her a halfhearted leer.

Janeen was old enough to notice, and giggled.

"Shay must've left again," Audrey said. "Well, Pam's place'll be open tomorrow night. Go get yourself a eyeful, 'cause all I got for you's a menu."

"Never was no good at flirting," Freddie said.

"Maybe that's why she's always taking off. Speaking of which, I saw her mama the other day."

"Nelly was out and about?"

"She and some light-skinned fella come in for breakfast."

"A white man?"

"Naw, he was colored. Just had lighter skin than most."

"Shay wasn't with them? Who was he?"

"Damned if I know. Ain't never seen him before. So you gonna eat, or you just come in to jaw? Flatheads are fresh today. Henry caught a couple of fat ones this morning."

Freddie nodded. "And a Barq's."

"I know, and pecan pie, 'cept we're out of pecans. Apple cobbler? I'll make it nice and hot, with caramel sauce. Pull the chill right out of your old bones."

Nothing could pull the chill out of his bones today.

He ordered, and ate in silence, and Audrey knew enough to leave him alone. When he was done, he motioned her over for the bill.

"Your money's no good here," she said. "Look after yourself, you hear?"

****

It was still pouring when Freddie accepted a ride home from Audrey's husband Henry, changed into dry clothes, and drove himself to Townsend's Rack and Cue. The pool hall was open Sundays, but couldn't serve alcohol. He leaned over the table and banked the five ball into the side pocket. His twisted fingers served him almost as well as a bridge in aiming the cue, maybe the only advantage of his disfigurement.

Ironhead and Screech stood by, Screech in the game, Ironhead waiting to play the winner. The cousins didn't talk about the Bluenotes. They didn't talk about the Roth strike. They didn't talk about anything other than the game. It was like nothing affected them but what they were doing now, like the past was a black wall and the only future was what was being invented in each moment.

Freddie scoffed at the notion, yet envied it, too. No ghosts of *was* or fear of *will be*.

"Man, that's like cheating," Screech said.

"Trade my fingers for yours," Freddie said, then promptly missed a straight-on shot on the seven. Pool was a game of straight lines and angles. He had the angles down, but sometimes getting from point A to point B gave him trouble.

"Easy shots are hardest," Ironhead said.

Screech chalked his cue. "Lemme show you how it's done." He sank the nine, thirteen, and eleven in quick succession, but then Freddie's balls blocked any other decent shot. Instead, Screech tapped the cue ball so it came to rest behind a cluster Freddie couldn't get around or through without risking the game.

"Shitty thing to do," he said, walking around the table, looking for any kind of possibility. "I was thinking of stopping over at Leon's tonight. Wanna come?"

"Why?" Screech said.

"Why?" Ironhead said.

"Strike starts in the morning."

"Okay, and?"

Freddie thought *the hell with it*, and blasted the cue ball through the cluster, scattering the balls, sinking one of Screech's and none of his own.

"Thanks," Screech said, then ran the table. "Shame you gotta cheat just to be this bad."

"Kiss my ass. Two out of three?"

"Byron's up," Screech said.

Freddie returned his cue to the rack.

"You mad?" Ironhead said.

"Nah," he said, but he was, and didn't know why.

****

Leon was at the union hall, planning. His wife Cindy— Dee—invited Freddie in for coffee, but he declined.

"Leon didn't even want the strike," he said.

"Takes a hell of a man to go against his own wishes to help others," Dee said, the light of pride in her eyes.

"What're you two gonna do?"

"The Lord'll look after us." She winked at him. "'Course, you could give Him a nudge by booking more gigs."

"Do what I can," Freddie said, tapping the brim of his hat. "'Night, Dee."

As he walked to his car, he felt a touch of resentment. By doing the right thing for their fellow union workers, Leon and 'Fish had made Freddie responsible for feeding their families.

****

For the next two nights he sat in Ruthie's office at Narlins and made phone calls, because sometimes when a man didn't have hope, he had to have faith. Most of the contacts were busts, but he did manage to arrange bookings at Iowa State Teachers College on the 13th and Upper Iowa University on the 14th. School wasn't in session, but the students of both were mostly local kids, so there should be plenty of folks around. Tim Piper at Electrical Park didn't have an open slot until October 9th, but that was all right. Scheduling that far in advance assumed there was a future. He even got the band into Curtis's Gardens at the end of November, where both the management and customers liked the music but hated the musicians.

Four bookings weren't nearly enough, but four was better than none. Now, if he could only field a band to fulfill those obligations.

His next call was to Sue Acheson to ask about Thump, and to make sure she'd be available to drive for the two college gigs.

"Earl's okay," she said. "I'm kicking him out today. He's not as bad as Toad, but he's still a pain in my ass." For years Sue had been common-law married to Thump's brother. And then suddenly Toad was gone, and Sue stopped using his last name. She got Emmaline out of the deal, which was all that mattered to her. Freddie didn't know the whole story, and didn't want to.

"He gonna be able to play?" he said.

"Ask him. He's right here." Sue must have put her hand over the receiver to muffle her voice, but he still heard her say to Thump, "Hey, Cowboy, it's Freddie."

"Yeah?" Thump said into the phone.

"Why Cowboy?"

"I ride horses."

Freddie knew what he meant. "Ever gonna quit that

shit?"

"Probably not."

"Horse is gonna kill you, man."

"It's the only reason I know I'm not already dead."

Freddie thought how sad that was, then changed the subject to his original reason for calling. "When you coming back? Roth's is on strike, and Leon and 'Fish really need the gigs."

"What about the cat Dwayne got to play for me?"

"You heard about Davenport?"

Thump laughed, and coughed, and laughed. "Yeah."

"He took off after that."

"Don't blame him. Still no one for Spits?"

"Calvin Arcineaux. Goes by Bullet. He's over here from Omaha, don't know how long."

"Find us anything?"

"Here and there."

"I'm in. But I got my eye on this pretty little filly..."

"Goddamn it, Thump—"

Thump hung up.

Freddie called Dwayne to bring him up to date, then Janae to see when Catfish would be done on the picket line.

Turned out, he wasn't walking the line. "He voted against the strike," she said. "He's no scab, but he's not going to help the union, either."

"So what's he do all day?"

Janae let out an exaggerated sigh. "Tries to increase the fish population. All the time, Boneman. *All* the blankety-blank time. Holy shit, I'm tired. Get him some gigs. Far away, where he'll be gone for, I don't know, weeks. How about Paris? Paris would be good."

"Is he home now?"

"No, praise be to Allah, or Whoever's listening."

"Know where he is?"

"Nope."

He could hear her smiling. "Know when he'll be back?"

"Nope."

Children were screaming in the background. Freddie suspected she wasn't smiling anymore. "Well, I did get us some gigs," he said, "but not too far out of town."

"It's a start. I swear, Boneman, I can't wait till the change is on me. No more cramps, no more kids. Heaven."

"Good luck," Freddie said.

Chapter 16

K.C. SAT BETWEEN JACK'S parents at their pre-church breakfast. It was just the four of them: Dick and Patti Schoonover, Jack, and her. Jack's two older brothers lived out of state, and K.C.'s family hadn't been invited. The Schoonovers and Browns ran in different social circles, not higher or lower, necessarily, just different. K.C. was the only connection between them—and she wasn't much of a connection, since her own parents didn't want much to do with her these days.

She'd only been to church with Jack a few times. The Schoonovers were Lutherans. Nothing wrong with that—if K.C. went at all, it was to any Protestant church her family didn't attend. But this morning Dick had cajoled her into filling in on the organ, since their regular accompanist was down with gout. K.C. wasn't as proficient on the organ as she was on sax and piano, but she could play one. She just didn't like to. She hated the double keyboard, the settings, the bass pedals, and the foot-controlled volume. Mostly she hated the sound. Organs were so... churchy.

"It certainly did rain a lot last night," Patti said.

"Looks like more's coming," Dick said. He bent an entire

slice of bacon into his mouth and winked at K.C. He was just being dopey, but it gave her the creeps.

Yes, let's talk about the weather, K.C. thought. *And maybe the best bleach for washing whites. And what shenanigans the neighbors are up to.*

"K.C. auditioned for a professional jazz band a couple weeks ago," Jack said.

Or why not that? She couldn't believe she'd sunk so low that she'd tried to use a sick man to further her ambition. *Please forgive me, Thump. And Mrs. Thump, if that's who you are.*

"I wish you'd stayed with the violin," Patti said to Jack. "You could be playing with the Waterton Symphony. I know the conductor."

"Violin," Dick snorted, as if his son was too good to waste his time on music. He was a bigwig at Landon & Co., Waterton's other major employer. Landon's made farm implements.

A ceiling fan above the table circulated air, despite the morning cool. K.C. watched it with disinterest, then looked around the house. It was a Colonial-style home built around the turn of the century. *Way* too spacious for the three people who occupied it now. The most it had ever held at one time was four. Jack came from a two-generation family. His brothers Art and Gregory had been born in 1908 and 1910. For reasons unknown, the Schoonovers then waited seventeen years before starting over with Jack. Maybe he was an *oops*. Art was in the service by then, and Gregory left a year later, leaving Jack to be raised as an only child most of his life.

It seemed an odd way to go about things, but then, K.C.'s family had its quirks, too. Such as starting each child's name with the letter "K." Her mother's name was Rose, but her father was Kenneth Senior. So: Ken Senior, Ken Junior, Kathryn, Kristina, and Kasey. Poor Mom must have felt like the odd person out. On the other hand, if she hadn't liked all the "K"s, she could have lobbied for something else.

"My sister in Chicago has a television," Dick said out of the blue. "If we ever get a station here, I'm buying us one."

K.C. hoped that didn't happen. If televisions caught on, they'd put movie theaters right out of business. "Kenny said New York was broadcasting during the war. He saw it during his training."

"You should eat, Kasey," said Patti. K.C. knew the woman didn't approve of her, but she was being sugary nice this morning because K.C. had agreed to play at church for them. K.C. had agreed to play so Patti would have to be sugary nice to her.

She scooped a small portion of scrambled eggs onto her fork.

A family portrait hung above the fireplace in the living room, taken when Jack was still a baby. Dick was a military man, and his first two sons had followed in his footsteps. Art and Gregory wore their Army uniforms, although neither saw action. They served in the late '20s, slipping in between wars, and Jack, of course, just missed the second one. There was little chance he'd be called up now. It was 1948. The world was at peace. Except for Berlin. And the Middle East. And China. And.... Well, in any case, he'd get an educational deferment.

They finished breakfast and freshened up for church. Dick and Jack rode in the front of the Packard, Patti and K.C. in back. Patti always did her best to interpose herself between K.C and Jack. She probably suspected what went on in K.C.'s apartment.

Trinity Lutheran was in West Fourth Street's "church

row." First Congregational, St. Demetrios Greek Orthodox, and Sacred Heart Catholic churches stood next to it in succession, and Christian Fellowship Baptist was just down the road.

One thing about Lutheran churches, they had lovely architecture, or at least Trinity did. It was so much bigger than her parents' Methodist church. Jack led her upstairs to the organ in the balcony. The choral director greeted her. "Kasey, isn't it?"

"Close enough," K.C. said.

The woman handed her a brown American Lutheran hymnal. "We'll be doing the marked passages. Gladys can play anything we put in front of her. Are you Lutheran, dear? If not, I'll have someone stay with you to cue when you play. Do you know these songs, or can you read music?"

Can I read music? Seriously? "I have a basic idea," she said, thinking words that couldn't be spoken in church.

Once the service began, she only screwed up a couple of times, coming in too soon once, and letting the congregation dictate the tempo instead of moving them along with a quicker accompaniment. Although she didn't care for organ, she was glad she was up in the balcony, because then she didn't have to do all that standing and sitting. Besides, she was getting paid to play. A paying gig was a paying gig.

She was curious about why Lutheran pastors announced how many Sundays past Pentecost the date was. Turned out August 1st was the eleventh one. Oh, those silly Lutherans...

The service was uneventful, nothing she hadn't seen before. The Schoonovers dropped her at her apartment afterward. Jack went home with them, and K.C. spent the rest of the day alone, doing nothing. That gave her too much time to dwell on her embarrassing gaff at the hospital.

Only two directions to go: up or sideways. She was feeling

pretty sideways at the moment.

How could it sound any other way?

Kenny?

She has a point, Squirt.

On the other hand, Sue had asked for her name and number to give to Thump.

****

The Roth strike started at 12:01 Monday morning. Not that it mattered too much to K.C. It didn't affect her, except that Jack predicted the price of pork would skyrocket if it lasted too long. He'd be swamped in the meat department as people rushed to stock up while the prices were still low.

Annoying little Davy continued to pester her at Dale's. His father was on strike, and he wanted to tell the world about it, loudly, which was the only volume he seemed to know. K.C. doubted he understood what a strike was, but at least he wasn't guessing her bra size.

Throughout the next few days she heard various customers discussing what was going on at the picket lines. Apparently there were fifteen or sixteen picketers at each of the plant's thirteen entrances, including some women. The rank and file had already begun vandalizing the scabs' cars, although there hadn't been any injuries to people yet.

As she clocked out at five on Friday she wondered if the Bluenotes had ever gone on strike, or ever would. She could see the headline: "CITY IN UPROAR: K.C. AND THE BLUENOTES HOLDING OUT FOR MORE MONEY."

Except she'd probably never get into the Bluenotes at all, let alone be their front man. Woman? Anyway, the shitty way she felt about herself now, "K.C. and the Hershey Squirts" would be more like it. With herself as the lead squirt. That was appropriate, since Squirt had been Kenny's nickname for her—although he better not have meant it that way…

She could hear him chuckling.

"Shut up," she mumbled.

Jack got off work at the same time. He had his truck, but her apartment was so close she wouldn't let him drive her. He left his pickup in the Dale's parking lot and walked her home. She let him hold her hand.

"Someone might call your house looking for me," K.C. said.

"Who?"

"One of the guys from the Bluenotes."

"You gave him our number? Is he black?"

"He's the bass player."

"What if Mom answers? She'll go nuts if a Negro calls the house for you."

"I don't have a number. What else could I do? She doesn't like me anyway."

Jack sighed. "Don't you ever give up?"

She squeezed his fingers. She'd made a fool of herself at the hospital. Thump wouldn't call anyway. "No," she said.

They walked a block without speaking. "Listen," Jack said finally, "a couple of my friends are going over to Roth's tonight to watch the strike. Wanna go?"

"What's to see?"

"I don't know—it'll be something different. There'll be music. And beer."

"You can keep the beer," K.C. said. "What kind of music?"

****

Five Roth employees struck up a band in the evening to entertain the onlookers. There were three black men, on trumpet, guitar, and sousaphone, and two white ones, on banjo and fiddle. They were playing Dixie tunes.

K.C. and Jack sat in folding chairs in the parking lot of the pastry shop across the street from Roth's. His friends didn't show. The crowd loved the music, and spilled out onto the street to dance and drink. After a long day of picketing, some of the strikers joined them. Even the cops assigned to maintain order seemed to enjoy the diversion. They kept time by tapping their billy clubs against their palms.

But K.C. could feel the anger and resentment underscoring the festivities. The scabs were not only hurting the cause, Jack explained, they were hurting themselves. Defiance of the union came with a cost, apart from the threat of physical violence. Friendships broken now would never be healed. Once a scab, always a scab.

At 10:45 p.m., fifteen minutes before second shift got out, the music stopped and the picketers returned to their lines, including the musicians. The celebration was over.

Although additional Waterton policemen showed up to escort the strikebreakers out, they were still outnumbered a hundred to one. As the men emerged from the plant, they were greeted with taunts, profanity, and threats. Most were smart enough to keep their heads down and their eyes straight ahead.

One of them, though—there was always one, K.C. thought —had to cause trouble. He was an imposing black man, six foot-five and maybe two hundred and fifty pounds. He'd parked close to where she and Jack were sitting, so they got a close-up view. His car had been painted with the words "SCAB," "JUDAS," and "DIE." "I'm gonna kill you sumbitches," he said.

A cop slapped his ear and said, "Could you be any dumber? Shut your mouth, and maybe we'll both live through this night."

The man got into his old Buick. As he pulled onto the

street, someone threw a rock that cracked the driver's side window. His brake lights flashed on. "Motherfucker," he shouted, but the same cop slammed his hip against the door to prevent the man from exiting.

"Drive, goddammit. Get *out* of here."

Roth's had suspended third shift for the duration of the strike due to the worker shortage, so the strikers' business was done for the day. They'd be back at 5:00 a.m. When the last of the scabs had escaped, K.C. said, "The trumpet player looked familiar."

Chapter 17

JULY'S COOL AND RAINY end had been replaced by brutal heat and humidity the first week of August. Freddie pulled into the lot closest to Roth's and lowered the visor against the sun.

Leon was marching in the picket line. He'd once hated big companies and unions for what they'd done to his father. He'd voted against the strike. And yet, there he was. When Freddie had spoken to Dee on the phone this morning, she said he'd been taking double shifts on the line. Somehow he'd become an activist for the United Packinghouse Workers of America. No one had seen that coming, probably not even Leon.

The scabs were inside, safe for the moment, and there were no newspaper photographers to mug for. Leon had paired up with a white woman to picket. Despite the heat, they seemed to be having a pleasant conversation, him with that smile of his and her looking giddy, the way ladies got around him.

Freddie wasn't the kind to take much notice of a man's appearance, but he had to admit that Leon was one handsome dude. Movie star handsome, if Hollywood would've let colored folks be leading men. Thing was, Leon knew he was good looking. He spent more time in front of a mirror getting himself *just so* than any cat Freddie ever met, except maybe Spits.

He was smart, too, finishing two years at Fisk College in Memphis. Didn't graduate, but two years made him an intellectual in Freddie's eyes.

Then there was that European gig, when he hooked up with the Jimmie Lunceford Orchestra for the '37 tour. He learned Lunceford's vaudeville shenanigans and comedic timing, sometimes using them with the Bluenotes. That, along with his looks, made him the most popular band member.

Meantime, Freddie had deformed fingers, an AWOL wife, and too little humor left in his soul. The farthest music had ever taken him was to St. Louis. Once.

He waved when he thought Leon noticed his car, but his friend was too busy being admired. Leon didn't have any real interest in other women, but he did love the attention. Freddie wondered if Dee ever got jealous.

Wasn't for Freddie to worry about.

Even with the window down, his car was too hot. He got out and found shade and a little breeze under the awning of the pastry shop. He lit up a cigarette. Tasted good, but tobacco didn't ease his joint pain like reefer did.

A passing car slowed next to the Roth entrance where Leon was picketing. The driver shouted, "Screw you, union pricks!" then squealed his tires and sped away. Several of the strikers, including Leon and the lady he was with, held up their middle finger.

From a glamorous European gig to a picket line at a sweaty Iowa packing plant. When his mama got sick, Leon came home. To pay for her care, he took that college education and all his worldly experience and used them to cut up hogs.

He was a good son. His mama died anyway.

And now that job, for now, was gone, too.

Freddie took a puff of his cigarette. Damn, it was hot—too hot to stand and wait. The humidity had to be about 112%, leaving him slimy as a frog. He walked out from beneath the awning and approached the picket line. Leon and his lady friend paused by the chain link fence door at the entrance when they saw him. Both were carrying signs. She had her free arm wrapped around him.

"Boneman," Leon said, "you here to march with us?"

"In this heat? I don't like you that much."

"Freddie, Rachael. Rachael, Freddie. You know which is which."

The woman's skin looked dangerously red. White folks burned so much easier than blacks. She was going to be on fire in the morning. "What happened to your fingers?" she said. "Your wife close her legs on you?"

Freddie was surprised. Most people weren't that direct. "Me and a household tool had a argument. The tool won."

"That must've hurt."

Physically, it was the worst pain he'd ever endured. Emotionally... well, he'd lost the piano that night. Freddie nodded. *Yeah, little missy, it hurt.*

"You get us some gigs?" Leon said.

"Four, so far."

"That's it?"

"Here's the thing—I'll keep on it, but I gotta know you'll be there. You know, in your head. No more Davenports. When you're on stage, you gotta let the strike go."

"I got me a responsibility to my union boys." He playfully

pushed Rachael's shoulder. "And girls."

"You gotta feed your wife, too—" Freddie glanced sideways at Rachael, "—and you ain't doing it out here."

Rachael let go of his arm.

Leon gave him a *this-ain't-your-business* look. "Who'd Dwayne get for T.J.?"

"Thump."

"No shit, he's back?"

"Just talked to him."

"That's something, anyway. Where's the gigs?"

Freddie told him. "Not much in town nowadays. Other bands already booked most of the good places, and the bad ones don't pay enough to be worth our time. Gonna have to start looking farther out. Mason City, Fort Dodge, maybe Minnesota."

"Sue's gonna bitch."

"Is Sue your wife?" Rachael said, emphasizing the word *wife*.

"Sue's the bus driver," Leon said. "Dee's my wife."

"Didn't know you had one," Rachael said, and she stormed away to march with a couple of other ladies.

"Thanks, Boneman—you messed that one up for me."

"Always first with a kind word and a helping hand. You weren't gonna jelly-roll her anyhow."

Leon laughed. "Nah, I guess not. No good when the man's prettier than the woman."

"Hell," Freddie said, "why don't you just come on over to my car? You can jack off while you admire yourself in the rearview mirror."

Chapter 18

"SIT DOWN," PATTI SAID when they got to the Schoonover house. "You, too, Jack." She looked unusually stern, even for her.

K.C. and Jack sat at the dining room table. They exchanged worried glances. "Mom, what's wrong?" he said.

K.C. knew.

"Mrs. Schoonover—"

"Be quiet. There are so many things I want to say." She paced around the table, and back, stopping next to K.C. Her body trembled, like a bomb was about to go off inside her. She squeezed her hands together and took a deep breath. "Kasey, we are not your answering service. I know you don't have a phone in your apartment, but if you need someone to take your messages, give them your own parents' number."

"Mom, you know she can't—"

"I wasn't talking to you, Jack."

"The store calls here for her."

"I still wasn't talking to you, Jack." Patti sat in the chair next to K.C.'s. The woman leaned in so close K.C. could smell the Listerine. "Do you know *who* called here for you?"

"Yes."

"A Negro. Did you hear me? A *Negro*. You gave our number to a black man." Her voice started to rise, her fuse burning shorter.

"Did not. I gave it to a white woman named Sue."

"The person who called was a man, and he talked that black gibberish."

"What did you tell him?"

"What do you think? That he had the wrong number. He sounded like a criminal, Kasey, *and he has our number*. How *dare* you?"

"He's a musician. His name is Earl. His band is the Bluenotes, the one I tried out for. They play jazz."

Patti rose and loomed over her. If she could've expanded her neck into a hood, she would've looked like a cobra. "You want to play nigger music? With niggers?"

Your own people gonna call you a nigger-loving whore.

"I just want to play."

"You need to leave my house."

K.C. stood up and headed toward the door. "Nobody will call here again."

"Mom, what are you doing?" Jack said, following K.C.

"Jack, sit down," Patti said, "If you go with her, don't come back."

K.C. walked as far as the sidewalk before stopping and turning around. Jack stood in the doorway, looking at her, looking back at his mother.

What's it going to be? she thought.

Choose.

Choose, Jack.

He lowered his eyes and chose, stepping out onto the porch and closing the door behind him. His face was fierce with anger. With disbelief. With regret. With uncertainty. But mostly, she thought, with love.

"Wait," he said. "I'll give you a ride."

She didn't want to go to her apartment, so he drove her to Crusoe's Island, where she'd played as a child. The drive wasn't far, just over the river from Electrical Park. Crusoe's wasn't really an island, just a narrow strip of land that jutted into the Oak River. It had gotten its name because it had a fake ship buried in the sand, as if it had run ashore. Paths through the woods led to enclaves with cement jungle animals, and, mixing metaphors, to cables hung from tree limbs so kids could swing like Tarzan on a vine.

Once there, she climbed to the bow of the ship, where she could sit and overlook the river, her legs dangling over the edge. A painted turtle sunned itself on a log. Bubbles of air rose in the green water, from frogs or rotting plants or fish. She couldn't see them from her perch, but she knew water bugs were skittering across the surface because fish made blooping sounds as they ate them.

The August heat wave hadn't broken. The flies were bad, the mosquitoes not as much, yet. The little vampires would come out at dusk.

Jack sat beside K.C. She rested her head against his shoulder. He'd chosen her over his mother. What he said next was going to make all the difference.

"I told you this would happen," he said, but without anger.

"It was petty and stupid. All because of a phone call."

Jack nodded and stared into the water. "Dad will talk to her. She'll cool down..."

"But?"

"You did give our number out. A black man did call."

K.C. scooched away from him, only a few inches, but she made her point. "What's wrong with that?"

"Mom's not the same as us. She doesn't like Negroes."

"Has she ever met one?"

"I don't know—probably." He tried to pull her back to him, but she pushed his hand away.

"Anyway," she said, "it's not like I gave out your address."

Jack stood up and leaned against the fake mast protruding from the fake deck. He spoke so softly she could barely hear him. "I can't go home, Kase."

"Yeah, and how shitty is that?"

"I hate it when girls say 'shit.'"

"So?"

He walked down the sloped deck to the sand, then around to the bow where she was sitting. At its highest point the ship never rose above chest height from the ground. He put his elbow on the bow, his wrist brushing her thigh. "Tell me something," he said.

At first she didn't know what he meant. She watched his face as he tried to find the words, and then she knew. "You don't want me to join a colored band, either."

"I didn't say that."

"Or is it because they're all men?"

"I only played violin, Kase, and not very well. I don't understand jazz. I can't feel what you feel. All I know is it's something standing between us."

"What if I said I didn't want you to teach economics?"

"That's different."

"How?"

He put his hand on her knee. "Whether Mom was right or wrong, you had to know how she would react."

His eyes were misty, like he was going to cry. Didn't he ever get mad? "Don't you ever get mad?"

"I'm mad now, Kase. I don't have a place to live."

"Then show it, goddammit." She felt a pinprick of pain as

she slid back from the edge and stood up. "Take me home."

She stomped off toward the car. He followed right behind, grabbing her arm and spinning her toward him. "Don't make me lose you, too."

"Ow!" she cried.

He released her arm. "I didn't mean to hurt you."

"You didn't," she said. "I think I have a splinter in my ass."

****

In her apartment, K.C. set Kenny's picture down, undressed, and lay on her stomach on the bed, a pillow under her pelvis to raise her butt into the air. Jack came out of her bathroom with tweezers and a Band-Aid from her medicine cabinet.

He took one look at her position and laughed out loud.

"If you ever, *ever*, tell anybody about this," she said, "I will murder you in your sleep."

"You don't have to ass me twice," he said.

"Very funny."

"No ifs, ands, or ... oh, wait."

"Stop."

"I feel like I'm falling behind."

"Dammit, just get it over with."

"Well, bottoms up."

She buried her face in her blankets. Was this what married people did? Was this ordinary love? Not the sex, not the dancing, not the laughing or the good times, not even the PTA or listening to the radio on Sunday nights? In sickness and in health, and the sickness wasn't just the flu or a cold, with a warm towel across the forehead and a glass of Pepto Bismol, but removing a splinter from your spouse's ass?

What if something happened and he had to help her go to the bathroom? What if she had to help *him*? Oh, yuck...

She felt him cup one hand over her right butt cheek.

"Don't move," he said. "It's a major splinter. This'll hurt."

She held her breath as she felt the points of the tweezers touch her skin. There was a sharp pain, but it was over quickly, and the sliver came out on his first attempt. He placed the Band-Aid over the wound.

"Look at the size of this thing," he said, showing her the splinter. He gave her left cheek a playful tap. "Just don't ask me to kiss it where it hurts."

How many times had she wanted to tell him to kiss her ass?

"Get me my jammies," she said.

"Are we staying in for the day?"

We?

Where *was* he going to stay until his mother got over being stupid? Mr. Somers didn't raise a stink when she brought Jack over for an occasional night of frolicking, but there was no way he'd let him move in. An unmarried boy and girl living together in an apartment he managed? The city would probably have him arrested.

Jack threw the splinter away and brought her pajamas.

She put them on and raised Kenny's picture.

Sure glad I didn't see that, he said.

You and me both, she thought.

It hurt to sit, but not as much as it had on the car ride back from Crusoe's Island.

"You could run out and get me a hamburger," she said. "We'll go from there."

"The works?" he said.

"And a Pepsi. Thanks."

She watched him walk out the door. What an entirely

crummy day it had been.

On the bright side, Thump had tried to call her. That was a good sign—wasn't it?

Chapter 19

THE SESSION AT NARLINS was the best they'd had since Spits had left. Leon, Screech, Bullet, and Ironhead wailed. 'Fish was a whirlwind on the eighty-eights. Freddie slid the 'bone like he was born to play it. Syd pounded out powerful rhythms that pulled the whole group forward, and Thump sounded like he'd never left.

Dwayne had swallowed his pride and incorporated a few elements of bop into some of his old charts. Their next two gigs were for college kids, who wanted the fast stuff.

When they finished, they were sweaty and exhausted, but elated. They pulled tables together around Dwayne's. Ruthie joined them, bringing them all beers, except Syd, who took a Dr. Pepper. "I'm going broke anyhow," she said, "so these're on the house. Never heard you boys play like that. You were on fire."

"Feels good, Ruthie," Leon said. "Like old times."

"Bah," Dwayne said.

"Don't start that again," Freddie said. "Your charts are genius."

"Yeah," Dwayne said, "but it's not what I do. It's like selling my soul."

Ruthie laughed at him, something the band rarely dared. "White folks thought swing was devil music till they started playing it. Now you're spouting off about bop."

"My swing charts are the best in Iowa."

Syd took a swallow of Dr. Pepper. "Maybe it's time for your bop charts to be best. Bop's fun to play, boss."

"All I know," Freddie said, "is I thought the Bluenotes was dead. Now I know we ain't."

"Still need more gigs," Leon said, opening his spit valve, giving the horn a final blow, and shaking the last drop of saliva out of it. Then he polished the bell with his shirttail, and looked at his reflection. "I'm back on the line tomorrow. Me and 'Fish are dying till this thing's settled."

"You could've played here tonight," Ruthie said, "if I hadn't already booked somebody else."

"You don't pay for shit, anyway," 'Fish said.

"Bad luck when the rehearsal goes this good," Bullet said.

"Maybe," Ironhead said, "but, God *damn*, man, that was the first time I didn't even miss Spits."

Uh-oh, Freddie thought. Everyone took a deep breath to see what Dwayne would do.

His face went from pissed to sad to what-the-hell and back to sad in a couple of seconds. His shoulders slumped as he said to Bullet, "You were great."

Then he set his glasses on the table, sort of folded up into himself, and went quiet.

"About them gigs," Bullet said, "I'm okay till Upper Iowa on the 14th, but then I'm gone. Manager of my band in Omaha lined up a western tour. Doing the loop. Start in Lincoln, end in Denver."

"We gotta have an alto horn," Screech said.

"You needed one before I came," Bullet said. "Nothing's

changed."

"Um," Thump said, as if about to make a profound pronouncement. He'd doghoused his ass off in the session, but now looked like he was sinking back into his post-O.D. stupor. He'd only had the one beer, so maybe he was just tired. "A white girl came to see me at the hospital. I was asleep, but Sue got a number to call."

"How the hell'd she find your real name?" Freddie said. He already knew where this conversation was headed. Damn girl wouldn't give up.

No idea."

Did you?"

Did I what?"

Call."

Thump nodded. "But I didn't get to talk to her. The lady who answered was a mean bitch, man."

"What'd the girl want?" 'Fish said.

"Told Sue she plays alto."

"We met her," Freddie said. "K.C. Brown. White Bird—at the audition?"

"Same girl who was here with her boyfriend the night Screech and Ironhead was supposed to play?" Ruthie said. "Ahem, if one of them had bothered to show up..."

Ironhead looked at her like *What*?

"Yeah," Freddie said. "She played 'Amazing Grace' on the piano like angels singing in heaven. Almost made me cry."

"Me, too," Ruthie said.

"Thought she was sax," 'Fish said.

"She ain't after your job."

Dwayne stirred from his silence. "Fuck it," he said. "Hire her."

"You're shitting me," Freddie said. "We don't even know

where she lives."

"We got a number."

"A wrong one."

"Find her."

"She's just a kid," Freddie said. "Probably still lives with mama and daddy. Know how many Browns there's gonna be in the phone book?"

"Man, I don't know," Ironhead said. "A white girl? Was I there?"

"I remember her," Syd said. "Had a brother who died in the war."

"A chick playing horn in my place? You serious?" Bullet said, as if offended by the notion. A replacement worrying about a replacement.

For the first time it occurred to Freddie that if the band was like Roth's, Bullet himself would be the scab, for stepping in for Spits.

"Find her," Dwayne said again. "I don't care. Put another ad in the paper."

****

Freddie pulled his car into the parking lot of the *Waterton Record*. He didn't know what to do. Personally, he liked K.C. She was a nice girl who had the hunger and maybe the talent. He understood the hunger. He respected the drive. She just wasn't the right fit for the Bluenotes. He'd tried to explain the problems she'd face with an all-male black band, but she was young. She wanted what she wanted, and screw everything else.

He understood that, too.

He got out and half-sat on the hood of his car, one foot on the ground, the other on the bumper. The sky in the west was a little darker shade of blue, clouds so distant they didn't have shape yet, only color. Maybe rain would come to break the heat wave.

The *Record* building was just across the Fourth Street Bridge on the west side. He watched the current roll by peacefully, recalling downpours when the river swelled and churned muddy waters over the banks, covering the roads and swamping low-lying properties on the east side. He didn't want rain that much.

In a way, though, a flood was just what K.C. was facing. Wherever she came from, whatever her life was like, she wasn't black. The Bluenotes was a force that would roll over everything she knew and leave nothing but muck in its wake. A lot of white kids liked to listen to black jazz on weekends, but after they played at being hepcats they could go home to their nice white lives, thrilled by their brief exposure to a different world but never threatened by it.

Little White Bird. Freddie knew she had a boyfriend. He knew she had a brother who taught her sax before he was killed. And that was all. What about her parents? Grandparents? Other brothers or sisters? Even if they were one of those progressive white families that supported the Negro, it wouldn't matter what they said they believed. Push come to shove, none of them wanted one of their own living black. Being fair-minded was fine, long as it involved someone else's kid.

Your boyfriend, your family, your friends, your life, Freddie thought, *it's all gonna be gone. All gone, White Bird.*

Ready to give that up?

Not to mention what it would do to the members of the band. Freddie was married, sort of, and so were Leon, 'Fish, and Syd. Thump used to be, before he found out horse gave him a better buzz than women.

Syd had been in the military, and still had that military discipline. Didn't drink, use dope, or chase women, so Marlye didn't have to worry. He'd be okay with K.C. around.

Leon was so good looking that Dee was probably used to the female attention he got. Still, no woman had ever traveled with the band before—well, except Sue, who everyone was afraid of. Would Dee trust Leon with a pretty girl traveling with him for hours, and sometimes days, at a time?

Janae might be grateful if 'Fish would expend his energy somewhere else for a change, but whether or not she cared about the reality, she wouldn't like the rumors, the whispering behind her back. A lot of people thought a cheating husband was a reflection on the wife.

Screech and Ironhead were a different breed of cat, but they had needs like everyone else, and why not a white girl?

It was too hot to be dawdling outside. Freddie pushed himself off the hood and walked toward the *Record*'s entrance.

He'd never touched another woman after Shay, never really considered it, even at Grits 'n' Tits, where temptation was right in front of his face. Didn't matter to Shay. He could cut his own nuts off and go live in a monastery, and she'd still accuse him of screwing around. Imagined infidelity might be why she'd left this time, or maybe she just wanted a change of pace and went to fight with Nelly instead. Whatever the reason, when she came back, if she came back, having K.C. around wasn't going to make his life any easier.

Shay didn't like white women, and she downright hated white men.

He removed a paper from his pocket and went inside to the classified department.

No doubt Dwayne would regret his words. The man

wasn't thinking, he was just pissed off or hurt. Ironhead had dared to suggest Bullet was as good as Spits on the sax. Dwayne had been so dead set against K.C., and now all of a sudden he wanted to hire her. Wasn't there a saying, something about cutting off your nose to spite your face?

They were all going to suffer for this, especially K.C.

Freddie stopped at a desk.

"What do you want?" said a dour white man.

"Seeing as how you're sitting at the classified ad desk, what d'you think?"

"How many words?"

"Four."

"How long?"

"A week."

"Three cents a word, fifteen cents per day minimum."

Freddie fished out a dollar and a nickel, then looked at the paper one last time before handing them over.

White Bird call Freddie.

Chapter 20

THEY WERE AT THE Starlite Drive-In Theater to watch a Red Skelton double feature, *Four Faces West* and *The Fuller Brush Man*. A lot of people with pickups backed in so they could watch from the bed of the truck, but K.C. didn't like doing that, so Jack pulled straight in.

"If you murdered somebody," K.C. said, "your mom would hide you in the basement and lie to the police to protect you. But I do this one little thing—"

"It *was* a little thing," Jack said, hanging the speaker on the edge of his window. "What I did was a big thing. I chose you over her."

K.C. had to admit that meant a lot to her, even more so since she hadn't asked him to make the choice. He'd done it of his own free will. Of course, if it had been her making the demand, he might have gone the other way. The one who demands loses.

And, of course, she knew all about unreasonable parents.

Jack was temporarily staying with his former boss, Will Hammon. Mr. Hammon had owned a service station until war rationing had forced him out of business in '43. Jack had been an attendant there in high school. He later recommended Mr. Hammon to his father when Landon's converted from tractors to tanks during the war and needed mechanics. He was an odd-looking man with only one eye—which kind of gave K.C. the creeps—but he and his wife Elaine were super nice people, and their little daughter was adorable.

Hopefully Dick would talk sense into Patti, and Jack could go home before he wore out his welcome with the Hammons.

It was 8:45, still twilight—fifteen minutes until the cartoons before the first movie. Jack turned the sound down on the speaker so they didn't have to listen to ads about overpriced concession stand goodies. Everybody snuck in their own food and drinks anyway. "Let's talk about something else," he said.

"Such as?"

He slid his hand under her sleeve and over her shoulder to her left breast. "This."

"Don't get me going tonight," she said. "Aunt Flo is visiting."

"Huh?"

"What punctuation do you use to end a sentence?"

"A period. Oh."

"Why get all undressed if there's nowhere to go?"

"You mean we have to watch the movies?"

"We could look for coins."

The Starlight was Iowa's first drive-in theater. K.C. and Jack had been here a few times since it opened in September of '47. Truth be told, sitting—or any other verb—in a car for that long got uncomfortable. If they kept the windows rolled up, it was too hot, and if they rolled them down the mosquitoes ate them alive. K.C. liked to explore the parking lot for money. It was surprising how much change people dropped, sometimes enough to pay for both of their admissions. Anyway, mosquitoes had a harder time with moving targets.

She reached in the glove box for his flashlight.

"Scrounging quarters?" he said. "We're adults. What will people think?"

"If you were worried about that," she said, "you wouldn't let me do this." She ran her hand up his leg to his favorite body part and gave a playful squeeze through the material. Then she opened the car door and sprinted away, leaving him in an unfortunate state. It was almost dark, but not dark enough to hide his condition should he decide to follow her.

The gravel lot around the concession stand was the best place to look, especially near the restrooms. There was only one stall in the ladies', so the girls lined up outside before the shows. While fiddling with their purses for cigarettes or makeup, they often dropped coins without knowing it. K.C. only had to wait until the cartoons started for the line to clear out. She never stooped to pick up pennies, but everything else was fair game.

It wasn't really stealing. Even if someone realized they'd lost a coin, which they wouldn't, most people wouldn't waste their time looking for it.

She passed car after car of high school kids necking, usually two couples, one in the front and one in the back. Where did they go before there was a drive-in?

K.C. smiled. She knew. High school was just last year for her. She and Jack had managed to find plenty of places, back when making out was the goal, not the warmup, when anything more than kissing was a rumor girls giggled about in the locker room.

One year. It seemed like forever ago. Everything was different now. She and Jack were no longer like these kids in the cars. Had they fallen from grace, or grown worldly, since then? Or were those two aspects of the same thing—couldn't fall without growing, couldn't grow without falling?

There was no doubt how her parents felt: K.C. was on the road to hell, and the devil was holding the door for her.

Not that K.C. cared about their opinion.

The day's light was almost gone now. Woody Woodpecker was on the screen, taking up half the sky and blaring that annoying laugh from every speaker in the lot. The girls in the line outside the restroom had made it in, out, and returned to their cars. K.C. flicked on the flashlight and looked for shiny blips in the gravel beside the fence that prevented anyone from seeing into the restroom. It wasn't too long before she found a nickel and a quarter.

My, how worldly she'd grown...

Around back of the concession stand she caught a flash of another coin. As she bent to pick it up, somebody poked her ribs and said, "Boo."

She screamed and whirled, ready to... what? She wasn't a fighter. But it didn't matter, it was only Jack. "Don't sneak up on me like that."

"That'll teach you to leave me with a boner the size of a baseball bat."

Maybe a golf pencil, she thought. In school she'd once overheard a couple of boys teasing each other on the playground. One said, "If you put your pecker on the edge of a razor blade, it would look like a string on a four-lane highway." Funny she should recall that now, especially since she didn't have anything to compare Jack's with. He was her one and only. She'd imagined them being bigger, but for all she knew Jack set the standard every boy dreamed of.

"Well, you shouldn't have grabbed my boob. No fair getting me hot and bothered when we can't do anything about it.”

“I didn’t know you were riding.”

“Shut up and turn off that flashlight,” a male voice yelled from a nearby car. K.C. didn’t see which. When Jack displayed his middle finger in that direction, a door slammed and a massive blond kid strolled up to them. He looked like he was still in high school, but he was a good four inches taller and fifty pounds heavier than Jack. A football player, judging by his “East High Trojans” jersey. “Do that again,” he said.

“Mind your own business,” Jack said, trying to sound brave. He wasn’t a tough guy in real life, although as an assistant manager at Dale’s, he did have to handle his share of problem customers.

K.C. heard people in the cars around them going, “Oo-oo-ooh,” and egging Mr. Linebacker on.

“Wow, you’re all kinds of stupid,” he said. He eyed K.C. “Maybe I’ll just me take some of that.”

“Like hell,” Jack said.

The boy coldcocked him, knocking him flat. “How ’bout it, babe? You game?”

K.C. screamed for help, which within moments brought a security guard from inside the concession stand. He was a black man even bigger than Mr. Linebacker. “What’s the trouble?”

“He hit my boyfriend,” K.C. said.

The guard looked at Jack, who was struggling to stand up, then at the boy. “That true, Gorgeous George?”

“Asshole fingered me.”

“You talk to your mama like that?”

“Ugh,” Jack said.

“You okay?” the guard said.

Jack was woozy. His bottom lip spouted blood like a fountain, and he had scrapes from the gravel on his palms and elbows. "Yeah," he said. "Barely felt it."

K.C. helped him up, holding onto him so he didn't fall again.

"Here's what's gonna happen," the guard said. "Gorgeous George, you're going back to your car. One more word and I'm throwing your butt out of here. We clear?"

Mr. Linebacker—K.C. liked "Gorgeous George" better—gave Jack the evil eye and said, "What about him?"

"Did you mistake that for a request?"

The boy lumbered away, muttering "jigaboo" loud enough for the guard to hear.

"Thank you, officer," K.C. said.

"Want an ambulance?"

"I'm fine," Jack said.

The guard handed him a handkerchief. "Don't need it back. You and your gal go on. Keep your finger to yourself."

K.C. pulled Jack's arm around her shoulder to steady him as they returned to his Dodge. "That was brave," she said. "But like he said, all kinds of stupid."

He touched his lip and winced. "We're both bleeding now."

"Trade you."

"Nope."

Chapter 21

SYD AND MARLYE INVITED Freddie for supper with them and their son Nat, who Freddie was meeting for only the second time. Hanging with Syd anywhere but on the bus or onstage could be scary. Not because he was wild, but because he wasn't. He didn't have vices anybody ever noticed, except maybe a lack of humor. With his military bearing, he was a by-the-book, *"yes, sir, no, sir"* kind of cat. It was a strange trait in a jazzman.

"What's wrong with your hands?" Nat asked Freddie. He was twelve or thirteen.

"Hush, child," Marlye said, setting a plate of potatoes and chicken gizzards in front of them. "That's not polite."

"It's all right," Freddie said.

"No, it's not," Syd said.

"Sorry, Mr. Ross," the boy said.

"I got us gigs on September 3rd, 17th, and 18th," Freddie said. "Busy those nights?"

"The Bluenotes always come first."

Unlike the rest of the band, most of Syd's income came from gigs. He was the best drummer in the Midwest, so when he wasn't playing with them, he was filling in with someone else. Despite the steady work and government payout, though, he had to look up to see the poverty line. His home, paid for with the help of the G.I. Bill, was shabby on the outside but spotless inside. He always wore his clothes pressed and neat, always had his shoes shined, but they were patched clothes and fourth-hand shoes.

It was kind of sad.

It was kind of inspiring.

"These smell great," Freddie said to Marlye. Chicken guts were cheap, but they were still probably more than Syd could afford.

"Better than what they fed us in the Navy," Syd said. He'd enlisted right in the middle of the war, but never left Hawaii. While there, he played in service bands and toured the islands with John Coltrane and Clark Terry.

Freddie ate a kidney. Loved that spongy texture. "What was 'Trane like?"

"Just another good saxophonist then. I did the clubs with him, but you know what they say: Nobody cares who you played with or opened for. I think he made his first record in '46 when he was still in the Navy, but I was out by then. He went and did what he did, and I came home and did what I did."

Freddie held up his gnarled fingers. "I was the right age for the first war, but they wouldn't let me in."

"You would've spent your time on latrine or guard duty," Syd said. "Don't get me wrong—I was proud to serve."

Syd's back straightened just a little when he said that.

"Gravy for your potatoes?" Marlye said, looking like she needed his approval of her cooking.

He held his plate out for her to ladle some on. "Thick as my mama's. Bet it tastes as good, too. Thanks."

"What do you play, Mr. Ross?" Nat said.

"Trombone now, but I used to get around real good on the eighty-eights before I got these fingers."

"Somebody shut the lid on you?"

Freddie chuckled around a mouthful of potatoes. "Something like that."

"Okay, I'm curious," Marlye said. "Do you mind talking about it?"

"Don't you start, too," Syd said.

Freddie chewed the potatoes several times more than necessary before answering. "I was greedy and stupid. Mostly stupid. Tried to get funny with people who don't smile much."

"Like me," Syd said.

"You ain't nothing like them."

"They did *that* to you?" Marlye said.

Freddie jabbed his fork through a chicken heart. "I loved playing piano. I could've given 'Fish a run for the money back then, and I was only nineteen. Me and Scott Joplin, man, me and Scott Joplin."

"Was he the one who broke your fingers?" Nat said.

Even Syd smiled at that. "I would've broke my own fingers before I played ragtime."

"What's wrong with rag?" Freddie said.

"Nothing, I guess, if you're old." Syd was twenty years younger than Freddie.

"Kinda what people are saying about us and swing."

Syd finally took a bite of food, his first of the night. Freddie watched him eat. He'd not only never lost his military bearing, he never lost his physique. The dude's muscles had muscles. "Dwayne really going to hire that girl?" Syd said.

"I put a ad in the paper," Freddie said. "Ain't heard anything yet."

"What girl?" Marlye said.

Syd ignored the question. "You know, I got to thinking about her. That night she tried out. She wasn't bad. I mean, the kid's got something. You saw it, too—don't tell me you didn't. Came out to do 'Ko-ko,' but we changed things on her."

"Couldn't keep up."

"It wasn't a fair test. We let her play with us a few times, and she could."

Freddie looked at Syd, then at Marlye, and back to Syd. *Do you know what it'd mean to have a white girl along with us?* he thought, but what he said was, "Maybe."

Hopefully little White Bird wouldn't call back, and no one would have to worry about it.

But she would.

****

When he stopped in to Narlins to see if any more gigs had confirmed, Ruthie yelled at him to get his own phone. She shoved him a handful of notes and said, "Got more people calling here for you than me. Do I look like Bell Telephone?"

"You're a pretty sweet little operator..."

"Don't try that schmoozing shit with me, mister." She was trying to sound angry, but didn't quite pull it off.

He looked through the messages—two yes, three no, one *Can we negotiate price?* Nothing from K.C.

"Thanks, Ruthie. Have a beer on the house."

"It's my beer and my house."

He left, got in his Ford, and drove home. A light was on in the kitchen window. He never left lights on.

He went inside to find Shay sitting at the table, petting Washington.

"Can I come back?" she said.

"You already did."

Washington flicked her tail, once. The newspaper was on the counter where Freddie had left it. He picked it up and went into the bedroom.

Chapter 22

K.C. WAS STRUCK BY an old photograph that hung on the wall in the Hammons' living room. It showed a teenage boy in a foreign military uniform, standing in a landscape that looked like it had been bombed to hell. By the boy's uniform and the age of the photo, it must have been the first war.

"I talked to your dad," Will Hammon said to Jack. He wore glasses with a frosted left lens to hide his missing eye. "Your mother will let you come home now."

"What about Kase?" Jack said. He was sitting on one end of the couch, K.C. on the other. Mr. Hammon was in his recliner across the living room. "I won't go back if she isn't welcome."

"You'll have to discuss that with them. Would you two like something to drink? I've got milk or Pepsi."

"Nothing for me," Jack said. "Kase?"

"Maybe a Pepsi, if it isn't too much trouble."

"Bottle or in a glass?"

"Glass, please."

As he went into the kitchen, K.C. wondered how he navigated with one eye. She doubted walking would be a problem, but how was he able to drive a car? Not only would his field of vision be more limited, but it seemed to her that he wouldn't be able to focus. But Jack said he was born like that, so he didn't know anything else.

Mr. Hammon's wife and daughter were at the grocery store shopping. The girl's name was Katie. She'd fit in perfectly with the Brown family. Kenny Sr., Kenny Jr., Kathryn, Krissy, K.C. and Katie.

"You're going home whether I'm welcome or not," K.C. whispered. "You can't impose on the Hammons forever."

"Not without you. I'll get an apartment if I have to. You can afford one, and I make more than you do."

K.C. was looking at the photograph again when Mr. Hammon returned with the pop. "That's my Dad in the Big One," he said, handing her a glass. "Ypres, Belgium. He fought with the British before America entered the war. I was one when the picture was taken."

"Did he make it back?"

"Eventually."

"Is he here in town?"

"Not sure where he is now. I haven't seen him in better than ten years."

K.C. took a sip of the Pepsi. "My brother Kenny was killed in North Africa."

"So Jack's told me. Sorry to hear that. I had a friend, whose name was also Jack—he died in a Japanese prison."

"That's the only reason he hired me at the service station," Jack said. "I had the same name as his friend."

"That had nothing to do with it," Mr. Hammon said. "It was pity. Your boy here was the bumsiest clastard I ever saw. I felt sorry for him."

He winked at K.C., then sat in his recliner with his father's picture looming over him.

"Bumsiest clastard?"

"Clumsiest bastard," Jack said.

"Can you stay for supper, Kasey? Elaine and Katie should be home in a few minutes. We'd love to have you."

"Thanks, but I need to practice my sax."

"You could miss this once," Jack said.

"Mr. Pierson makes a special trip to open up the band room for me. I can't just not show."

"What are you practicing for?" Mr. Hammon said.

"Nothing, probably," she said. "A dream."

"Nothing wrong with that."

****

White Bird call Freddie.

K.C. didn't believe what she was reading. Mr. Pierson had brought the *Record* with him. She was looking through the ads while she waited for Jack to come back for her. Maybe there were other people with the nickname White Bird. There had to be lots of other Freddies. But how many men named Freddie knew someone called White Bird?

Her hands shook. What could it mean?

Mr. Pierson must have noticed her excitement. "Kasey, are you all right?"

She closed the paper, folded it, and set it on a chair. "Last time I spoke to him on the phone, he cursed at me."

"Who?"

"Freddie Ross."

"Was he a student here? I don't remember him."

"No, he must be about your age. He's with the Bluenotes."

"That jazz band you have your heart set on?"

K.C. nodded. "There's an ad in the paper for me to call him."

Mr. Pierson picked up the paper and scanned the classifieds. "Where? Oh. Who's White Bird?"

"I played a Charlie Parker tune at the audition. His nickname is Bird, so their manager called me White Bird."

"That's not very respectful."

"He didn't mean it to be, but I kind of like it. White Bird. It's better than 'Kansas City' Brown. I still have Freddie's card."

"Are you going to call him?"

"Soon as I get back to my apartment building."

He put a fatherly hand on her shoulder. "Are you sure this is what the ad is about?"

"What else could it be?"

He sat in the chair next to her. "Whatever it is, it's trouble."

K.C. took a deep breath. "Freddie told me all that. Traveling with all those older guys, how both black and white people would hate me... I don't care."

"Maybe you should listen to him."

"He *wants* me now, Mr. Pierson," she said as Jack appeared in the doorway.

"Who wants you?" Jack said.

****

She dialed the number on Freddie's business card. This time a woman answered.

"Narlins, this is Ruthie."

"Is Freddie Ross there?"

"Damn it, anyway. Who is it this time?"

"White Bird."

"The hell kind of name is that?"

"He wanted me to call him."

"I'm not him."

"This is the number on his card. He answered last time."

"He's not here."

"Could you tell him I called?"

"This about a gig?"

"Maybe."

"Either it is, or it ain't."

K.C.'s nickel was running out. "I don't have my own phone. Could you tell me when he'll be at Narlins?"

"He comes and goes. Take your chances."

Click.

K.C. stood looking at the phone, as if it personally had broken the connection. Why couldn't anything ever be easy?

Jack was leaning against the wall down the hall, close enough that he could see her, far enough away not to eavesdrop. She hung up the phone and nodded him toward the stairs.

"Well?" he said.

"Shut up," she said.

Chapter 23

SHAY SEEMED CONTENT TO sleep on the old couch they'd bought at Goodwill ten years ago, although it sagged in the middle and wasn't comfortable.

Freddie didn't ask her to come to bed. There was nothing physical between them anymore. He could barely remember a time when there had been. When they were both home, they met in the kitchen, she to make her food, he to make his. They waited for each other to use the bathroom. She always complained about the stink when he came out, although he never did that with her. He let her listen to her programs on the radio if she got to it first. She read or sewed if he had a Cubs game on, or did until the announcer's jabber drove her crazy enough to get up and sweep the floors or wash clothes.

It was like living alone without living alone.

At least she had Washington.

Shay never told him why she left this time—her mama, or something he did, or just general principles. It didn't matter. Freddie knew he wasn't the best husband on the planet. He wasn't much of a romantic, but, in his defense, she didn't give him much of a reason to be one.

He understood why she did some things, but none of that trouble was his fault. He just had to accept that she did what she did. Maybe she wasn't even doing it to him. Maybe he just happened to be in the way.

For better, for worse.

For nothing at all.

He felt like shit, but that was normal these days. Some men had wives who would care for them in sickness, wives who were *wives*, not part-time roommates.

The only thing of substance she had said to him since her most recent return was, "We should get rid of that old piano."

He said, "No," and they went back to silence.

She was laughing at Amos 'n' Andy—a program he hated —when he left for Narlins. She didn't ask him where he was going, and he didn't tell. There wasn't a rehearsal tonight, just some of the band getting together for drinks and conversation. But that wasn't for another hour. For now he just needed to get out of the house, somewhere he could breathe.

Waterton wasn't New York or Chicago, with their beautiful skylines, but he still liked seeing the lights at night. Block's and the Waterton Building, across the river, were the only two structures that stood eight stories or taller. They jutted like towers above the horizontal city, monoliths silhouetted against the stars, dark except for security lights in the lower windows.

He thought about stopping at the Diminished Fifth or Grits 'n' Tits, but decided against it. Instead, he took random streets, thinking, or trying not to. He rolled the window down to feel the humid breeze on his face. At a stoplight a ten-dollar whore approached his car. Even a small town like Waterton had them, not as many and not as much variety as the big cities, but always there, prowling the underbelly. This was the east side. On the west side, near the Fifth Street Bridge, the twenty-dollar whores sold their wares from the shadows. From what he'd heard, ten or twenty bucks, their services were the same, a quick suck job in the front seat, in, out, gone. Even for whores, location was everything. "Looking for a date?" this one said, sticking her face through the window.

She was too pretty to be in this line of work, but, then, what was a whore supposed to look like? Pretty, thin, ugly, fat—a needle didn't care how a person looked.

But that was too simple. Maybe instead of supporting a drug habit, she was supporting a baby in the only way open to her. Or, like Shay, caring for her mother.

Freddie gave her a ten. "I don't need nothing. Buy yourself something to eat. No dope."

"You a fairy or something?" she said, but she kept the money.

At Lincoln Park some teenagers were hassling an older man, probably a robbery—just another night on Waterton's east side. Nothing he could do. With his twisted fingers and aching joints, they'd make quick work of him. He honked his horn, hoping it might distract them and give the man time to escape. It didn't. They looked up long enough to determine he wasn't the cops, then knocked their victim down and took something from him. At least they didn't beat him. They laughed and strolled away.

Freddie circled the block and came back to see if the man was all right.

"Goddamn kids," the man said as he brushed himself off. "Joke's on them. Ain't nothing in my wallet."

"Need a ride?"

"I'm almost home. Thanks anyway."

Freddie drove away. Hoodlums and whores. Sometimes it seemed like there was a hole in the city that drained straight into hell. It was still better than places like Chicago, where the flow went both directions.

He avoided going anywhere near Roth's, where the gawkers would still be clogging the streets. After another twenty minutes of aimless turns, Shay being the elephant in the room he was trying not to think about, he pulled into Narlins. The parking lot was full when he arrived.

As he entered the building, he heard familiar music. Of all the bands Ruthie could have booked, she'd brought in the Edgar Robbins Eight from Cedar Rapids. Most of the tables were occupied, with several couples on the dance floor.

Dwayne, Catfish, Screech, and Sue were sitting together at a table in the back. "Didn't they open for us at the Harlem?" Freddie said.

"What Ruthie pays won't even cover their gas," 'Fish said.

"Means they net nothing from the deal," Dwayne said, "which is what they're worth."

"All these people came to hear these cats? We don't get crowds like this here."

"No accounting for taste, Boneman," Screech said.

Freddie was surprised he was here without Ironhead, since he hardly ever saw one without the other. He asked about it.

Screech shrugged. "Byron got himself a woman."

"*Ironhead*?"

"Hard to believe, but that boy's oiling the dipstick tonight."

"Watch it," Sue said, "there's a lady present."

"Where?" Screech said.

"Pig." She drank Hamm's right from the bottle. 'Oiling the dipstick.' Jesus."

The Robbins band was playing "Cherokee."

"Hear that trumpet?" Dwayne said. "He's *way* outside. Somebody shoot me."

"Better if somebody shot *him*," Screech said. "It'd put us all out of our misery."

Yet the crowd tapped their toes, the dancers danced, and Ruthie smiled as she delivered beer after beer to paying customers. She dropped a Schlitz off to Freddie without him asking. "This is what I'm talking about," she said, and off she went.

"Anyone heard from Thump?" Freddie said.

Sue nodded. "Toad says he's having a hell of a time staying off the horse, but so far, so good. Pretty much just drinks, sleeps, and farts."

Freddie turned to Catfish. "Leon must be on the line?"

"Things're about to get ugly," he said. "Almost had a riot today."

"What happened?"

"Goddamn scabs, man. Lots of pushing and shoving. Ain't gonna take much before someone burns this town down. Tomorrow the mayor's gonna ask the governor to call in the National Guard."

Freddie didn't think 'Fish had much room to criticize, since he wasn't out there fighting for the cause like Leon. "Didn't know anything about it," he said. "Never left the house today."

"You and that devil cat," Dwayne said. "Thing's gonna stick a claw in your throat one of these days. You'll just bleed out and lay there till the cat eats you."

"Shay'd find me. She came home."

"No shit?"

"'Course, she'd probably be the one that set Washington

on me in the first place."

"Did she say anything?" Sue asked.

"Like what?"

"I don't know—why she left, where she went, if she's going to stay this time."

"Nope."

"Why aren't you home talking to that woman? Wasting your time here with these idiots, when you could be patching things up with her."

Freddie looked at the water condensing on the beer bottle. He didn't drink from it, just ran its cool surface across his forehead. As he did, he noticed a new bruise on his wrist that he couldn't account for. The hell? "Don't know if I want to," he said. "Don't know if she does."

"Then kick her ass out for good. It's your house."

"That what you did with Toad?"

"I still talk to him because of Emmaline and Thump, but we'll never live under the same roof again. We knew when it was time, and we stuck to it."

"Hear, hear," the others said, clinking their bottles together.

The Robbins band finished "Cherokee" and went right into "Stars Fell on Alabama."

Dwayne lowered his head to the table and covered his ears. "I've died and gone to hell."

Freddie's body was on fire. He was weak, he was sweaty, and now there was a new bruise. Damn it. "I don't know what time it is for us, Sue."

Chapter 24

JACK HAD BEEN ACTING weird all day. Once Dick talked sense into Patti he was allowed back into their house, although K.C.'s status there was still uncertain. Maybe it was the uncertainty, but something was bothering Jack.

They were in K.C.'s bedroom. He stood next to her, holding the picture of Kenny, staring at it like he'd never seen it before.

"Put that down," K.C. said. She was sitting on her bed, fully dressed, and intended to stay that way.

He returned the photograph to the dresser. "How come you don't have a picture of me?"

She checked the glass to make sure he hadn't smudged it with fingerprints. "You're not dead."

"Is that what you want?"

"Don't be stupid."

"It's not my fault I wasn't old enough to be in the war."

"Who said anything about that?"

"I stood up to that guy at the drive-in."

What the hell? she thought. "What the hell?" she said.

"I might not be a big hero like Kenny, but I'm not chicken."

"What are you talking about? Nobody expects you to be like Kenny."

"You're always comparing us."

"I am not."

He sat next to her. "You don't say anything, but I can see it in your face. 'Kenny died, and what have *you* ever done?'"

"What is wrong with you?"

"You probably wish I'd been the one to die. Then you'd have your precious brother."

K.C. thrust herself off the bed. "Are you fucking crazy?" she screamed, although the question was more complicated than she wished it was. One life couldn't be swapped for another, and if it could, it would be wrong. She didn't want anyone's life for Kenny's. She just wanted Kenny.

But did Jack really think he was competing with him for her affections? It wasn't even the same thing.

Jack lifted his feet onto the mattress and wrapped his arms around his knees. "I don't know what you want," he said. He was crying.

Crying.

She'd never seen him do that before. It was unsettling. "Jack, don't."

"I'm sorry," he said, and burst out of the room.

She caught up with him before he got to the door, grabbing his arm and spinning him around. "Jack," she said, "listen. Listen."

He swiped at his cheeks with his sleeve. He wouldn't look at her. Boys were supposed to be tough. Crying was weakness. She wanted Jack to be tough, not weak, and yet, it was the bravest thing she'd ever seen him do.

"What?" he said.

She was the cause of his weird behavior.

K.C. hugged him hard enough to hurt. "I don't know,

either."

****

After Jack left, she called Narlins again from the pay phone. The same woman, Ruthie, answered. K.C. could hear the sounds of a band playing swing in the background, and lots of voices. Narlins must be busy. She asked for Freddie.

"I'll get him," Ruthie said. She seemed to be in a better mood than the last time they spoke.

While K.C. waited, she thought about Jack. She should appreciate him more. He was a good guy who chose her over his mother. Not all boys would do that. That part of the problem was resolved, but she didn't know what would happen if her own exile from the Schoonover house was permanent. Would Jack have to choose again?

Would she even want him to?

"This is Freddie."

"Hi, Mr. Ross, this is K.C. I saw the ad."

There was a long pause. A very long pause. All she could hear was the background noise. Freddie sighed. "Hey, White Bird. Dwayne said to give you another try."

Even though she suspected that was why he'd placed the ad, hearing him say it out loud took her breath away. She had a million questions, but the only one she managed to put into words was "What changed?"

"Can't talk now," he said. "Can you meet me sometime?"

"I have tomorrow off."

"How about the public library? Can you get to the east side?"

"What time?" She couldn't believe this was happening. Jack was worlds away from her thoughts.

"Three?" Freddie said.

158

"Should I bring my sax?"

"Why? You plan on giving a concert there? Meet me at the desk where they check out books. We'll talk. But I ain't gonna lie—I still think this is a bad idea."

"I know," she said, and it probably was, but oh, sweet Jesus, they were giving her a second chance...

****

Waterton was such a divided town that when Carnegie was funding libraries, just after the turn of the century, Waterton had to ask for two grants because they couldn't decide on east or west side. As far as K.C. knew, it was the only city its size that got two Carnegie libraries. The one on the east side wasn't too far to walk, just across the Fifth Street Bridge and up four or five blocks. But it was hot, so she took the 2:20 bus. Even if Freddie was on time, she'd have to wait over a half hour.

The lobby had a poster advertising children's reading hour. They were doing *Little Black Sambo*, which struck her as a little ironic. K.C. sat by the card catalog, where she could see both the entrance and the circulation desk. She fidgeted with her hands, folding them in her lap, straightening her hair, practicing imaginary scales. Anyone looking at her would think she was some kind of lunatic.

Jack wandered into her thoughts, and she chased him out. *Not now, Jack. Focus.*

Kenny whispered, *Go get 'em, Squirt.*

And then Austin Tyler, from Dale's, interrupted her nervousness. "Hey, Kasey, what are you doing over here?"

"What do people usually do at libraries?" she said.

"West is closer to your apartment."

"Yours, too." She looked away, acting like she wasn't interested in talking to him, only she wasn't acting.

"Ooh," he said, "you're having a secret rendezvous."

"You're not my supervisor here, Austin. Get lost."

"Maybe I'll tell Jack."

"Go ahead."

Austin pulled a chair in front of hers, facing her. Damn it. "I'm checking out the brainy girls," he said. "You're pretty smart."

He probably came to the east library because his pervert act had worn thin with the west side girls. Just her luck that it happened to be today.

"A brainy girl wouldn't look at you twice."

A group of small children passed by—most white, but a few black—herded toward the Youth Department by one of the librarians. *Sambo* was about to begin.

"So, are you two serious?" Austin said.

"Don't even think it."

He put his hand on her knee. "Come on, whaddaya say?"

She pushed his hand away. "Fuck off."

"I love it when women talk dirty."

"What a surprise. Leave me alone."

"Too good for me, is that it?"

Too good for me? It was like a line from a bad romance movie. "Austin," she said, but then Freddie walked through the door. *Thank you, Mr. Ross.* She waved and called his name.

Freddie headed her way.

Austin turned to see who she was waving at. "You're meeting a *nigger*? Whoa, you just got crossed off my list."

"If I'd only known it was that easy."

"Hey, White Bird," Freddie said.

"She doesn't want to talk to you, buck," Austin said.

Freddie might have gnarled fingers, but he was a big man. "What did you say?"

"You heard me."

The circulation desk attendant, a middle-aged woman, must have been watching them, because she rushed over to K.C. "Miss," she said as she glared at Freddie, "I can call the police if this man is bothering you."

"No," K.C. said, indicating Austin, "*this* one is."

"I was just leaving," Austin said. When he stood up, K.C. swore he was going to spit at them. He didn't, but his expression told her that their next shift together at Dale's wasn't going to be pleasant. He stormed up the stairs to the second floor to look for brainy girls with whiter tastes.

Freddie waited until the library lady huffed back to the desk, then moved the chair next to K.C.'s and sat down. "See?" he said. "It's already started."

****

"What changed Dwayne's mind?" K.C. said. They'd gone to a table on the lowest floor where there were fewer people to see them together.

"Can't say for sure anything did," Freddie said. "For him nobody can take Spits's place. Bullet's good, but Dwayne don't like him, either. He don't like any horn player who ain't Spits."

"So why did you want me to call you?"

"Ironhead said something stupid, hurt his feelings. But thing is, Bullet's gone after our next two gigs, so we're gonna need someone again. That's when Dwayne said to hire you. I don't know if he meant it, or was just mad. You still got to show him something..."

"I don't get it."

Freddie hesitated, like he was trying to decide what to say. Then, "Let me tell you about Dwayne and Spits. They're both Chicago boys. Went to the same high school, but didn't

161

really know each other till later. I think Dwayne's a couple years older. Yeah, I'm fifty, so Dwayne's forty and Spits is thirty-eight—"

"Wait, you're older than Dwayne? He looks like he's sixty."

Freddie grinned. "Best not tell him that. Anyway, you ask me, next to Yardbird, nobody can blow a sax like Spits. Plus, he got himself a degree. Chicago Musical College. Not even Leon finished college, but Spits did. Probably could've gone big-time, but he's like Thump. Started shooting horse. Man, that shit's poison. Don't know how many times it's almost killed him. Well, the gigs dried up for him because of it, so he had to take a job at the Regal Theater in Bronzeville, playing in the house band for silent movies. That's where he met Dwayne. Dwayne was the organist. They got to be friends. I mean, *real* good friends. See what I'm saying?"

K.C. recalled her phone conversation with Tim Piper. *Dwayne doesn't like girls. At all.* "You mean, he's a homo?"

"Guess that's what you'd call it."

"How's that, um, work between men?"

"Love's love, little Bird. Ain't just about sex."

Maybe not, but she envisioned two naked men together, and couldn't get the image out of her mind. There were only two places it could go, and one would hurt. "Yuck," she said.

"Whatever you or me think, Dwayne was good for Spits. Got him off the horse for a while. They split from the Regal and formed their own band. Played all the clubs in South Chicago—DeLisa, the Rhumboogie Cafe, Green Mill, Villa Venice—clear out to Evergreen Park. But by the time the war started, Spits was back on the needle.

"One night, him and Dwayne had a meeting with W.C. Handy, but Spits never showed. They found him strung out in a Dumpster. That was the last time he almost died.

"Horse was too easy in Chicago, so Dwayne brought him here. Turns out horse is easy here, too. They started up the Bluenotes, but Spits and him fought all the time about the dope. Finally Spits said 'Fuck it' and left."

"Dwayne knows W.C. Handy? Wow."

"We ain't talking about W.C. Handy."

"Spits get his nickname because of the reed? What's his real name?"

"Jesse Bryant. So it wasn't only a alto sax Dwayne lost, it was like, I don't know what they call each other, not a husband, but...?"

"And that's why he hates me? Because I'm a girl?"

"Because you're a white girl who thinks she can run with black cats. But mostly because you ain't Spits."

"Do I have a chance?"

Freddie shrugged. "Who knows what's in the man's head now? Maybe. I don't know if he cares anymore."

"Will Spits ever come back to the Bluenotes?"

"Nah. I saw him a couple Sundays ago. Dumb motherfucker's still using. Shot up right there in Audrey's bathroom."

"Him and Dwayne?"

"I don't see it happening. Spits ain't like my Shay. When he's gone, he stays gone."

K.C. didn't know who Shay was. "What do I do next?"

"We got out-of-town gigs on Friday and Saturday. The one on Saturday's a hour away, but it's a six-to-nine gig, so we'll be back that night. I'll see how many of the boys I can get to come to Narlins Sunday afternoon. You can run through shit with them before we show you to Dwayne again. Four o'clock?"

Dale's wasn't open on Sundays, so work wouldn't be a problem. Buses didn't run, though, and she wasn't sure how things stood with Jack. Maybe he'd drive her, maybe he wouldn't. She'd find a way. "I'll be there," she said.

Freddie stood up. "Good luck."

She wondered if Dwayne and Spits considered themselves married. Maybe it was more like they were engaged, only with no way to make it official. Did they kiss and cuddle and go to movies like regular couples?

As Freddie turned to leave, she looked at his left hand. He wasn't wearing a ring, but then, with his fingers, how could he? "Mr. Ross?" she said. "Can I ask a personal question?"

"Depends on the question."

"You said a name. Shay. Are you married?"

He chuckled. "I'm too old for you."

K.C. felt her cheeks redden. "I didn't mean that."

"Does it matter?"

"Not really. Just curious. My boyfriend and I..."

"Not that punk with you today?"

"God, no. That was Austin. My boyfriend's Jack. You saw him at Narlins."

"All white boys look alike to me."

"Really?"

"You got to learn when somebody's shitting you, kid. I only saw him for a second."

"Well, we might get married."

"Might?"

"That's the thing. I was wondering—"

"You looking for love advice from this old broke-down boneman?"

"I don't know. Got any?"

"Sorry, White Bird, I ain't the one to ask. You wanna know do I got a wife?" He nodded. "This week I do."

Chapter 25

THE POLICE STATION WAS on Mulberry Street, just down the street from the East Side Public Library. The courthouse was across the street from that. In his teens Freddie had spent plenty of time in both. It was during a freak March ice storm when his father came to bail him out the night his fingers were wrecked, the night he was arrested instead of the people who attacked him.

He stopped at Mulberry and Fifth for a red light. The station hadn't changed much since 1917, the courthouse not at all. Now, as then, cops came and went through the back door of the station, civilians through the front. He didn't have to do much mental subtraction to see the buildings the way they were then. Even the August sun couldn't erase his memory of that bitter night.

Although it was the worst thing that had ever happened to him, some good also came of it. At the time his plan for the future was playing Joplin at Narlins and shooting dope. Nothing more. He didn't need anything else, except a little hootchie-coo from Shay a couple times a week. That changed when he lost the use of his fingers. Seemed like music was gone forever, so he was forced to look ahead, to make decisions. Some young musicians might load an O.D. into the needle or put a gun in their mouth, but Freddie didn't. Instead, he stepped away from hard drugs and the people who sold them. He made an honest woman out of Shay.

There wasn't much physical labor he could do, but he could drive. His father used to be a coachman for Kline's Livery before cars put the company out of business around 1920. Freddie followed in his footsteps, except it was taxis instead of carriages. Wasn't a lot of money, but they got by. He did that for years, until he was fired for too many traffic violations. That's when the music bug bit him again.

Most instruments required functioning fingers, but all he needed with the trombone was talent and the ability to grip and blow. He had the talent and he learned the grip. Much to Shay's chagrin, he practiced every night. Then he met Dwayne and Spits. As it happened, the Bluenotes were looking for both a boneman and a booking agent.

Just as the light turned green, several squad cars pulled out of the police parking lot in the back and sped east, lights flashing and sirens screeching. Roth's was east of the station. 'Fish said things were getting bad there.

Freddie had steered clear of Roth's since visiting Leon on the line, but with only Shay's silence to look forward to the rest of the day, he decided to investigate. He headed in that direction. Traffic was unusually heavy, probably folks who were also curious about all those police cars.

Everything ground to a halt about two blocks from Roth's. The cops had to run their squads up on the sidewalks to get there. Freddie couldn't go forward and he couldn't turn around, so he put the Ford in park, shut it off, and got out. Others were doing the same. From here he could see hundreds of people in the streets, maybe thousands, vibrating with an edginess that made him nervous.

National Guard trucks were already there, men in uniform with rifles, either protecting the picketers from the crowd or the scabs from the picketers.

Freddie saw the puff of smoke before he heard the gunshot, and then all hell broke loose. Everybody screamed and stampeded away from Roth's in all directions. Freddie ducked back into his car and let the madness flow around him. He didn't know if a Guardsman or cop had opened fire, or what, but Leon was on the line today. He hoped he wasn't hurt.

People bumped and rocked the Ford as they rushed by. He caught bits of angry and frightened conversations. He heard enough of the same phrases to piece together what might have happened.

"Jigaboo scab."

"Shot."

"White striker."

Oh, shit, Freddie thought. Goddammit, God *damn* it. Catfish was right. This town was gonna burn.

****

It was two hours before order was restored enough for traffic to move again, and another hour of snail driving before he got home. Shay was listening to the radio in the kitchen. No Amos 'n' Andy tonight. KXM had interrupted its regular programming with news of the riot. Cops and National Guard got it under control tonight, but a calm wind today didn't guarantee there wouldn't be a tornado tomorrow.

"Anybody die?" Freddie said.

"One."

"They say who?"

"Not his name."

"White guy?"

"Yup."

"Black shooter?"

"Yup."

"Shit. They're gonna kill us all."

Shay turned off the radio and looked up at him. She'd gotten so old, worn out. "Coffee's on the stove."

Washington came out of the bedroom and meowed at Freddie. She even brushed up against his leg in a way he liked to think was affection. Now that Shay was back, the cat must think he was okay. But she didn't care about who shot who, or much of anything that went on in the human world. Feed her, give her a litter box, do everything she wanted the instant she wanted it, and stop doing it the instant she no longer wanted it. Life was simple for Washington.

Freddie poured himself a cup and sat at the table next to Shay. He studied her face a long while before speaking. "What're we gonna do?"

"Lay low and hope nobody comes after us."

"That ain't what I meant."

Shay went to the refrigerator. "It's what I meant," she said. She took out a leftover tenderloin and came back to the table.

"Why'd you leave this time?" Freddie said.

"'Cause I did."

"You gonna stay?"

"Unless I don't."

Her eyes went watery. Freddie put his hand over hers. "Shay," he said.

"No," she said.

He slid his hand away. "What can I do?"

"Can't think of anything."

In The Blood

****

Leon said he'd had it. With the strike, with the strikers, with the union, and with the scabs. Roth's rejected the union's latest proposal, a nineteen cent raise, down from twenty-nine. Word was that management sensed the workers were about to crack, and wouldn't budge from their original nine cent offer. "Least they could do," Leon said, "is give us ten or eleven cents. They're trying to embarrass us. I was hit, spit on, knocked down, and almost trampled, all for nothing. Well, piss on that. I'm just going to play music till the thing's settled."

Which meant Leon was all in for their gig at the State Teacher's College. So was 'Fish, who'd never taken much interest in the strike anyway. He just wanted to be able to feed Janae and those five kids.

The rioting had flared back up the next night, but not as bad as feared, and by the night after emotions had calmed to a simmer. Still, it was a good time to get out of Waterton. The college wasn't far, maybe eight or ten miles, but Sue drove them over in the bus to save them from having to find separate transportation. The gig wasn't really on campus, but at the Lutheran Student Center across the street. Freddie had thought it was an odd setting when he'd booked it. Turned out the stage was in a small auditorium in the basement, which was fine for preaching and making speeches, but not so good for music. The place couldn't hold all that sound. Waves bounced off the walls and ceiling and echoed back on themselves.

Still, the crowd was about as big as they could have hoped for, since school wouldn't be in session for another two or three weeks. Pretty easy going, too. They danced to the swing, sat back to appreciate the bop, and applauded after every number.

Freddie thought Bullet put a little extra into his changes, this being his second-to-last appearance with the Bluenotes. Everyone else was good, too, although not as hot as they'd been at their last rehearsal.

Afterward, while Dwayne collected their fee, Freddie approached the others about rehearsing with K.C. at Narlins on Sunday. Bullet was out, since he'd be getting ready to go back to Omaha for his band's western tour. Leon and Syd had made plans with their wives. Thump said maybe, which meant maybe. Ironhead and Screech said maybe, which meant no. Only Catfish promised to come. "Janae's starting to walk bow-legged," he said. "She needs time off."

A trombone, a piano, and possibly a bass to work with K.C.'s horn. Wasn't much, but it'd have to do. "Don't tell Dwayne," Freddie said.

"Don't tell me what?" Dwayne said, stepping up onto the bus. He gave Syd back his union card and held on to the rest.

"We're having a surprise birthday party for you," Freddie said.

"My birthday was in February."

"That's why it was gonna be a surprise."

"You want to keep secrets, the hell with you." Despite the harsh words, Dwayne seemed to be in a pleasant mood. He counted the money and divvied it up, including Sue's share. "Kind of a crazy place to hold a gig," he said, "but we did all right. Boneman, you'll have to book us somewhere on campus with a real auditorium after school starts. Think how well we'll do when all the students are back."

Sue fired up the bus. "Think how well you'd do if you were any good."

****

In The Blood

Even after midnight, the National Guard was locking down Waterton in a twelve-block diameter around Roth's. The strike was still going, and the picketers would be back in the morning, although Leon wouldn't be among them. Why risk dying for a union that was going to sell out the workers anyway? As soon as Sue pulled into the lot on Newton Street, everyone in the band got into their cars and headed home, not wishing to be caught in the streets this late. Dwayne got a ride with Leon.

Freddie's house was a five-minute drive. Inside, he turned on the kitchen light and found Shay snoring on the Goodwill couch. Her face was buried in the back cushion, so she didn't even stir when the light came on.

Washington was curled up on the *Waterton Record* on the kitchen table. When Freddie slid the paper from under her, she hissed, growled, and batted at his hand. Indignant, she hopped off the table and ran into the bedroom.

Nothing but Roth in headlines on the front page. In one of the stories the name of the dead man was revealed. Gilbert Hoyle, 38, married with three children. Hoyle's photograph showed a smiling man wearing work overalls. He'd been shot by Albert Bender, 55, a local widower. According to the paper, the men didn't know each other. Bender claimed he was aiming into the air to scare off picketers who were trying to overturn his car with him in it. Witnesses said he fired pointblank into Hoyle's face when Hoyle stuck his head through the passenger window.

The cops had moved Bender to a jail in LaPorte City, fifteen miles south on 218, to protect him from mob violence.

Shit. Shit. Shit.

Freddie put the paper down. Didn't matter if Bender did it on purpose or not. He was black, Hoyle was white. That's all a jury would need to know. The man was going to hang.

Freddie opened the refrigerator and took out leftover catfish filets that hadn't been deboned. He picked around them with a fork and ate slowly. Fish bones were like swallowing toothpicks. Washington was back, sitting at his feet, staring at him with those spooky glowing eyes. She'd never come when he called her by her human name, but apparently her cat name sounded exactly like the smell of fish, because that brought her running every time.

After a few bites he realized he wasn't hungry, which was strange after having just done a three-hour set in a hot church basement. He dumped the remaining fish on the floor for Washington and got up to use the bathroom.

Damn, he felt lousy. One of these days he should go see a doctor over at the free clinic, find out why he hurt all the time, why he sweated so much, why he bruised so easily. Probably all they'd do is give him some aspirin and tell him he's getting old. Well, okay, but fifty wasn't *that* old. His daddy lived to be seventy-six, his mama sixty-six. He ought to have at least another fifteen or twenty years in him.

He paused at the couch to gaze at Shay. Good Lord, that woman could snore. He got a big towel and draped it over her as a blanket. Sometimes when she slept she frowned, like the demons that drove her during the day tormented her at night, too. Other times she looked like the sweet-faced girl he knew as a teenager, peaceful and pretty as an angel— although her life then had been neither peaceful nor pretty.

Shay.

Freddie nearly stooped to kiss her cheek, nearly reached down to caress her hair. Instead, he let her be and went to take a piss.

****

Freddie had been in Fayette, Iowa, before. He'd even

played Upper Iowa University. But until now he'd never seen an Amish person. As Sue drove them up Highway 150 a horse-drawn buggy pulled up to the stop sign on a side street. Despite the heat, the driver was wearing black pants and a heavy, long-sleeved shirt. A straw hat kept the sun out of his eyes. The man had a long beard but no mustache, like Lincoln.

"Interesting folks," Sue said. "They don't use zippers or buttons, just metal fasteners. Don't fight in wars, don't send their kids to public schools. No cars. No electricity."

"Damn, man," Thump said, "what's the *point*?"

The man tipped his hat at them as the bus passed. If Freddie thought culture on the west side of Waterton was different, these Amish might as well be visitors from the moon. They'd be more foreign to Waterton's white population than the coloreds were.

"Farmers like us," Screech said, and Ironhead nodded.

"They're farmers," Sue said, "but they are *nothing* like you idiots."

"Why wouldn't they use buttons?" Leon said.

"Too showy. Vanity's a sin to them. Unlike you, pretty boy."

Freddie watched the buggy until it was out of sight. The Amish had to be foolishly stubborn to live like they did—that, or they had such rock-solid beliefs that they forced the entire weight of the world to flow around them. Either way, it must be a hell of a life.

Syd had been half dozing in his seat, a Fedora pulled over his eyes. "Don't have time for people who refuse military duty," he said to no one in particular. "They live in this country, too."

"It's their religion," Sue said.

"No excuse."

Good thing they were playing an early set. Fayette was more than an hour from Waterton. It was a nice little Iowa town, lots of trees and pleasant houses, so white Freddie needed sunglasses to look at all the faces. The college might have some black students, but he doubted it. Still, there hadn't been any trouble the last time the Bluenotes'd played here.

Sue pulled into the parking lot of a brick building too small to be called a university. Dwayne went in to get someone to open the auditorium. It was only 4:30, an hour and a half until the show started, but that left plenty of time to set up and tune.

Sue took a cigarette and the novel *The World of Null-A* from her purse. "I've tried to read this shit about twelve times," she said to Freddie. "Can't make head or tail out of it, but when I start a book, I have to finish it. Anything's better than listening to you clowns."

Freddie read the cover. A.E. van Vogt. *Never heard of him.* "Suit yourself," he said.

They set up, warmed up, and waited. The crowd started wandering in at 5:45. It was smaller than at the Teachers College, and less appreciative, which wasn't surprising, since the band's performance was lackluster. They weren't "catastrophe at the Cobana" bad, but they didn't play with the energy they'd had last night. Even Bullet, in his final performance with the Bluenotes, seemed to phone it in. But they got paid and they weren't lynched, which was the best they could hope for on a night they weren't at their best.

Sue was asleep when they got to the bus, head back on the driver's seat, an unlit cigarette in her mouth, and *The World of Null-A* on the floor where she'd dropped it. Freddie woke her up by clapping in her ear, which caused her to jump and swing her fist. He'd known it was coming and dodged the blow.

"I hate it when you do that," she said.

They reloaded and were back on the road to Waterton by ten o'clock. When Sue stopped to drop Screech and Ironhead off at their farm outside Lesterville, Freddie got an image of them in Amish clothes, plain and dark, with straw wide-brimmed hats, and suspenders holding their pants up. Oh, and long beards without mustaches.

Was there such a thing as colored Amish? Freddie laughed.

"What?" Ironhead said.

"E-I-E-I-O," he said.

"Fuck you," Ironhead said, "and old MacDonald, too." He and Screech collected their instruments and went into the house.

The parking lot in Waterton was only ten minutes away. Bullet was the first off the bus. Tipping his hat he said, "It was fun, boys. I ain't going back to Omaha for a couple days, so maybe I'll still see you around. But probably not."

Chapter 26

WORK WITH AUSTIN AT Dale's on Saturday was worse than awkward. He wasted no time sauntering behind the soda fountain to whisper, "Nigger lover." Just as Freddie had warned her. Austin had always made disgusting comments when Jack wasn't around, but now he openly pinched her butt and squeezed her breasts. She pushed him so hard he nearly tripped over the cord to the ice cream freezer. "Slut," he said. "That how the jigaboos like it? Rough?"

"I thought you crossed me off your list."

"I wouldn't take you home to Mom, but I'd let you suck me."

Jack was at the meat counter. If she said anything to him, he'd probably punch Austin in the face. That would be satisfying to K.C., but she didn't want him to get in trouble.

"I'm telling Dale," she said.

"Go ahead. He won't care."

So she did.

And he didn't. Dale, grandson of the original owner, was around forty and nice looking for an old guy. "Boys will be boys, Kasey. You're a pretty girl. Of course they're gonna make passes. Just say no."

"You mean it's okay for him to grab my boobs?"

"I didn't say that."

"Sure sounds like it to me."

"What do you want me to do, fire him?"

"Well, yeah."

"Austin's a hard worker. He's no Einstein, but that means he won't go to college. I might get to keep an assistant manager older than twenty-two for a change. Just don't provoke him."

"That's your answer? 'Don't provoke him?' Jesus Christ."

"Watch your language, young lady."

When she got back to the soda fountain, her face must have been red as a flaming coal. She wanted to explode. Davy better not come in today, or she'd twist his head off.

Austin was still there, leaning against the counter and smiling. "Told you," he said.

She wanted to crush his balls in a waffle iron. "Fuck you," she said.

"Someday," he said, and walked off whistling.

****

K.C. hadn't planned to go to church. Her state of mind wasn't going to get her closer to heaven this morning. She was pissed off at Austin and Dale. She fretted over her second audition at Narlins. Her status with Dick and Patti Schoonover was still up in the air.

Alone in her apartment, she wasn't expecting visitors, so it took her by surprise when someone knocked on her door. Krissy, her husband Ben, and their son Micah stood in the hallway.

"Hey, baby sis," Krissy said.

"Hi, Aunt Kasey," Micah said. He was four.

K.C. looked at the clock above the door. "It's eight-thirty."

"Yeah. Church is at nine."

"Okay…?"

"Your mom and dad invited you," Ben said.

Whoa. "Mom and Dad? Why?"

"I told you they wanted to see you again," Krissy said. "Here's your chance."

Just like that? K.C. thought. She was still in her pajamas. "They could've given me some warning. I'm not even dressed."

"We'll wait," Krissy said.

Bathroom, bath, make-up, hair, nice clothes… No. "Tell them next week. If they say they're sorry."

"This *is* them saying they're sorry. Then you have to say it, too."

"For what?"

Krissy sighed her exasperated spoiled housewife sigh. Her glasses perched halfway down her nose, making her look like a librarian.

"When she makes that sound to me," Micah warned, "I get spanked."

"Not today," K.C. said.

"You are so pig-headed," Krissy said.

"I know, but you love me anyway."

"All right, but no excuses next Sunday. We'll be here at eight-thirty sharp to pick you up. Be ready." She paused to look over K.C.'s pajamas. "And, really, you should get yourself some decent PJs. Aren't those for boys?"

K.C. was so tempted to stick her finger through the slit in the front and waggle it to wave goodbye. "Say hi for me," she said.

****

"No way I'm driving you to the east side," Jack said. "The strike isn't over."

Other than at work, she hadn't seen him since before she met with Freddie. "Narlins is nowhere near Roth's," she said with her best whine. "If you won't do this one little thing, I'll walk. Don't worry that I'll have to lug my saxophone all that way."

"Like hell. It's not safe."

"I walked to the East-Side Library the other day." It was a lie—she'd taken the bus—but she was making a point.

"Why'd you go to the east one?"

"Meeting somebody about auditioning with the Bluenotes again."

They were both at her tiny kitchen table. Jack shook his head, then walked to the chair next to her window. He gazed out on the street below, as if there were an answer there. "Dammit, Kase, Mom's never going to accept you if you keep associating with Negroes."

"That's none of her business. Or maybe you have a problem with it, too?"

"Stop it."

"Then what? You don't trust me?"

"I don't trust them. Whether they're black or not, they're men. Older men. You don't know them."

"Look, all middle-aged men aren't lusting after young female flesh."

"Not all of them, but what about these?"

"What about Austin?"

"Tyler?"

"Do you know any other Austins?"

"What about him?"

"Other than having his hands all over my boobs and butt, nothing."

Jack spun toward her. She'd never seen him get this

furious this fast. She kind of liked it. "When?"

"Well, I mean, he's talked dirty to me before, but…"

"And you didn't tell me?"

"I was afraid you'd kill him, so I told Dale"

Jack's clenched and unclenched his fists. "What did he say?"

"That it was my fault."

"That's bullshit. You're right, I'm going to kill him."

"Austin's not worth hanging for. Just don't schedule me at the same time with him." She paused to give him a coquettish smile. "And drive me over to Narlins this afternoon…?"

Jack frowned at her like she was a crazy manipulative bitch.

Okay, this one time, she was, using a serious situation as leverage to get her way. But playing for the Bluenotes was serious, too. More serious than an idiot pawing at her in the grocery store.

"All that just to get a ride?" he said.

"It's all true," she said, "but, yeah, I want a ride."

"Can I stay and listen while you audition?"

"Keep your eye on me, you mean."

"On them."

"There's nothing to worry about, but you can stay if you want."

"Fine. Just don't tell my mother I took you to meet with Negroes."

"She probably won't let me back into your house anyway."

Jack looked at the clock. "How soon do you have to leave?"

"Need to be there by four, so three-thirty?"

"Good," he said. "That gives me two hours."

"For what?"

"To go beat the shit out of Austin."

Yes, she thought, wanting to give him her waffle iron to take with him. "No," she said. "You'll get yourself fired."

"I'm going back to college on September 10th anyway. Dale's got nothing I need."

"I've got something you need," she said, and managed to keep him at her apartment until it was time to go to Narlins.

****

Freddie was there. So was the piano player—Charles Elliot, was it? Catfish. No one else. That was disappointing. Like the first time she'd been here, the place was dark except for a light above the stage.

"Hey, White Bird," Freddie said. "Just you, me, and 'Fish now, but I got one more coming. This Jack?"

K.C. nodded and introduced them.

"Mr. Ross," Jack said.

Freddie shook Jack's hand, his crooked fingers barely moving. "This here's Catfish."

Catfish nodded from the piano bench.

"You want to warm up, Bird?" Freddie said.

"Got anything in mind?"

"'Rhapsody in Blue,'" Catfish said. "I hear you know your way around the eighty-eights."

"I'm not auditioning on piano."

"You know the number or not?"

"'Rhapsody?' Sure. Two- and four-handed version."

Catfish smiled. "Well, we got a little time. If it's okay with your boyfriend, come on over here and show me what you got."

K.C. glanced at Freddie, who shrugged, then at Jack, who

looked a bit alarmed.

She joined Catfish on the bench, sitting on his right so she'd have the higher notes if he decided to play along.

"Start us off, little missy."

She led with a three-count trill on the F and E below middle C, followed immediately by the diatonic glissando up the keyboard. Instead of single notes, however, like when the clarinet played it, she went big and did the run in unison octaves in the right hand. Once she got to the melody, she intentionally held the opening B flat chord a tantalizing two counts too long—a fermata Gershwin didn't call for—before continuing the predominantly descending melody in syncopated eighths.

After that she just closed her eyes and let the music take her. She'd played this piece in the final spring concert every year in high school. She preferred the single-piano version, although it was fun in practice when she staged a little duel with her chief competitor for featured pianist, Debbie Neuhaus. Debbie could play, but never quite feel, the different piano styles.

K.C. thought Catfish might take the lower notes, but he got up and stood behind her, probably watching her fingerings. Without skipping a beat, she switched to the solo version, playing the whole thing through its umpteen key and tempo changes, from flighty to majestic, comical to dramatic. When she finished she was sweating like the proverbial pig.

"God *damn*, girl," Catfish said. He started applauding, followed by one, two—three?—other sets of hands.

K.C. turned to see who else had come in. It was a black man she didn't recognize, dressed in out-of-date clothes that he made look stylish. He was carrying a sax case.

"Wow," Jack said. "I never get tired of hearing you play

that."

"And you don't even like jazz," K.C. teased.

"Man, I ever gotta miss a gig," Catfish said, "Dwayne's gonna snap you up in a second. Might not let me come back."

"I don't want your job," she said. "I want Spits's."

"Well, well, well," the stranger said. "Let's see about that, young lady."

Freddie cleared his throat and said, "White Bird, this is Spits."

"Jesse Bryant at your service." Spits held out his hand. K.C. hesitated. He was a *homo*... She didn't think the condition was contagious, but where had that hand been?

Nowhere hers hadn't.

She stood up and shook with him.

"My real name's K.C. Brown."

"I must say, K.C. Brown, that was impressive. If you blow horn that well, Dwayne would be a fool not to hire you. Come on, you and me are going to jam."

Suddenly K.C. was more nervous than she'd been before. Spits wasn't famous, but she'd heard his name so often that it felt like he was. And now that she knew the nature of his relationship with Dwayne, it would be even harder to win Dwayne over. It would be like her replacing Jack with a girl.

She removed her sax from its case, moistened the reed, and adjusted the mouthpiece.

Freddie took a seat with his trombone. Catfish returned to the piano bench.

"You using Ricos?" Spits said.

"Always."

"Good girl." Spits turned to Catfish. "Charlie, you and Freddie lay out for a while. Just us two are going to play to start with. K.C., Freddie tells me you know 'Ko-ko.' You got the front."

She blew a few notes to limber up, then started in on the intro. After a few measures, Spits came in, but instead of unison like their trumpet player that first night at Narlins, he played a countermelody, creating wonderful and unexpected harmonies. Harmonies she'd never have thought of in a million years.

As if reading her mind, Spits said, "Now switch it up. I'll do the melody, you see if you can stay with me."

They started over. She tried to imitate what he had done, but it just sounded stiff and amateurish to her.

"No," Spits said. "Don't do what I did. Make it yours. The music knows the way. Don't think it, *feel* it."

The next time through was better, and the third better still. K.C. started to understand the connection between the notes in a new way. On the fourth take, Spits signaled in Freddie and Catfish. They went beginning to end, with Spits giving her all the changes. Unlike the first time she'd played with the band, she was able to keep up, even taking the lead in places.

She was satisfied. She'd not only held her own, but she'd been so caught up in the music she nearly forgot Jack was there. He might like "Rhapsody in Blue," but he hated bop.

Too bad.

"Well," Spits said, "technically, you're good. Nice articulation and you listen well. But I'm not hearing on sax what I heard on piano. Piano's inside you, sax is still outside. Let it in, K.C. Sax can't just be something you play, it's got to *be* you."

Mr. Pierson had told her the same thing. *You aren't a player until it becomes an extension of your body, a third arm, a piece of your soul.*

"Is there any hope?" she said.

Spits smiled. "Don't give me that pout—we're not done here. You're already better than I was at your age. You know the swing tunes Dwayne does?"

"I know all the swing tunes."

This time she was smart enough not to admit she used to play along with records.

PART THREE

CAT BIRD

Chapter 27

THE NEXT TIME SHE worked at Dale's, Austin was back with his comments and his pawing. This time K.C. didn't hesitate. She delivered the most magnificent knee-to-the-groin the world had ever seen. He crumpled behind the soda fountain, struggling to catch his breath. She thought he might vomit—almost hoped he would, except that she'd have to clean it up. There were no customers in the store. He never would have tried anything with her if there had been, but that was in her favor, since she could retaliate without offending anyone. Well, except Austin, who she very much wanted to offend.

"Fucking bitch," he moaned. "You're fired."

"You can't fire me."

"Dale can."

"I'll go get him."

She found the owner in the break room drinking coffee. She requested that he come out front without telling him why. When he saw Austin on the floor, still clutching his testicles, she expected him to support Austin and fire her. She almost didn't care. It was worth it.

"She kicked me in the nuts," Austin said. He was still a

pleasant shade of green.

This was the big moment. K.C. started untying her work apron in anticipation of her impending unemployment, but Dale surprised her. "From what I've heard, you deserve it. Get up and leave her alone. K.C., don't kick him in the nuts anymore. I don't want to have this conversation with either of you again."

They spent the rest of the day avoiding each other, although she could feel his glare from afar. In the parking lot after work Jack took off his work apron and put it in his pickup before walking her home. He'd just relocked the door when Austin came out of the store. Jack strolled up to him and, without a word, punched him in the face, just like the ape at the drive-in had punched Jack. Austin went down, nose gushing blood.

"If you ever touch Kasey again," Jack said, "I'll break your arms. If you ever talk to her about anything but work, I'll break your jaw. We clear on that?"

Austin wobbled to his feet. "You know she sucks niggers, right?"

Bam, down he went again.

"Kasey is the truest girlfriend in the world," Jack said.

Austin lay back on the pavement, sprawling his arms out like he was about to make a snow angel. He laughed. "Have it your way. I wouldn't fuck that whore with Dale's dick."

Jack looked like he was about to kick Austin in the head, but Kasey pulled him away. "Enough," she said.

"Fuck you both."

Dale always stayed after the store closed to do the bookwork. K.C's job had survived her violent outburst this morning, but Jack's probably wouldn't tonight.

"I'm walking Kasey home," he said to Austin. "Be gone when I come back."

On their way to Wellington Court, she told him what'd happened behind the soda fountain. "That felt sweet," she said.

"Good job. Going to West tonight?"

"Yeah. I need to talk to Mr. Pierson anyway."

"Want to go out somewhere for supper?"

"Save your money. Just pick me up afterward. By the way, thanks for what you said."

He nodded and held her hand, but his expression was troubled, as if he wasn't *entirely* sure she was the truest girlfriend in the world. Since he'd just defended her honor, she let it pass this time, but she knew they had more talking to do.

****

The band couldn't practice at Narlins all the time. Some nights Ruthie had live entertainment, other nights music piped in through loudspeakers. Neither allowed for rehearsal. K.C. didn't know what all the band members did for regular employment, but she'd been told Leon and Catfish were involved with the Roth strike. She also still had the job at Dale's, for now, which made it difficult to coordinate a time during the day when all the musicians could get together.

She went downstairs from her apartment and used the pay phone to call Mr. Pierson. She figured what his answer would be, but it didn't hurt to ask.

"I'm not even supposed to let Jack in," he said. "I had to make a special case with the school board to get permission for you."

"I know," she said, "but the Bluenotes are giving me another chance. We need somewhere to practice."

"Where do they practice now?"

"The place they usually go is busy, and with my work schedule..."

There was a long pause at the other end, long enough that K.C. became hopeful. Then he said, "I'm sorry, Kasey. If the school board found out, I'd lose my job."

"How would they find out?"

Don't press it, Squirt, Kenny said.

Mr. Pierson sighed. "I'd have to sneak them in, which I won't do. You know how delighted I am that you've stayed with music. Your brother would be proud of you. But there has to be another place. Somebody's basement?"

"All I want is to be in a jazz band," she said, tempted to slam the receiver down. "Why is everyone standing in my way?"

"I'm sorry if it seems that way. You're still welcome to practice there on your own."

"Maybe I shouldn't play my sax at all. I'll just sell it and use the money to get married and make babies."

"Don't be childish."

"*Childish*?" K.C. said. "Goddammit, everyone *but* me is being childish. All they say is 'you can't, you can't, you can't.' Well, why can't I?"

There was another pause before Mr. Pierson said, "There's no reason to swear at me. I've always supported you, and I still do, but I'm responsible for helping all my young musicians, not just you. It's my life. If I lose my job..."

"I get it. I'm not a student anymore, so I don't count. Okay, fine. You won't have to worry about me anymore."

"Kasey—"

She hung up the phone.

He's one of the good ones, Squirt. Don't turn on your friends.

"Shut up."

****

Jack's mood was as bad as hers when he came back to pick her up. "He scratched my truck," he said. "The son-of-a-bitch scratched my truck."

She let him in and closed her apartment door behind him. She was still angry about Mr. Pierson and didn't need to hear his problems. "Calm down."

"Don't tell me to calm down. Know what else? I got pulled over for it."

"For a scratch?"

"He wrote 'nigger lover lover' on my hood and driver's door. Cop said, what was I trying to do, start another riot? Shit."

How she hated Austin. She was pretty sure she hated everybody tonight. "He give you a ticket?"

"A warning. I have a week to get it fixed. I told him I wanted to file a complaint, but he said, 'Did you see him do it? Otherwise it's his word against yours.'"

K.C. led him to the kitchen chair and sat him down. "Take it to Ben. He can paint over it good as new. Krissy likes you, so you know he won't charge much."

"He'll have to sand it first. That'll cost a fortune, even from Ben. It's almost brand new."

"This is my fault," she said, because she thought that's what he expected to hear.

"It's Austin's fault," Jack said, pounding his left fist on the table. "But why do you insist on trying to get in with those people?"

"*Those people*?"

"You know what I mean. Dammit, Kase, that's not your

world. This is your world. Here. With me."

"My world is wherever I am. I don't want to fight about it. You're not the only one having a crappy night."

"Let's go, then."

"I'm not going to West tonight. I talked to Mr. Pierson on the phone. He's being a jerk. He won't let the Bluenotes practice there."

"Why would he? They'd fire him."

"So you're on his side, too."

"I'm on *our* side." Jack stood up. He shook his right hand, which was swollen and red. "Probably broke my hand on that asshole's face."

Translation: Look what I did for you.

****

She felt like she was drowning. Yes, her little temper tantrum was self-defeating. Yes, refusing to practice because Mr. Pierson wouldn't give her what she wanted was childish. She was standing in her own way, but she was so frustrated...

Instead of the school, they drove to Krissy's place so Ben could look at Jack's truck. They lived on St. Martin Street in a good neighborhood not far from the golf course. Ben's auto body shop was downtown, but he had a double garage behind his house where he worked on a '32 Alpha Romero in his spare time.

The house was a two-story Georgian with blue aluminum siding and a chain-link fence enclosing the yard. Their dog, a black and white Boston terrier named Sir Reginald Bear, barked at them as the truck pulled into the driveway.

Micah must have heard the dog, because he rushed out to greet them, followed by Ben.

"Hi, Aunt Kasey and Uncle Jack," he said.

"Shhh," Ben said to Sir Reginald. He gave him a biscuit, which made K.C. and Jack uninteresting to him.

They got out of the truck. "Hey, Micah," she said.

"My second favorite Brown girl," Ben said to K.C. "What brings you?"

When they told him, he shook his head and claimed he had a three-week backlog. Then Jack showed him what Austin had scratched into the truck.

Ben whistled and said, "Micah, go inside."

"Do I have to?" the boy whined.

"Tell Mommy we'll be in in a couple of minutes. Maybe she could make us some lemonade."

When he was gone, Jack said, "I got a warning ticket."

"I see why. What's this all about? 'Nigger lover lover?'"

"A guy at work was pinching my butt and stuff," K.C. said. "Jack punched him out."

"I would have, too. How soon do you need it back?"

"I don't work tomorrow, so Thursday maybe?"

"Got too much going on at the shop, but you can't drive around like this, so I'll work on it here at night. The red should be easy enough to match. I'll just need thirty bucks for the paint. Won't charge you for the labor."

Jack's face lit up. "Really? I was expecting a lot more."

"That's a family price." He winked at K.C. "'Course, you can give me more if you had your heart set on it..."

Jack took out his wallet. "I got forty-two on me."

"I was kidding, dipshit. Thirty's fine. I'll get started while it's still light."

Jack stayed out with Ben while K.C. went inside for lemonade with Krissy. She always felt a little uncomfortable here. Dick and Patti, her own parents, even Mr. Hammon, all lived in nice houses, but they were older and established, so that's what she'd expect. But Krissy was only four years older than her, and Ben maybe ten or twelve. For her sister to have so much, so young, was annoying, not because K.C. wanted it, but because that was how her parents defined success for a young woman.

Krissy was dressed casually in cotton slacks and one of Ben's undershirts. No shoes. Ordinary reading glasses from the five-and-dime. It was unusual to see her when she wasn't trying to set fashion standards for the world. "Hey, baby sis. Don't forget church on Sunday."

"Can Jack come?"

"Jesus doesn't close any doors."

"It's not Jesus I'm worried about."

"Let's go outside on the deck."

Micah wanted to come too, but Krissy found a baseball game for him to listen to on the radio. He didn't know a thing about baseball, but liked the announcer's voice when he got excited.

The screened-in deck wrapped around the north and west sides of the house. From the west side was a lovely view of other houses with manicured lawns, trimmed hedgerows and trees and, in the distance, a corner of the golf course. The overhang provided shade, and the screen kept out the mosquitoes and flies. A little round tea table had already been set up with place mats and glasses.

K.C. sat down and waited for Krissy to bring the lemonade.

The sun was still an hour from setting, but it was low enough to cast long, neat shadows across long, neat yards. A westerly breeze was pleasant but humid. Late-model cars were parked in driveways all along the block, except at one house, where some boys were shooting baskets at a hoop attached to a double-car garage.

All this, K.C. thought.

Krissy filled their glasses, placed the pitcher on the table's center mat, and sat across from K.C. "Now," she said, "what's going on? Did you and Jack have a fight?"

"Not with each other." K.C. didn't feel the need to explain the situation to her, because she knew what her sister's responses would be.

K.C.: Austin fondled me. Jack beat him up.

Krissy: Good.

K.C.: Austin scratched Jack's truck.

Krissy: That was mean.

K.C.: Mr. Pierson won't let the Bluenotes practice with me at West.

Krissy: You shouldn't be associating with coloreds anyway.

In other words, pretty much what everyone else had told her.

In Krissy's defense, she didn't actively hate Negroes. She would never hurt them or call them niggers. She didn't want to take away their rights. She didn't want to bring back slavery. But she didn't want them living next to her, either. They were just a different kind of people she had to look down to see, a bother she'd prefer to avoid. The only time she thought about them, K.C. was sure, was when K.C. herself mentioned them.

Krissy took her reading glasses off, wiped the lenses with a handkerchief, and put them back on. "Hate these damn things," she said. "Lucky I'm married. No one notices girls with glasses."

"Those are nothing to write home about, but the tortoise-shell ones were nice."

"Hmmph." Krissy sipped lemonade and looked in the direction of their garage, although she couldn't see it from the deck. "I wonder what men talk about when we're not with them."

"Beer, sports, and women," K.C. said. Or dope, jazz, and women, if Freddie was telling the truth.

"Not Ben. He likes beer and football, but only has eyes for me."

Of course he does, K.C. thought. *You buy negligees for him to take off you.* "Will you be able to drive us home?" she said. "Ben needs to keep Jack's truck a couple of days."

"Dressed like this?"

That was the Krissy she knew. K.C. was surprised Krissy wore casual attire at all, let alone let herself be seen outside in it. She sometimes thought Krissy went to bed in a formal evening gown. "You look fine."

"I'm sure Ben will, though. So. You and Jack are okay?"

"As okay as we've ever been."

Chapter 28

FREDDIE HAD DOZED OFF in the chair. He awoke to Shay's voice. He opened his eyes a slit and saw her at the kitchen table, stroking Washington's fur with a brush. The damn cat was purring like an electric motor. Washington never did that with him unless food was involved, and then only until she got what she wanted.

"Pretty kitty," Shay sang, a tuneless melody. "Pretty little baby kitty."

Washington did have interesting coloring—but 'pretty'? Freddie wasn't so sure about that. And she certainly wasn't a little baby kitty. She was probably seven years old and shaped like a bowling pin, all her weight at the back end.

He continued to watch while pretending to be asleep. He'd never seen Shay dote like this over the cat. Maybe it was like brushing the hair of their daughter, except that they didn't have a daughter. Or a son. That lack in their lives was a gift from a hooded group of men in Spring Valley, Mississippi, a long time ago. While some of them hung Shay's father Sloan, the rest busied themselves finding uses for her body. Her mama Nelly's, too. A wire in a midwife's back room had spared her a white man's child, but left scars that kept her from having any other man's child either.

Shay continued to brush and sing. She must have sung these words before, because the rhythm was too even for her to be making it up on the spot.

"Pretty kitty, pretty kitty,

Pretty little baby kitty,

Pretty as a angel on a Christmas tree.

Pretty kitty, pretty kitty,

Pretty little baby kitty,

Pretty as the girly no one sees but me."

She suddenly stopped, picked Washington up, and set her on the floor. "I know you're awake," she said to Freddie. "You ain't snoring no more."

Freddie sat forward, stretched, and yawned. "Just woke up."

"You must think I'm a crazy woman."

"Never been a time I didn't." He smiled to show he was joking, but when she didn't smile back, he said, "Cat ain't much of a substitute for a real child."

"Don't get yourself all teary-eyed over me. Never said it was your fault."

"I'm just saying—"

"Well, don't. Truth is, you ain't much of a real husband, neither."

Freddie lay back in the chair and closed his eyes. "You sure don't make this easy," he said.

****

There was nothing like pounding piano keys for blowing off steam. Unfortunately, Freddie could no longer do that, unless he used his elbows. Music was still the way, though. He just had to take a different path.

In The Blood

He climbed the stairs to the second floor at Narlins, where he kept his trombone in a locker. No matter how many times he came up here—several times a week for years—it always brought back memories. Back in the 'teens, apartments were located where the storage space was now. He used to live in 2-A. That one-room pit had been so filthy that rats were ashamed to live in it, but anywhere was better than home, where he had to listen to his father's constant criticism. They fought about dope, music, girls, his attitude, his mother's disappointment in him, one of his father's white friends... damn near everything. If Freddie breathed wrong, he got yelled at.

That must have been about 1916. By then he wasn't home much anyway, playing ragtime at Narlins almost every night till dawn. Easier just to go upstairs afterward to blow dope and sleep.

Shay was part of these memories, too, something he didn't need right now. She stayed with him in 2-A about half the time. The other half she spent with her mama Nelly at the house of a man named Harley Mimms. Mimms had brought them up from Mississippi after Sloan was lynched for saying something impolite to a white girl. Then he ran off, leaving Nelly and Shay to fend for themselves.

Nelly never got over Sloan's death, so she wasn't much help with anything.

Freddie sighed and inserted his key into the lock. He pulled out the case with his trombone.

To make ends meet, Shay took to the streets. Back then Freddie was just another john with a pocketful of change.

All those men, all those sweaty nights on her back or on her knees, and now she wouldn't do for her own husband what she'd done for strangers. Maybe she used up her energy supporting herself and Nelly, or maybe it was only Freddie who turned her to stone. The times she left him and she never said where? Could be to see Nelly. Could be she had some big stud on the next block making her groan and scream.

Freddie trudged back down the stairs. He was surprised to see Catfish there.

'Fish took a look at Freddie's face and said, "You look like you just ate a bowl of dog shit."

"Thing is," he said, "it wouldn't bother me all that much. You know, if somebody else is doing it for her... I sure as hell ain't."

"Got no idea what you're talking about," 'Fish said, and Freddie saw no reason to explain.

Ruthie would be opening Narlins at four. No live music tonight, just tunes piped in over the loudspeaker. Freddie removed his trombone from its case and fit the slide into place.

'Fish sat at the piano.

"Long as you're here, play something loud—anything," Freddie said. "No, hell with it, play 'Twelfth Street Rag.'"

"Thought you hated that number."

Freddie sat down in the chair next to him. "Yeah, but I need something to make me mad."

"Ever told you you're a strange dude, Boneman?"

'Fish started in. Freddie winced with every note, each one reminding him of the thump of the hammer on flesh, the cracking bones, the crushed fingernails, the dislocated joints, the blood. Then the merciful faint that delayed his pain for a few moments, followed by the awakening, the vomiting, the tears...

He lifted the trombone to his shoulder. He was plenty mad now. After the attack, he was the one arrested. Not the thugs who ruined his ragtime career when they ruined his fingers. Yeah, the cops were white, but the hoodlums were as black as Freddie. It wasn't like they were protecting rich white men against the accusations of a poor colored kid. Black was black to them. The least they could've done was arrest everybody.

But no. The lowlifes walked, Freddie went to jail, and his father had to bail him out.

He blew the tenor line as loud as his lungs could muster, keeping up with 'Fish's left hand as it glided across the keyboard.

He was so caught up in his memories and anger that he kept playing after Catfish had finished.

"Whoa, Boneman, cool it down. You're gonna pop a vessel."

Freddie lowered the trombone. "None left that ain't already popped."

'Fish turned to look at him. "This about Shay?"

He didn't want to talk about her now any more than he had before "Twelfth Street Rag."

"Nah, 'Fish, it's about me. Don't trouble yourself. Janae and the kids okay?"

"The tagalongs've been passing a cold between them, but otherwise, everything's good."

'Fish's two youngest, Harvey and Sarah, were three and two. Then it skipped up to Sally, who was ten, Lenny, twelve, and Chuck, Jr., fourteen or fifteen. "Which one of them was mine again?"

"Take them all, if you want. 'Specially Junior. There some kind of pill teenagers take that turns them into assholes? Tell him it's hot and he puts on a coat. Tell him it's dark and he puts on sunglasses. Tell him about girls, and, well, the little shit's probably got more kids than me. See what I'm saying?"

Lewis must have thought the same thing about Freddie,

and Freddie had hated him for it. Now he was on Catfish's side. Funny how age changed the way a person looked at things.

"How's the strike going?"

'Fish slammed the piano lid down, a strong reaction for a man who didn't get too excited about much of anything. "Don't get me started," he said. "Damn union's gonna cave. A man gets shot in the face walking the line for them, and they're gonna say, okay, nine cents is fine, sorry we bothered you."

"I don't think Leon's been back since the killing."

"I met Al Bender a couple of times. State's gonna hang him, so two men'll be dead over nine cents."

Freddie disassembled his trombone and put it back into its case. Ruthie would be coming to kick them off the stage soon. "Would it be better if they died for twenty-nine cents?"

****

It was Sunday morning and Freddie was at church. Shay had insisted not only that he go, but that they bring Nelly, too. They sat in the back row, where her mother felt the congregation wouldn't look at her.

Nelly Wiggins was a seventy-year-old woman who looked ninety. She was tiny, maybe eighty-five pounds, and frail as wet tissue. She dyed her hair black, but there was nothing she could do to disguise the crushing look of hard experience she carried in her face and posture. She folded her hands in her lap. She didn't look up, didn't sing, didn't pray. The only sound she made was an almost inaudible mumble. The few words Freddie was able to make out were "Sloan," "ungrateful," and "let me go," separated by long stretches of nonsense syllables or words spoken too softly to hear.

He knew about her husband Sloan, dead these forty

years. Maybe "let me go" referred to the white men who'd killed him and raped her and Shay, but Freddie could only guess at who she thought was ungrateful. Everybody, probably. A person only had to meet Nelly once to understand that Shay came by her bad attitude honestly.

Reverend Hahn was preaching about Christ and how His suffering applied to the Roth strike. Every time Freddie came to church, which was seldom, Hahn said something to try to give 2,000-year-old scripture meaning in the modern world. It was his job. Freddie had no problem with Jesus, but He wasn't walking the picket line.

While Hahn rambled, Nelly mumbled, and Shay participated, Freddie thought about their rehearsal session coming up this afternoon at Narlins. White Bird had called him a couple of days ago to tell him the Bluenotes wouldn't be allowed into West High School. She sounded mad as hell, but the band didn't really need another place to practice anyway. The school had been her idea. If she couldn't make it at a time they were getting together, too bad. The way he looked at it, she'd come begging to them, and that hadn't changed because of the newspaper ad. They weren't about to adjust their schedules for her.

Reverend Hahn started shouting about the laws and the prophets, about letting his people go, about oppression and not-so-ancient slavery. Like call and response in a song, the congregation chanted back at him, "Yes, Lord," "Lord have mercy," and "Amen."

Spits had said he'd be at Narlins today. He'd done so well with K.C. last time that some of the band members were already becoming believers. Freddie wasn't ready to go that far yet, but the girl did have talent. With Spits teaching her, there might be hope for her.

Everything came down to Dwayne. He was the one who'd

said to hire her, but how would he feel if he knew Spits was involved? It could help her, it could hurt her.

Shay elbowed him in the ribs. "Pay attention," she whispered fiercely.

"I am," Freddie said, and he was, inasmuch as he was aware Hahn was speaking. He tried to stop thinking about the Bluenotes and concentrate on the pastor's words. In the end he wasn't sure what the message was supposed to be. Was Christ on the side of the strikers? The scabs? Roth management? The Good Book said all of them, but Freddie didn't see how they all deserved the same grace. Somebody had to be wrong. God could be a slippery character when it came to figuring out exactly what it was He was trying to get across.

Whatever Reverend Hahn intended, he sure was passionate. His voice had almost a musical rhythm to it as it rose and fell with each righteous exhortation. He finished his sermon with thunder and fire, and then it was time for the real singing. Shay stood, pulling Freddie up with her. Nelly remained in her seat, eyes down.

Freddie wished he could plug his ears. This was the part he hated most about church. A few people could carry a tune, but too many sounded like they were changing keys on every note so they never had to change notes. "Wade in the Water" came out as lines of separate monotones, each on a different pitch, although every tone-deaf, salvation-seeking one of them would swear they were spot on the melody.

By the time the singing was over, he had a headache of biblical proportions. Hahn went on about a few more things after that, and then, Lord have mercy, released them from their Sunday bondage. Freddie needed some weed. It had always eased the pain in his joints, but sometimes it worked better than aspirin on headaches, too.

He rose, but when he reached to help Nelly up, Shay slapped his hand away. "Don't you touch my mama," she said.

"Don't you touch your mama, neither," Nelly said. "Can do it by myself."

She did, too, gangly as a newborn fawn trying out its legs for the first time. Once she was on her feet, she swayed like the earth was shaking beneath her. After most of the congregation had left, Freddie led the women to his Ford.

Nelly's house was the same one she and Shay had shared with Mimms all those years ago. Since Mimms was long gone, Freddie had no idea who was paying her bills. When they got there, Nelly again refused help. Shay offered to stay and visit for a while, but Nelly said no. "Just wanna be let be," she growled, and hobbled without help into the front door.

"She mad at you?" Freddie said as he backed out of the driveway.

"No more than any other day."

"Why wouldn't she let you come in?"

"She never does. Hardly, anyway. She don't like me much. Says seeing me's like watching Daddy swing all over again."

Freddie stopped in the middle of the block and stared at her. If Shay didn't stay with Nelly all those times she left him, where *did* she go?

"What?" she said.

Thing is, it wouldn't bother me all that much.

Easy to say, maybe not so easy to mean. He shook his head, stepped on the gas, and said, "Never mind."

Chapter 29

"HOW DARE YOU SHOW up here?" her father, Kenneth, Sr., bellowed at Jack. They were in the parking of the Waterton Methodist church.

Jack looked away. Maybe he could stand up to someone like Austin, but he'd never been able to stare down her father. "She invited me," he said to his feet.

"We thought it would be okay this time," Krissy said. She wasn't wearing her glasses, and had to squint, which made her look worse than glasses did. "You said you wanted to see Kasey."

"We did want to see *Kasey*," he said. His face had that look of disgust K.C. so hated, jutting chin, lips clenched tightly together and bent into a frown so formidable that the focus of his scorn couldn't help but feel intimidated. Jack was the focus of his scorn.

Her mother, Rose, little more than half his size, stood behind him, neither nodding nor shaking her head.

Pastor Thronson was greeting people at the church door. If he noticed the Brown family confrontation, he chose to ignore it.

"I'm sorry," Jack said. "I'll go."

"I'll go with you," K.C. said. She was so angry she wanted to slap somebody.

"Maybe if Jack sits in the back...?" her mother suggested.

"He's not a nigger," Ben said, holding his hands over Micah's ears.

"Not all niggers are black," her father said.

K.C. and Jack had ridden with Krissy's family in Ben's 1947 Studebaker Starlight. There were no buses on Sunday. It was a hot day and a long walk back to her apartment, but she'd rather do that than suffer her father's attitude. Her parents hadn't seen her in how long, and now the first thing he could think of to do was yell at them?

To hell with that.

"Come on, Jack," she said, tugging his arm, away from the church door.

"Wait," Ben said, "I'll drive you. Krissy, take Micah inside with Mom and Dad. Hold a place for me. I'll be back in a few minutes."

"Bah," her father snorted, and stormed into the church with her mother following.

"That went well," Ben said.

K.C. pushed the front seat forward so she could ride in the back. Then Jack climbed in next to Ben in the passenger's side.

Ben shifted into reverse and backed out. "Any reason they treat you like that?"

"Our moms went to school together," Jack said, rolling his window down to let some air in. "Let's just say they ran in different circles."

"Or we could say they hated each other," K.C. said. "Something about the cheerleading squad and the captain of the football team."

"Kind of a long time to hold a grudge for something like

that."

"That's the excuse," K.C. said, "not the real reason. They think Jack corrupted me."

Ben gave Jack a friendly slug on the shoulder. "You old devil, got the cart before the horse, did you?"

"Um," Jack said.

"Jeez, what did they expect? This is the twentieth century. Nobody waits anymore," Ben said.

"Nobody?" K.C. said, thinking *Krissy, you little floozy, I love you. Weren't such a little Goody Two-Shoes after all, eh?*

"You didn't hear it from me," Ben said. "She'd have my ass."

"Sounds like she already did," K.C. said.

"Well," Ben grinned, "not my *ass...*"

"How come they don't hate you?" Jack said.

"We weren't stupid enough to tell them."

"We didn't, either," K.C. said. She leaned her face up behind Jack's seat. Ben drove slowly, so there wasn't much of a breeze, but what little there was felt nice.

"You moved into your own apartment when you were eighteen," Ben said. "Not too hard to figure out what was going on."

"Krissy never did."

"Didn't she?" Ben said. He stopped for a red light at the six-way intersection at Fourth, Campbell, and Kimball.

"She knew?"

"We didn't *know* know, but yeah."

"So everybody knows what a slut I am."

"Knock it off," Ben said.

"Yeah," Jack agreed, rather weakly, she thought.

When the light turned green, Ben shifted into first and

crept through the intersection. He did that every time he came this way, as if he didn't trust the cars on the other streets to stop.

K.C. looked at the back of his head and smiled at the idea of her sister's pre-marital deflowering. Krissy made no secret that they had sex now—the negligee incident—but before they tied the knot? Delicious.

But then, *How dare you show up here*?

Who did her parents think they were fooling? It wasn't her reputation they were worried about, it was their own. Good heavens, what would their friends and neighbors think?

It made her furious. On the other hand, it might be a good omen for Jack. Whatever she thought about their relationship, her parents' disdain for him was an argument to stay together.

Are you aspiring to, or rebelling against?

Mr. Pierson had been talking about music, but it could as well have been love. Marriage shouldn't be an act of rebellion.

Ben turned left onto Wellington and pulled to the curb across from her apartment complex. "We have arrived at your domicile, madam," he said in the worst British accent ever. "Any message you'd like me to deliver to your mom and dad?"

"Yeah, they're buttholes."

"Anything... else?"

"Tell them she'll see them later," Jack said. "Without me."

"Not any time soon," she said.

****

She and Jack had their usual fight about him driving her to Narlins. Since Mr. Pierson was being a creep, it was the only place they could practice, and Sunday afternoon the only sure time they could all get together.

"What's it worth to you?" he said with sort of an angry leer.

Okay, maybe she did use her body as a bribe sometimes, but she shouldn't have to do that for every little thing. More to the point, he shouldn't expect it. "Why can't you just say 'Yes, I want what's best for you'?"

"I would, if I thought jazz was best for you. Let's say these guys hire you. What's it going to get you? Playing in cheap dives the rest of your life? Living out of somebody's car?"

"Not everybody wants to teach economics when they grow up."

Jack shot up from the kitchen table. He'd looked this angry when he'd punched Austin. "Oh, now it comes out. At least there's a future in teaching. All you can do is fail."

"Then let me fail. Goddammit, Jack, let me fail. I have to try. I have to *know*. If you love me, you'll drive me over there."

"I can love you *and* not drive you to Narlins."

This was so frustrating. Every damn time. "I need my own car," she said.

"Then you wouldn't need me at all."

He didn't realize how close to true that was. "Just do it. Please. Your truck is fixed, so you don't have any excuse. Do you have anything better to do this afternoon?"

"Than listen to black men play music I hate?"

"This shouldn't be this hard."

"You're the one making it hard. It's *my* truck, *my* gas, *my* time..." He stopped, but the damage was done. He knew it, too. His expression was a mixture of horror and regret. Too late. Too, too late. "I didn't mean it to sound like that—"

K.C. wanted to clobber him like Gorgeous George had at the drive-in. Instead, she went into her bedroom and got her purse. She came back, pulled out a dollar bill, and set it on the table. "This will pay for five gallons of gas, with a ten cent tip for wasting your time. Will that be sufficient?"

Jack sat down, but turned the chair so she could only see his face in profile, a dark silhouette against her apartment's only window. "What are we going to do, Kase?"

She weighed her words, speaking each one slowly so she could maintain her control, "I think you should go now."

"I'm so sorry."

"Just. Go."

"What about Narlins?"

"I'm not going to say it again, Jack."

"Can I come back?"

"I don't know."

He nodded and stood up. Without looking at her, he walked out the door, closing it gently behind him.

She didn't cry often, and didn't now. But she felt like someone had carved a hole in her soul, a strong wind blowing right through her and echoing in her bones.

My truck, my gas, my time.

"Kenny," she said, but he didn't answer.

****

K.C. thought of herself as a nice person, which made her wonder why she didn't have many—any—friends. She hadn't kept in contact with her high school classmates, even though some of them were still in town. She didn't really know anyone else in her apartment building, other than to say hi. Her coworkers at Dale's were too old, too young, too different, or too Austin.

She was mad at Mr. Pierson, but he couldn't be considered a friend anyway, since he was so old. Jack was Jack and, at least for the time being, in the rear-view mirror. Kenny was dead. Her parents, Jack's parents... nobody liked her. Well, Krissy and Ben, but they would never drive her to Narlins. A black neighborhood to meet with black men? Not in this lifetime.

She still had two hours. It was a long walk, one she could make, but in this heat carrying a saxophone? She'd be too exhausted to play her best, and she'd stink to high heaven.

So she took a chance. She called Narlins, hoping Freddie would be there early.

He was.

"You been smoking giggle-puffs?" he said. "Colored man's gonna drive over to the west side and let a white girl into his car? A white *teenage* girl? Shit, they'd hang me right next to Bender."

The Bender name was familiar. K.C. had seen it in the paper. "I don't have any other way over there," she said.

"What about that boyfriend?"

"We won't talk about him."

There was a pause, then Freddie said, "Well, that's something I know a little bit about. You know that alley behind the Paramount? Just over the bridge. Can you make it that far?"

"It's only a few blocks from my place."

"Meet me there in an hour. I'm driving a black '40 Ford. You see it, you get into the back seat, you hear me? I used to drive a cab. Maybe folks'll think that's what we're doing."

"Thank you, Mr. Ross."

"Thank you, my ass. Still can't say as I want you, but what the hell, you was good with Spits."

He hung up without a goodbye. K.C. checked the coin

return, and for the first time ever found a nickel. Her lucky day... except five cents wasn't enough to offset her mood. She went upstairs to sulk for forty-five minutes.

Sulking wasn't a good plan. It just made her angrier with everybody, especially Jack, so she collected her sax and walked toward the Paramount. The sky was clouding over, although it didn't look like rain. She turned left onto Fourth Street. Dale's was on Third, but she didn't deign to look in that direction. It was closed on Sundays, so Austin wouldn't be there anyway. That was assuming he still had a job. He hadn't been scheduled the only day she'd worked since Jack had coldcocked him, and she hadn't heard any scuttlebutt from the other employees—other than Dale, that was. He was aware of what'd happened in the parking lot that day, and promised "heads are going to roll."

Heads hadn't rolled. At least not yet. In Jack's case, it didn't really matter. He was going back to college in a couple of weeks, so he was planning to cut back on his hours at the store. If Dale fired him, oh, well, no great loss. Jack's father would make sure he had spending money.

At the bridge she looked to see if kids were playing around the drainage tunnel at Sixth Street, but they weren't. Other than an occasional car passing over the river, she seemed to be the only person out and about. Not even anyone fishing, although she saw several dead carp down on the banks. Carp were a junk fish, inedible. She'd heard once that if somebody caught one, there was a law against throwing it back in the water. Seemed kind of cruel to let them die in the sun, but, then, they were only fish. She could smell the rot from the bridge. And see those dead fish eyes staring up at her, or at least she imagined she could.

The Oak River rolled on its course southeastward to merge with the Iowa River. It was lovely, except for the dead carp and the smell. That made her mad, too. Why did every nice thing have to have an "except for" after it?

She crossed the bridge, refusing to be comforted by the river's gentle murmur.

You sure are a sour puss today, Squirt.

"Now you show up."

I never left.

"You left. Five years ago. Boy, did you leave."

Except for that.

"Just like everything else."

K.C. stepped off the bridge onto the sidewalk leading to the Paramount. Freddie wouldn't be here for at least fifteen minutes. A small green area overlooked the water, with park benches where people could sit and enjoy the view. There were no dead carp on this side. She placed her sax case next to her and draped her arm over it as if it were her lover. Pleasant little puffs of wind from the west cooled the back of her neck.

You were pretty hard on Jack.

"He put a *value* on me."

That's not what he meant, and you know it.

"Why do you men always stick together?"

Take him back.

"Mind your own business."

You are *my business, Squirt. You are my only business.*

"Because you're dead, and this conversation is all in my imagination?"

K.C. slapped her forehead, as if that would dislodge five years of grief, expel Kenny's spirit from her memory and resurrect it as flesh and blood.

No flesh and blood materialized, but a horn honked when a black Ford pulled off Water Street into the alley behind the theater.

She got up and ran to Freddie, hugging her sax to her chest with both hands.

"Back seat," he whispered, then, loud enough for anyone to hear—although there was nobody around—he said, "Where to, miss?"

The car reeked of smoke, not cigarettes like her Dad's, but something else. It was thick as fog and hot as a furnace. She coughed and wondered if she could die of smoke inhalation. "It stinks in here."

"Roll your window down." He drove through the alley and turned right onto East Fourth.

"That's not tobacco, is it?"

Freddie laughed. "I think you white folks call it juju sticks, something like that. Reefer. Weed. Marijuana."

He had warned her that most of the band members smoked it, but she'd never tried it. She supposed she was going to have to get used to the stench and the irritation in her eyes.

"Thanks for picking me up," she said. She plugged her nose at the smell, which made her voice sound funny. "Is it expensive?"

"What, weed? Nah, not really. Not where I get it."

"What's it like?"

"Ever been drunk? Oh, I forgot, pretty white girls can't hold their beer. Well, never mind, it ain't nothing like being drunk anyway. Mostly it helps the aching in my joints. Getting old's a pain in the ass. And everywhere else. I'm telling you, White Bird, don't do it."

Weren't there only two choices? Die young or grow old. Both were bad. Boy, life was bleak sometimes.

They crossed Franklin Street and headed northwest into the heart of North End, where the worst of Waterton's slums were. It was not a nice place. The houses were more rundown than the ones she saw on the way to Allen Hospital. Half of them looked like plywood shacks, the lawns like junkyards. Until last Sunday, she'd only seen the area at night, when darkness softened its edges. In the daylight… well, she could understand why Jack didn't like coming here.

But that still didn't excuse him.

A police car stopped at the light on a cross street. Freddie eyed him nervously. "He pulls me over, he's gonna smell the weed and throw my ass in jail. He sees you, and he'll have a reason to pull me over."

He drove by as casually as a person could while in a car. K.C. held her breath, as if that would make a difference. Luckily, the officer wasn't paying attention to them, and turned onto East Fourth going the opposition direction, toward downtown.

"Whew," she said, leaning forward toward him. "Got any gigs coming up?"

"Next one's September third in Fort Dodge."

"That's Jack's birthday. Not that it matters anymore."

"Ain't no way you're gonna be ready by then, anyway. I mean, if you ever are."

"I might surprise you."

"I might grow feathers and shit gold bricks, too. But who knows. Maybe Dwayne'll cancel Fort Dodge. Roth strike's gonna be over by the end of the week, so Leon and 'Fish'll be getting regular paychecks again. They won't need so many gigs. That'd be okay by me. Fort Dodge ain't my favorite town."

He turned right, and left, and left again, on streets she'd forget the names of, before they got to Narlins.

K.C. looked out the window. Two crows lit on a road-killed rabbit and squabbled over pecking order.

"Where do you get it?" K.C. said.

"You still going on about reefer? I know a guy."

Freddie turned into the Narlins lot. The place was closed, but a number of cars were there. He counted them with a perplexed look on his face.

"Something wrong?" she said.

"It ain't even four yet." They got out and approached Narlins' door. "The hell? That's Sue's car. What's she doing here?"

They walked in to the sound of weeping. The whole group was gathered around two tables that had been pulled together—Thump, Catfish, Ironhead, and Screech at one, Leon, Syd, Sue, and Dwayne at the other. Dwayne had his head down, glasses on the table, his face buried in his arms. Sue and Syd were on either side of him, each with a hand on his shoulder. He was weeping something awful. His voice was deep and terrible and heartbreaking, expanding to fill the entire room, surrounded and magnified by silence.

No one said a word.

Freddie ignored K.C. as he hurried to join them. She followed a step behind. Sue looked at him with infinite sadness. "Spits," she whispered.

K.C. understood immediately that Spits was dead. She knew from her conversations with Freddie that dope had probably killed him. She'd only met him the one time, last week, but he'd been so good with her, so smart, so patient. She set the case with her sax on the floor and knelt next to it as if in prayer.

Listening to Dwayne's lamentations, she understood something else: his weeping was no different than her Grandpa Brown's had been at Grandma's funeral. No different than the war widows' in the newsreels they used to show before movies. No different than anybody who'd just lost a spouse. Dwayne loved Spits. It was simple as that.

She wasn't the only white person here, but she felt like an intruder. She had no right to grieve with them, yet she grieved. She had no right to cry, yet she cried.

You know what to do, Kenny said.

She could play a piano like nobody's business. She could play a sax better than most. Her singing voice was no more than average, but that's what Kenny was telling her—what she was telling herself.

K.C. sang. Softly at first, so only she could hear herself, but gradually louder, a spiritual that spoke of pain she could never know, not of death but of a loss bigger than death. It might not be proper for the occasion, but it felt right.

> Sometimes I feel like a motherless child.
> Sometimes I feel like a motherless child.
> Sometimes I feel like a motherless child,
> A long way from home,
> A long way from home.
> True believer,
> A long ways from home,
> A long ways from home.

When her voice was loud enough for the others to hear, some looked at her with resentment, but others—Catfish, Syd, Sue—nodded their approval.

Sue and Catfish joined in.

> Sometimes I feel like I'm almost gone.
> Sometimes I feel like I'm almost gone.
> Sometimes I feel like I'm almost gone,
> Way up in the heavenly land,
> Way up in the heavenly land.

True believer,
Way up in the heavenly land,
Way up in the heavenly land.

The next time through everyone sang except Dwayne, raising their voices to that heavenly land. They were musicians. They added harmony. It was magic.

Dwayne lifted his head. His eyes were puffy, his face wet with tears. K.C. could see his profound devastation. He put his glasses on and gazed at her. "Thank you," he said.

Chapter 30

SPITS'S BODY WAS GOING to be shipped back to Chicago, where he had a sister, but Dwayne wanted a local service, too. Jorge Martinez, the director at Gindt Funeral Home, arranged for his house minister to come the night of the visitation and speak a few words on behalf of the deceased. The Bluenotes had asked to play a tribute, but Martinez turned them down, citing the other visitations going on the same night. Instead, he piped soft organ music into the viewing room, which also served as a chapel. Although Freddie didn't care for the instrument's slow, fluty tones, it seemed appropriate, since Dwayne had been an organist at the Regal Theater in Chicago when he'd met Spits.

The Reverend Ralph Cornwell hadn't known Spits, so he'd delivered a generic, one-size-fits-all eulogy, which he obviously found distasteful. Martinez had told Freddie the minister was aware of Spits's "special relationship" with Dwayne, and strongly disapproved. In Cornwell's mind, he was offering prayers for the soul of a man already in hell.

Sometimes Freddie thought that instead of denominations like Lutheran, Methodist, and Baptist,

Christianity should be divided into groups according to which part of the Bible they chose to ignore.

Spits lay in his coffin, dressed to the nines in his best 1930s suit. At first glance he looked handsome and dapper, but a closer examination showed the ravages of horse—the hollowing beneath his cheeks, the sharp jawline, the sunken eyes.

All of the Bluenotes' wives were here—except Shay, of course—as well as Sue, Emmaline, Toad, a handful of people Freddie didn't recognize, and White Bird. She stood in the back, head down, never approaching the coffin. Almost everyone who knew Spits also knew Sue, so her presence wasn't unexpected, but for the strangers who'd never met K.C., a teenaged white girl was definitely out of place, making her the subject of glares and whispers. Freddie would talk to her after the visitation.

Dwayne sat in a folding chair three feet away from Spits, his eyes blank, his body slack, his will broken. It didn't look like he'd ever find a reason to move again. As the visitation wound down, Thump got in line with folks to say their last goodbyes. When he reached the coffin, Dwayne shocked everyone by exploding from his chair and grabbing Thump by the back of his neck, forcing his face down into Spits's. "You see that?" he cried. "You see that? Jesus Christ, you stupid motherfucker, that's what's gonna happen to you! That's what horse does. It *kills* you. It kills everyone around you."

White Bird gasped at the outburst. Everyone else seemed to be in stunned silence.

"What the hell, Dwayne?" Thump said, nose-to-nose with death. "Let go, man."

"Spits is dead, and you're gonna keep shooting up that poison?"

Freddie figured what he meant was, *You both use. Why is Spits dead and you're alive? It ain't fair.* Freddie didn't wish anything bad for Thump, but he wondered the same thing. Why had the same circumstances claimed one but not the other?

Reverend Cornwell, who'd been chatting with some of the strangers, reacted with outrage. "Mr. Hite, this is a chapel," he yelled. "You will not take the Lord's name in vain here."

Dwayne released his grip on Thump and charged toward Cornwell. "You sanctimonious piece of shit."

"You are an abomination, sir. *He* was an abomination."

"Gentlemen," Martinez said, stepping between them. "Quiet, please. There are other bereaved relatives in the building."

"What was I thinking, Jorge?" Cornwell said. "Why did I allow myself to be persuaded to speak for these sodomites?"

"It's your job, Ralph."

Dwayne reached into his pocket and thrust a dollar bill at Cornwell. "Go buy yourself a ham sandwich, you goddamn hypocrite."

Freddie stepped out of line and tugged on Dwayne's sleeve, guiding him back toward his chair. "Come on, man. It's okay. We all miss him."

"Not all of us," Cornwell said. As he headed toward the exit, he said to Martinez, "If this is the kind of vermin you serve, you'll have to find yourself another minister."

"I serve all who come to me, Ralph. And so should you."

When Cornwell was gone, the mourners Freddie didn't know finished their farewells and filed out. Thump paused long enough to look down on Dwayne and shake his head. "Damn, man, don't blame me."

"It's not you," Dwayne said. "Goddamn Spits."

Thump left, along with Toad, Catfish, and Janae. 'Fish

never had liked to be anywhere near death. Dwayne wept a little, then fell back into his forlorn trance.

Freddie sat next to him. The remaining Bluenotes—Dee, Marlye, Sue, and Emmaline—gathered in the rows behind him, murmuring the usual words of condolence. Dwayne showed no sign that he heard.

White Bird was still standing in the back. Freddie motioned to her to join them, but she shook her head. When she refused a second time, he went to her.

"Why you hanging back here all by yourself?" he said. "You're one of us now."

She looked at him with those big teary eyes teenagers got. "I am?" she said.

"I just said so, didn't I?"

"I only met him once. He was so nice."

"He was the best. That's why you got to be the best for him. Every note you blow is gonna be for Spits. Spits and Dwayne."

Freddie nudged her toward Spits's casket.

"Why did he leave Dwayne?" she said.

"This ain't the right time for that story. How'd you get here?"

"Bus, but they stop running at six."

"Sue'll take you home."

"Thanks," she said, and then they were at the coffin, looking down at Spits. "He's almost as handsome as Leon."

"Nobody's that good looking," Leon said, the twinkle in his eye the first glimmer of humor all night.

Dee play-slapped him on the back of the head. "You must be the infamous White Bird," she said. "I'm Cindy, Mr. Dreamboat's wife. I've heard a lot about you."

"Uh-oh," K.C. said.

Marlye also introduced herself.

"Quite the prodigy," Syd said.

Ironhead and Screech nodded in agreement, although Freddie doubted they knew what prodigy meant.

K.C. turned to Dwayne, knelt, and laid her hand over his. "I'm so sorry, Mr. Hite."

She was not Spits. She would never be Spits. Freddie knew it, Dwayne knew it, White Bird knew it, everybody here knew it. But after another round of heaving shoulders and guttural sobs, Dwayne said, "Me, too, kid."

****

t was Monday, August 30th. Dwayne had accompanied Spits's body on the train to Chicago, giving no timetable for his return. The Fort Dodge gig was canceled, but he'd picked up a two-night gig in Lakeview, Minnesota, on the 17th and 18th.

Freddie lay on his couch and read the *Record* about the Roth strike. It had officially ended the night before at 11:59 p.m. Waterton had not burned, although there was still plenty of tension. He assumed Leon and Catfish had returned to work this morning. Just like 'Fish predicted, the company'd held firm to their offer of nine cents per hour, and the union, despite all the picketing, name calling, and violence done in its name, had given in. Not only would Hoyle still be alive if the strike had never happened, but all the Roth workers could have been earning that nine cents extra for the past month, rather than going without paychecks.

Washington sat on the armrest by his feet and batted at his shoestrings. Freddie turned the page. Albert Bender had been formally arraigned for first degree murder in the shooting death of Gilbert Hoyle. He was still being held in

LaPorte City, and probably would be until his trial.

There was an article about Whittaker Chambers accusing Alger Hiss of being a communist on television a few days ago. Whoever they were. Freddie didn't own a television. Nobody in Waterton did, because there wasn't a television station in the area. He wouldn't watch congressional hearings anyway. Calling somebody a communist was just another excuse for folks to shout at each other.

Freddie checked the sports. The Cubs had split a doubleheader with the Phillies yesterday, winning 10-4 and losing 1-0.

Washington was now biting his shoelaces. He wondered what it was about laces that fascinated her. Maybe she liked the taste. That wouldn't surprise him. She turned up her nose at perfectly good food, but then licked her own butt. Cats were strange creatures.

He closed the paper and set it on the floor. He was feeling more and more worn down. His physical problems—aching joints, fatigue, easy bruising, bloating, nosebleeds, the list went on—were made worse by his distress over Shay.

It didn't seem possible she could grow more distant, but she had. She'd refused to attend Spits's visitation because she "couldn't abide faggots." Near as Freddie could tell, she couldn't abide anybody, except maybe for whoever it was she stayed with when she left him. Since he'd found out it wasn't her mother, he'd been curious. He wouldn't admit it could be jealousy. Why be jealous now? Wasn't her fault what happened to her when she was a kid. Wasn't her fault Mimms had abandoned them, forcing her to take to the streets to support her and her mama. That was how Freddie first knew her. Wouldn't be right to hold it against her now, since he used to take advantage of her services himself.

She'd given up that life, or so she claimed. She'd certainly given it up with Freddie. It shouldn't matter. He was fifty years old. What did an old man need with sex anyway?

Unless it wasn't the sex he was missing.

He sat up. Washington hissed at him and scuttled into the bedroom. Goddamn it, Shay. He could recall her in that apartment above Narlins, naked in his bed, saying "Come on, baby." She was young and pretty. His body wasn't broken. Nothing hurt.

They were alive and together then.

They were still alive, and sometimes still together in the same house. But there was an ocean of nothing between them now, an ocean of nothing inside them, and he wasn't sure how the saltwater had leaked in.

****

Screech and Ironhead were cousins, but it was Ironhead who'd acquired the land by Lesterville through some kind of foreclosure. Over the years previous owners had divided, subdivided, and sold off so much of the property that by the time Ironhead got it, only thirty acres of tillable farmland remained, plus another thirty of greenbelt along Dry Run Creek.

Three generations of Grangers lived in the house, although Freddie never knew who was going to be there when, and couldn't remember most of their names anyway. Everyone called Screech's father Pap, but after him there was a revolving group of nephews, nieces, and distant cousins who came and went.

Screech and Ironhead raised pigs, chickens, a few dairy cattle, and a couple of horses. They grew just enough corn and hay to feed the animals. A vegetable garden with tomatoes, carrots, cucumbers, and radishes provided for their own needs. If anything was left over, they took it to a farmers' market in Waterton. In the winter they harvested the greenbelt for firewood.

Their annual hog roast should be coming up soon, although they hadn't said anything about it yet.

Two days after Spits's visitation, Freddie drove out there to buy eggs, among other things. Ironhead sold them to his friends for half what any of Waterton's stores did. The price difference more than made up for the extra gas he used. He wasn't like Shay, who used to think nothing of spending a dollar on gas to go to a sale in Cedar Rapids in order to save a dime on two pounds of bacon.

The Granger house sat a good hundred yards off the road. The gravel driveway snaked its way over small rises, between elm trees, and through a lawn that looked like it hadn't been mowed since last fall. Behind the house stood an unpainted but otherwise sturdy barn, a garage, a hog house, a storage bin, and a chicken coop.

Of the thirty acres where they could grow crops, half were field corn for the chickens and pigs, the other half hay for the cows and horses. Their only farm implement, an unusable Model D Landon tractor, had come with the property. It had rusted to flakes outside the barn, where it had probably sat for twenty-five years. They couldn't afford to replace it with a working model, so they hitched their plow, baler, and combine harvester to horses.

The operation wasn't as backwards as the Amish up by Fayette, but Freddie still felt like folks should set their watches back fifty years when they came here.

He pulled around back and parked in front of the garage. As he opened the car door he was greeted by the smell of cows, which he didn't mind, the smell of pigs, which he hated, and the smell of chickens, which was the most diabolic stink in the world.

When he was a boy his father Lewis sometimes brought him to Kline's Livery, where he worked as a coachman. When Freddie complained about the stench, Lewis always said the same thing: *That's the smell of money, son*, and Freddie always thought, *That's the smell of shit, Daddy.*

The corn was full height, just needing to dry out before being cut and ground into feed. But it was what was planted between the rows that interested Freddie. During the war the government had encouraged farmers to grow hemp for use in making parachute chords. The war was over, but there was still plenty of seed around. Some smart farmers—or stupid, if they were caught—continued to plant hemp for uses that had nothing to do with parachutes.

Which was the other reason Freddie had come. The Grangers made more on weed than they did on milk, eggs, produce, meat, or wood. What they didn't sell in the summer and fall they stored and sold in the winter.

As he approached the house, a gigantic Saint Bernard came charging out of the barn. Ironhead had named the dog Clarence, but usually called him Dumb-Luck. It had been Dumb-Fuck, but sometimes the nomadic relatives brought children. Either way, even the dog had a jive nickname: Clarence Dumb-Luck Granger. Dumb-Luck was more sound than fury, barking but never following through. Freddie knew that, but any poor stranger who happened out this way would probably piss themselves when they saw that furry dinosaur galumphing toward them.

"Why do you bark at me?" Freddie said. "I don't bark at you."

Dumb-Luck sniffed at him, decided he was okay, and trotted back to the barn.

Pap opened the door. "Damn dog. Hey, Boneman. The usual?"

****

Freddie and K.C. met at the East-Side Library again.

"First thing," he said, "you got to dress like a jazz player."

"How does a jazz player dress?"

"Not in a house dress. I don't know with a girl, since one never played horn with us before, but it ain't that."

"That doesn't help me much. This is what I wear to work."

"Not this kind of work. We'll figure something out. Oh, yeah, and get yourself a hat."

He picked up his Fedora and put it on her. Her head was smaller than his, so it dropped down over her eyes.

"You don't like my face, or what?"

Freddie smiled. "You got a pretty face. Just need a hat that fits. I bet Vincent DePaul's got one. Mind you, that's just for before and after gigs, to show you got style. We can't wear hats on stage."

"Say I get the look. Great, but what I need is practice. When can I play with the band?"

"Saturday and Sunday afternoons at Narlins. Ruthie's open at night during the week and Saturday, and Leon and 'Fish are back at Roth's during the day. We got gigs on the 17th and 18th."

"Doesn't leave much time."

"Then you better catch on fast."

Three rough-and-tumble white men walked by their table and gave them a hard glare as they turned a corner.

"What about Dwayne?" White Bird said. "Will he be back?"

"C'mon," Freddie said, "we need to move around. I think those boys're looking for trouble, and I ain't got the hands to give it to them."

"What boys?"

"Just go on over to the bookshelves. Pretend you're looking for something. I'll go to the other side and talk to you through the books."

They got up from the table. K.C. went to the nearest shelf, but Freddie wandered around a bit, as if browsing. When he ended up across from her, she said, "Is this necessary?"

"Ain't the white girl who gets lynched."

"This is Iowa. Nobody lynches anybody here."

"Oh, they don't gather around and hang us from a tree, but that don't mean they're gonna let things slide. There're other ways."

She pulled a book and opened it, as if she were reading. "When's Dwayne coming back?"

"Don't know. He called Ruthie and said he left our union cards with Sue, so I'm thinking it'll be a while."

K.C.'s cheeks went even whiter. "Jeepers," she said, sounding just like the teenager she was, "I don't have a union card yet."

"That's why I wanted to see you." He reached into his pocket, pulled out a card, and reached through a gap in the books to give it to her. His hand was shaking. Dammit, he felt worse every day.

"It's got my name spelled right and everything. "K" dot "C" dot."

"Little present from Dwayne. He appreciated it when you sang for Spits."

"Is this legal? What does it cost?"

"All you got to do is sign. Dwayne knows people. And it won't cost nothing. He pays all our union dues, except Syd's, because he's got other bands, too."

Freddie walked away and stopped at the other end of the

row. She waited a few seconds, then did likewise.

"Speaking of which," she said, "where are our gigs?"

He didn't want to admit it to himself, but he liked it that she referred to the gigs as *our*. Damn kid, anyway. He was starting to like her. "Lakeview."

"Where's that?"

"North of Owatonna, in Minnesota. It's a long ways, so make sure your ass ain't scheduled at the grocery store that weekend. We ain't gonna work around you."

"You work around Leon and Catfish."

"They earned it. You ain't yet."

"The 17th and 18th? I don't think I'll still be working there then."

"Trouble?"

"It's a long story."

"I got nowhere to be."

She changed the subject. "Your hands are shaking. You weren't feeling good on the way to Narlins on Sunday, either. You okay?"

"I told you, just getting old."

"Why don't you go to the doctor?"

"So he can charge me twenty bucks to tell me I'm getting old?"

"Isn't there a free clinic?"

"That's my business, White Bird. If I need to go, I'll go." She shrugged like kids did to pretend they didn't care, but he knew she wasn't going to let it go. "So Fort Dodge is canceled on Friday. Be at Narlins Saturday morning. We're gonna go all day if we have to."

K.C. sighed. "It's Jack's birthday on Friday. He'll be twenty-one."

"I thought we weren't talking about him."

"We're not."

"Long as you're at Narlins during the day, do whatever you want that night. We'll be back at it on Sunday, too."

She got a far-away look, like she was trying to listen to something she could hardly hear. "Shut up," she mouthed. She didn't seem to be talking to him.

"There something you need to tell—?"

Freddie stopped mid-sentence when a movement to his right caught his attention. He turned to look. A light-skinned black man in a hundred dollar suit was walking into the magazine room with a black woman. He only caught a glimpse before they disappeared, but it was enough.

White Bird must have seen something in his eyes, because she said, "What? Who were those people?"

"Never saw the man before. The woman's Shay. My wife."

"Uh oh," she said.

"Nah, it's okay by me," Freddie said, fairly certain it wasn't.

On the other hand, he was here with a 19-year-old white girl. There was no chance of anything happening between them, but try telling Shay that. White was her least favorite color.

Maybe nothing was happening between Shay and her friend, either, he thought, knowing he'd never been very good at lying to himself.

Chapter 31

"I'M SICK OF YOU two," Dale whispered to K.C. and Austin.

"I caught her stealing," Austin said.

"That's a lie," K.C. said loudly enough to startle a nearby customer.

"Keep it down," Dale said. "What did she steal?"

"A candy bar. I saw her eating it."

"I paid for it," K.C. said. "Check the tape."

Dale stepped to the cash register. "Here's a five cent sale," he said to Austin.

"I didn't see her ring it up."

"Kasey, you know you're not supposed to ring up your own purchases."

"I didn't want to ask him to do it," she said.

"And Austin, I had hopes for you, but I won't tolerate lying in order to make trouble for someone. Get out."

"You can't fire me for that. What about when she kneed me in the nuts? What about when Jack sucker punched me in the parking lot?"

"You got what you deserved," Dale said.

Austin untied his apron and threw it down. He jabbed a

finger in K.C.'s face. "You are dead, you cock-teasing bitch."

As he stomped out the door, a regular customer named Mrs. Lauren said, "He's always been such a foul-mouthed boy."

"I apologize if he's offended you, ma'am. He won't do it anymore. Grab yourself an extra pound of hamburger. Second one's on the house."

"Thank you, Dale," Lauren said and headed toward Jack in the meat department.

K.C. tried to hide a smile.

Dale glared at her. "Don't look so pleased with yourself, young lady. You're done, too."

"What did I do?"

"Officially, you rang up your own purchase."

"I've seen you do that."

"Unofficially, you're a pain in my ass."

"I've got rent to pay."

"Not my problem. If you can't afford to lose a job, then don't get yourself fired."

Well, dammit all anyway, she thought, but it was hardly a surprise. She'd known this was coming since Austin had grabbed her boobs. It was a wonder Dale had waited as long as he had. "Can I finish my shift, or do you want me to leave now, too?"

"I *want* to have never hired either of you in the first place. My mistake. You can finish the day, but once you check out, you're through here. I'll mail your last paycheck."

K.C. fumed as Dale walked away.

Jesus.

Just when she finally got her chance with the Bluenotes, everything else this week had turned to shit. Gigs wouldn't pay her rent. Her parents still hated her. Spits had died. She and Jack were on hiatus.

And tomorrow was his birthday, the first in four years when they weren't *them*.

She needed ice cream. Lots of ice cream.

She was at the soda fountain, and there was no one around to ring it up for her.

****

Jack had been watching her all day like a man with a broken heart. Which he was. This was the first day she had worked with him since she'd kicked him out of her apartment, and now it would be her last. He looked so devastated, but he didn't approach her, even during the confrontation with Dale and Austin. She knew he wanted to. By now he would have heard what happened. Did he go to bat for her with Dale to save her job? Probably. Did he turn in his own resignation?

When it came time to clock out, they met briefly in the break room. He started to say something, but didn't.

K.C. started to answer, but didn't.

On the way out, they brushed shoulders. She thought he did it on purpose. She knew she did. He followed her out the door. She turned right to walk home. He turned left toward his truck.

"I'd drive you through hell if you asked me to," he said, just loud enough for her to hear.

She paused. "I'm asking," she whispered, but kept walking.

His truck started. She heard its wheels crunch on the pavement as he backed out, then shifted into first.

Knucklehead, Kenny said.

This time she didn't tell him to shut up. She had to stuff her hands beneath her armpits to keep them from shaking.

Anyone seeing her would think she was cold, and she was.

She kept her eyes on the ground all the way home, trying to find a way to turn her brain off. It was no use. Jack was gone, her job was gone, and the first time she missed rent, a week from Friday, her apartment would be gone. Mr. Somers looked the other way when she snuck Jack in overnight, but he wouldn't when it came to money.

She got to Wellington Court and climbed the steps to her apartment, but then stood there outside the door, key in hand. What was she going to do?

She leaned against the wall and slid to the floor. She had no idea how long she'd sat there staring at the door across the hall.

Mr. Somers came by at some point. "Are you all right?" he said.

"I don't think so," she said.

"Anything I can do?"

Might as well just come out with it. "I just got fired. My last paycheck'll be next week."

She expected a "no pay, no stay" speech. Instead, he said, "What happened?"

"Lots of stupid people happened," she said. "Including me."

He studied her for a few moments. "I can let you carry over for a couple of weeks until you find something else."

"I'm not asking for favors."

"I'm not offering any. Once you land on your feet, I'll expect back rent. A couple extra bucks a week till we're square."

"Thanks," she said, although she didn't feel gratitude or relief. She didn't feel much of anything.

"What about that boyfriend? Could he help you out?"

"Boyfriend?" she said.

"Ah. Well, don't sit out here too long, Kasey. People will think I changed locks on you."

You will soon enough, she thought, but she stood up. He continued down the hall and knocked on the door to 4D.

Instead of entering her apartment, K.C. went back down the stairs to the pay phone on the first floor. It was after 6:00, so Krissy would be home from the Cream Separator.

She dropped a nickel in the slot and dialed the number.

Ben answered on the second ring. She hadn't expected him, since he usually worked late at the body shop.

"Is Krissy there?" K.C. said.

"Sure, sis, hang on."

A moment later she heard Krissy's peppy voice. "Hi, Kasey, what's the occasion?"

She took a breath, gathered her courage, lost her courage, almost hung up, and then didn't. "I need help," she said.

****

"It's obvious," Krissy said when she learned of K.C.'s firing. She pushed her reading glasses up her nose. Otherwise she had to look up to look down. "Come to work for Dad at I.C.S.C. The pay's good."

"And be a secretary?" K.C. said. She'd taken the bus over. Micah was sitting on her lap at the table on the deck, playing with a glass stegosaurus the size of a blackboard eraser.

"What's wrong with that?" Krissy said.

"It's exactly what I *don't* want."

"There's nothing shameful about being a secretary."

Micah tugged on K.C.'s sleeve. "Gr-r-r-r," he said, thrusting the dinosaur toward her face, like an eagle rising up and swooping down for prey.

"Pretty sure stegosauruses didn't growl," she said, "or fly."

"Mine does. Gr-r-r-r-r."

"I didn't say there was," K.C. said to Krissy.

She heard Ben swearing. He was in the back, working on his '32 Alpha Romero, as usual. Sir Reginald Bear barked at the loud voice.

"Probably smashed his knuckles with a wrench," Krissy said. "Happens all the time. Good thing he's got ten fingers to work with."

K.C. thought about Freddie's hands. "Do you have a Pepsi? I'm dying of thirst."

"When do I not? But don't change the subject. I'll be right back."

As Krissy went into the kitchen, K.C. glanced at Micah's toy as he continued to gr-r-r-r. Her mother used to have it on the mantel at their house when she was a kid. It had been Grandma Stickfort's. When she died, her mother kept it because Kenny was so fond of it. Then Micah had come along and thrown a fit until she'd given it to him.

K.C. had always thought it odd that someone would make a dinosaur out of glass. Not a practical toy and not an especially attractive decoration.

Krissy came back with three cups on a tray.

"I get pop, too?" Micah said. "Oh, boy!"

He set the stegosaurus upright on the table and gulped his down. Okay, the little dinosaur was kind of cute.

"Thanks," K.C. said. She took a sip. It was Coke. Some people couldn't tell the difference between that and Pepsi, but she could. Mixing cherry Cokes at Dale's had trained her taste buds, and in the process made her really sick of Coke. She drank it anyway.

"Now," Krissy said, setting the tray down, "you said you

needed help. If not a job, what?"

"I, uh...." She glanced at Micah.

"Micah," Krissy said, "take Steggy into your bedroom to play, okay?"

"I want to stay with Aunt Kasey."

"You can talk to her later."

"Poop head."

Krissy's eyes narrowed. "What have I told you about that kind of language, young man?" She stood up and grabbed his arm, lifting it above his head as she paddled his bottom. He wailed at a pitch only children could find. She dragged him inside the house. A door slammed shut, followed by, "And stay there until I tell you you can come out."

"I hate you," Micah cried.

Krissy returned a few moments later with her purse. "That boy. He listens to his father too much. Jesus, I need a cigarette. Do you mind?"

K.C. couldn't have been more shocked if her sister had announced she robbed banks for a living. *Holy crap*, she thought, *Krissy smokes? Krissy?* Sure, there were ashtrays scattered about the house, but she'd always assumed they were Ben's. The things she didn't know. Maybe she'd never wanted to know, or never cared enough to.

She picked up Steggy and absently stroked his smooth tummy. "Go ahead."

Krissy took a lighter and a pack of Chesterfields from her purse. "Want one?"

"I don't smoke," she said, and put Steggy down on his side. His little black dot of an eye stared right at her.

Krissy lit up. "Try it. It'll calm your nerves."

And make her breath stink. Not that she'd be kissing Jack again anytime soon anyway. Micah was still carrying on loud enough to be heard on the deck. K.C. finished her Coke.

"You're full of surprises."

Krissy drew in a deep breath and blew the smoke out the side of her mouth. "That's better. So. About that help...?"

K.C. leaned back on the chair's back two legs. "I don't know what I want, but it's not to type and file."

"What, then? A place to live? You could stay in the basement for a while if you get kicked out of your apartment. We'll set up a cot or something." She put the Chesterfields and lighter away. "Or you could move back in with Mom and Dad. You'd just have to... I don't know, be more reasonable?"

"Even if they'd let me, I wouldn't go."

"Why are you so contrary?"

"You got what you wanted. Ben, Micah, the house, the dog. That's great, but why do I have to want the same thing everyone else does?"

"There's a reason everyone else wants it, silly."

"I really should talk to Kathryn."

"If you can't afford long distance, write her a letter." Krissy took several drags on her cigarette, then crushed the butt in the closest ashtray. "But she can't help you right now, Kasey. She can't get you a job, and she can't find you a place to live."

"Do you ever think about Kenny?"

Krissy looked surprised. "What brought that up?"

"Just wondering."

"Well, sure. I mean, he was our brother, why wouldn't I? But you can't spend your life moping, or you might as well be dead, too. Kenny wouldn't want that."

I know what Kenny wants, K.C. thought. I talk to him. She doubted Krissy would understand, though, so she didn't say anything about that.

Really, Squirt? She talks to me, too. Everybody does,

when they think no one else is listening. Even Mom and Dad. Keeps me from getting too lonely.

That was nice. It made her feel better thinking her family had the same delusion she did. After all, Kenny's voice was just her own mind conversing with itself.

"I miss him."

"We all do, sis." Reeking of tobacco Krissy leaned over and kissed her on the forehead.

There was another thump outside, followed by, "Go-o-o-o-o-o-o-o-od *damn* it." Ben stretched out the syllable like Steggy growling.

"Sounds like he needs to take a break," K.C. said. "Think he'd mind giving me a ride back home?"

"That's it? You came over here to ask for a Coke, and now you want to leave?"

"Actually, I asked for a Pepsi."

"Same difference. Look, whatever we can do for you, we will. Just don't be a....?"

"Poop head?"

"Yeah, don't be a poop head. Sometimes you have to be the one to give in first."

Jack. Mom. Dad.

Shit. Krissy was probably right. But still, shit.

****

Ben hadn't said much on the way to her apartment. He was sweaty and covered in grease. The knuckles on his left hand were swollen. He had dirt under his fingernails. The Brylcreem in his hair was smeared with engine oil. His clothes were filthy, and he smelled bad enough that K.C. had to roll her window down.

As he pulled to the curb across from her building, he said,

"So what was this all about? Something going on with you?"

K.C. watched two squirrels play in the yard outside the Studebaker's window. The big one chased the little one, which then turned around and chased the big one. Both scurried up to the lowest branch of an elm and flicked their tails at each other, chittering excitedly. Squirrels were cute.

She liked Ben, but wasn't sure how much to tell him. "I got fired today, for one."

"That's not the end of the world. You didn't like it there anyway, right?"

"It paid the rent."

"There are other jobs. For two?"

"Jack and I broke up."

Ben leaned closer to her, bringing with him the scents of gasoline, burnt oil, and antifreeze, mixed with body odor. "What happened?"

She told him how Jack complained about the price of gas. "Like I'm not worth sixteen cents a gallon."

"Kid, you got to knock that shit off. It's stupid. You sound like a spoiled little kid. It's not like he was seeing other girls."

She wanted to explain everything she felt about Jack, but she didn't know herself. He was a good guy, a guy who loved her, a guy with a future, who could give her stability and comfort. There was nothing wrong with him, nothing at all.

And maybe that was the problem.

"He's boring," she said.

"Boring is good sometimes."

The squirrels came back down the tree. "It's his birthday tomorrow."

"Victory over Japan today, Defeat for Jack Day tomorrow. You know what I think? I think I should take you straight to his place and drop you off so he has to drive you home. Tell him you're sorry."

K.C. wasn't good at apologies, but she wasn't bad at excuses. "His mom won't let me in the house."

"Then Jack will have to come out."

Without waiting for her to respond, Ben pulled away from the curb, turned around in a driveway, and headed toward Fourth Street. She wanted to go, and she didn't. As they passed Church Row she glanced at Trinity Lutheran. It seemed like ages ago that she'd played the organ there.

What was she going to say to him? Knock knock, who's there? Surprise, I'm back.

She watched the houses go by, the picket fences, the children in the yards. It was getting late. The sun would be down soon, and all the children would have to go inside.

Ben turned onto Sheridan.

The closer they got, the more nervous she became. It would probably be okay if Dick answered the door, but what if Patti did?

"Maybe I should call first," she said. "There's a pay phone at the Standard a couple blocks from him."

"And give him the chance to say no? Nope, you just show up, force his hand."

"How do I do that?"

Ben stopped at the corner of Fairway and Sheridan, several houses down from Jack's. "Tell him you have a birthday present for him."

"But I don't."

"Sure you do."

"What?"

"This." He lay his hand on her arm, then suddenly pulled her toward him and kissed her square on the lips, not passionately, not forcefully, but not brotherly, either. "Only do it right with Jack. Use a little tongue."

"Jesus, Ben." She pushed him away and hopped out of his car.

What the hell?

What the hell?

What the hell?

She almost ran toward Jack's house, thinking, stupidly, that she was going to smell like car parts and body odor.

On his porch she paused to calm her breathing. Ben drove by and waved, giving her a thumbs up. When the Studebaker was out of sight, she straightened her dress, sighed, and knocked on the door.

Moments later it opened and there, of all the luck, was Patti. She looked K.C. over as if she were vermin that had just crawled up from the slime. "You've got some nerve," she said.

"I'm sorry." That was all K.C. could think to say. She couldn't even bring herself to ask for Jack.

Patti shook her head and closed the door. K.C. heard her call, "Jack, your whore is here."

Approaching footsteps on the hardwood floor, Jack's angry voice said "Don't you ever call her that again."

The door opened again, and Jack stepped out onto the porch. "I don't know whether to yell at you or hug you."

"A hug would be nice."

Jack wrapped his arms around her. He was trembling. She thought he might cry again, but he didn't. He held her like that for a long time. He couldn't grow a very good beard, but his cheek had patches of thin stubble. She could still smell traces of the Aqua Velva he'd used the last time he shaved, probably this morning. Normally she could take or leave Aqua Velva, but tonight the scent was sweeter than cologne.

"How'd you get here?" he said. "Did you walk?"

"No," she said, and she told him the story of Austin, Dale, Krissy, and Micah, leaving out the last part about Ben.

****

Storms moved in overnight. K.C. lay in her bed listening to the thunder and rain while Jack slept beside her. He was more of a teeth grinder than a snorer. The quiet was good for her, but he frequently woke up with a sore jaw.

It was 6:00 a.m. on Friday, September 3rd, Jack's birthday. He was twenty-one, legal everywhere, although he was scheduled to work at 6:45 and wouldn't be able to celebrate until later.

He told her Sunday would be his last day at Dale's. He'd quit to protest her firing, but agreed to stay through the weekend to help out. Why he'd be nice to Dale after what he'd done was beyond her, but that was Jack.

He would register for classes on the 8th, then school started on the 10th. That was a Friday, which seemed like a weird day to start classes. Jack would be a junior, halfway through his journey to becoming an economics teacher.

There was another floor above hers, but the rain was coming down sideways, because she could hear it on her walls. She loved rain, especially the different layers of sound that came with it. Small drops went tap-tap-tap, while larger ones splatted, and all of them flowed down the gutters to the drain pipes with a whoosh. Beneath it all was a kind of peaceful silence that only made the rain lovelier.

Ben had made a pass at her. She didn't know what that meant. Should she tell Krissy? Her sister wasn't the prim little china doll she'd imagined her to be, but K.C. didn't think she could hold up under that kind of shock. There was also Micah to consider if their marriage went south because of this.

Another possibility was that Krissy would accuse her of encouraging Ben. Some wives—and Krissy was one of them, K.C. suspected—believed their husbands would never stray, unless seduced by a wicked woman.

She certainly hadn't seduced Ben, nor said anything that could have led him on.

On the other hand, it wasn't like he'd grabbed her boobs like Austin had. But he did kiss her. On the lips. He said he was only giving her an idea for Jack's birthday. As if Jack wouldn't have thought of that himself.

Dammit.

Why did men have to be so stupid? Why were their brains controlled by their thingy? She had desires, too, but Jesus.

One thing was for sure. She wasn't about to tell Jack. If his reaction to Austin was any indication, he'd go after Ben. That couldn't happen. If she did end up marrying Jack, they couldn't afford to alienate the only family members on either side who liked them both.It was dark in her apartment. When lightning flashed in her living room window, it lit up the doorway to her bedroom. She counted to three before she heard the thunder. She couldn't remember if one second or five meant the lightning was a mile away.

K.C. rolled to her side and shook Jack.

"Huh?" he muttered.

"It's six. You have to work in forty-five minutes."

He sat up and rubbed his head, ruffling his hair so it stuck out in all directions. "My breath tastes terrible."

"Yeah, well, you don't have to smell it. Get up, you'll be late."

"What's he going to do, fire me?"

Jack kept spare razors, Burma-Shave, Aqua Velva, and Colgate in her medicine cabinet. He got up and trudged to the bathroom. His boxer shorts had little fire engines printed on them, which was cute. They were too big for his skinny butt, and they sagged. *That's my man*, she thought.

The two of them had made up, after a fashion. When she asked if he wanted anything special for his birthday, he said no. Just the usual, from her knees to her back. Because it was his birthday, she didn't make him reciprocate the pre-everything canoodling.

He closed the bathroom door. She rolled back toward the wall to concentrate on the rain. One of the problems with being in close quarters with him was that she could hear every sound he made in the bathroom. The other was that he could hear every sound she made in there. She always turned on the faucet in the sink full blast, but that probably just called more attention to her indelicate noises.

It was something married people had to get used to, she supposed. That, or buy a house big enough to have the bathroom on one end, the bedroom on the other, and a lot of space in between.

Chapter 32

IT WAS RAINING LIKE hell, and had been all day. Freddie got home from supper at Audrey's to find Shay sitting on the front step, barefoot, her plain gray dress soaked through.

"What're you doing?" Freddie said, pulling his yellow raincoat up over his head as he got out of his Ford.

"What's it look like?"

"You'll catch your death."

"Why would you care?"

The cement in his driveway was pitted with holes and puddles. He ever came into cash, he'd have to get that fixed. He offered Shay his hand. "Come on, baby."

Her hair had gone completely gray, and had lost most of its kink in the rain. She looked up at him with puffy eyes. "Don't you 'baby' me. I saw you at the library, pretending you wasn't talking up that white girl."

Freddie didn't think she'd noticed them, but it didn't matter. "And I saw you there with a black man. Must have money with that fancy suit he was wearing."

"He's only part black. We wasn't doing nothing."

"Neither was we. We hired her for the band."

"A white girl? What's she gon do, suck you all off after the show? She swallow or spit?"

"Lord, you're a sick woman. K.C.'s our alto sax, that's all. She's taking Spits's place."

"Shit, a whore for a faggot. What kind of story's that? Like a nigger band's gonna take on a white girl. Why not just say you're screwing her?"

Freddie climbed the steps around her. "Because I ain't," he said, "and I ain't gonna. Anyhow, you got no room to talk. When I found out you wasn't staying with your mama those times you leave me, I wondered where you went. Guess now I know."

"Just leave me alone."

Freddie went inside and spoke through the screen door. "The library was yesterday. How come you didn't say nothing till today?"

"Had other things on my mind."

"That other man, you mean."

Shay turned ever so slightly in his direction, her dark face silhouetted against the grass of their yard. "Mama died yesterday."

Freddie took a step back as the news sank in, then came outside and sat next to her on the porch. Spits and Nelly in the same week. He hadn't cared for Nelly, and she hadn't cared for him. Shay and Nelly hadn't seemed to care much for each other, either. Yet she was Shay's mother. Freddie remembered what losing his mama had been like. He pulled Shay closer and draped his raincoat over both of them. Neither said anything, but she leaned her head onto his shoulder and wept.

****

She lay naked in the bed with him that night, curled into

the contours of his body like when they were teenagers. Nothing was right between them anymore but their shared history. History was why she came back every time she left, and history was why he let her. He felt a long absent stirring, but now was no time for that.

She hadn't said another word about Nelly, so Freddie asked.

Shay sighed. "She just got tired. I'm tired, too."

He knew what she was talking about: 1908, Spring Valley, Mississippi, the lynching, the rape. "That was a long time ago, baby. I figured you was past all that now."

She rolled away and sat up. "*Past* it? You never get past it. When they killed Daddy, they took out my heart, but what they did to me and Mama after..."

"It ain't like you was ruined forever. I mean, I know what happened was terrible—"

"You don't know nothing." She stood up and faced him. "Look at me. See this skin? That's all there is to me. Ain't *nothing* inside. It's like they opened me up and threw my guts and bones away. I don't feel a thing. So when I was flopping with men for money, they might as well've been fucking a dried up orange peel, much as it meant to me."

"But when you was with me, when we was young... You liked it good enough."

She sat down again. "Well, you come as close as anybody ever did. For that I'm obliged. But Mama, she never even had that. She kept on breathing 'cause she didn't know how to stop. Good Lord finally came and showed her how."

"What about Mimms?"

"Harley? The hell you talking about? He was married. White woman named Ginny. Anyhow, he wasn't around but a short while."

"Black man married to a white woman in Mississippi?

Bullshit."

"Never said Harley was black. He was mixed. His daddy was whiter than sugar in snow."

Freddie was shocked. Thirty-some years with this woman, and he never knew that. "I don't believe it."

"Think what you want. His daddy was Isaiah Mimms. Even as white men go, he was the vilest man ever to breathe air. Probably why Harley tried so hard to be good to us."

"Good, how? He brought you and Mama Nelly out of Mississippi, but soon as he got you up here, he run off."

"Run right to his grave, is what he did. Man was born with a bad heart. He wasn't even thirty."

"You told me he abandoned you."

"That's what you heard, ain't what I said. What I said was, he left. Didn't say how."

Freddie got up and started toward the bathroom. "Got to micturate," he said, recalling Spits's word. "How did I not know all this?"

"When did you ever ask? Know what else? Harley and Ginny had a boy together. Jeffrey Jacob Mimms. He was three when his daddy died. That was Jeff at the library with me."

"What'd he want with you?"

"Ain't your business."

****

At Narlins Ruthie yelled at Freddie to come to the phone. When he answered, White Bird asked if he'd pick her up early for rehearsal. She had something she wanted to talk to him about. Freddie was leery, because it sounded like one of *those* kind of talks, one where she spilled her guts over some so-called catastrophe that in ten years would seem like a trifle. Hell, the girl didn't even know what a problem was.

Being a teenager, she didn't have anything else to compare her troubles to, so every little bump was the end of the world. All she had to do was grow up to learn that life usually straightened itself out.

Except that it didn't. No amount of growing up had fixed his fingers or healed Shay's pain. All time did was wear down the rest of the body and mind.

Still, didn't she have a friend she could turn to? Why did she need to tell her story to Freddie? Being old didn't make him wise. Anyway, he had enough troubles of his own. He didn't need hers.

He parked behind the Paramount again. She'd have to walk in the rain, but that was okay. It might cool her off.

While he waited, he sat in his Ford, listening to the rain and wipers and smoking some weed. His muscles and joints were on fire. There was no reason for it. All he'd done yesterday had been sit at home, sit at Narlins, and sit at Audrey's. Then he came back to sit some more and lie down to sleep. Although he did toss and turn. Shay had taught him what a stupid, oblivious man he was, and it ate at him all night. He knew she didn't want his touch now, but he'd always told himself she'd enjoyed it back then. All those years...

Maybe he was better at lying to himself than he realized.

Nelly had died. There'd be another visitation, and probably a funeral here in Waterton. He doubted she'd want to be sent home to Mississippi. Why would she want her body covered by that hateful dirt? Unless it was to rest next to Sloan...

Well, Shay would figure all that out. She'd tell him where to be, and when to be there, and that would be it.

Or she might not tell him. He didn't know how he felt about that.

Cars splashed by on East Fourth. He could hear them more than see them. The rain-cooled air was condensing on his windshield while reefer smoke accumulated from the car's roof down.

He thought about Shay's absences again. She didn't go to Nelly's, and it didn't seem possible she'd stay with someone who was any part white, even if his daddy did do them a good turn. He was just starting to get himself worked up when White Bird knocked on his window. She had an umbrella, but she'd used that to protect her sax case more than herself.

He rolled his window down a crack. "You know how it goes. In the back. You look like a drowned rat."

She dripped water all over his upholstery in the back seat, but he couldn't really complain, because he was the one who refused to pick her up on the west side. "Reefer stinks," she complained.

"Makes getting older tolerable."

He rolled his window back up.

She held her hand over her mouth and nose. "You got heat in this thing? Crank it up, I'm freezing."

"Yass'm," he said.

"Don't use that slave talk with me."

"Then don't order me around like I am one. You want something, ask."

"Will you *please* turn on the fucking heat?"

"Ooh, you do got a mouth on you, girl. You do know it's still summer, right?"

"You do know it's raining, right?"

"Attitude, too. You might just fit in with the boys yet."

"Sorry. It's been a bad week."

"You got that right."

The car had been idling for fifteen minutes, so the heat blasted out as soon as he turned it on. The windshield cleared off pretty quick, too, but there was nothing he could do about the smoke except open the window.

She coughed and put the fabric of the umbrella to her nose, using it as a filter against the smoke. "Can you even see through all this?"

"I could roll the window down."

"I'm cold enough."

"You can be warm, or you can breathe, not both."

"Serve you right if you got pulled over."

"Well, ain't you little Miss Blow-Some-Sunshine-Up-My-Ass?" Since she was on the other side of the car, he lowered his big window a crack and opened the smaller side window all the way. He pulled out of the alley. The banks of the Oak River seemed almost bright. "Ever notice how the grass always looks greener on a cloudy day? Good Lord trying to cheer us up, you think?"

The rest of the band wouldn't get to Narlins for another hour, hour and a half. Although Freddie wasn't a heavy drinker, a few shots would cheer him up a lot better than bright green grass. Ruthie would sell him beer, but he needed something stronger. A lot stronger. The Diminished Fifth was on East Sixth and Franklin, not too far out of their away.

But no. He couldn't bring K.C. in there, because she was nineteen and she was white. The drunks would attack them both, in different ways. "What was it you wanted to talk to me about—Ow!"

Freddie felt a sharp pain in his thumb and index finger on his left hand. He flicked the reefer butt out the side window, then blew on his hand. He'd got himself yakking too much to remember to smoke the rest of it. Damn thing burned down to a nub and took some skin with it.

K.C. chuckled. "That'll teach you."

"Girl, sometimes you can push my buttons good as my wife. And by 'good,' I mean bad."

"I've got buttons, too," she said.

Freddie went around the block, back to Fourth Street. If anything, the rain was coming down harder. It was early afternoon and almost dark as night. He switched his headlights on. No sense giving the police a reason to stop him. Wasn't any law said folks had to have their lights on in the day, but a cop could always say he was driving under "unsafe for the conditions." And once he asked Freddie for his license, he'd smell the weed and see K.C. in the back, and Freddie's life would get uglier than it already was. Like that was possible. He'd been a guest of Waterton's finest before. He didn't want any more of it.

As they passed the KXM radio station he noticed how low the clouds were hanging, how fast they were moving, even though the wind at ground level was slight. There was no thunder or lightning, no danger of the storm going severe, but it was some spectacle to watch. Heaven moving while the Earth stood still.

At Narlins he parked as close to the door as he could get. White Bird handed him her umbrella and horn. "I'm already wet," she said. "Just keep my sax dry."

Without waiting for an answer, she jumped out of the car, slammed the door, and rushed inside.

****

She told him about Jack. About Dick and Patti. About her parents. About Kenny. About Austin. About Dale. About Krissy. About Ben. About Jack again. Freddie had seen Jack and Austin maybe once. Kenny was dead. The others were just names to him. But one thing his years had taught him was to listen. Most people didn't need advice, they just wanted someone to tell their troubles to.

Freddie led her upstairs to the lockers to get his trombone. "Don't meant to change the subject, but you ought to get a locker from Ruthie. Long as your music teacher ain't letting you practice at school anyway, might as well keep your horn here so you don't have to lug it around everywhere."

"How much?"

"Seeing as how you're between jobs, she won't charge you nothing."

Poor thing, she looked so bedraggled, small, and wet, her dress clinging to her, her hair in dripping straggles. He really did like her.

And that was sort of funny, when he thought about it. His father used to have a young white friend named George who worked with him at Kline's Livery. The boy was about Freddie's age. When he was killed in the first war, Lewis was just beside himself. Freddie, being a kid, had been jealous of the attention George got.

The big confrontation happened right here, in Narlins, back when the storage space was apartments. He didn't officially live in 2-A, but he spent most of his time there. It was Christmas morning, 1916. Freddie was lying on a bed next to Shay. They both were naked. She was sleeping while he puffed on weed and stared at the ceiling.

The door was unlocked. His father walked right in without knocking. First thing out of his mouth wasn't "Hello, nice to see you, son," but, "You're smoking again? That reefer?"

"Ain't your business."

"Who's the girl?"

"Ain't your business, neither."

Shay woke up long enough to pull a blanket over herself and mumble at Freddie to be quiet.

"It's Christmas morning," Lewis said.

Freddie sat up, took a long drag, and said, "Well, hallelujah."

Lewis rushed at him, grabbed his arm, and jerked him to his feet. "Don't you take that tone with me."

"Let go of me. What're you doing here?"

"I come to take you home before your Mama wakes up and finds you gone."

"Mama knows where I am."

"It's Christmas morning," his father said again.

Freddie blew smoke into his face. Lewis slapped the joint from his hand, then crushed it under his boot.

"Goddammit, that shit ain't cheap," Freddie cried.

Lewis looked like he wanted to hit him, but didn't. "Sometimes I wish you never got your mama's gift with the piano. Only thing music ever did was land you with bad people. Should be home with your family today, not laying down with a whore and blowing dope."

"She ain't a whore." Except that, then, she still was.

"She's naked and in bed with a boy she ain't married to."

Shay stirred, opened her eyes, and blinked at Lewis. "Who the fuck he?" she said to Freddie.

"Nobody, go back to sleep."

"Come home," Lewis said. "This one day. It'd mean a lot to your Mama."

"Don't need no speech about family," Freddie said.

"That's all we got," he said.

"What '*we*'? That white boy means more to you than I do."

"George?"

"Hell, yes, *George.* You talk about him every goddamn day, and now you go boo hoo hoo 'cause he get his stupid ass killed in the war. And all the time your own son's right in front of you going 'Hey, Daddy, here I am.'" Freddie sat on the bed next to Shay and glared at him. He patted Shay's hip, leaving his hand there. "Well, you can have your dead white boy. I ain't coming home."

"Freddie," his father said, "listen. That ain't true. It ain't true... George was my friend, but you're my own blood."

Freddie didn't go home that morning, and wouldn't until his father bailed him out of jail the night his fingers were ruined.

Who the fuck he?

Those were the first words Shay had ever spoken to Lewis, a fine introduction. The hell of it was, they got along pretty good once Freddie married her—at least as well as Shay got on with anybody.

"Freddie?" White Bird said. "You kind of went away there."

"Just remembering stuff I ought not to." He unlocked his locker and took out his trombone. "So what you gonna do about Jack?"

"What do you think I should do?"

"Look, little Bird, I ain't got no magic wand. I got my hands full with Shay."

K.C. leaned against the lockers and squeezed water out of her hair, leaving little puddles on the floor. "What's she like?"

"She ain't like nobody but herself."

He headed toward the stairs. Going down hurt more than climbing up. It was like getting his fingers crushed all over again, except it was all his joints, and felt like knives instead of a hammer.

"You didn't answer my question," K.C. said.

"Shay's got her reasons for being how she is. Guess we all do."

K.C. must have noticed him limping, because she asked if he needed help. She took hold of his elbow, but he was damned if he was going to accept pity from a nineteen-year-old. He jerked his arm away.

"You should see a doctor," she said.

He turned to her at the bottom of the steps. She really was a good kid. Seeing her as he did now, he could imagine what his father saw in George. "I want you to kick some ass on that horn today, girl. You hear what I'm saying? Kick some motherfucking ass."

Chapter 33

SHE DID KICK ASS. She found the rhythm, found the wave, and found the notes, and even when the notes were the wrong ones, she brought them back into the number as if that was what she intended all along.

Dwayne's old standards were easy. His new experiments that incorporated bop were more challenging, but also more fun.

The fellas were impressed. Catfish told her she was almost as good on sax as she was on piano, and she knew how much he'd loved her piano playing. Leon flashed her that handsome smile of his and gave her a friendly wink— much nicer than the stink-eye she got the first time they'd met.

Leon, Thump, and Syd had to leave right after rehearsal. Thump gave her a thumb's up on his way out, and Syd patted her on the shoulder. "You'll be all right, kid," he said. "I already knew you were good, but you were better than good today. Spits would've been proud of you. Dwayne, too. See you tomorrow."

That left Freddie, Catfish, Screech, and Ironhead sitting around a table. Ruthie brought beers for herself and the men and a Pepsi for K.C.

"You're really something, little Snowflake," Ruthie said. "The way you took the changes in 'Cherokee'—whoo-ee, that was sweet. My late husband was a horn man, so I know what I'm talking about."

Snowflake was a cute nickname, not said in derision this time, but it was too delicate for alto sax. K.C. liked White Bird better. It didn't exactly conjure images of fire-breathing dragons or ass-kicking, sweat-dripping soldiers of jazz, but it did have the connection to Charlie Parker. Who could argue with that?

"Thank you, ma'am."

Ruthie broke into a wide, white-toothed grin. "Ma'am? That shit's gotta stop right now. Call me Ruthie. 'Ma'am' sounds like I'm running a whorehouse."

"It was sometimes, back in my time," Freddie said.

Ruthie ignored Freddie. She looked K.C. over. "Damn, girl, did you wear that dress on purpose?"

"What's wrong with my dress?"

"You look like one of them mousy housewife gals selling Tide in a newspaper ad."

"I think she needs a hat," Freddie said.

"That'd be a start. Now, drink up fast. I gotta open in an hour."

"Any reason we can't be here?" Screech said.

"No, but I'll have to start charging you for the beers."

"Who's playing tonight?" Catfish said. "Not that Robbins bunch out of Cedar Rapids again?"

"Local band, just starting up. Somebody and the Diatonics."

"Donald, I think," Catfish said. "Haven't heard them, but I know Piper wouldn't book them over at Electrical Park."

"I can't afford the likes of Garber. Why do you think I hire you?"

"Oughta make us your house band," Ironhead said.

"I would, but I want to keep my customers," Ruthie said. She winked at K.C.

"On a brighter note," Screech said, "our hog roast's the first Saturday in October."

"I was wondering if you were gonna do that again," Catfish said.

"You coming, Bird?"

K.C. looked to Freddie for an answer. "Am I invited?"

"Why wouldn't you be? Any time after two. Takes that porker all morning to cook. You know where we live?"

"Freddie told me, but I don't have a car."

"I hear you got a boyfriend," Screech said. "Bring him, too. We got plenty."

Even after giving Jack his birthday nookie, K.C. wasn't sure if she and Jack were back to being she and Jack. "I'll ask him, but..."

"He don't like colored folk?"

"More than most white people do," she said. "I don't know, he might be nervous."

"Tell him the pig's white. That oughta make him feel better."

They all laughed at that.

"Hope the weather's better by then," Ruthie said.

K.C.'s clothes had almost dried until she'd gotten them wet with sweat again. Even if Freddie drove her to the alley behind the Paramount, she'd drown walking the rest of the way home.

As if he was reading her mind, Freddie said, "I'll drive you to your place. It'll be dark, maybe no one will see."

Ironhead, who was sitting next to her, inched his chair closer. He was a big guy, radiating hot stink from his performance. In his low gravelly voice he said, "Like what you see, White Bird?"

K.C. leaned away from him. His voice was sexy, but what kind of question was that?

"Tell him no, Snowflake," Ruthie said. "He thinks telling him yes is an invitation to bed."

"Don't say nothing," Freddie said. Screech had said Ironhead had found him a woman. Must've fallen through. "Byron, you remember what happened with Sue? When she told you she'd kick you so hard your nuts'd fall out your butt? Well, that's how it's gonna be with K.C., except I'll use a blowtorch first. We understand each other?"

Ironhead smirked, shrugged, and pulled his chair back. "Didn't mean nothing by it. No harm, right, White Bird?"

Watch yourself, Squirt.

"I just want to play music," she said.

"And that's what we're gonna do," Freddie said.

"To jazz," Catfish said, holding up his bottle as a toast. They clinked theirs against his.

"That's what I'm talking about," Freddie said.

****

They sat in Freddie's car in the Narlins parking lot, just the two of them, him in front, K.C. in the back as usual. Though the sun wouldn't set for another couple of hours, the clouds turned the sky dark as dusk. Rain was still coming hard, but maybe a little less than earlier. She could listen to it all night. The rhythm was so soothing, yet it also filled her with a familiar, almost pleasant, melancholy. All she needed to complete her mood was a little thunder and maybe a distant train whistle. It didn't make any sense to be comforted by sadness, but that's how she felt.

She hugged herself for warmth and laid her head back against the seat while she waited for the heater to kick in.

Freddie was watching her in his rearview mirror. She smiled at him. "I like the rain, too," he said, "but it don't stop soon, houses by the river gonna get flooded out."

As soon as the heater started spitting warm air, he put the Ford in gear and pulled out onto the street. There seemed to be a lot of traffic for a Saturday afternoon. The oncoming cars were dark shapes with parallel streaks of light stretched out like watercolors in front of them on the wet asphalt.

"Thank you," she said.

"For what?"

"What you said to Ironhead."

"Don't pay him too much mind. He wouldn't really try nothing with you. Thing is, he's a lonely man. He's got Screech and Pap out on the farm, and whoever else stops by, but in his head he's all by himself. I know what that's like."

"Me, too." She could be talking about Jack or either set of parents, even Krissy, Micah, and now, especially, Ben, but at the moment she meant her sax. Ruthie had given her a locker. Knowing she was going to be separated from it felt weird. Narlins may be only a few miles, but that was the farthest she'd been from her sax since high school. Freddie was right, though. With Mr. Pierson being a crumb, she had no place to practice other than Narlins. She couldn't do it in her apartment because the walls were thin. It probably wasn't going to be her apartment much longer anyway.

"You want me to bring a blowtorch for your brother-in-law?" Freddie said. He was really good at sensing her thoughts.

"I don't know what to do about Ben. He's never done anything like that before. Never treated me like anything but an annoying little sister. And then all of a sudden, *pow*."

"You gonna call him out on it?"

"If I did, he'd probably just laugh and say it was all a big joke."

"Don't seem too funny to me. Someone ought to bust his balls."

K.C. studied him in the mirror. Freddie was a tall man, but he must have weighed more at one time, because his skin sagged at his jowls and neck, as if everything solid had melted away beneath the surface. When she'd first met him, she thought he looked younger than Dwayne. Up close, he looked older. The stubble on his cheeks still had some pepper with the salt, and his hair was mostly dark, but there was no doubt that at fifty Freddie had already grown old.

Whatever had aged him had not made him cruel. No one she knew would believe that a middle-aged black man had defended the honor of a teenaged white girl against the advances of another colored man.

He'd be a good father or grandpa. Maybe he was.

"Do you and Shay have any children?"

Freddie's face became somber. "No."

"Ever going to tell me about your wife?"

"That's something you can't fix, little Bird. Nobody can."

"I told you about Jack and Ben."

He turned onto East Fourth. "And I listened."

K.C. nodded. "None of my business," she said, "but I know how to listen, too."

"I appreciate that." Freddie drove a few blocks without speaking again, but at a red light near the bridge he said, "That day at the library? Shay's mama died. She's kind of broke up about it."

A wind had come up from the west, blowing the rain hard against her window, a tommy gun more than a lullaby. K.C.

didn't know what to say, so she said the wrong thing. "I didn't know her mother was still alive in the first place."

The light changed. Freddie shifted into first and pushed on the gas. "She wasn't, really."

"I'm sorry. I didn't mean to—"

"No worries, White Bird. Just remember, you ain't the only one who's lost somebody."

Nobody had lost anybody like she'd lost Kenny. It wasn't the same thing at all, a young man dying in the war, and an old lady dying of being old.

But then, plenty of other boys were killed in the war, too. Maybe their families loved and missed them as much as she did Kenny. Maybe Shay missed her mother that much. All K.C. knew was that losing her own mother would be nothing like losing Kenny. She certainly wouldn't keep *her* picture on her nightstand.

"When's the funeral?" she said.

As Freddie crossed the bridge, he said, "Wouldn't hurt my feelings if you ducked your head down till we get to your place."

She laid down on the seat. "Turn right on Wellington."

"Don't know if there's gonna be a funeral. Don't think Shay'll want me there if there is."

"That's sad. Wellington Court's on the left, past Third. You can park across the street."

She felt the car stop at Third Street, then pull through the intersection. When Freddie got to the apartments, he slid in next to the curb, braked, and shifted into neutral. "Okay," he said, "talking's done. Get away from the car quick. If you need a ride tomorrow, you best hope it ain't raining. I ain't having a white girl in my car in the light, not on this side of the river."

"I'll call Narlins and let you know," she said. It would

depend on Jack. Driving her would be his first test to see how the whole mess stood between them.

****

She rested on her side in her jammies and stared at the photo of Kenny. Would she really not want her mother's picture here?

Did Shay have a picture of her mother?

Were people ever too old to grieve? Maybe there was a magic age when the death of a loved one became easy.

She recalled what her father had told her when Grandma Stickfort was dying and K.C. didn't want to go to her house: *Spend as much time with her as you can now, sweetie, because you'll be sorry you didn't after she's gone.*

K.C. had been a little girl then. She had no idea what dying was, or why she wouldn't be able to see Grandma. It wasn't until she was ten that she understood that the grave they visited on holidays was her grandma's new home, or maybe prison. No one could go in and Grandma couldn't come out.

All her other grandparents were still alive then, so Grandma Stickfort was her first experience with death. Then there was Kenny. That's when her father's words really hit her. She hadn't spent nearly enough time with him. If she could go back fifteen years, she'd crawl inside his skin and live with him there.

Who knew, Squirt? But even if you'd never left my side, I'd still be dead and you'd still be sad. There's only one thing you can do.

"What's that?"

You know.

She did know.

K.C. got out of bed. She draped a house robe over her

pajamas, rummaged through her purse for a nickel, and went downstairs to the phone.

Krissy answered on the first ring.

"Hey, it's me," K.C. said.

"Hey, baby sis. What's going on?"

"You busy?"

"Ben and I got a babysitter for Micah. *The Loves of Carmen* is at the Strand. It's got Glenn Ford and Rita Hayworth. Sounds kind of sexy. Wanna come with? It's in color."

"I'm tired tonight, but I was wondering, can I go to church with you tomorrow?"

"Wow, that's swell. Mom and Dad'll love it. Maybe no Jack this time? Oops, Ben's ready to go. We'll pick you up at eight-thirty. Bye-bye."

K.C. trudged back up the stairs, hoping she'd made the right decision. Dad and Mom on one side, Ben on the other, and her in the middle with the power to harm or heal in both directions.

Ugh.

****

That power began with an awkward ride to church. Krissy insisted on sitting in back with Micah, leaving K.C. and Ben in front, glancing at each other out of the corner of their eyes. All she had to do was speak, and everything would change. Krissy would either banish Ben from her life, or K.C. Or both.

She didn't say anything. Ben didn't say anything. Instead, they rode to church to Krissy's chirpy monologue about the virtues of *The Loves of Carmen*. Micah must have been rambunctious for the babysitter last night, because he'd been asleep when they'd picked K.C. up, and he was still asleep when they pulled into the parking lot.

K.C.'s parents were waiting there for Krissy, Ben, and Micah so they could go in together. They must have been shocked to see K.C. get out of the car, and delighted that Jack didn't get out after her.

The rain had stopped sometime in the night. Breaks in the clouds allowed a few rays of sunshine through, which reflected off pools of rainwater that had accumulated in low spots in the pavement and yards. The morning air was still cool and humid enough that wisps of mist rose from the ground, and the scent of the air had that odd combination of freshness and worms. K.C. avoided the puddles, but Micah, now fully awake, ran ahead of Krissy and splashed through every one he could find. Ben caught up with him and lifted him under his arm, holding him sideways so his feet wouldn't drip onto Ben's Sunday clothes.

Her father looked at K.C. as if he were going to say something disapproving, but her mother stepped in front of him and said, "Hello, dear. It's wonderful to see you."

"Hi, Mom, Dad," K.C. said.

"What's the occasion?" her father said. "I thought you were done with us."

"She's never been done with you, Daddy," Krissy said.

K.C. was glad for the interruption, because she didn't know what to say.

"I'll take Micah in," Ben said. Krissy went with them.

"Is everything all right?" her mother said.

She wanted to say that the death of Freddie's mother-in-law had made her realize that her time with family was limited, and that she couldn't afford to waste any more of it. But that would seem too much like capitulation, like she was apologizing for living *her* life, not the one they demanded of her. "I just didn't like the way things ended last time."

"We didn't either, dear. Thank you for coming. You're

welcome here. Isn't she, Kenneth?"

"As long as Jack isn't—" Her mother stomped on his toe, and he changed in mid-sentence. "Let's go on in."

"I have a pork roast in the oven," her mother said. "Will you have dinner with us?"

"I've got somewhere to be later, but okay—you know how much I like your roast."

Inside, K.C. endured the meet-and-greet with people who were as surprised as her parents to see her. Many of their "welcome backs" had an accusatory tone, as if to say *Why haven't you been coming to church, young lady?* She didn't owe them an explanation, and didn't give them one.

After the opening prayer, Pastor Thronson launched into First Corinthians, of all things. *Oh, for Christ's sake*, K.C. thought, followed immediately by, *Oops, I meant "golly,"* and a repentant glance upward.

Love is patient and kind, yadda yadda, love doesn't do this and isn't that.

She looked around at the faces of the congregation, trying to find some in which love was, and didn't, and wasn't. She knew most of these people. They were as messed up as she and her family were.

She thought about that during the silent meditation time, concluding everyone was a hypocrite. But when the donation plate came around, she put in a dollar, much to her parents' approval.

Then came the Lord's Prayer. K.C. hadn't *Our Fathered* for a long time, and rather enjoyed the choral aspect of it, everyone chanting together. It was almost like music—which reminded her, she hadn't yet asked Jack for a ride to this afternoon's rehearsal.

Pastor's first name was Ashleigh, which K.C. thought was a woman's name. His sermon was long-winded, as they usually were. He lost her during his repetition of sin, sin, sin, but got her back when he invited everyone to sing. She picked up the *Methodist Hymnal* and turned to number 562 as instructed, "Jesus, Lord, We Look to Thee."

> Jesus, Lord, we look to thee;
> Let us in thy name agree;
> Show thyself the Prince of Peace,
> Bid our strife forever cease.

Bid our strife forever cease. What a nice thought. K.C. kept a running commentary in her mind of pithy little retorts to each verse, right up until the final couplet.

On the wings of angels fly,
Show how true believers die.

That was the thing with religion. It was all about hurry up and die. Kenny did just that, and look where it'd left everybody. Maybe he was gigging with Fats Waller in heaven, but here on Earth his family was wallowing in grief and, at least in church, calling their misery joy.

****

Kenny's room looked the same as it had on that last day of furlough before he was shipped overseas. His bed had been made, although the pillow was on top of the covers, still bearing the impression of his head from the final time he slept on it. His guitar was in one corner, beneath the picture of Jane Russell he'd cut from a movie magazine and taped to his wall. On his dresser was the Glenn Miller program of a concert he'd seen in Kansas City, signed by Miller himself. There was an unopened letter next to it, written in a girl's hand and postmarked just after Kenny left. The return address bore only a first name, , Betty who'd dotted the "i" with a little heart. K.C. wondered why her mother hadn't forwarded it, since Kenny had still been alive at the time. She was so tempted to open it and find out who Betty was, but couldn't do it. She wasn't aware of any girlfriends he'd had then, and didn't want to find out about one now. It would be too much to bear, knowing he'd also left behind a sweetheart.

On the wall opposite Jane Russell, Kenny had pinned two college banners: ISTC and Iowa Hawkeyes. He'd intended to enroll in the music program at Iowa State Teachers College when he got out of the Army, and for some reason that escaped K.C., despite all his artistic sensibilities, he liked football.

Most of his clothes still hung in his closet. She held the sleeve of one of his shirts to her nose and inhaled deeply. His mother had starched the hell out of it, but K.C. still imagined the scent of Kenny. She let the sleeve drop before the smell made her cry. *The Problem of Pain*, by C.S. Lewis, was on his writing desk, with a bookmark where he'd left off reading. His favorite slippers were under the bed. He probably felt they were "too girly" to take into the Army with him.

And finally, the thing she'd waited until last to examine: nestled between the headboard and his dresser his alto sax rested upright on a stand. It had been polished to mirrored perfection. Her mother never could tolerate a speck of dust. K.C. was almost afraid to touch it, to defile it with her own fingerprints, so she contented herself with looking at her curved reflection in the brass. She was doing all this for him.

All for him.

When she most wished Kenny would speak with her, to reassure her she was doing the right things, he chose to be silent.

Risking her mother's wrath, she sat on the edge of his bed and took in the ambience of him.

Krissy popped her head in the door. "How can you stand coming in here? Makes me too sad. Dinner's ready."

It made K.C. sad, too. Funny how they'd fought over the room after Kenny left. Before then, Kenny and Kathryn had their own rooms, while Krissy and K.C. shared one. Both wanted to move into his, but their parents said no. It was as if their parents had known in advance that he wouldn't be coming home and were already preparing it as a shrine.

K.C. stood up and smoothed the blankets on the bed. As soon as she stepped out of the room, she caught the aroma of pork roast. If there was one thing she missed about living at home, it was her mother's cooking.

At the table Micah was squawking about having to sit in the high chair. He was small for his age and couldn't comfortably reach his plate on a regular chair, so there really wasn't much choice. "Quit fussing," Krissy said, "and I'll bet Grandma will let you have some ice cream for dessert."

"Promise?"

"Cross my heart."

"Sit down, Kasey," her father said. "How about you lead us in grace?"

K.C. figured it was some kind of test, but she didn't argue. They all folded their hands together under the table, except Micah, who was reaching for his glass of milk. She did the "Come, Lord Jesus" bit and asked Ben to pass the mashed potatoes.

Ben was looking mighty sullen down there at the other end. Sometime soon K.C. would have to figure out what to do about him.

"Dale Rodgers called the other day," her mother said. "He asked me to tell you he's sorry and to remind you to pick up next week's schedule."

Well, whaddaya know, she thought. *Didn't he just fire*

me? The great Dale Rodgers comes crawling back.

"What's he sorry about?" her father said.

"We had an argument," K.C. said. "Nothing, really."

It hadn't been "nothing, really." He'd booted her off the payroll, not for anything she did but because Austin was a jerk. Unless the Bluenotes panned out big time, she'd need the money, but she wasn't about to forgive him just yet.

"Where's that worthless boyfriend of yours?" her father said.

"Kenneth," her mother warned, even though it was her longtime spat with Patti Schoonover that had turned them against Jack in the first place.

Her father apologized, then cut a slab of pork roast laden with fat trim. He always claimed that fat was what gave meat its flavor, but even the sight of that much white turned K.C.'s stomach.

"We heard through the grapevine," her mother said, "that you still hope to play your saxophone with a Negro band."

The grapevine, she'd be willing to bet, was Krissy. K.C. cut a small piece of meat with her right hand, speared with the fork in her left, and chewed slowly, letting her mother stew a bit before answering. "Not 'hope to,'" she said, "am."

"I wish you wouldn't."

"Quit being so namby-pamby," her father said. "We won't have you keeping company with niggers."

"Mr. Brown," Ben said, nodding toward Micah. The boy didn't seem to care. He had as much applesauce on his face as in his mouth. Krissy, probably wanting no part of this conversation, kept her attention on cleaning Micah's face with his napkin.

"We've been through this," K.C. said.

"Not enough, obviously." Her father scooped green beans onto his plate. "No daughter of mine is going to be seen in public playing with a bunch of—" He glanced at Micah—"*jazz musicians*. And that's all there is to it."

"You wouldn't have complained if Kenny did."

"Like hell. Music is no occupation for a man, either. Anyway, Kenny was a better player than you. And no one was going to make a pass at him."

K.C. thought about Dwayne and Spits, then, glaring directly at Ben, said, "They don't make passes at me. They're nice men."

"The next nice colored man I meet will be my first."

K.C. set her fork and knife down. "So nothing's changed. You hate my boyfriend and you hate the only thing I want to do in my life."

"What parents wouldn't be concerned?" her mother said.

"Ben, cover Micah's ears," K.C. said. When he did, she said, "Let's get this straight. I am not a slut. He's been my one and only, and I did it because I loved him. If any of you pretend you didn't do it before you were married, then you're big fat liars."

"Kasey Anne Brown," her mother cried, "you apologize this instant. How *dare* you?"

"And *you*," K.C. said. "You and Patti were on the cheerleading squad in high school. You both wanted the same football player. Did she get him into bed before you? That's why you hate Jack. If he'd been someone else's son, you wouldn't have cared."

Until now, K.C. wasn't exactly sure how one "burst into tears," but that's just what her mother did as she fled the dining room.

Her father slammed his fist on the table. "Get out," he said.

"Fine by me."

K.C. thrust herself out of her chair and marched toward

the door.

"Kasey, wait," Ben called, "I'll drive you home."

Wasn't that just swell? Oh, well, she was in a rotten mood anyway. Why not have it out with him, too, and get it over with?

****

She demanded that he take her to Narlins, and he didn't argue. After she gave him directions, he said, "You know it's because you're the baby of the family, the last one they could have dreams for. This is the first time they've had an empty nest."

"Screw their empty nest. If they wanted more kids, they knew how to make them. Just because I'm the youngest—"

"I know. I know. I was just saying."

"Yeah, well, save it. If they're lonely, it's their own fault. They threw me out, I didn't choose to go."

They got through all of west Waterton and well onto the east side before Ben spoke again. "What's it going to be, Kasey? I didn't offer to give you a ride so we could talk about your parents. This is driving me crazy."

She looked straight ahead and thought derisively *Poor thing.* "What do you think it should be?"

"That I should say I'm sorry and it should go away. I don't know why I did it. I'd never even thought of kissing you before. It was just, I don't know, an impulse? I mean, I didn't hurt you, did I?"

"Why? Because I don't have cuts and bruises?"

"You know what I mean."

"Yeah, I do. Turn here."

The sky had cleared, and there were a number of people out walking around, enjoying the break from the two-day deluge. Many of them were black. "I gotta admit," he said, "I don't like this part of town."

"What if I say your penance is driving me here whenever I need you to?"

Ben stepped on the brakes in the middle of a block. "No, Kasey. Either tell Krissy or shut up about it, but I'm not going to have you holding this over my head forever. This time it's drive you to Niggerville. Next time maybe you'll want me to buy you your own car. That's not going to happen. If you're going to blackmail me, I'll tell her myself."

"Jesus, Ben. She wouldn't believe me anyway. That, or she'd blame me for it. It can't ever happen again. If it did, I'd have to stay away from you forever. I don't want to do that. You and Krissy are about the only friends I have."

Ben's expression got all sincere. He looked like he wanted to clasp her shoulders in a sincere manner, and sincerely vow he'd never do it again. He actually started to reach for her, but then pulled his hands back. "Kasey," he said, sincerely, "I swear to God it will never happen again. I was wrong. I was dumb. I don't know how many ways to say it. I'm sorry."

K.C. sighed. She wasn't about to forget, but on the stupid-shit-o-meter his transgression was pretty low. Less damaging than her parents' rejection. Less worrisome than the situation with Jack—who she still hadn't called, and wouldn't need to now—and nothing compared to losing Kenny.

But it had happened. And because it had, it would be hard for her to look at anything the same way again. Her world was narrowing instead of expanding, with fewer and fewer people she could turn to, fewer and fewer places she could go to feel safe. At the moment the only person she felt she could trust was Freddie, and she really didn't know him all that well.

Chapter 34

FREDDIE WAS SURPRISED WHEN Jeff Mimms knocked on their door just after noon on Sunday. If his father Harley had been half colored, and Harley's wife had been white, then by Freddie's reckoning, Jeff's blood was only a quarter black. His skin was as light as a tanned white man's.

"Jeffrey Jacob Mimms," Freddie said through the screen door.

Mimms was taken aback. "Have we met?"

"No, but I've heard all about you."

Mimms smiled. He was wearing a Fedora and a different hundred-dollar suit than the one he'd worn at the library. "Oh, I doubt that," he said. "Is Shay back from church?"

"Didn't go today. She was up, but went to lay back down. Her mama's passing is weighing heavy. Something I can help you with?"

"I need to talk to her about the estate."

"What estate? How's that your business anyhow?"

"I'm an attorney."

"Where in hell'd Shay get the money for you?"

"No charge, Mr. Ross."

"Ain't no lawyer ever breathed that did anything for free."

"Call it a family obligation. Nelly Wiggins was my aunt."

"My ass. Nelly didn't have a drop of white blood in her."

"No, she didn't. May I come in?"

Freddie opened the door and stepped aside. What the hell? He still wasn't sure Mimms and Shay weren't up to something, but it was worth letting him in to hear his story— even if, as he suspected, it was going to be a lie. "Have a seat at the table."

Mimms removed his hat. "Shay didn't tell you?"

"She said your daddy Harley was mixed. I can see it in you, but what's that got to do with Nelly?"

Washington came out of the bedroom, hissed at Mimms, and went back in.

"Never developed a fondness for cats," Mimms said. "Evil things."

"You should see her up close. Claw your nuts off if you're not careful. You was about to say about Nelly?"

"My dad was her brother."

"Bullshit. Nelly's daddy was Ambrose Jennings. Her mama was Dorothy. They was both black as coal dust, from what I hear. They couldn't've had no white kids."

"*They* didn't. Not both of them, anyway. Ambrose died in '83. Sometime after that Dorothy had the misfortune of being alone with my granddad Isaiah Mimms. Isaiah was a white man who forgot the Civil War was over. Ambrose and Dorothy had been working his plantation as 'indentured servants' during Reconstruction. You know what that meant."

"They was slaves all over again."

"In everything but name."

Freddie wasn't convinced, but being Nelly's half-brother did answer why Harley Mimms would bring her and Shay all the way up to Iowa. And, he had to admit, he'd been learning a lot of shit lately that he hadn't known before. Why couldn't Shay have had a half-and-half uncle? Maybe she had another something-or-other that was part kangaroo.

"I need a scorecard. So Isaiah raped Dorothy after Ambrose died, and Dorothy had a kid."

"Who was my dad Harley."

"And Harley tried to make it up to Dorothy because of what his daddy done to her?"

"Not Dorothy. He couldn't. She died in oh-five. He did it to make it up to Shay because he felt terrible about what happened to Sloan at Spring Valley."

"If he felt that bad, he would've got them out of Mississippi before the lynching."

"How was he supposed to know that was going to happen?"

"Because it was Mississippi." Freddie went to the refrigerator. "Want a beer or something?"

"Never developed a fondness for alcohol, either. Got a soda? Or water will do."

Freddie filled a glass from the tap for Mimms and opened a bottle of Schlitz for himself. After he returned to the table, he took two long swallows and said, "How is it they never came for your daddy? Those folks don't like mixing down there."

"Because my father's father was Isaiah Mimms. And Isaiah Mimms had money. Dad was the only blood family he had left. And me, of course. Isaiah was a first-class polecat in almost every respect, but he did look after his own."

Freddie wondered how much was true and how much was smoke. He looked Mimms over. Would Shay really go for a (mostly) white man fifteen or twenty years younger than her? Maybe he was hung better than Freddie. That wouldn't take much.

"What's Nelly need a estate lawyer for?" he said. "She couldn't've had two nickels to her name."

"Who told you that? A black stepdaughter meant nothing to Isaiah, so he didn't leave Nelly anything, but my dad did. She was his sister. The house he bought for her goes to Shay now, as does the remaining money in Nelly's trust."

Freddie shot up from the table and took a step back. "Man, you're messing with me now. He wouldn't buy her a goddamn house."

"That's exactly what he did. Dad and Mom were set for life, so they could spare the money. After he died, his accountants paid the property taxes. Now that she's gone, her will says the house goes to Shay. Free and clear."

"Accountants still gonna pay the taxes? 'Cause I sure as hell can't. I can't hardly afford this house."

"Won't need to," Shay said from the bedroom doorway. She was holding Washington, scratching her under the chin. "I'm gon' sell the house and cash out the trust."

"You mean we gonna be rich?"

Shay put Washington down. "What d'you mean, *we*? I'm going to Chicago. You just skedaddle on over to Narlins now, let me and Jeff talk. Ain't your little white chicky gon' be there?"

There was nothing Freddie could think of to say. His throat felt closed up like a vice. He walked out of the house to a bright cheery sky.

He looked up at the sun and muttered, "Piss off."

****

Practice had a few more glitches than yesterday. Guess it was to be expected. No one could be that good two days in a row. White Bird was moody, even by her standards, and

Freddie himself felt like he'd just stepped in front of a train. Worse, toward the end of "In the Nude" his nose began to bleed for no apparent reason. He hadn't picked it, hadn't even touched it. Just a hard blow into the 'bone had set it flowing.

Ruthie brought some cotton and made him lean his head back. The bleeding stopped after a few minutes, but by then whatever spark the band had had was doused, and they shut it down early.

It wasn't dark and it wasn't raining, so he dropped K.C. off behind the Paramount again. As she got out she said, "Go to the doctor, or I'll kick your ass."

Freddie chuckled. "Yass'm."

When she was gone, he sat in his car thinking. No place could sell liquor on Sunday, or else he'd go to the Diminished Fifth. Only thing he knew was: he didn't want to go home. This time when Shay left, it would be forever. Chicago. Where streets were lined with dreams for the plucking. Except she'd never been there. Chicago dreams would wilt on the stem just like they did in Waterton. And Spring Valley, Mississippi. And everywhere in between. Shay carried that death with her.

Truth was, Freddie didn't like her much.

She didn't like him.

But, goddamn, he didn't want to be alone again. No sensible lady would look at him now and say *Oh, I gotta get me some of that.* He'd just be an old crippled-up old man to them. Like he was to Shay, only she was used to him.

He couldn't remember if he ever told White Bird that being lonely was worse when you're not alone—but if he had, it was bullshit. There was just something about waking up in the morning and knowing there was another person in the house, even if they didn't speak or smile.

There was something about it.

In the end he put the Ford in gear and drove back to Smoky Row, parking in his driveway. It wasn't even 6:00, yet he thought about sleeping in his car all night, in case she was still in there with him.

Jeff Mimms probably was a lawyer. And her cousin. That story was just stupid enough to be true. Which meant Shay wasn't snizzling him.

Mimms offered her more than sex or love, more than Freddie could ever give her: freedom from poverty, at least until the money ran out.

He was about to climb into the back seat, when he said out loud, "Hell, no."

It was his house. He wasn't going to let her scare him off. If they were having at it on the kitchen floor, he was going in. She was still his wife, and if that didn't mean anything to her, well, he was going in anyway.

He worked himself into a fighting mood and yanked open the door. He was ready for the best shot either Shay or Mimms could give him.

But she was already gone.

****

Now that he didn't really care, Freddie went to the free clinic in the morning. Rows of jars lined a shelf on the wall, full of cotton balls, tongue depressors, gauze, and applicators. Every doctor's office he'd ever been in had a sick smell like formaldehyde. It was one of the excuses he used to avoid the clinic.

A young white doctor whose nametag read P. THOMAS MD listened to Freddie's symptoms and said, "Hmmm," while his nurse, L. BEERMAN RN, wrote on a clipboard. He had Freddie lie back on the table while he pressed on his stomach. "That hurt?"

"A little."

"Spleen feels enlarged," he said to the nurse. "You can sit up, Mr. Ross. Want to tell me about those fingers?"

"Long time ago, doc. I fucked with the wrong people, then they fucked with me. Sorry for my language."

The nurse smirked and shook her head: No need to apologize. She was a round black woman who looked like she'd ironed the curls out of her hair and flattened it with half a jar of pomade.

Dr. Thomas lifted Freddie's right hand and examined it. "Bones never set right. Why didn't you get medical help? These could have been fixed with the right treatment. Might not have been good as new, but they'd work a helluva lot better than they do now."

"My daddy did what he could, but he wasn't no doctor."

Thomas looked at his other hand. "We'd have to re-break them to set the bones properly, but I'm afraid you've got too much arthritis in the joints. Likely just make things worse."

"Ain't here about my fingers, doc. What do I got?"

"Right now, just symptoms. I have some ideas, but I won't know for sure until we do some blood tests." He looked at the crook of Freddie's elbows. "Glad I don't see needle tracks here."

Freddie thought about Thump and Spits. "Why, you think all black people shoot dope?"

"Stop talking shit," the nurse said. "Doc isn't like that."

Thomas sighed. "Of course not. But too many poor people do. Working at the clinic, I wish I got paid by the needle marks we *didn't* make. Right arm or left?"

"Don't matter."

The nurse tightened a rubber tube around Freddie's left

bicep and tapped for a vein, then swabbed the skin of his elbow with an antiseptic cotton ball. "You'll feel a pinch," she said.

Freddie always looked away when needles were involved, but he usually didn't even feel the poke. When he looked back, she was removing the rubber tube, causing Freddie's blood to flow into the syringe.

"How soon'll I know?"

"A week," Thomas said. "What's your phone number?"

"Ain't got one. You can leave a message with Ruthie at Narlins."

"Narlins?—Oh, the New Orleans. Nightclub or something, right? You a musician?"

Freddie held up his hands. "Used to be a better one, but I can still get by."

"Figures," the nurse said.

"Lindy, shhh," Thomas said. He lit up a cigarette, a Camel. He offered one to Freddie, who declined. "With those fingers, let me guess, trombone?"

"They call me Boneman."

"Well, Boneman, let me see you back here in a week."

"Am I gonna get bad news?"

Thomas shrugged and blew out smoke. "You're going to get news, one way or the other."

Nurse Lindy placed a Bandaid over the puncture wound. Freddie might have thought her parents named her for the dance, the Lindy Hop, but the nurse was too old for that. The dance had only been around twenty years. However she got her name, he liked her. She had sass.

"Can you tell me what you think it is?" Freddie said.

"In a week," Thomas said.

****

He sat on the bench in front of his mother's piano and lifted the lid. He wanted to play it so bad, but with *his* fingers that would seem like an insult to her memory. Whatever problems his father had with him, his mother never wavered in her love and kindness. Mama could get frustrated with him, too, but at least she made an effort to understand. Unlike his father, she remembered what it was like being young—the rebellion and the mistakes—and knew it was all just part of the process.

Washington was at his feet, but in two quick hops launched herself on top of the upright. Her first hop landed squarely on the keys, clanging notes like he did when he tried to play at Narlins. The second brought her to rest above his eye level, glaring down at him, tail swishing. Furious, Freddie swept her onto the floor and closed the lid.

She hissed at him.

If Shay was going to leave, why didn't she take the goddamn cat, too? He kicked at her, missing, and she fled into the bathroom.

Shay wasn't gone for good yet. Most of her clothes were still in the bedroom closet, most of her underwear in the dresser drawer. Her toothbrush was gone, but her makeup and shampoo were here. That made sense. Her mama had just died. He was no legal expert, but he knew estates didn't get settled that fast. It would be a while before she had the money to plant her roots in Chicago.

So. Wherever she'd run off to this time, it was probably with Mimms. If it was true they were related, then he could be sure she wasn't making whoopie with him. And maybe it answered the question of where she'd gone all those other times. Could it have been that simple? She was mad at him and went to stay with her cousin for a spell?

Freddie tried to feel bad for all the things he'd thought

about her, but couldn't. Even if her whereabouts were innocent enough, that didn't change the fact that she left him so many times without so much as a toodle-oo, taking off with no warning and returning with no explanation.

He got up, went to the mailbox for the *Record* and bills, and sat at the kitchen table. He kept hoping Dwayne would write, but he hadn't yet.

The main headline in the paper was Queen Wilhelmina abdicating the Dutch throne. Beneath that, something about communists in China. Neither was of any interest to Freddie. A story on the bottom of page one, however, said that Gilbert Hoyle's wife Helen planned to sue Albert Bender for wrongful death after the criminal trial was over. What good would that do? Bender was probably going to hang. If by some miracle he didn't, he'd get life. Either way, he wouldn't be able to pay her.

He flipped through the rest of the newspaper. The Iowa State Teachers College's football schedule was printed. Their first game was with Iowa State College in Ames on the 18th. Iowa State Teachers College versus Iowa State College. The names were so similar he wondered if the cheerleaders got confused about which side to cheer for.

He glanced at the crossword puzzle. The first clue was deep fried squid, eight letters. Having no idea, he closed the paper and went into the bathroom. Washington was in the bathtub, poking her head around the shower curtain. She hissed at him again.

"I oughtta piss on you," he said, but didn't, lifting the lid on the toilet. As he went about his business, he noticed a lump on one side of his groin. It wasn't big and didn't hurt, but he didn't remember feeling it before. A week, the doctor had said.

Either he had something, or he didn't. At this point, what

did it matter?

Freddie shook off the last drops and tucked himself back into his jeans. Nelly's obituary hadn't been in the paper yet. Maybe it never would be. Weren't too many people who'd care.

****

"I'd hurt myself if I tried that," Sue said. She was at a table at the back of Grits 'n' Tits with Freddie, Thump, and Toad, watching a young white stripper shake her breasts for the men next to the stage. The girl was wearing black cowboy boots, a white cowboy hat, a discreetly placed patch of cloth, and nothing else. "'Course, my boobs look like two string beans sagging on the vine. Probably hit myself in the face and poke my eyes out."

"Damn near blinded me with them," Toad said.

"I sure tried."

The jukebox cranked out country music. The cowgirl on stage called, "Yee-hah," and pranced from one end of the platform to the other pretending to be holding reins and riding a horse.

Thump took a swallow of Schlitz and farted.

"Damn, man," Toad said, fanning the air with his hand.

"Now you see why I chose the brother I did," Sue said to Freddie. "Not that Toad can't uncork a few himself." She shook her head as she watched the stripper gyrate. "Really, boys, that's interesting to you?"

Thump and Toad looked at each other, then broke into wide grins.

Freddie shrugged. The girl was pleasant enough to look at, but she only reminded him of what he couldn't have.

"Hey, Boneman," Sue said, "not living up to your name tonight?"

"Not sure *that* bone even works anymore."

"Sounds serious," she said, but she looked amused, like, *What's the big deal? It's only sex.* "Haven't gotten any for a while?"

"Unless I slept through it."

Sue laughed and patted Toad's shoulder. "That's what I did. Whenever I saw this black bear coming at me with that look in his eyes, I downed a couple of goofballs and told him not to wake me when it was over. Pretty sure that's how I came by Emmaline."

"Shit," Toad said, "you were begging for it."

"For it to end. Luckily, you were always thoughtful. I think your record was three minutes. I used you to time an egg once. When I was awake."

"Ooo-ee," Thump said, "look at that ass. Shake what your mama gave you, girl."

Freddie glanced at the stage. It was a fine view indeed, and he couldn't have cared less if the stripper had been selling encyclopedias.

"Pigs," Sue said. "You're all pigs. She's not your lover. She doesn't give a shit about any of you. You know that, right? So what's the point? You like sitting in a room full of men with boners?"

"Long as one of the boners is mine," Thump said.

"The point is *that*," Toad said as the girl gyrated her hips and waved her hat over her head as if she were riding a bucking bronco.

"Jesus," Sue said.

Freddie wondered if it was hard to be a stripper. Did she enjoy it, or was it just another job, like waiting tables or taking dictation in an office? Maybe when her shift was over she'd go home, just like anyone else, and make herself a club sandwich and a milk shake, then listen to a late-night radio program. Maybe she went to college during the day. Maybe she had plans to get married. Maybe she'd live to be a hundred. Maybe she'd die tomorrow.

He'd never know. The only time they would ever connect was during these few minutes, here, with her mostly naked and him mostly bored. His life seemed to stretch out forever compared to this brief peek at hers.

It wasn't just the stripper. It was true of every strange face he saw in cars, in stores, on the streets: lives that popped into existence and then vanished, frozen in his memory, or not, at whatever age he first glimpsed them.

Then he got to thinking, how many times did he meet someone he'd seen before without realizing it? Was there a list somewhere in the universe that kept track of true things that would never be known? Something like *Freddie Ross has met 100,000 people in his life,* or *Freddie Ross has pissed exactly 55,727 times.* There must be an actual number, but if it was unknowable, was it real?

This was way too deep for a man watching a girl wiggle on stage. "Damn it," he said.

"What?" Thump said.

"Guess I ain't having a whole lot of fun."

"Aren't you a Gloomy Gus tonight?" Sue said. "Problems with Shay again? Still?"

"Always."

She smirked as a white man by the stage slipped a bill into the small triangle of cloth over the stripper's privates. "Hey," Sue called, but not loud enough for the gawkers at the stage to hear, "why don't you stuff some cash down *these* pants?"

She pulled her slacks out a little from her waist to show them where, as if they couldn't find the way on their own.

"I will," Toad said. "Then I'll go fetch it."

"Not even with a signed order from God Himself. I learned my lesson with you." Then, turning to Freddie, she said, "Maybe it's time you moved on, little buckaroo. Shay's more trouble than she's worth."

"Too late," Freddie said. "She's gone again."

"For good?"

"Don't matter. She ain't there when she *is* there. Says she's going to Chicago."

"Good riddance." Sue signaled to Pam, the owner who doubled as waitress.

"Whaddaya want?" she said.

"Another beer for my friend."

"How about a Pabst this time?" Freddie said.

Pam checked a list on the back of her order pad. "Says here we got Schlitz, Schlitz, Schlitz, and Schlitz. Oh, and just this morning a fresh shipment of Schlitz came in."

"Guess I'll have a Schlitz," Freddie said, nodding his thanks to Sue.

One beer became several, more strippers came to shed various costumes, and several beers became too many. Freddie found himself thoroughly pickled, something he didn't do often.

When it came time to leave, Sue followed him home to make sure he didn't kill himself or anyone else with his car. She pulled in behind him and guided him into his bedroom.

"Gonna help take my clothes off me, too?"

"You got nothing I want to see, Boneman. Sleep. If she isn't coming back, to hell with her, right?"

****

He found a note in the mailbox the next afternoon when he woke up sometime after noon. Shay must have stopped by, although she could have come in and told him.

Mama's body was burned, it said. *She didn't want no words spoke for her. She said for Jeff to throw her ashes in the river so she can see her home one last time before she passes on to the sea. You can keep the cat.*

The Oak River emptied into the Mississippi in southeastern Iowa, which flowed south to the Gulf, passing between Louisiana and the state of Mississippi on the way. Maybe Nelly thought her ashes would somehow put themselves back together, that her body would rise up from the dark waters to take revenge on the surviving kin of the men who'd hung Sloan and forced themselves on her and Shay.

Or maybe there was something down there she still longed for, some memory of home before the grief and pain. Freddie had lived there, too, until the railroad strike in Waterton had brought his family north. He'd been a young boy then, and didn't recall much of it, except the smells of magnolias and honeysuckle and the heat of the summer sun on his back.

Mississippi probably still had the magnolias and honeysuckle, and surely the sun blazed as hot, but that state couldn't hold anything for Nelly that wasn't black and bitter as her ashes.

Oh, I wish I was in the land of cotton,
Old times, they are not forgotten,
Look away, look away,
Look away, Dixieland.

Freddie's head and stomach ached. He lit up a reefer from Ironhead's farm. *Holy shit*, he thought. *Holy shit.*

He didn't want the damn cat.

Chapter 35

DALE'S APOLOGY WAS LESS sincere than Ben's, but he admitted he'd acted hastily and was willing to give K.C. her job back.

"As long as you don't rehire Austin, too," she said. She sat across the desk from him in his office, her work schedule in hand. "And I need Fridays and Saturdays off to play with the band."

"Same conditions as before," he said. "If you can give me two weeks' advance notice when you're going to need a weekend off, I'll try to accommodate you. Best I can do."

"September 17th and 18th, October 2nd and October 9th."

"I haven't scheduled that far ahead. The 17th and 18th will be okay, but two weekends in a row in October? That's not fair to the ones who'd have to cover for you. Pick one."

The second was the hog roast at Ironhead and Screech's farm. Hardly essential, but she wanted to go because it would make her feel more like one of the boys, so to speak. And the 9th was Electrical Park. That was as big time as Waterton got. "If I don't come back, someone's going to have to cover for me anyway."

"Look, I'm going to be honest with you. Jack begged me

to take you back. I agreed, but only if he'd stay on, too. I'm short on assistant managers."

"He told me he quit."

"He did, for about ten minutes, until he offered the deal for you. 'Both, or neither,' he said. He'll be cutting back for school, but he'll still be here some weeknights and on weekends."

K.C. clenched her fists under the desk, where Dale couldn't see. *Jack, you son-of-a-bitch*, she thought. *You said you quit in protest.*

He did it for you, Squirt.

I didn't ask him to, she answered silently.

Don't be a crumb-bum, Squirt. For once, when someone does something nice for you, just say thank you.

"Let me think about it," she said, not knowing if she was talking to Kenny or Dale.

Little beads of sweat popped out on Dale's forehead, as if his struggle to remain calm took a lot of effort. "Kasey, you're not doing me any favors either way," he said. "Stay or go. You have five seconds."

She stood up and looked at her schedule. "Okay. I'll give it a try. See you Monday morning. And thanks."

K.C. didn't really want to work at a grocery store anymore, but it was a concession to necessity. Until she knew what kind of money the Bluenotes paid, she'd need a dependable income.

As she turned toward the door, she whispered so softly not even Kenny could hear, "Jack, you are *dead*."

****

Jack slammed his fist against the frame of her apartment door. "What the *fuck* do I have to do?" he screamed.

K.C. had never seen him so angry, and never, ever heard him say *fuck*.

"You're going to wake the neighbors."

"To hell with the neighbors."

"Somers will throw us both out."

"He'd throw you out anyway if it wasn't for me getting your job back."

"You lied to me," she said. "You said you quit over Dale firing me. Was that supposed to impress me?"

"I did quit."

"Wow, what a sacrifice. That'll teach him a lesson. 'If you fire my girlfriend I'll quit for ten minutes.' Jesus, Jack, did you think I wouldn't notice you when I came in to work?"

"I thought it wouldn't matter. I thought you'd be grateful, and maybe things could be like they were before."

"You mean with Austin grabbing my boobs and that little creep Davy guessing my bra size? *That* way?"

Jack leaned against the wall and slumped to the floor. "You're not going to make me cry again."

K.C. sat at the kitchen table, hands folded, head bowed. "Good. I'm not worth it. Face it, I'm a bitch. You haven't said it, but that's what you're thinking. And you're right. You're better off without me."

"This isn't about what's best for me. It never has been. Don't you fucking *dare* claim you're doing this for anyone but yourself. If you want out, then at least have the guts to say so. Say, 'Jack, I want out.'"

She looked up from the table. Her anger over his lie was an excuse. She knew that. He offered her everything any sane American girl ever dreamed of. He was nice, most of the time. He didn't belittle her, usually. He didn't hit her, ever. He didn't make passes at other girls, like a certain brother-in-law did. He opened doors for her. He helped her on with her coat. He beat up Austin for her. He didn't force her to have sex when she didn't want to, and tried hard to please her when she did. He remembered her birthday, and that she liked Pepsi better than Coke.

He loved her.

"Jack," she said, "I want out."

He sat silently on the floor for a long time. Two minutes, three. It seemed like an hour. Finally, he said, "Okay," and stood up. He left, pulling the door shut behind him, gently, not the slam she deserved.

She stared at the space left by his absence.

Knucklehead, Kenny said.

"Shut up." K.C. said. "You're not even real."

We need to talk about that.

"Not now."

She willed herself to move. Into the bathroom. Into the bedroom. She set Kenny's picture down and changed into her pajamas.

Jack's first day of the fall term was tomorrow. She had rehearsal Saturday and Sunday. On Monday she was supposed to be making sundaes and Green Rivers behind the soda fountain at Dale's again. Jack still worked there. It would be too cruel if their schedules overlapped. She wouldn't put him through it. She wouldn't put herself through it.

That whole scene with Dale today had been unnecessary. No way she could go back now. She'd rather be broke and living in the Sixth Street drainage tunnel.

****

Freddie got pulled over by the police on the way to rehearsal Saturday, and again on the way home. Both times for a broken taillight, both times on the east side, both times by a white cop. The first one gave him a warning ticket and told him to get the light fixed. If he noticed K.C. in the back seat, he didn't say anything. The second cop, shining his flashlight on Freddie's driver's license, said, "You know what you smell like, Mr. Ross?"

Freddie had smoked a reefer at Narlins. "No, sir."

"You smell like jail time. If I did search your car, what do you suppose I'd find? I mean other than this girl, who I'm going to pretend is a taxi fare. Even though this isn't a chauffeur license."

"You can look, sir. I don't have anything on me."

"What happened to your hands?"

"Lost a fight. Long time ago."

K.C. didn't know if the officer felt sorry for Freddie or was just a nice man, but he nodded and said, "Okay, Mr. Ross. Fix that taillight. And lay off the weed. I pull you over again in this condition, I'm gonna have to arrest you."

"Thank you, Officer."

The cop stooped to look in the back seat. "By the way, could I get your name, miss?"

K.C. kept her eyes down and said, "Kasey Brown," pronouncing it like her family did, like Mr. Pierson, like Jack.

He wrote on his ticket pad. "No trouble here?"

"No trouble, sir. Mr. Ross is just giving me a ride home. He's not coming in."

"Uh huh. All right, Mr. Ross, Miss Brown, you can be on your way."

Freddie waited for him to drive around him, then pulled slowly away from the curb. "Whew," he said. "This was Mississippi, I'd be swinging from a tree right now. You, too, maybe, for fraternizing. That, or the cop would be filling you up with babies in the back seat of his car. But this ain't

Mississippi, and I ain't Sloan Wiggins."

K.C. didn't know who Sloan Wiggins was, and didn't ask. "Lucky twice in one day," she said.

"Good luck or bad, it comes in threes. Wonder what's next?"

"What's next" was he dropped her off at her apartment, she got out, and spent the night alone, listening to her records, Bird and Dizzy, Monk and Miles.

You gotta sweat it, Freddie had said, *you gotta bleed it.*

You aren't a player until it becomes an extension of your body, Mr. Pierson echoed "*... a third arm, a piece of your soul.*"

Rehearsal had been good tonight.

Two days after The End, she felt bad for Jack. He'd be over being mad. By now he was blaming himself and trying to figure out what he'd done to push her away and what he might do to get her back. He'd be brokenhearted and lonely.

K.C. turned up the volume on her record player. Poor Jack. He really was a good guy.

She'd never felt freer in her life.

****

The next day was their last practice before her debut with the band in Lakeview. As they were warming up, Ruthie came out of her office, escorting Dwayne. "Lookie what I found," she grinned.

K.C. had assumed he'd come back eventually, but nobody'd thought it would be this soon. They all set their instruments aside and rushed down from the stage to greet him with slaps on the back, handshakes, and hugs.

Dwayne sat at a table. He was dressed in a suit, the only way she'd ever seen him. "First thing," he said, "don't anyone blubber over Spits to me. I know how you all feel, but he's gone." He touched his chest. "I got my own feelings for him here, and a little something else for... Lakeview, is it?"

Freddie nodded.

Dwayne pointed at K.C., then at the chair across from him. "White Bird, you're no blacker than last time I saw you. Don't suppose you grew any man parts, either."

"Afraid not," she said, taking the indicated chair. The others pulled another table next to his and joined them.

"I appreciate you singing for me," he said. "At the funeral home. That meant something."

K.C. felt her cheeks redden.

"If you was black," Catfish said, "we couldn't see you blushing."

"Shut up," she said.

"Drinks?" Ruthie said.

"I'm buying," Dwayne said.

"No charge. Beers and a pop?"

"Pepsi," K.C. said.

"Root beer for me," Syd said, and Ruthie scooted away.

"Second thing," Dwayne said. "Thump, sorry about giving you the business at the visitation."

"Never even happened, man," Thump said. "Sue and Toad've been keeping me pretty straight since Spits. I know it ain't been long, but it's something."

"How's it feel?"

"Like someone's lighting cherry bombs in my brain. I'm shaking all the time."

"You can still doghouse?"

"Was there any doubt?"

Dwayne pulled a folded score from inside his suit coat. There were several pages, parts written out for each band member. "Wrote a new chart on the train coming home. A couple of versions. One's private, just for me. The other's for the band. We're gonna end with it at Lakeview."

Ironhead took the score from him and passed out the parts to the others. "Sweet," he said. "Words got a bluesy feel to 'em. Man, I love this. You're finally gonna let me sing again."

"This for Spits?" Freddie said.

"Who'd you think?"

K.C. checked out her sax part. The piece was called "It Ain't Wrong If It's Right."

"Wow, Mr. Hite," she said. "Look at that alto. I get to play this?"

"Too much for you?"

K.C. hesitated a second, so Freddie spoke up. "Hell, no," he said, winking at her. "She's been giving us what's-what these last couple rehearsals."

"I think we got us a prodigy," Catfish said, and nobody disagreed. "And you ought to hear the little shit tickle the eighty-eights, too."

"Why?" Dwayne said. "You looking to move on to a new band?"

"I'm not a little shit," K.C. said. "And I'm not here to play piano."

Ruthie came back with the drinks on a tray, already opened. She took one for herself, set the empty tray on another table, and slid a chair over to join them. "Screech and Ironhead's hog roast is on the 2nd," she said.

"That was the third thing," Dwayne said.

"Got a nice fat one picked out," Ironhead said.

For some reason K.C. thought about Sue. *Kick you so hard your nuts will fall out your butt.* She could imagine her saying that. She liked Sue, and was really glad she was going to be with them in Lakeview. That overnight stay would be the first time they got to test all of Freddie's, and Jack's, fears about how folks would react to a young white girl keeping company with older black men.

"That's what I like to hear," Dwayne said. "Now get your asses back up on stage. We're going do this till we get it right."

The first few attempts to make it through the chart were rough on all of them. Everyone was tentative. Different players dropped out at different times, unsure of the exact feel Dwayne intended. Sometimes the piece sounded like jazz, sometimes gospel, sometimes undefinable. Most of his arrangements, while genius, were fairly straightforward. But this one was for Spits, and nobody wanted to screw it up.

During a lull, Ironhead asked Catfish to run through it with him alone, trying to work out the melody against the piano. Then Dwayne told everybody to lay out except Syd, Thump, and Catfish. He made them do the rhythms over and over again. "You feel that? How it comes and goes? It's our *life*, goddammit. Play it that way."

After twenty minutes frustration was starting to boil over, and any sentimentality over the chart's meaning was lost. While the others bickered and cursed, Syd put his head down on the snare drum and K.C. sat on the edge of the stage.

This was *hard*.

"Cut the whining," Dwayne said. "Time to put this bitch together."

They took a collective deep breath and went through it again. And again. And again. Eventually K.C. thought they were beginning to feel it, although she didn't think she'd nailed the sax part yet.

Dwayne knew it. "Better," he said, "but, White Bird, you

got to do your part, too. The boys tell me you're something special. Show me."

K.C. showed him. The whole band did. He was clearly satisfied with their playing through A and B, giving them a thumbs up, but his tears didn't come until C, when Ironhead started to sing the lyrics in earnest, enunciating them with a sensitivity K.C. hadn't known he possessed. His brooding tone squeezed shadows from the notes.

It ain't wrong if it's right.
It ain't wrong if it's right.
Ain't no darkness where there's light,
And it ain't wrong if it's right.

Can't nobody tell us no.
Can't nobody tell us no.
When our hearts tell us it's so,
Can't nobody tell us no.

This old world can be unkind.
People's hatred makes them blind,
But the two of us were fine.
We had no enemy but time.

The grave don't get the final word.
It don't get the final word.
If your memory is preserved,
The grave don't get the final word.

By then everyone was trying to hold it together. Ironhead was slaying them with his voice. K.C. didn't know Spits like they did, but she knew Kenny, and she knew how it felt to lose him. It was her turn.

She lifted her sax for her next entrance, tapping the pads. At the pickup notes she thought *This is for you, brother*, and she blew her soul through her lips, past the reed, through the neck, and out the bell. If there'd been a house to bring down, she would have brought it down. Everyone stopped to gape at her. Although there was more to the chart, nobody came back in after the bridge, letting her take the number home by herself.

She outshined even Ironhead's devastating stylings. As the final note rang through the hall, there was an audible silence. All she heard was the involuntary drumming of her left thumb against the octave key.

Now her own tears were flowing.

Dwayne and Ruthie stood to applaud, and the band members joined in. "God *damn*." Dwayne took off his glasses and wiped his eyes. "Remember when I said you weren't a player? Never been so full of shit in my life."

Two sentences.

K.C. wiped the sweat from her face and smiled. Despite all the turmoil in her life, all it took was those two sentences to make her feel something she hadn't felt in a long time—happy.

Chapter 36

SHAY'S CLOTHES WERE GONE, so she was gone. For good. No way her mother's inheritance could have come through yet, but she'd had enough. She couldn't stay one day longer with Freddie. He didn't know—he had never known, and never would—what he had done to become so unsatisfactory to her.

He stood at the door with his car keys in his hand. He was going to pick up White Bird for what she thought was going to be another discussion at the library. Washington stood at his feet, glaring up at him, hissing. He opened the door. She looked outside. Her tail flicked nervously.

"Go on, get out," he said.

She crouched as if she were about to pounce. She meowed.

And then she was gone, just like Shay. The last he saw of her was her tail and her little round butthole as she disappeared into some hedges across the street.

Good riddance. If the damn thing wanted to act like a wild animal, let her be one.

Freddie stepped onto the porch and pulled the door shut behind him. He didn't lock it. His neighborhood was safe. He didn't have anything worth stealing anyway.

On his way to the west side he stopped at the St. Vincent DePaul and bought a little something he figured K.C. might like. He put it in the trunk. He'd give it to her in Lakeview, or maybe save it for Electrical Park on the 9th.

Freddie had told K.C. he'd pick her up outside her apartment. In broad daylight. The hell with it. She was one of the band now. She was going to be seen in public with them in a couple of nights anyway. Besides, two white cops had pulled him over when she was with him, and neither had harassed him about it. Maybe things weren't as bad as they seemed.

Or maybe he just didn't care anymore.

He crossed the river at Fourth Street, noticing a couple of fishermen in a rowboat beneath him. The Oak was usually low enough this time of year that all anyone needed was a pair of waders, but the recent rains had swollen it, and the water was only now starting to recede. He envied those fishermen their carefree bobbing, the lull of the river and the heat of the sun, drinking beers and swapping lies. He hoped someday he could relax like that again, free of the pain of Shay and the ghosts of Nelly and Spits.

He turned onto Wellington. K.C. was already on the curb waiting for him. She waved and smiled when she saw his car approaching. Freddie shook his head. The girl was wearing a checkered blue dress like Dorothy's in *The Wizard of Oz*. That had to change before they brought her out on stage in Lakeview.

Without being told, she climbed into the back seat. "Hi, Freddie," she said in a breezy tone.

"You're in fine form today."

"Better than I've been in ages. How are you?"

"We'll see," he said.

She chattered all the way across the bridge, peppering him with questions about Lakeview. Despite it being only one state away, she'd never been there.

How big a town was it?

Five or ten thousand, he guessed.

Were there a lot of black people?

Probably not.

How was the audience going to react to her?

Do your part and we'll be all right.

Where were they going to stay Friday night?

He'd found a cheap motel for them.

Did it take black people?

He had a book, *Directory of Negro Hotels and Guest Houses in the United States*. According to it, yes.

Did it take *white* people?

Hope so.

On and on, right up until he drove past the east library.

"You missed your turn," she said.

"Got one stop to make first—"

"Where?" she said, and he detected a hint of alarm in her voice.

What he had to say was harder for him than anything she might be thinking. He tried to find the right words. "I didn't want to be alone."

"For what?"

"Remember how you told me to see the doctor? Well, I did."

"What did he say?"

"Should have the blood tests back today."

"What did you have blood tests for?"

"If they knew, I wouldn't need the tests."

"I don't like the sound of that."

"You and me both."

"How about your friends? Your wife? Wouldn't they come with you?"

"Shay ain't an option anymore."

"Why not?"

"And the boys, I don't want them to see me if things go bad."

"They're your friends, Freddie."

"You gonna go in with me or not?"

"If they'll let me."

He didn't see why they wouldn't. The clinic was for poor people of any race. Plenty of whites and coloreds sitting together there. Even some Mexicans and Orientals. And that nurse, Lindy, told him Dr. Thomas wasn't a prejudiced man. They wouldn't care if he brought a white girl in to hear the diagnosis. And if they did, so what? "Ain't gonna ask their permission," he said.

From behind, K.C. put her hand on his shoulder. "You scared?"

"Worse thing he could tell me is I'm dying, and what's the big deal about dying?"

"Don't say that."

Freddie could feel her fingers trembling. She was scared, too.

****

"Acute lymphocytic leukemia," Dr. Thomas said.

White Bird gasped.

Freddie perched on the examination table, legs not quite reaching the floor. K.C. sat in a chair next to him. The nurse wasn't Lindy today. This one was an older white woman who eyed the two of them with disdain. Her nametag read C. ST. CROIX, LPN.

He'd heard the word leukemia before, but had no clear idea what it was. "What the hell's acute lim-fo-what-the-fuck leukemia?"

"A disease of the blood," Thomas said.

"Like sickle cell?"

"Cancer. This particular type is more common in children."

Cancer. The C-word. Freddie's stomach lurched. He'd never found out what killed his parents, although his father went quick, so it was probably his heart. But Mama.... Once a large woman, she just melted away in her final years. She wouldn't go to the doctor when she was alive, and forbade an autopsy after her death. "Ain't nobody cutting this body up," she'd said, "just to tell you I'm dead. You'll already know that."

The doctor who came to their house wrote "natural causes" on the death certificate. Freddie figured that meant old age, even though she was only sixty-six. But in the back of his mind he always wondered if it might not be cancer. He'd heard scary stuff about that shit. He didn't want to go like Mama went.

"You're saying I got a kid's cancer?"

"I'd need to do a biopsy to be sure, but yes."

K.C. was sobbing. She jumped up and threw her arms around him, hugging him so hard he couldn't breathe.

He gently pushed her away. The nurse, still hostile, nevertheless helped K.C. back to her chair and got her a cup of water.

Freddie felt like his muscles were turning to Jell-O, like his whole body might ooze into a puddle on the floor. *Good luck or bad, it comes in threes.* Well, first there was Spits, then Nelly.

What's the big deal about dying?

Tough-talking words. "Got a pill for that, doc?"

"Standard treatment is radiation, arsenic, and thorium-

X."

"Arsenic? Ain't that poison?"

"It's all poison. That's what kills the cancer cells."

"Don't do me much good if it kills me, too."

"There's a brand-new drug called aminopterin, just developed last year. It's showed some promise in inducing remissions in children. I don't know if it's been tested on adults. I don't even know if it's legal to use on adults."

"If it ain't?"

"The poison."

"Ain't much of a choice."

"Spontaneous remissions have been known to happen," Thomas said.

"What's that mean?"

"It's when people get better without medical intervention. You'll have to talk to God about that. Miracles are His business."

"Me and Him ain't on such good terms lately."

"If nothing else, we can still treat the symptoms."

That didn't sound good at all, like *We'll make you as comfortable as possible.* "How long?" he said.

"Until what?"

"*How long, Doc?*"

Thomas sighed. "I'll be honest with you, Mr. Ross. Your blood looks bad. Your liver and spleen feel enlarged, and you said you've been displaying other symptoms for some time. If the biopsy shows what I think it will..." He stopped to take a deep breath, like he didn't want to finish answering the question. Must be hard to be a doctor sometimes. "Left untreated, it could be quick. A few weeks if you're lucky."

K.C. screamed.

Freddie was afraid he might faint, and what kind of thing

was that for a grown man to do? "A few *weeks*, Doc? I got things to do."

Thomas held up his hands in a placating gesture. "It won't be untreated. We're going to get after this thing. I'll call about the aminopterin today, but there's not much hope there. Otherwise, we've still got the standard treatment. An oncologist visits the clinic once a month, or as needed. Doctor Buckles, usually. He's a good man."

"What about the biopsy?" White Bird said. Freddie was glad she asked, because he wouldn't have thought to.

"We draw bone marrow from the hip."

"That sounds like it'll hurt," Freddie said.

"You'll be anaesthetized," Thomas said. "You won't feel it."

Now he wished she hadn't asked. "You ain't drilling no hole in my hip."

"Would you rather die?"

"You already told me what I got."

"Freddie, you have to," White Bird said.

"It gonna hurt? Dying, I mean."

Thomas pulled out a cigarette, but didn't light it. "Probably. Other forms of cancer can be worse, but, yeah. You're already feeling it."

Like a daughter comforting an ailing father, White Bird caressed his back.

"Well, shit," Freddie said. "Say you drill, what's next?"

"Now you're talking sense." Thomas lit his cigarette. "I'll consult with Buckles. We can't do a marrow test here, so you'll have to go to St. Francis. Or Allen, if you prefer. We have an arrangement with them, too. We'll go from there. You don't have a phone, right? Is there anyone I can call?"

He looked at K.C.

"Only a pay phone in my apartment building," she said. "There's usually nobody around to answer it."

"Call Ruthie at Narlins," Freddie said. "Leave a message. Got a pencil?"

"I do," the nurse said, and Freddie gave her the number.

"Good," Thomas said. "I'll call when I know something. In the meantime, let's get a chest X-ray today—see how those lymph nodes are doing."

****

The lymph nodes were as bad as his blood. Freddie felt so weak from the shock of the diagnosis that his legs could scarcely bear his weight. K.C. had to help him back to his car, holding him up like he was crippled. He was really glad none of his male friends were there to see him like this.

After she seated him on the driver's side, she got in on the front seat of the passenger side.

Freddie put his head on the wheel. "You can't tell nobody," he said. "I don't want no fussing over me."

She cupped his right hand in hers. She was weeping something awful. "What about your wife?"

"I told you, she ain't an option. She run out on me again."

"What a bitch."

"Don't call her that. She didn't know I was sick." He started the car. "I always knew she'd leave for good someday. Now was the time."

"Freddie, what are you going to do?"

He drew his hand away to shift into reverse. As he released the emergency brake, he said, "Shush now. Don't you be crying for me."

"I can't help it. I don't want you to die."

He shifted back into neutral. "Funny thing about that," he

said, although there wasn't one thing funny about it. He couldn't believe he was about to unload his feelings on a nineteen-year-old girl. He didn't do that with anybody. "After all my troubles, I said to my dumb-ass self I didn't care about dying. But that's easy to say when you ain't dying." He paused as the truth sank in. "I don't want me to die, neither, little Bird."

And then Freddie let go. He blubbered like a child. K.C. joined in for another round of her own. They leaned into one another, head to head and shoulder to shoulder. He put his arm around her. When they were both spent, they sat for a while longer in the clinic's parking lot. Patients came and went. Doctors. Nurses. No one took much note of them. They had their own problems.

There wasn't much more for either of them to say. Freddie drew a measure of strength from her silence. He hoped she did the same with him.

Finally he said, "Will you go to Narlins with me?"

It was still afternoon. Narlins wasn't open yet, so Ruthie wouldn't mind letting them in.

"I thought you wanted to go to the library."

"I need to play. Ain't nothing music can't make better."

"It can't cure cancer."

"Nah, but for a little while it takes you away from this world. You felt it with Dwayne's new chart. You know you did. *That's* the miracle. Can't find that kind of holy in no church."

"I know what you mean, but you have to stop playing sometime. Then the world's back again, the same old shithole."

"I said for a little while, Bird. But what a glorious while it is. And after, you got the memory to keep you going a while more."

"Yeah," she said, her eyes far away, "I remember."

Freddie guessed she was thinking of her dead brother. He put the car in reverse. "Narlins?"

"Narlins."

David Hoing & Roger Hileman

PART FOUR

SWAN SONG

Chapter 37

IT WAS 175 MILES to LAKEVIEW, but K.C. had no idea what kind of facilities they had there, so she had to get ready now, even if it meant sitting all dolled up on the bus for four hours.

She couldn't afford a beauty salon. Since she didn't have any girlfriends to do her hair for her and Krissy was at work all day, she spent most of the morning in front of her bathroom mirror. Although it probably wasn't appropriate to a jazz venue, she went for a Rita Hayworth look, hair swept up and away from her face. She used rag curlers for the sides and back. Even curled, her hair hung to her shoulders. It was held in place on top by lots of bobby pins, which were a nuisance. Bobby pins had been hard to come by during the war, so women were mad for them these days, but K.C. regarded them only as a necessary evil.

With her hair as done as it was going to be, she applied her makeup. No telling what the lighting would be onstage, but she decided to wear extra rouge so her skin wouldn't bleach out in case of harsh lighting, with a deep red lipstick that went with the teardrop ruby earrings she planned to wear.

She dressed in a light blue evening gown with spaghetti straps, rayon hose, and high heels. The gown had red sequins on the bodice, which was cut low to show some cleavage. She'd been sent home for wearing this dress to a high school dance during her senior year, and had never worn it since. She hadn't gained any weight in the past year and a half, so why not wear it now? It wasn't out of fashion yet.

She pushed up on her boobs to accentuate them. Jane Russell had nothing to fear.

Wow, Squirt, look at you. When did you grow up?

Embarrassed, she let go of her boobs. "Going to Lakeview tonight."

You sure you know what you're getting into?

"It's what I want to do."

It's what you think I wanted to do.

"Isn't it?"

You can't live my life for me. You have to make your own way.

"This is my way." She heard Freddie honk his horn across the street. "Gotta run. Wish me luck."

You don't need luck, Squirt. You got talent.

She hurried outside, carrying a small suitcase with her toiletries, pajamas, and casual clothes to wear before tomorrow night's second show. Freddie had already picked up her sax from Narlins and placed it in the back seat. His trombone was next to him in front. She took the hint and sat in the back. She'd thought they were past that now, but apparently not. At least she didn't have to walk to the Paramount.

Freddie whistled, then laughed. "What? You don't think being white's gonna be enough to make folks notice you?"

"Am I overdressed?"

"Not if we're going to a prom."

She didn't think he meant it as criticism, but she took it that way, especially since he'd commented on her clothes before. "What should I have worn?"

"We'll have to work on that. I should've talked to you more about it, but I kinda had other things on my mind."

"Have you heard back from the doctor?"

"Ruthie said he ain't called. I don't feel any worse than I did then, so maybe I'm having one of them 'spontaneous remission' things."

"You're still getting the biopsy."

"Whether I do or don't, remember what I told you—don't tell nobody."

K.C. watched his hands on the wheel, his fingers bent this way and that. They were swollen at the joints, especially the middle ones, and crooked in places bones shouldn't be crooked. "You ever going to explain your hands?"

Freddie glanced over his shoulder at her. "You think this leukemia shit's the worst that's ever happened to me? Ain't even close. Only thing worse than dying and being dead is dying and still being alive. Just ask my wife Shay."

"What did she have to do with your fingers?"

"Not a thing," Freddie said.

As they crossed the bridge, he gave her an account of Spring Valley, Mississippi, in 1908, and what a white mob had done to Shay's father, and then to Shay and her mother.

"Jesus, Freddie," K.C. said, "that's the most awful thing I've ever heard."

She couldn't imagine watching someone she loved die— and then she thought about Kenny. Kenny, North Africa, 1943. A German shell so close they had to ship his body back in pieces. She bit her lip. And after she'd seen the horror of that, what if those same Germans had then torn her clothes off and forced themselves into her, one after another?

She cried, and to hell with her makeup. Lakeview had restrooms, and restrooms had mirrors. She'd fix it there.

"It ain't no easy thing," Freddie said, "having the woman you love say 'No, you won't do.'"

Shay must have been broken in every way a person could be. K.C. hadn't witnessed Kenny's death. She'd never been raped. Yet there still was no getting over her loss. Poor Shay. Poor Freddie. "Some people can't be healed," she said, and it occurred to her that she might be one of them.

"I know. Probably Shay does, too. She's gonna keep looking, though. Going to Chicago."

"A woman couldn't hope for a better man than you."

Freddie chuckled without mirth. "Shay can."

K.C. sniffled. "You deserve better than you got."

"So does Shay. But ain't no such thing as '*deserve.*' You get what you get."

Hearing the pain in Freddie's voice made her realize how much she must have hurt Jack—and for what? A little white lie?

Ain't no easy thing, having the woman you love say 'No, you won't do.'

Poor Jack.

She leaned back in the seat and stroked her sax's case. "Hey, you sneaky devil, you never did tell me about your fingers."

"No time now, little Bird" he said, winking into the rearview mirror and turning into the Newton Street parking lot. She'd been so preoccupied with Shay's story and her own thoughts that she hadn't been paying attention to where they were.

If the doctor was right, there weren't going to be many

other times. Freddie looked like he was thinking the same thing. They got out of the car.

The rest of the band had already arrived and were loading their instruments into the back of the bus. Sue was leaning against the door frame, smoking a cigarette. K.C. was surprised to see Emmaline was there, too, also smoking.

The catcalls and whistles started as soon as the men saw K.C.'s outfit.

"Uh oh," she said. "How's my makeup look?"

"What do you think? Like you been crying. Everyone's gonna wanna know why." He handed her a handkerchief, then shook a bent finger at her and whispered, "Not a goddamned word, you hear? Promise me."

K.C. nodded. "Are you sure you're up to playing this weekend?"

Freddie smirked at her. "Am I dead yet?"

"Don't say that." She tried to tap the furrows in her rouge flat. "Better?"

"Now you look like a clown, all that black liner shit dripping down. Here, let me."

Freddie took back the handkerchief and dabbed at her face, smoothing the eyeliner and rouge together. Then he stepped back, studied her face, and laughed. "Too much black. Girl, we ain't putting on a minstrel show."

"Is it that bad?"

He gave her a hug. "Nah. Sue or Emmaline can help you when we get up to Lakeview."

He had a small duffle bag, which he threw over his back. Then he grabbed K.C.'s suitcase and his trombone and limped to the bus. K.C. got her sax and followed.

"You'd been any later," Sue said to Freddie, "and you'd've ridden to Lakeview with my shoe up your ass." She looked at K.C.'s outfit. "Good heavens, girl. You look like a twenty-dollar whore in a five-dollar flophouse. What's with the makeup?"

"It got smudged on the way over."

"I hope you brought a change of clothes."

"Not that I can wear on stage."

As Freddie put the instruments and bags in the back of the bus, Dwayne ambled up to K.C., said, "Damn, White Bird," and got onto the bus.

"Don't listen to them," Catfish said. "You look pretty."

"Yeah," Ironhead said, his voice a little too creepy.

"Watch it," Sue warned. "Enough yakking. Get in, it's a long drive."

Syd was already on the bus. He offered his hand to help Sue, then K.C. and Emmaline up the steps. The rest followed them in, sitting toward the back with Dwayne. Emmaline slid in behind Sue, across the aisle from K.C.

"Surprised to see you here," K.C. said.

"Everyone says you're amazing," Emmaline said. "I wanted to hear for myself. Mom said I could. You can call me Emmy."

"Which reminds me," Sue said after starting the bus. While it idled, she stood up and faced the guys in the back. "Listen up, pigs. There are two young ladies present. I hear so much as an oink from you this entire weekend, I swear to God I'll dump you in the middle of a cornfield. You got that?"

At which point Ironhead, Screech, Catfish, and Leon started oinking, of course. Freddie would never do that, Dwayne's tastes did not include girls, and Syd had always been a gentleman. It was a little surprising that Thump didn't join in, but then again, maybe not. He was Emmaline's uncle.

"Keep it up," Sue said.

She sat down and put the bus in gear, and they were on

their way to K.C.'s first gig as an official Bluenote.

"I'm nervous," she whispered to no one.

It's what you wanted, Kenny said.

****

They were halfway to Lakeview, and all K.C. and Emmy had talked about was girl stuff, the latest fashions, hairstyles, movies, and boys. Emmy had a lot to say about the latter, but K.C. wasn't in the mood to discuss Jack, especially with someone she hardly knew.

She looked between Sue and Emmy, saw a facial resemblance, then back at Thump and saw the family resemblance there, too. She wondered, though, why the girl's skin was as dark as her uncle's. If she'd ever given it any thought, which she hadn't until now, she would have guessed that Emmy's coloring would be somewhere in between.

"Wanna know a secret?" Emmy said. "I like white boys better than black ones. 'Specially the ones with blond hair and blue eyes. They're so beautiful."

"I heard that," Sue said. "I better not find out you've been with *any* boys."

"Oh, you know I'm pure as snow, Mom," Emmy said. She winked at K.C., then crossed the aisle to sit in the seat next to her so they wouldn't be as easily overheard.

K.C. studied the contrast in their color. "What's it like having a white mother?" she said.

"Why, isn't your mom white?"

"I meant, what's it like when your mother's a different color than you?"

"It's all I ever knew. She says anybody gives me trouble about it, knock them in the head."

K.C. smiled. She really liked Sue: an unbiased, no-nonsense woman who didn't tolerate bullshit from anyone, even men much bigger and stronger than she was—stronger if strength was measured by muscles alone. Sue was so, so different from her own mother. Mrs. Rose Brown never had the backbone to do anything but support her father's tirades, whether she agreed with them or not.

The thing was, K.C. didn't really know what her mother thought about anything, because whenever she spoke, she just repeated whatever Dad had just said.

"You've got a killer-diller mom," K.C. said. "I wish mine was like that."

"*Killer-diller*?" Emmy shook her head and smiled. "You white people talk funny."

"I heard that, too," Sue said.

"Oopsie-daisy," Emmy said and rolled her eyes. K.C. guessed "oopsie-daisy" was one of Sue's phrases, proving Emmy's point.

"So why did your mom let you come?" K.C. said.

"So you had someone your own age along on the first trip. Who wants to get stuck talking to *old people* all weekend?" She emphasized "old people" to make sure Sue would hear.

"You little shit," Sue said.

Dwayne made his way to the front of the bus. "Who's a little shit?" he said.

"Wasn't talking to you."

"Good. I'm not here to talk to you, either," he said. "Listen up, White Bird. Me and the boys have been working out your entrance on stage tonight. Place we're at is called the Bullhead Ballroom."

"*Bullhead* Ballroom?" K.C. said. "Really?"

"It's Minnesota. Anyway, it's a nice joint. Maybe not as good as Electrical Park, but classier than Narlins. We're not sure how the crowd's going to take you, so we've got to play this thing just right."

In The Blood

****

Dwayne struck an "A" in octaves on the house piano for the rest of the band to tune, then herded them all into a small room to the side of the stage, to wait there until they were ready to play.

"What's the order tonight?" Syd said.

Dwayne passed around a list with the numbers they'd be playing.

Freddie looked it over. "Where's 'It Ain't Wrong?'"

"Don't think we're ready to go with that one," he said, which K.C. interpreted to mean that Dwayne wasn't ready yet to hear it performed in public. "Besides, nobody in Lakeview knew Spits. I think we should save it for Electrical Park."

K.C. felt jittery. High school concerts had been nothing compared to this. She'd always been the best musician on stage then. It had all been so comfortable. But this was something else entirely—her first professional gig, playing an instrument white girls weren't supposed to play, with musicians she wasn't supposed to play *with*.

She was terrified. Sweat smeared her makeup again.

But then she saw the first number on the list and smiled. *Thank you, Dwayne.*

By showtime the dance floor and seats were already full— white people in a white town thirsting for black music. The stage was brightly lit, the wings and the audience were in the dark. While the band members remained in the side room, Dwayne stepped up to the microphone and faced the audience. Like she had at that first audition at Narlins, K.C. thought he looked like an overweight Cab Calloway in his black suit and bow tie.

"Ladies and gentlemen, meet the Bluenotes," Dwayne

323

announced. "Our hideman, Syd Clayton." There was polite applause as Syd walked onto the stage, which grew more enthusiastic when he dazzled them with a short riff that would have done Gene Krupa proud.

"Catfish Elliot on the eighty-eights."

Catfish displayed his virtuosity with a medley of some of the numbers on their list, then Syd joined him in a sort of "holding pattern" while the rest were introduced.

"Thump McLemore on the doghouse."

Thump added a walking bass line that virtually ran.

"Boneman Ross on the trombone."

Freddie limped out onto the stage and added harmony to the bass lines Thump and Catfish were already playing.

"Screech Granger on the guitar."

After Screech plugged into his amp, he started off with rhythm but switched to lead, his fingers flying up and down the neck.

"Ironhead Granger on tenor sax."

Ironhead added innovative coloring above Freddie's trombone, sometimes discordant, sometimes so beautiful that the lines melted together.

"Leon Finch on trumpet."

By now the audience was cheering wildly. Leon played in a register so high it could shatter crystal.

And then the music stopped, except for Catfish rolling octaves in his left hand and Syd tapping quarters on his hi-hat.

Oh, Jesus, K.C. thought. *Here we go. Deep breath. Deep breath.*

"And now, ladies and gentlemen," Dwayne called, raising his voice dramatically, "making her professional debut with the Bluenotes, playing alto sax, our own little White Bird,

Miss K. C. Brow-ow-ow-ow-own!"

K.C. clutched her sax and stepped onto the stage.

The crowd went silent. The rest of the Bluenotes were dressed like Dwayne: black suit coats and trousers, white shirts, black shoes, black bowties. K.C. was wearing a blue evening gown and heels. That wasn't what shut the audience down.

She was young and female, the others older men. That wasn't it, either.

As Dwayne stepped away from the mic and headed to the side of the stage, the boos started. Then the laughter, the Bronx cheers, and the wolf whistles. She heard cries of "white nigger" and "trash," mixed in with other words even worse.

They want to hate you, Squirt, Kenny said. *Make them love you.*

What the hell. She was going to kick some motherfucking ass...

Leon winked at her. He placed a beer glass in front of the bell of his trumpet, using it as a cup mute. Syd pounded out two measures of hard rhythm, and then K.C. and Leon broke into "Ko-Ko" with an energy that took the audience by surprise.

They'd come to dance. Problem was, people didn't dance to bop, they listened. They continued to curse for another minute or so, but by the time K.C. started to take the changes, she had their attention. At the bridge they were crowding the stage, their jaws hanging slack in amazement, and by the final chords they were cheering like teenaged girls at a Sinatra concert.

And it was only the first number. Dwayne had chosen his list well, giving the people cool swing to dance to and hot bop to boil their blood.

At the end of the night K.C. was a star, at least in Lakeview, Minnesota. That was all she'd ever wanted.

"Did you hear, Kenny?" she whispered in the side room by the stage after the show.

You surpass me, Squirt.

That was just what Mr. Pierson had told her, only this time it was Kenny. *Kenny.* Damn.

She grinned as she packed her sax into its case and followed the other band members out. A throng of awestruck fans surrounded her, trying to touch her and shake her hand, begging her to autograph their tickets.

It was heady stuff, but they pretty much ignored everyone else, a snub she was sure the guys noticed.

At the bus Emmy threw her arms around K.C.'s neck. "Wow," she said.

****

Several cars followed the bus out of the parking lot and to the motor hotel Freddie had booked for them. It was called the Stop-N-Snooze. Although it was listed in his Negro hotels directory, "hotel" was stretching it. "Sewer with windows" was more like it. The manager's nametag said Leroy. Leroy was a meek-looking little white man in a plaid shirt, somewhere on the other side of fifty, with a salt-and-pepper hairstyle that had never been in fashion and several teeth missing from his lower jaw. He wasn't the least bit curious about his guests. As long as they had the money, he accepted anyone, colored people, white people, men, women, children, and probably dogs and horses. The place sure smelled like it accepted horses. Leroy didn't ask how the men were going to work out the sleeping arrangements with the women. He did give K.C. and Emmy a bit of a strange look, though.

"We're twins," K.C. explained.

"Cute," Leroy said.

Dwayne paid in advance for three rooms, two nights. They weren't planning to return to Waterton until Sunday.

Ironhead, Screech, Thump, and Leon took the double beds in room 7. Freddie, Syd, Catfish, and Dwayne would be in 8, and the women in 9.

"You sleep two to a bed?" K.C. said, wondering who would be with Dwayne. She and Krissy had shared a bed when they were younger, but that was different. They were just kids.

"We're lucky it's only two," Syd said.

"Some places don't have beds," Catfish said.

"We've stayed in barns before," Freddie said.

"Hey," Leroy said, "this place may stink like a barn, but it ain't no barn."

The others headed to their rooms. K.C. hung back to have a word with Dwayne.

Cars pulled into the lot, followed by slamming doors and loud voices. She'd noticed them trailing after the bus when they'd left the Bullhead, but had figured they were just going the same way, or were her new fans hoping for another look. Well, maybe some of those people were fans, but most of them were angry, calling out the usual ugly words. The glow of the Bluenotes' performance at the Bullhead was going to be short-lived. Since Freddie's directory listed the motel as a place where black people were welcome, the good citizens of Lakeview, Minnesota, ought to be used to all types staying there.

"You niggers send that white girl out!" someone cried.

Leroy sighed. "Here we go again."

"I want to be here," K.C. yelled back from the office's door. She couldn't see their faces, as the headlights were behind them.

"Jesus, Bird," Dwayne said as he finished signing the register for all of them. "You trying to get us killed?"

"They can't say that," she said. "It's not right."

"Welcome to the world, little girl."

"Shut the hell up," Leroy called to the mob.

Someone threw a rock through the office window. "All right, that's it," Leroy said. He jumped up and pushed K.C. out of the doorway. "Which one of you dumbass fuck-buckles broke my window? You know I keep my pistol here. Was it you, Andy?"

"We don't like white women mixing with niggers," a big man in overalls said. K.C. felt the violence building, like at the Roth strike. Hopefully it wouldn't end the same way, with someone dead.

"Me, I don't like Lima beans," Leroy said, "but that don't mean other people can't eat them. Would any of you screw a white girl who sleeps with blacks?"

"Hell, no," Andy said to grunts of agreement from the others.

"Well, then, what's your complaint? You wouldn't want this gal anyhow."

K.C. took offense at the implication, but Dwayne put his hand on her arm. "Let it go," he whispered.

"We don't want them in this town."

"Yeah, well, I ain't too excited about a bunch of drunk Norwegian butter-fucks howling in my parking lot, either. I take them as they come at my place. Don't make me use my gun. You've seen me at the range. I could pick off your nuts easy as wings off flies."

"You'd shoot me over a bunch of niggers?"

"I'd shoot you on general principles."

"They're not gone by noon tomorrow," Andy said, "we're

coming for them."

"Blow it out your ass."

"We have another show tomorrow night," K.C. whispered.

Leroy looked at her like she was the stupidest human to walk the planet. "Don't count on it," he said.

Hate me, love me, hate me, K.C. thought.

Freddie *had* warned her.

She wanted to rage at these bridge trolls, but they were too much for one teenaged girl to overcome.

"Better still, I'll take your whole pecker off, Andy," Leroy said, "such as it is. Your wife'll be baking me cookies for years."

After a few more insults back and forth, Leroy convinced Andy and his gang to get in their cars and go home. K.C. was impressed.

"We gotta leave in the morning?" Dwayne said.

Leroy closed the door and switched off the vacancy light. "If you're smart." He returned to the desk, then checked the guest register. "Look, Mr. Hite, I put up all kinds here, but they're all the *same* kind. Black with black, Mexican with Mexican, Chinamen with Chinamen. You play hide the salami with someone a different color, folks around here get themselves all riled up. I can't tell you what to do, but...."

"I get a refund for tomorrow night?"

"No, but I won't charge you for the busted window."

"That's really white of you."

Leroy smiled and sneered at the same time. "Might wanna rethink who you travel with next time."

"Might not," Dwayne said. "Still's a free country."

"Since when?"

Dwayne took K.C.'s elbow and led her toward the hall. "Come on, White Bird."

"Wait," she said, turning to Leroy. "Just so you know, I'm not sleeping with them."

"Beg pardon?"

"These guys are my friends. We don't… you know."

He gave K.C. a hard look. "Who the fuck cares?"

****

The second night in Lakeview didn't happen. Dwayne had them all on the bus by 11:00 Saturday morning. Everyone but Freddie was furious about it. The men argued in the back of the bus the entire way home, a discussion K.C. wasn't invited to join in. She and Sue stewed at the front. Emmy tried to cheer K.C. by telling her how wonderful she was, but neither of them was in the mood for happy talk, and they spent the last two and a half hours in silence.

To make matters worse, the manager of the Bullhead refused to pay them for either night, since they'd broken their contract.

The group was glum when they arrived in Waterton by mid-afternoon. Dwayne offered to take everyone to shoot snooker and drink beer at Townsend's Rack and Cue.

Freddie wasn't feeling up to it, and K.C. didn't know how to play pool. Sue was still fuming, not only at the apes in Lakeview, but at Dwayne for backing down to them. "You get me with a stick in my hand," Sue told him, "and I'll use one of your nuts as the cue ball."

"Take Bird home for me?" Freddie said.

"What's wrong?" Sue said.

Freddie glanced at K.C. and mouthed, *Not a word*. "Just under the weather, I guess. All I need's a good night's sleep."

Chapter 38

FREDDIE TOOK A NEWSPAPER from a rack in the clinic's lobby to read while he waited to see Dr. Thomas.

In the four days since Lakeview, his body had ached so bad he didn't want to move. He was hot, he was cold, sweating every night between chills. His hands were blotched with new bruises, caused by no more than the pressure of holding his trombone. He felt dizzy and sick to his stomach. Was it really worse, or did it only seem that way now that he knew what it was?

Whichever, he was worn out and beat down in ways he'd never been before. Until this morning the only reason he'd gotten out of bed was to use the toilet. He tried to eat, but it just came back up.

A gig had never done that to him before. When everything else was against him, music had always uplifted him, made him whole.

And yet, here he was.

He went alone this time. Not even White Bird could comfort him today. He wasn't sure he'd have the energy to handle her weeping again anyway.

He lifted the paper from his lap. The headline of the story

on the bottom half of the fold read "ROTH MURDER SUSPECT KILLS SELF."

"Albert Bender, 55, arrested in August for the murder of Gilbert Hoyle during the Roth strike, was found dead in the LaPorte City jail last night."

Freddie shook his head as he scanned the article. According to the deputy who found him, Bender had hanged himself with a noose he'd fashioned from his bedsheet. He'd asked for a pencil and paper to write a letter to his lawyer. Instead, he'd left a note on the bed that said, *I didn't see him.*

He'd always claimed that he'd fired his gun out the window of his car to scare away the strikers who were harassing him, and that Hoyle had just happened to stick his head in the window at that very moment.

Freddie folded the paper and put it back on the rack. The dumb shit proved he didn't want to hang—by hanging himself. On the other hand, he got to leave on his own terms. His trial had been scheduled for November. It would likely have been open and shut, two or three days, a guilty verdict and a death sentence from the judge. But then there would've been appeals to higher courts, and denials, and the whole thing could have stretched out for a year or two. Maybe Bender didn't want to have to think about dying for that long.

Still, Freddie wondered what had gone through his mind just before the final fall. Fear? Anger? Regret? Relief? Prayers?

When Nurse Lindy called his name, he hobbled into the examination room and sat on the table. The nurse took his temperature and blood pressure. "You look like a long stretch of bad highway," she said. "Temp's high, but your blood pressure's not too bad for someone your age."

He'd liked Lindy the first time they met. Sassy and

unsentimental. "Glad it's you," he said. "Didn't care much for that nurse Saint-something."

"St. Croix. Celeste is okay, just got into nursing a little later than most."

He looked at her nametag, L. BEERMAN, RN. "Your name really Beerman?"

"No, it's Hattie McDaniel—the hell kind of question is that?"

"Schlitz or Pabst?"

"Hilarious. Like I've never heard that before. I hate beer. I married into the name. So what's going on?"

"Didn't doc tell you? He says I got leukemia."

Lindy shook her head. "I haven't seen your charts. You must be the one he called Buckles in for."

"He's the cancer doctor, right?"

"Oncologist, yeah. Had the needle biopsy yet?"

"Ain't looking forward to it."

"Nobody does."

Dr. Thomas opened the door and strolled in carrying a clipboard. "Ah, Mr. Ross, I was hoping we'd see you soon." He looked at the readings Lindy had written down. "Ouch—a hundred and one? Bet you're feeling lousy."

"Ain't been able to keep anything down since Sunday."

He placed a stethoscope to Freddie's chest. "That's just nerves. Your pulse is a little fast. Lungs are okay." He pulled a chair next to the table. "Nurse, can you step outside for a moment?"

As soon as Lindy pulled the door shut, Freddie thought, *Here it comes.* He took a deep breath. "Go on, doc, you can tell me."

"No way to sugarcoat this, I'm afraid. I spoke with Dr. Buckles. He looked at your blood test and X-rays. That, and the fact you're symptomatic already, led him to doubt the necessity of a bone marrow biopsy."

For a moment Freddie allowed himself to hope that meant good news. But no one had to sugarcoat good news. "How about that new drug?"

"Aminopterin. Can't get it. It's still experimental. Even if we could, there'd be no guarantee it would work on you. It's only been tried with children."

"Why would it work on them but not me?"

"Doesn't matter. It's not available. The only other treatment option is radiation, arsenic, and thorium-X. We could try it, but Dr. Buckles and I are in agreement that your disease is too far progressed for that to be effective. It might extend your life by a month or two, but you'd feel miserable the whole time."

"So what are you saying?"

"You know what I'm saying, Mr. Ross. I can prescribe pain killers. A fever reducer. Anti-nausea medication. Those will help with the symptoms."

"So I just gotta go home and die?"

Thomas patted him on the shoulder. "I hate this part of my job."

Freddie threw up on the floor. He didn't have time to make it to the trash can three feet away. The doctor gave him a box of tissues. Freddie's hands shook too much to hold them. Thomas wiped his mouth for him.

Then they sat in silence for a few minutes, facing each other with a pool of vomit at the doctor's feet. Thomas probably had other patients he needed to see, patients he could help, but for now he was content to stay with Freddie.

"How can I go from 'not dying' to 'dying' so fast?" Freddie said. "Maybe if I'd come in sooner?"

"It's cancer, Mr. Ross. No one knows how it's going to go,

even if you get after it early."

"Guess I don't need to make plans for Christmas?"

"Maybe Halloween. *Maybe.* If you haven't already, you'll need to get your affairs in order soon. Let me write you those prescriptions. You can pick them up at the pharmacy. I'm so sorry, Mr. Ross. These are the times I wished I'd been an accountant."

Freddie stood up on legs that were already weak. Thomas caught him before he fell, and called Lindy in to get him a wheelchair.

"I can walk," Freddie insisted.

And he did, unaided, one wobbly step at the time.

He got his medicine and stumbled to his car. He put the key in the ignition but didn't turn it. Instead, he leaned forward and put his forehead on the wheel. Sometimes a man just couldn't catch a break.

Now he knew what Albert Bender must have been thinking in that moment before the fall.

****

Freddie took his pills and sat on his bed.

He was angry.

He was furious.

He was enraged.

First at Dr. Thomas, a healer who couldn't heal him, but later at God, His angels, or anyone else who had the power to pull a dirty trick like this. In the end, though, he saved his deepest layer of bitterness for Shay. Whatever his failings, for more than thirty years he had tried to comfort her. It hadn't been enough, but he'd stuck with her no matter what. Now, when he needed her, she was a memory, a bad taste, an unscratchable itch.

"*She didn't know I was sick.*" That was what he'd told

K.C.

Shouldn't have mattered that he was sick.

Shouldn't have *mattered*.

Shay was his wife, goddammit. That meant something, or should. If marriage didn't guarantee love, it should at least require decency.

He wasn't hot, but Freddie turned his fan on for the noise. The sound of cars going by outside annoyed him. Some of the drivers were likely among the hundred thousand people he might have glimpsed in his life, encounters so brief he seemed immortal by comparison. Only now he knew he wasn't. Yet those people drove past his house on the way to the rest of their lives, unaware that they might or might not have seen Freddie—unconcerned, just going about their normal business.

He didn't have a "rest of his life," and the ones who did pissed him off.

He lay on his side. He didn't know what to do—he'd never been dying before. Was there a way he was supposed to feel?

Fear? Check.

Anger? Check

Regret? Check.

Relief? Hell, no.

Prayerful? What for? God could click His fingers and make the cancer go away, but He wouldn't. Why waste a miracle on a broke-down nigger in Waterton, Iowa? Nobody would know about it. Nobody would care. Nobody would be converted. Got to save them fireworks and magic shows for people who make the headlines.

Maybe Freddie didn't yet understand what Bender'd been thinking. Bender knew the exact moment of his death. Freddie's was somewhere out there in the near but nonspecific future. Maybe nobody knew anything until that moment, and then it was too late.

He couldn't sleep. He couldn't get out of bed. He didn't want to be alone and he didn't want company. K.C. had gone with him for the initial diagnosis. She'd never know how much that meant to him. But thinking about *her* pissed him off, too. Shay blamed him for not healing the trauma of her life, but what did K.C. blame Jack for? By all accounts he was a nice kid who loved her and would do right by her.

But White Bird was a kid, too. She didn't have the experiences that allowed older folks to put things in perspective. She threw him out for some little lie? Stupid, but molehills and mountains. She'd learn.

And because she'd learn, and because she was young, she'd live long enough to regret leaving Jack. Shay never would. She'd go to her grave resenting Freddie for not being able to unhang Sloan or unrape her and her mother.

She'd come and gone several times over the years. He'd never learned to like it, but he'd accepted that it was going to happen. Experience—no wringing of hands or gnashing of teeth, just another day in the life.

But no amount of experience had prepared him for *this*. Nobody got practice runs with their own death. It would come, and he would go. There wouldn't be any bargaining.

Freddie put a pillow over his face. He was paralyzed by a creeping dread. Maybe Bender had had the right idea.

No, he thought. *Goddammit, no.* That way was for cowards, and he was no coward. The pain pills were kicking in, better than reefer ever had. He didn't feel sick to his stomach, and for the moment he wasn't sweating with fever. He still felt battered and worn out, but how was that different than any other day in the past few years?

Fuck it. Fuck it all. The leukemia was going to get him, no way around that. But not today. Not this week. Not next week. He was going to make it to the hog roast at the farm on the second. Then he was going to play the Bluenotes' gig at Electrical Park a week later. After that, who knew? But hell or high water, he *would* hold on that long.

Chapter 39

SHE WAS SEVEN AND her sisters wouldn't dance with her. Kenny let them listen to the radio while their parents were out celebrating their anniversary. K.C. had forgotten all but one of the songs from that night. Twelve years later, however, she still remembered how she felt when Kathryn and Krissy, then fifteen and twelve, danced the Lindy Hop with each other but not with her. "You're too little," they said. "This dance is hard. It's only for grownups."

When crying and stomping her feet only made them yell at her, she flopped onto the sofa and sulked.

Then the station played "The Glory of Love." K.C. would never forget that. The Benny Goodman Orchestra. Kenny got up from studying at the dining room table and held out his hand to K.C. "I'll dance with you, Squirt."

He was nearly a foot taller than her, so he picked her up and hugged her to his body. As vocalist Helen Ward crooned on the radio, Kenny sang softly in K.C.'s ear so only she could hear.

> You've got to give a little, take a little,
> And let your poor heart break a little.
> That's the story of, that's the glory of love.

When the song was over, Kathryn and Krissy were glowering on the sofa, and K.C. was the happiest little girl in the whole world.

****

It wasn't 1936 anymore, and K.C. didn't know how to feel. She lay on her bed in her jammies, twisting strands of her hair as she tried to make sense of Lakeview. There was no question that most of the people at the Bullhead Ballroom had loved her. One of the Bluenotes had told her that when a band rode the wave on a number in front of an enthusiastic audience like that, the experience was better than sex. Having now done both, she had to agree. The way they crowded the stage, applauding, cheering, pleading for her autograph... She'd never known anything like it. Except maybe that dance with Kenny.

But then some of those same fans had followed the bus back to the motel. They'd reacted just like Freddie'd said they would. Was it going to be that way every time? Love her onstage and hate her off? Or would some audiences skip the adoration part and go right to "nigger-loving whore"?

"Kenny?"

Hi, Squirt. Or should I call you K.C. now?

"You saw what happened at the motel?"

If a ghost could sigh, Kenny sighed. *I see everything you see. I hear everything you hear. I am you, K.C. There is no Kenny anymore. Kenny is dead.*

"Don't say that. I need you. We all need you. You said Mom, Dad, and the girls talk to you, too."

You said that to yourself. You're still doing it.

"Shut up."

Remember when you said "You're not even real?"

"Shut up, shut up, shut up." She covered her ears with her hands, but there was no sound to block out.

You need to move on. Not as us. *As* you.

"I can't live without you."

You've been doing it since 1943. Gotta go, Squirt.

"I can bring you back anytime I want."

Let me go.

"I'm not ready."

If not now, when?

"I don't know. It'll never be just me. It's always going to be us."

Not always.

"Don't go. Please please *ple-e-e-ease*."

There was no answer.

****

Inside the issue of the paper that proclaimed "ROTH MURDER SUSPECT KILLS SELF," K.C. came upon an ad. It was a large, quarter-page attention-getter.

ELECTRICAL PARK BALLROOM
SATURDAY, OCTOBER 9
NINE P.M. 'TIL MIDNIGHT
ONE SHOW ONLY
THE BLUENOTES
FEATURING K.C. "WHITE BIRD" BROWN
YOU'VE NEVER HEARD
OR SEEN
ANYTHING LIKE THIS!

Next to the ad was a brief story about a "near riot" in Lakeview, Minnesota, that had broken out over a white girl who played in a black band.

K.C. read the story twice. Honestly? First, yes, it had been ugly, but it had hardly been a riot. Second, why would anyone in Waterton care what had happened in a small town a hundred and seventy-five miles away in another state?

She suspected Dwayne was the source of the ad, and probably the story, too, to drum up advance publicity for their gig. He didn't seem to be tight with his money, but a quarter-page ad had to cost some serious dollars.

Or maybe the story came from another source and that manager of Electrical Park, Tim Piper, figured to cash in on the notoriety.

Either way, she wasn't sure it was a good idea. Sure, the more people, the better, if Dwayne had somehow wrangled a piece of the gate. But Waterton had the largest percentage of minorities in the state. It was a divided town. The whites had hated the blacks since at least '09, when the railroad had brought trainloads of them up from the South as strikebreakers. And the blacks hated the whites, well, because the whites hated *them*. A white girl in a black band might be seen as salt in the wound to both sides.

Whoever was responsible, she hoped they knew what they were doing.

K.C. got dressed and went down to the pay phone to call Narlins to find out when the next rehearsal was.

Ruthie answered. She must have had a bad day, because she was surly. "Bird, I got no idea," she said. "Haven't seen more than two of them at a time in here, and they're always bickering."

"About what? Was it me?"

"I heard your name come up. That's all I'm saying."

"Even Freddie?"

"He ain't been in all week."

K.C. didn't like the sound of that. "Can you give him a message if you see him?"

"Hell, yes, I love being the answering service for all you freeloaders. Need to buy your own damn phones."

"Will you ask him if he can meet me at the library on Friday at 3:00."

"If he doesn't show, that means I didn't see him."

"Fair enough. And one more question. Do you know if Sue will be at the hog roast?"

Ruthie hesitated, then said, "You don't wanna be the only white person. You don't got to worry. Sue'll be there. You won't be the only snowflake in the coal."

And she hung up.

K.C. stared at the receiver for a few moments before hanging it up and checking the coin return. What bug had got up Ruthie's ass?

****

The weather was nice, so K.C. walked to the East-Side Library. She got there plenty early and waited over an hour, but Freddie didn't come. She assumed that meant he hadn't been to Narlins to get the message, which worried her. It wasn't like him not to go there several times a week. She knew one reason that might keep him away, but she didn't want to think about that.

As she headed out the door, it occurred to her that she didn't know where any of the band members lived. All communication had gone through Ruthie, newspaper ads, or word of mouth. Now that it appeared Kenny was set on leaving, she needed to speak with Freddie.

A black car sped through the intersection of East Fifth and Mulberry, but it wasn't a Ford. Dammit, where *did* Freddie live? Smoky Row somewhere, but that only narrowed things down to a square mile or two south of the Illinois Central yards. If she knew his address she could take a bus there.

But she didn't. Depressed, she walked back home. The sweet stench of Roth's hog kill had settled in like invisible fog. The Oak River was still running a little high from the recent rain, although the current had calmed. A flock of Canadian geese floated on the surface, honking and preening.

She remembered a stupid joke Kenny had told her when she was little. She'd fallen for it every time.

"Ever noticed that when geese fly in a "V," one side is always longer than the other? You know why that is, Squirt?"

"Uh-uh."

"Because there's more geese on that side."

And then he'd ruffle her hair and laugh. Looking dumb was worth it just for that.

Where she should have turned right onto Wellington to go to her apartment, she turned left and went toward Dale's. She had no reason to go there, unless Jack was working. And if he was working, she had even less reason. It was late enough in the day—his classes would be over by now. She tried to talk herself out of it with each step, but somehow her feet kept carrying her forward.

What would she say to him?

What would he say to her?

What the hell are you doing? she thought. And then she strolled in anyway, trying to act casual, just another customer looking for pie filling or spaghetti in a box.

Jack stood in his usual place behind the meat counter. Although he was weighing sausages for old Mrs. Brolin, he noticed K.C. immediately. Even from across the store she could see his expression. Anger, heartbreak, hope? Maybe a little of each, but no joy. However he felt, he didn't acknowledge her presence. He simply turned back to Mrs. Brolin and wrapped her sausages in brown paper.

To her horror K.C. realized that Austin was behind the soda fountain.

Austin.

Why would Dale hire *him* back? Was he that desperate for assistant managers?

Then she wondered if Austin and Jack still hated each other, or were they bosom buddies now, united in their disdain for K.C.?

Whatever wild hare had prompted her to go to the store, it was gone now, and she fled out the door, nearly bowling over little Davy in her haste to escape.

****

Since the manager at the Bullhead hadn't paid them, K.C. had little money left in her purse and no income at all. Mr. Somers had been nice enough to give her a break for two weeks, but that had been two weeks ago. So when she saw an envelope taped to her door, she knew what was in it. She pulled it off and inserted her key into the lock. As usual, it took forever to work. Somers had promised to replace it some time ago, but she supposed there'd be no reason to now, at least not for her sake.

She placed the dreaded envelope on the kitchen table and checked her refrigerator for something to eat. All she had was a half-empty can of Spam, two bottles of Pepsi, and some droopy celery. Yuck.

A breeze brought Roth's in through her one window. She closed it, then opened a bottle of pop and sat at the table, staring at the envelope. She rarely got mail in her box downstairs, and now here was this note. Stuck to her door for the other residents to see. They'd all know what it meant, which was embarrassing. She took a deep breath, tore off the end the envelope and blew it open so she could pull out the letter.

Here it comes, she thought as she unfolded the paper.

Dear Miss Brown,

This is a letter I wish I did not have to write, but I have responsibilities to the building's owner and to my family. Financially, I cannot continue to carry you for much longer. Ethically, it's not fair to the other tenants who are on time with their payments.

I hate to do this, but if you have not caught up on your rent by the middle of October, I will have no choice but to offer your apartment to someone else. I hope you understand this is nothing personal, but simply a business decision.

Sincerely,
Herm Somers,
Superintendent, Wellington Court Apartments

Nothing personal? Couldn't get more personal than evicting a girl from her home, but she didn't hold it against him. She'd known this day was coming, and sooner rather than later.

What was she going to do?

There was no one for her to turn to for help. Dad and Mom would be happy to know she'd left Jack, but she'd burned every bridge that led back home.

Jack? No way.

Freddie, Dwayne, or any of the other Bluenotes? Not until she earned it as a band member. It wasn't their fault the manager in Minnesota wouldn't pay them.

Kathryn? *Dear sister, I realize I haven't spoken to you in ages, but I've meant to call, and oh, by the way, could you lend me some money to pay my rent?* Yeah, that would work...

That left Krissy and Ben. Krissy would be willing, but the situation with Ben was still awkward. He might think of it as blackmail.

She took a swallow of Pepsi. Nobody liked her.

Nobody liked her.

And whose fault was that? She listened for Kenny's voice in that question, but it was just her.

Things weren't hopeless yet. The middle of October took her past the Electrical Park gig. Maybe that would get her by until the next gig. Whenever that was. Curtis's Gardens in November was the only one she was aware of, but there had to be something before that.

Although it wasn't even 5:30 yet, K.C. decided to change into her pajamas. She couldn't justify spending her few remaining dollars to eat out or see a movie, and didn't have anyone to go with anyway. Another night alone, oh boy...

She went into the bedroom, laid Kenny's photo face down on the nightstand—he might think he was gone, but she didn't—and stripped down to nothing. Her laundry had been stacking up for over a week. Her favorite jammies were filthy. She rummaged through her dresser for something else to wear. Tucked into the back of a drawer was one of Jack's T-shirts, just right for his height, but long enough to be a nighty for her.

She held it to her nose. His scent was still on it, faint but enough to stir her feelings—one in particular that wasn't at all welcome.

She was naked.

Jack smelled good.

Twinge and squirm.

Good grief, not *now*.

She stormed out of her bedroom and past the open window. This high up, no one could see in, but, piss on it, so what if they could?

Furious and stupidly horny, K.C. ripped Mr. Somers's letter into small pieces. That'd fix him. She yanked opened the fridge and pulled out a piece of celery. Its droopy stalk reminded her of Jack again. She stared at it, entertained a wicked notion for about half a second, then said aloud, "Oh, hell, no."

She tossed the vegetable into the garbage and hurried into the bathroom for a long, long shower.

****

Morning came. After hours of tedium, K.C. took a bus to Narlins for their Saturday rehearsal, trusting that Freddie would drive her home. Except that Freddie didn't come. Neither did anyone else, except Syd.

It didn't surprise her that Ironhead and Screech weren't there, and Thump could have gotten himself involved with the needle again. But Catfish and Leon? Dwayne? Freddie?

Especially Freddie.

"Where is everyone?" she said. They sat on the stage, legs dangling over the edge.

"Little trouble in paradise," Syd said. "We'll work it out."

"Is it me?"

"We all knew what could happen at Lakeview, but it spooked some of the boys."

"A few hicks in a small town?"

"What if it happens here?"

"There are lots of colored people in Waterton. Whites ought to be used to you by now."

"But are they ready for *you*?"

"So I play one gig, and I'm out?"

Syd patted her shoulder. He was wearing a sleeveless T-shirt that showed off his muscular shoulders and arms. "Nothing like that. You're good, K.C. You're really good. We're all proud of you. But some think it could look like we're trying to make a statement by bringing a white girl onstage with us. We're jazz musicians. We entertain people. We don't want to make a statement."

"Are you one of the 'we'?"

Syd smiled. "I'm one of the 'they.' I've got no problem with it. I went to the army to make a statement."

"So did my brother."

Syd gave her a quick hug. "Yeah, I know, kid. Doesn't look like anyone's coming today. Need a ride?"

"Thanks, but it's early. The buses are still running. What about tomorrow?"

He hopped down from the stage. "They'll be here if I have to drag them by their shirt collars. See you then, Bird. Come ready to strut your stuff."

After he left she remained on the stage for a few more minutes, thinking, until Ruthie poked her head out and said, "Hey, I'd like to lock up for a couple hours before we open so I can get a bite."

"Okay." K.C. was hungry, too. Maybe she'd go to the S&S on West Fifth to buy a few groceries with what little money she had. It was a little farther away from her apartment than Dale's, but she'd learned her lesson about going back there.

She returned her sax to the locker upstairs and then trudged back down. On her way out, Ruthie said, "I called Sue to make sure. She *is* going to the hog roast. Don't know why you're nervous, though. We're all friends, ain't we?"

****

Sue picked her up the next day in a '39 Chevy. Freddie had asked her to.

Her car smelled like an ashtray.

Tobacco was better than reefer, but K.C. cranked down her window anyway. "Why didn't Freddie come himself?" she said, pretending ignorance.

"He said you'd know why." She drew in on her cigarette. "He wants me to drop you at his place after Narlins. He'll bring you home."

"Is he going to be at rehearsal?"

Sue stopped at the red light just before the bridge. Blowing smoke out the side of her mouth, she said, "Doesn't sound like it. So what's going on? I saw him at Audrey's. He looked terrible."

K.C. gazed out the window at the Sixth Street drainage tunnel. "He didn't tell you?" she said. "He made me promise..."

The light turned green. Sue accelerated toward the bridge. "But?"

"It's too big. I can't hold it anymore."

Sue reached out and squeezed her fingers. "You can tell me, sweetie. He's sick, isn't he? As in gonna-die sick?"

K.C. bit her lip and nodded. Maybe if she didn't say it out loud, it wouldn't count as breaking a confidence.

"Goddammit, goddammit, god*damn* it," Sue said. "Nothing they can do?"

K.C. shrugged. Maybe, maybe not.

Sue seemed to understand her silence. She turned the car toward the North End. "Son-of-a-bitch. I got my hands full trying to keep Thump out of the morgue and Toad out of my pants. Now I've got to look after Freddie, too?"

K.C. turned to the window again. She didn't want to talk about Freddie anymore, and she didn't want to not talk about him. "Ruthie said you're going to the hog roast?"

"It's just a bunch of people eating pig. Ironhead might be dumb as a sack of hammers, but you've got to taste his Southern cooking—it's almost as good as Audrey's. And Pap? Jesus, what a character."

"What about the wives?"

Sue crushed the remains of her cigarette in the car ashtray. "What about them?"

"I'm kind of scared what they think of me."

"You met them at Spits's visitation."

"That was before Lakeview."

"They know you were there with them, and none of them filed for divorce. So what's really bothering you? If it was their wives, you wouldn't've joined the band in the first place."

The only snowflake in the coal.

That's what Ruthie had said, and she was right. It didn't make sense. K.C. was comfortable with the band, but that was just playing music. She knew what to expect from them. At the farm there'd be dozens of black people she didn't know. It didn't matter how open-minded she thought she was, if *they* weren't.

Anyone would be nervous in that situation. "I'm not prejudiced," she said.

"We're all prejudiced, sweetie," Sue said. "It's just a matter of who. When I was your age, I thought I was hep, too, but I lived in a neighborhood where everyone was white. Pretty easy to be brave there. Then I started driving a school bus up in the North End. Dealing with parents was a bitch.

The black ones were no worse than whites, but they were, you know, black. Dad hated them because of the railroad strike. I guess some of that stuck with me, because for the first couple of months I damn near peed myself every time some colored mother looked at me crossways."

"What happened?"

Sue chuckled. "Toad happened. He's a pain in my ass now, but once upon a time... But that's another story. The way around being nervous is to stop thinking *black people* and start thinking *people*."

She turned into the Narlins lot.

"Then I don't have anything to worry about?" K.C. said. She made no move to get out of the Chevy. "They won't hate me or look at me funny?"

"So what if they do? Relax, I'll be there with you. Anyone gives you trouble, tell them to go suck a duck."

A poster on the door advertised Donald and the Diatonics. K.C. recalled them playing here before. A new band or something.

Syd and Dwayne pulled in right after them.

"He seems to be taking Spits's death well," K.C. said.

"Does he," Sue said. It wasn't a question.

"It's been five years for my brother, and I'm still not over it."

Sue shifted the Chevy into park and shut it off. They got out of the car. "Look a little closer," she said, holding the Narlins door open for her. "I'm surprised he hasn't shot himself."

The band practiced despite Freddie's absence, and sounded pretty good. K.C. didn't detect any of the animosity toward her that both Syd and Ruthie had hinted at, although there was a certain tension. Something was going on with them. She didn't ask, fearing an answer she wouldn't like.

Just before she and Sue left for Freddie's, Dwayne said, "Hey, White Bird, I got something cooking. I think you'll like it. Tell you more when I'm sure."

****

A spanking new 1948 Hudson Commodore Six was parked in Freddie's driveway, its breezy blue paint job a cheerful contrast to Freddie's black Ford. Or was it a '47? The two models looked almost identical.

"Whose car is that?" Sue said, but she declined to come in. She let K.C. out at the curb and drove off.

The house looked sturdy enough, although the roof needed new shingles and the paint around the windows was peeling. K.C. guessed Freddie's hands made it hard for him to do much manual labor.

As she approached the porch, the front door opened and a light-skinned black man came out. He looked familiar, but K.C. couldn't place where she'd seen him.

"Afternoon, Miss Brown," he said, tipping his hat at her.

"Do I know you?"

"You will."

Without another word he got into his Hudson and backed onto the street. K.C. watched him until he turned south at the intersection, then she knocked on the door.

"Ain't locked," Freddie called.

She found him sitting at a table next to an old refrigerator, legal-sized papers spread out in front of him. She was shocked by his appearance. How could he have deteriorated this much in only a week? So thin, so frail. Veins popped out on his forehead and hands. He was sweating. He smelled terrible.

K.C. nearly bolted. "Sue said you wanted to see me, but it looks like you're busy, so..."

"So what? You gonna walk back to the west side from here? Sit your ass down, Bird. This concerns you."

She took the chair across from him—his odor really was atrocious—and looked around. The kitchen and living room were one area, carpeted with a material that might once have been green. There wasn't much furniture, but the house was so small the room seemed cluttered. It all looked like second- or third-generation hand-me-downs: an old couch, a rocking chair, a radio console, and an upright piano. The piano surprised her, since Freddie couldn't play anymore. It had been agonizing that night he'd tried at Narlins.

Two doors opened to his bedroom and bathroom. A third might lead to a closet or a basement.

Freddie looked up at her. His eyes were yellow and bloodshot at the same time. "I'm dying, White Bird. Nothing they can do."

She'd guessed that deep down, but to hear him say it so bluntly was a hammer to her chest. "There has to be."

"Nope. It won't be long, neither."

She looked at all the papers on the table. "Who was that man leaving as I came in?"

"Shay's cousin. Jeff Mimms. You saw him at the library. He's a lawyer."

Mr. Mimms's skin was as light as K.C. thought Emmy's should have been. "What was he doing here?"

It was a stupid question.

He shook his head. Good Lord, he looked weary. "Dying men need lawyers." He tapped on the papers with a pen. "These here? I'm divorcing Shay and changing my will."

"It's about time. She doesn't deserve you."

"Whether she does or not, it ain't about that."

"What is it about?"

"You ain't working at the grocery store no more, right? Prick up in Lakeview didn't pay us. Your boyfriend's gone. I figure you got nothing left to pay rent."

"I'm not taking money from you," she said with as much indignation as she could muster.

"Ain't talking charity. What I'm saying is I'm gonna need someone to look after me. It'll only be a little while."

She felt something like horror. She knew what he was going to ask. Sue had already told her she had her hands full with Thump and Toad. "What about your friends?" she said.

Freddie leaned back and stretched, his joints popping like brittle twigs. "You ain't my friend?"

"Well, yeah."

"I can't ask them, little Bird. I *can't.*"

"I bet you went to see Thump in the hospital. Was he embarrassed?"

"I ain't him."

"Your pride is stupid. They love you. They'll come if you ask."

"You don't get what I'm saying."

"What if you need help peeing, or..."

"I can still do that my own self."

"I don't have a car, Freddie. Buses only run during the day. You'd still need somebody at night."

"So move in, be my nurse. You can take my car whenever you want."

K.C. gasped. The suggestion was ridiculous. She almost laughed. A nineteen-year-old white girl living with a fifty-year-old colored man in the heart of black Waterton? What a great idea that was. "You know I can't do that."

He drooped like the celery she'd thrown away. His voice trembled. "You got to. Ain't no one else. I'm begging."

I don't want to be the one who finds you dead, she thought. "Where will I go after you're gone?"

Freddie shuffled the papers. "Don't you worry 'bout that."

K.C.'s heart was breaking. "Really, seriously. You're asking me to move into this house with you?"

"That's the first part," Freddie said.

****

The day was sunny and almost eighty, hot for October. Ironhead and Screech had set up a volleyball net behind the farmhouse. The lawn had recently been mowed, but the cut grass hadn't been raked, except for on the volleyball "court." Judging by its length, it was the first time it had been mowed in months.

Several children and a few adults were batting the ball around. K.C. didn't know any of them. The women were trying to get the men and children to set up plays, but everyone just knocked it over the net from wherever they were, front row, middle, or back.

She sat at one of the six picnic tables set up in the yard and inhaled the sweet aroma of pig sizzling on a spit. Ironhead was brushing it with some kind of barbecue sauce that smelled delicious. A dog the size of a brontosaurus thought so, too, because Ironhead was constantly shooing it away.

Sue was next to her on one side of the table, watching the game. A teenager introduced to K.C. as Chuck Elliot, Jr., Catfish's oldest, was on the other side, by Emmy.

Catfish's boy must have been about fifteen. Some of his comments to K.C. were filthier than little Davy's at the store. Unlike Davy, though, Chuck had obviously had some experience with girls, because he wasn't shy about telling her specifically what he wanted to put where.

"Keep it in your pants, tiger," Sue said, "or I'll cut it off and cook it with the pig."

"Have to move the pig, then. Ain't room on the stick for both," he said. "Well, how 'bout you, Miss Emmaline?"

Sue glared at him, but Emmy only giggled. "Chuckie-boy," she said, "I'd still pluck out my own eyes before I'd give you a second look."

"Fuck you," he said, and wandered off to hustle someone else.

"Ain't gonna happen," Emmy called.

Catfish, Thump, Toad, and Leon were at the next picnic table over. The other tables were crowded mostly with strangers. K.C. recognized a couple of the wives of the Bluenotes from Spits's visitation, although she didn't remember which was which. The rest were just faces.

Two toddlers giggled as they chased each other between and under the tables.

Sue noticed her looking and said, "The little ones are Sarah and Harvey, 'Fish's youngest. They're two and three. Next table over, the gal in the middle is 'Fish's wife Janae. On the right is Leon's wife Cindy. She goes by Dee."

"I was introduced to her and... Marlye, is it?"

"Syd's wife. She's over there next to him by the house. Nice lady. The whole family is nice."

Marlye, Syd, Freddie, and Dwayne lay back in lawn chairs in the shade of an elm tree, drinking beer from bottles. They seemed to be having a good time, lots of laughing and toasting.

"Think he's told them yet?" K.C. whispered to Sue.

"Not carrying on like that, he hasn't."

"Told them what?" Emmy said.

"Nothing," K.C. and Sue said together.

Sue nodded back toward the picnic tables. "Anyway, the

boy next to Janae is Nat, Syd's son. 'Fish's middle two, Lenny and Sally, are playing volleyball. The rest are some relatives of Ironhead and Screech's. The only one I really know is Pap, but he's still inside."

"So Catfish and Syd have kids. What about Leon and Cindy?"

"They did. A little boy, Anthony. He died of a kidney infection before he turned one. That was back in '36, I think."

"That's sad. None since?"

"According to Dee, they've never tried. Leon's a big flirt, but... Well. Let's just say Anthony's death took a lot out of them both."

What a shame, K.C. thought. Leon was *so* good looking. Cindy was pretty, too. Their kids would have been heartbreakers.

Screech and an older gentlemen—Pap?—came out of the house, followed by four women and several teenage girls. They delivered bowls of food to the picnic tables.

"What's all this?" K.C. said.

"Must be the white table," Pap said, then winked at Emmy, "'cept for this pretty lady. Well, we got black-eyed peas, collard greens, mustard greens, and turnip greens here. Corn pone, hominy, and grits here. And just wait till Ironhead gets done with that pig. Hog jowls, chitlins, and maws. And chess pie for dessert. Sweet Jesus, that's eatin'."

One of the girls set a glass in front of each of them. "Sweet tea," she said without being asked.

"After," Pap said, "I'm gonna get out my banjo, and me and the boys'll play you some real music. Ever heard blue grass done right?"

And that's what they did. Once Ironhead carved up the guest of honor, the volleyballers were called to the tables, the children corralled, and a group prayer spoken, they ate. And ate. And ate. K.C. was so full she vowed she'd never touch food again. It was all delicious, even after they told her what chitlins and maws were made of.

The dog, whose named turned out to be either Clarence or Dumb-Luck, depending upon who she asked, did well for himself, too, bounding from table to table for scraps. By late afternoon he was flat on his side by the house, snoring away.

Pap retrieved his banjo. He finger-picked on the back porch. Screech strummed an acoustic guitar. One of the teenage girls sawed on a fiddle. Thump had brought his standup bass.

The music was joyous. Women and children danced on the lawn. Men slapped their thighs in rhythm.

It was the most fun K.C. had had in years. After all her silly fears, it was just a picnic like any other. She'd hoped to draw closer to the band members, and she felt like she had.

Then, as the festivities were winding down and the women carried the dishes to the kitchen for washing, Freddie hobbled toward K.C.

He leaned against the side of the table and cleared his throat. "Got something to say," he announced. He had to shush them several times before everyone quieted enough for him to deliver his message. They all looked at him with a sudden wariness, as if they sensed that whatever he was about to say was not going to be pleasant.

And then, in a steady, unemotional voice, he told them.

A few people tried to laugh, as if it were a bad joke. When it became clear he was serious, the sniffles and tears started, the protests and denials.

"Electrical Park," Freddie said. "Gonna be my last gig."

Chapter 40

HE LOANED HER THE FORD—gave it to her, for all practical purposes. The first three nights she wouldn't stay with him. She'd wait as long as it took for him to fall asleep, and return as early in the morning as she could, but spent the nights in her own bed.

She could do that because Freddie had sent Sue over to square her rent with the superintendent.

On the fourth night he took the car keys from her. He was half reclined on his Goodwill couch, with K.C. sitting on the rocker. "Help me up," he said. "Gotta piss."

"You said I wouldn't have to do that."

"I can hold my own pecker. All I need's for you to walk me there and back."

She felt his forehead for a fever. "You're burning up."

"Another reason you got to stay."

K.C. went into the bathroom for a wet washcloth. As she laid it across his forehead, she said, "What do your neighbors say about me being here?"

"Fuck the neighbors. They can see I'm sick. They ask, I'll just tell them you're my nurse."

"Where am I going to sleep?"

"You can have my bed. I like this old couch fine. Pretty sure leukemia ain't catching."

"My father will shoot me."

"Well, then, I'll shoot him."

K.C. smiled. Her chin was quivering but, just a little, she did smile. "Like hell."

"Lord's set aside a place in heaven for you, little Bird. But I still gotta pee."

****

Sue didn't work at the library the next afternoon, so she and K.C. went shopping for a "Bluenotes outfit." While they were gone, Freddie took more pain pills than he should and smoked a lot of reefer. His body hurt. The pills and the weed helped with that, but couldn't do anything to give him strength.

Weak as he was, he forced himself to walk, even if it was only to the mailbox to get the newspaper. It was silly, when he thought about it—what was happening in the world that could possibly matter to him now?

He sat at the kitchen table, even though lying down was more comfortable.

An earthquake in Turkmenistan—*where?*—killed a hundred thousand on Wednesday. Just that many more people to greet him in heaven or hell. Probably hell.

The Cleveland Indians beat the Boston Braves 4-1 to even the World Series at a game apiece. So what?

The Bluenotes, featuring "White Bird" Brown, was playing at Electrical Park on Saturday night.

Freddie was surprised Dwayne was continuing to run the ad. Considering the dissention in the band and the possibility of race trouble, he thought Dwayne might want to keep the event as low key as possible. But it was Dwayne's money, and the band's problem. Freddie's problems would be going away soon.

Before he knew it White Bird was home, carrying packages from Block's.

"Sue ain't coming in?"

"She thinks Thump's back on the needle. Toad's been with him, but he has to go to work."

"Whatcha got?"

K.C. smiled and headed toward the bedroom. "You'll see."

She went in and closed the door. When she came out, she was wearing a *real* Bluenotes outfit: white shirt, black suitcoat and pants, black bowtie, and mirror-shiny black shoes, just like the clothes the fellas wore. "Know how hard it was to find men's clothes in my size?" she said. "We had to go to the children's section. It was embarrassing."

Freddie tried not to laugh, but couldn't help himself. She looked like a white version of Nat Clayton, Syd's son. Except for the long hair she could pass for a boy. She wasn't well endowed, allowing the jacket to disguise her feminine attributes. "Take the car keys. There's a sack for you in the trunk. Bring it on in, but don't peek."

"Let me change first."

"No, I need you in them clothes."

She was gone and back in less than a minute. "What is it?" she said, handing him the sack.

"Little surprise I bought you. Sit down and close your eyes."

She was twitchy with curiosity. He was afraid she'd be disappointed when she saw the gift. Freddie opened the sack and pulled out the Fedora he'd bought for her at St. Vincent DePaul. He blew the dust off it and put it on her. Unlike his own hat, which had covered half her face, this one was a perfect fit.

K.C. reached up, examined it with her fingertips and broke into a wide grin. "My own hat!"

"Go on, take a look at yourself."

She rushed to the bathroom to admire it in the mirror. She came out a little teary-eyed. "Oh, Freddie, I know it's only a hat, but it makes me feel like I'm one of you. I mean, the rehearsals, playing at Lakeview, the hog roast—it was all good, but this..."

"Sweet child, you *are* one of us."

She ran back to the table and gave him a big hug from behind. In her gratitude, her grip was a little too enthusiastic. "Go easy," he said.

"Sorry. Can I wear this on stage?"

"We never wear hats when we play. Management don't like it."

"Never had a white girl in the band before, either."

"Sure haven't."

"Well, then, it's time to break more rules."

"What the hell," Freddie said. "Maybe we'll all wear them. Sunglasses, too. We'd be some real hepcats."

****

That night she drew him a bath, then left the bathroom while he undressed. Once he was in the tub with his lower half hidden by bubbles, he called her back in. She was hesitant, but he assured her she wouldn't see anything she shouldn't.

When she poked her head in the door, he told her to drag a chair in from the kitchen, which she did. She was clearly uncomfortable, keeping her eyes anywhere but on him.

"Little Bird," he said, "know anything about the numbers racket?"

"I've heard of tennis rackets."

Freddie chuckled. "When I was your age I didn't know nothing either. It's gambling where folks bet on numbers. Illegal as hell. What'd happen was, some thugs'd go where a lot of folks got together, like at a bar." He dipped a washcloth in the water and dragged it over the back of his neck and behind his ears. The hot water there felt so good it gave him goose bumps. "The ones who went to the bars, they was called runners. They'd say, 'Pick three numbers from zero to nine and write them on a slip of paper.' Everybody paid a dollar to bet. Then the runners'd collect the money and the slips and take them to the head man in town, called the banker."

K.C. peered at him. "What were they betting on?"

Freddie hadn't been naked in the same room with a woman in ages, other than that one night after Shay's mother died. Nothing happened then, and nothing was going to happen now. He didn't even have the urge. "Every Tuesday the newspaper ran the number of shares sold on the New York Stock Exchange the day before. Whoever got the three last numbers of it right, won. The banker kept half the money, the winner got the other half. If more than one matched, the winners split their half. If no one did, the pot carried over till the next week—see what I'm saying?"

"That's dumb."

"It's gambling. Easy way to make a few bucks if you win and you ain't out much if you don't." Freddie fumbled with the washcloth, dropping it into the bath. He retrieved it and wrung it out over his head, letting the bubbly water sluice down his face. After savoring the warmth, he handed it to K.C. "Here, make yourself useful. Wash my back."

"I'm not going to do that."

"C'mon, I can't reach."

"How do you reach when I'm not here?"

"I don't. Just walk around with a dirty back, I guess."

She reluctantly took the cloth and brushed it across his shoulders. "Your skin feels different."

"Than what?"

"Mine."

"It ain't contagious."

K.C. dropped the cloth over the top his head. "Wash your own self," she said, but she sounded more amused than mad. She stepped away from the tub and looked him in the eyes. "So what do these numbers have to do with anything?"

"I was nineteen, just like you. All I wanted to do was play Joplin on the eighty-eights at Narlins. I didn't know nothing about nothing. Never heard of no numbers racket. Till one night I did. I always thought people was coming to listen to me. Pissed me off they was mostly coming for the numbers."

"This is about your fingers, isn't it? Freddie, what did you do?" Her tone got to sounding like a mama scolding.

"I had this list I played from. Forty-nine charts. I only played twenty-five or thirty in a gig, different ones every night, and never in the same order. You know, mix things up so folks don't get bored. Well, I heard about this numbers game, and it seemed to me the gangsters was making more from me playing than I was. So I come up with my own little scheme. It goes like this: I number my charts oh-one to forty-nine, so every one has two—what d'you call 'em?"

"Digits?"

"Every one has two digits. Say one night 'Alexander's Ragtime Band' is oh-one, 'Bill Bailey' oh-two, 'L'il Liza Jane' oh-three, and so on, up to 'Beale Street Blues' at forty-nine. Then I just throw the sheet music up in the air and pick them up off the floor in whatever order they fall in. That way even I don't know what I'm gonna play when, and the charts would have different numbers every week."

K.C. leaned against the sink and cocked her head at him in exactly the same way a dog did when it heard a strange noise. "I have no idea where this is going."

"I go to these runners and I say I want a piece of the action. I tell them my idea. Instead of the stock exchange, why don't they use the order of my charts to bet on? We could pick one as the cue piece. Say that was 'When the Saints Go Marching In.' Whenever I played it, folks'd bet on the titles of the three charts that came next. The winning numbers would be the second digit of the number the pieces was given that night. After I played 'Saints,' if I played 'Alexander,' then 'Beale Street,' then 'Jane,' those numbers would be oh-one, forty-nine, and oh-three. The second digits were one, nine, three. So that's what the winning bet would be. One, nine, three. If I didn't play 'Saints' one night, then the pot would roll over until next time. "I said I'd do it for just a little cut, you know, maybe five percent. That way I make a little extra money, and I know the people are really coming to hear me play."

"What did they say?"

"What d'you think? They said, 'Listen here, you some kind of wise guy? Ain't nothing wrong with the system we got. Folks know it's fair. Now, what you say would never work. Besides it being stupid, how we gonna know you won't rig it for yourself? All you gotta do is pretend the songs're in random order. Then you tell an accomplice the winning numbers before the gig and you both clean up every time. Ain't happening, kid.'"

Freddie slid down further into the bubbles so that only his head, shoulders, and knees stuck out of the water. "I told you, I was nineteen and stupid. If I'd've just let it go, nothing would've happened. But I was mad. I wasn't no cheat. So I said, 'Well, you don't give me a cut of your game, I'm going to the cops.'"

"And?"

"Couple nights later I'm practicing at Narlins. 'Twelfth Street Rag.' Last chart I ever played on the eighty-eights." He lifted his hands from the water. "They came for me with hammers. Just for spite, they busted up the piano keys, too."

Freddie winced as he recalled that night, gun at his head, him on his knees, fingers placed one at a time over the edge of the piano bench. They'd not only shattered his fingers, but they'd shattered them in different directions. His hands had become a tangle of bloody and broken sausages.

He splashed water on his face to hold his emotions. Thirty-one years, and it still burned in his soul.

"Jesus." K.C. turned away. Maybe she was imagining it, too, except that no one could imagine it if they hadn't been through it. "Did they go to jail?"

"Hell, no," Freddie snorted. "*I* did. There was two of them, their word against mine. Cops came. Seeing as my fingers was busted every which way and the runners didn't have a scratch, they probably figured out what really happened. But, hey, we was all just niggers to them. Someone had to go to jail, and they didn't care who."

"Freddie, I'm so sorry."

"Yeah, me, too. Loved them eighty-eights. After that, the 'bone was the only thing I could play." Suddenly Freddie didn't want to be in the water anymore. He didn't want to be anywhere. Soon enough, he wouldn't be, not in this world anyway... "Help me outta here," he said

K.C. didn't argue. She braced her feet against the base of the tub and offered her hands. He grasped them as best he could and pulled himself up.

Chapter 41

THE NEWSPAPER ADS WORKED. Throngs of people already surrounded Electrical Park when the bus arrived two hours before the show. Sue dropped them in the back so they could unload the instruments and keep Freddie's condition from view. Syd had found an old wheelchair for him, which of course Freddie squawked about using. He could barely walk now, but he was damned if he was going to be rolled onto stage like a cripple.

K.C. went around to the front to check out if there was anyone she recognized in the crowd. She stopped near the outside ticket window and scanned the faces. Within moments she heard Krissy's voice calling her name.

Her sister fought her way through the people, no easy thing for a small woman. She was huffing and sweating when she arrived. "Hi, Kasey," she said, and slapped her, just hard enough to hurt her feelings.

"What the hell?" K.C. said, more surprised than angry. "What was that for?"

"Ben."

"He told you? So why slap me? I didn't ask him to kiss me."

"He didn't get off scot-free. I've been holding an aspirin between my knees at night, if you get my meaning." Then Krissy kissed the same cheek she'd struck. "You're still my baby sister, and I love you."

This was nothing new. Krissy had always run hot and cold with her. K.C. didn't know what else to say about Ben, so she didn't say anything. "I didn't expect to see you here. Anyone else come?"

"I think I saw Mr. Pierson."

Oh. That was nice. But, "I meant…"

"Mom and Dad?"

"Yeah."

Krissy looked at her feet and didn't answer, which was all the answer K.C. needed.

"Ben's back there in the crowd, though," Krissy said finally. "He doesn't approve of mixing, either, but so what? I made him bring me anyway. He owes me. Oh, and I talked to Kathryn on the phone a couple of days ago. She said she'd try to make it, but you know her. St. Louis is a long ways away, and this is dance lesson season."

From inside, Dwayne knocked on the door's window. *Come on*, he mouthed.

"Gotta go," K.C. said. "Thanks for coming. I'm sorry about Ben."

****

They were all waiting in the kitchen while Dwayne went to show their union cards. It was about a half hour before the show. K.C. had changed into her Bluenotes outfit in the restroom, her clothes identical to theirs. She was determined to wear the Fedora on stage. No one objected.

Freddie was so weak that Syd had to grease his slide for him. He'd need every bit of his remaining strength for the performance. Everyone kept asking him how he felt, if he was really up to doing this.

"Leave me the hell alone," he said. He looked thin and frail in his wheel chair, as if his bones were absorbing his skin and muscles. His eyes were always yellow and bloodshot now. His gums had receded, making his teeth seem longer, with wider spaces between them.

He'd gone further downhill in just the past couple of days, and he was getting cranky. If K.C. was dying she'd be cranky, too.

When Dwayne came back he said, "Damn Piper tried to stiff us again. We bring in his biggest gate in years, maybe ever, and he wants a discount on our fee. Shit."

K.C. adjusted her mouthpiece like usual. She looked out the kitchen door. Dwayne was right. The place was already full, and more were coming in every second.

"That's all for you, kid," Syd said.

"It's for us," she said, but she knew he was right. The Bluenotes were a known quantity in Waterton. She was not. She was a novelty, a sideshow, a freak.

She liked it.

"White Bird," Dwayne said, "step outside with me."

He held the kitchen door open and waited for her in the hall.

"Am I in trouble?" she said.

"The band is. There's stuff going on, and now Freddie's sick. I don't know how long I can hold us together."

"Look at that crowd. They can't wait for us."

"Yeah, I know." He walked her across the hall to a small office, probably Tim Piper's, although he wasn't in at the moment. They sat down on either side of the desk. "Remember at Narlins I told you I had something cooking? Well, I called a guy I know in Chicago."

"About what?"

"Look, White Bird, here's how it is. Except Syd, none of us boys got what it takes to go big time. Used to be I did, but it's not in me anymore. If it wasn't for that goddamned horse, Spits could've done it. But you, you got everything you need."

K.C. felt a tingle that signaled something good. "Thanks. So... what's this about?"

Dwayne removed a sheet of paper from his vest pocket and handed it to her. "I talked to John Hammond about you."

"Who's he?"

"Record producer from Mercury. He's in town for the show."

"To see me?"

"I vouched for you, so don't make me look bad. He can get you some studio work, backing up the big names."

"Studio work? I want to perform on stage."

"Baby steps, White Bird. Lots of folks make their name in the studio. Knock him out like you did me, and you could be headlining in a couple of years."

This was crazy, overwhelming.

Kenny?

There was no answer, just a slight breeze from somewhere, like a kiss on her forehead, like a ruffling of her hair, like a spirit leaving her body, but not before binding the hole in her soul.

She was okay. She was okay.

'Bye, Kenny.

"I don't know what to say."

"I think 'thank you' is customary." Dwayne spoke with an angelic smile, as if he, too, felt the magic in the air.

****

Freddie refused anybody's help as he shuffled out and sat in a chair next to Thump. Dwayne was introducing them one at a time, like he had at Lakeview, again saving K.C. for last. The crowd was restless. She heard anticipation, nervousness, amusement, skepticism, and anger. When she ran on stage, a white girl in a boy's suit and Fedora hat among older black men, some of them even laughed.

Whatever they expected, however much they may have doubted, K.C. knocked them flat on their asses when she took the changes in "Ko-Ko."

That chart set the tone for the rest of the gig. Maybe the night would end up like Lakeview, but while they were on stage they had them by the short and curlies, in the best possible way. The audience became more enthusiastic with each number.

Toward the end, Ironhead approached the mic. "We got something special for you tonight. This next piece, it was written by Mr. Dwayne Hite, for our friend, the late great Spits Bryant. Wasn't nobody like Spits."

Screech turned down the volume on his electric guitar. They started slowly, just him and Ironhead, like a blues ballad.

"'It ain't wrong if it's right,'" Ironhead sang. "'It ain't wrong if it's right. Ain't no darkness where there's light, and it ain't wrong if it's right.'"

Thump and Freddie—who was holding his own, buoyed by the music—came in on the second verse, low cool tones under Ironhead's voice and Screech's guitar. Syd brushed the hi-hat in steady fours.

By the bridge everybody was in. The tempo and volume increased, Leon screaming on his trumpet, Catfish pounding straight rhythm with his left hand and syncopation in his right. Syd swapped the brush for drumsticks and beat the hides till sweat gleamed on his arms. Ironhead switched to tenor sax and Screech cranked up his amp.

Then K.C. made the crowd forget all about "Ko-Ko" with her majestic annihilation of Dwayne's sax line. The number encapsulated everything the band felt about Spits and his death, the highs, the lows, the triumphs, the grief.

K.C. was in the middle of it, and it was *astonishing*.

They must have jammed for more than ten minutes before bringing it on down for the last verse, ending as they started, with Screech strumming softly and Ironhead crooning. He finished *a capella* on a long fadeout, holding middle C for four full measures.

The audience was stunned. For what seemed like an eternity, they said and did nothing, filling Electrical Park with silence. Then the applause started, the cheers and whistles, building to a crescendo louder than the music had been at its height.

K.C. absorbed the adulation like a flower breathing sunshine.

Jesus, she thought. *Jesus, Jesus, Jesus. This is* fun.

She couldn't count the number of bows they took before the crowd noise finally subsided. If this was to be the Bluenotes' last hurrah, they were certainly doing it up in style.

Dwayne walked onstage to thank the audience and bid them goodnight. "We are the Bluenotes," he said into the mic. "We would like to thank you all—"

Before he finished, Freddie did something unexpected and amazing—he got up and hobbled to the mic, nudging Dwayne aside. In a hoarse and dreadfully soft voice he said, "I got a favor to ask."

Dwayne looked at K.C. in confusion. The rest of the band looked at each other with shrugs and raised eyebrows all around. What was he doing?

He needed the microphone stand to hold himself up. "Was a time," he said, "I played the eighty-eights over at Narlins. I loved piano, but..." He held up a hand to show his mangled fingers. "Ain't played one in public in over thirty years. I'm retiring from the Bluenotes tonight, so this here's my swan song, as they say. I was wondering if you'd mind an old man doing one more number. It'd mean a lot to me."

As the audience applauded their approval, Freddie struggled the few steps to the piano. K.C. couldn't hear what he said to Catfish, but she could read Catfish's lips: "Anything you want, brother."

Catfish got up, helped situate Freddie on the bench, and stood aside.

The audience went quiet.

Freddie tentatively lifted his hands to the keys. He flubbed many of the notes, but the tune was still familiar. K.C. knew how much he loved ragtime. He was trying to play Scott Joplin's "Solace," a slow and poignant piece.

Because of its pace, Freddie probably thought he could pull it off, but he was struggling. K.C. felt a little embarrassed for him and a lot sad. She handed her sax to Leon and approached the piano just as Freddie looked like he was about to give up.

"Let me help," she whispered.

"No, K.C., I'm all right. It was just a thought."

"It was a good thought," she said. "Move over."

She sat to his right on the bench.

"You know Joplin?" he said.

"You do the left, I'll do the right."

Even using both hands, Freddie couldn't pull off the oompah bass line that had been written for one hand. K.C. stayed with him, playing at his pace. After a half minute or so, though, he shook his head and lowered his hands to his lap.

"Ain't no use," he said.

"My friend," she said, "you gotta sweat it, you gotta bleed it."

She lifted his right hand to her lips and kissed his fingertips, then placed her own hands over the keys. "Solace," when performed properly, made her weep. She performed it properly, and it made the Bluenotes weep, too, and the audience, and Freddie.

It was such a haunting, beautiful number—"Solace," solace—so appropriate tonight.

She closed her eyes and played by memory, with inspiration and love. As she did, Freddie put his arm around her shoulder, and he kept it there even after the final note.

Chapter 42

THE COUCH WAS MORE comfortable than the bed. Freddie watched from there as Mimms and K.C. finished the paperwork. He had no one else, so she got everything. He especially wanted her to have Mama's piano, so that it would ring out again. Mimms would sell the house for her and help her set up a financial plan.

K.C. had been crying, but she seemed composed now. The sound of her voice comforted him.

It was a sunny day. The windows were open. Freddie drew in a painful breath. The breeze was variable, sometimes bringing in the fumes of the west side factories, sometimes the stench of Roth's.

The band was coming this afternoon. So were Sue, Emmy, and Toad. Audrey and Henry were closing the restaurant for a couple of hours so they could visit, too. Freddie knew why.

He saw angels in the room, which was curious, because he didn't believe in angels. But there they were—Mama and Daddy, Spits, even Nelly—not dancing, not floating on silky wings, just standing around, like they were waiting for a bus.

Freddie heard—or thought he did—a scratching at the

door. It wasn't the first time this morning. He asked K.C. to answer it again. She'd already humored him several times, and no one had been there. This time, though, when she went to the door she said, "Well, aren't you cute?"

She opened the door and a gray striped and speckled cat rushed in. It was Washington. She ran right to Freddie, hopping up on his chest, meowing like crazy. She was hungry. She'd become a sack of skin and bones during her adventure in the wild. Even so, her weight on him was excruciating.

He found the strength to lift his hand. He tried to pet her.

Washington hissed at him.

Freddie chuckled and closed his eyes.

EPILOGUE

SWING DIDN'T DIE WITH bop. Bop didn't die with cool jazz. None of them died with rock and roll. Music diverged and converged and grew, everything part of something else. K.C. played it all. She hadn't yet achieved the nationwide public acclaim Dwayne thought she would, but she was well known in music's highest circles. Everyone wanted her for studio work. She met Dizzy a couple of times. Duke. Satchmo. Even Elvis. She often went out on tour with this orchestra or that, never the headliner for an entire concert, but sometimes the special guest attraction for a number or two.

Until she made it to the top of the bill, she was satisfied being a freelancer. She wasn't held to one schedule or one location. She could come and go as she pleased.

It was a good life. She was thirty, and it was good.

She had an apartment in L.A. now when she wasn't elsewhere. Stationed on the Coast, she rarely returned to Iowa, but when she did, she'd call Dwayne and Syd to chat. The rest of the Bluenotes had scattered to other bands, or given it up, or, in Thump's case, died. Ruthie was still making a go of Narlins. The concerts K.C. played never brought her back to Waterton, although she did find herself in Des Moines and the university towns of Iowa City and Ames a few times over the years. In the fall of '59 she was in Cedar Rapids, where a regional bandleader named Leo Greco invited her to perform on his live Sunday morning television show. It was shot in front of a studio audience.

Years before Dwayne had tailored the jazz version of "It Ain't Wrong If It's Right" for a Chicago up-and-comer, who turned it into a minor hit. K.C. had since adopted his own personal version of it as her theme song, with Dwayne's blessings. He'd written it for Spits, of course, but it always meant Freddie to her. Greco was happy to play it on the show, even though he was an accordionist and it wasn't his usual kind of music. His band welcomed the change of pace.

After the broadcast, the audience was invited to meet the musicians and have their programs autographed. Most sought out Greco and his regulars, who were local celebrities, but a little boy made his way through the crowd to K.C.

"Miss Brown?" he said. He was a cute kid, maybe seven or eight. He held out a pen and two programs.

K.C. was delighted. "You want *my* autograph?"

"Yeah, and my Daddy, too."

"What's your name?"

"Greg, but everyone calls me Egg."

How adorable. K.C. wrote on the first program, *To my best little buddy Greg the Egg, K.C. Brown.* She gave the sheet back to him and took the second program. "And what's your daddy's name?"

Greg the Egg pointed to a couple seated in the third row of the set. "Jack," he said.

K.C. looked up at Greg's parents. The man was wearing horned rimmed glasses and a gray suit he'd probably bought at Sears, his wife a pleasant blue dress with a pearl necklace. The woman was sitting where K.C. might have been, in a different world and a different life.

She smiled and signed the program:

To Jack and family,

God bless.

Kasey Brown.

THE END

CHARACTER NAMES

As is our customary in our novels, many of the characters were named for friends, relatives, and colleagues. These names have no other significance, and our use of them is in no way intended to reflect upon the actual character, behavior, or physical appearance of the real people. In fact, some of them aren't even the same race, sex, or in one case, species. It's just our way of saying hello. They are, in alphabetical order, Rachael Acheson, Albert Baker, Kristin Beerman, Dan Bender, Marlye Janae Bokhoven, Dorothy Brolin, Casey Brown, the late Dr. Robert Buckles, Colleen Bolton, Wayne Clayton, Whitney DeVilbiss, Charles Elliot "Uncle Chuck" Finch, the late Clarence Paul Finch, the late Kenneth Finch, Megan Hahn, the late Elaine Hileman, Richard (Dick) Hileman, Travis (T.J.) Hoing, Lauren Jagger, Ciara Lewis, Hayley Shay McCoy, Jake Miller, Patti Miller, Chris Neuhaus, Ellen Neuhaus, Diksha Ojha, Sue Olive, Thomas Pattee, Tim Pieper, Dave Ralston, Cindy and Greg Reyst, Keith St. Croix, Julie Schoonover, Lindy Helen-Marie Spore, Susan Stickfort, the late Ruthie Taylor, Ashley Thronson, Audrey Wallican-Green, Kathy (Kathryn) Williams, and Sidney Zepnak.

Not to forget our animal friends, Sir Reginald Bear was named for the dearly departed Boston terrier belonging to co-author Dave Hoing's stepdaughter Jovan Hampton. Finally, we would be remiss if we didn't acknowledge that Washington the Cat, although not named for anyone we know, was very much based on Dave's adorable but semi-feral feline, Squeakers.

A NOTE ABOUT THE SETTING

In common with one of our previous novels, *Hammon Falls*, this book is set primarily in the quasi-fictional town of Waterton, Iowa. Waterton bears a strong resemblance to the real city of Waterloo, Iowa. Much scrupulous research of the town and the times went into the writing of *In the Blood*. That said, readers local to the area may be surprised and/or dismayed to find that Waterton's history and place names don't always match Waterloo's. This is by design. *In the Blood* is fiction, and rather than obsessively adhere to the history of a real city, we used what fit the needs of our story and changed or invented what didn't. In other words, we made some of the history fictional, too.

However, locations mentioned that do, or did, exist in Waterloo include Allen Hospital, Iowa Cream Separator Company, the libraries (east and west side), the Paramount and Strand Theaters, the Sixth Street Bridge and its drainage tunnel, Smoky Row, the Starlight Drive-In Theater, Washington Park, West High School, and most of the street names.

Places that do or did exist, but for various reasons were given different names in the book include the Black's Building (here called Block's); the Cedar River (Oak); Electric Park (Electrical Park); John Deere tractor factory (Landon); Rath Packing Company (Roth); and Robinson Crusoe Island (Crusoe Island).

Places that are entirely fictional include Narlins, Dale's Grocery, the Diminished Fifth, Townsend's Rack and Cue, and the infamous Grits 'n' Tits strip club.

There are also some historical "rearrangements" involving real places and events. For instance, while there was a Robinson Crusoe Park in Waterloo, it didn't open until 1959. In the fictional Waterton it already exists in 1948. Also, there was a strike at Rath Packing Company from May to July of 1948, but we have it occurring in a single month, August, of that year.

The level of poverty on the east side has been exaggerated here, as (perhaps) has the overtness of the racism.

AFTERWORD

In this book the character Dwayne Hite loses his partner Jesse "Spits" Bryant to a heroin overdose. To express his grief he writes two versions of a song for Spits, called "It Ain't Wrong If It's Right." One is a blues piece geared for public performance by the Bluenotes, the other a personal ballad written just for himself. In accordance with Dwayne's wishes, we'll keep his personal version personal, but for anyone interested, the lead sheet and piano score for the blues version can be found on our website here:

www.hoingandhileman.net/in-the-blood/

ABOUT THE AUTHORS

Dave Hoing is retired from the University of Northern Iowa Library, where he was a Library Associate in the Special Collections and Archives unit. His tenure there could be measured on a geologic time scale, and he was often mistaken for one of the ancient artifacts.

He lives in Waterloo, Iowa, with his wife Joni, a dog named Tree who he calls Doodle, and a cat named Squeakers who he calls many colorful, and sometimes off color, names. His adult stepchildren, Jon and Jovan, have emigrated to the fantasy land known as California.

In his other life, from which he has not retired, Dave is a member of Science Fiction and Fantasy Writers of America, although he now concentrates on literary and historical fiction. In addition to writing, he pokes his fingers into a lot of other creative pies, dabbling in composing, drawing, painting, and sculpting. Music is his first love, but he concedes that he's better at stringing words together than notes, so there are times when he must tear himself away from one kind of keyboard to work at another. He also enjoys traveling—42 states and 27 countries to date—and collecting books printed before 1800

Roger Hileman divides his time between his two passions, writing and music. But with either, telling a story is the key. Roger prefers weaving tales with engrossing and inspiring landscapes. In *Hammon Falls* and *A Killing Snow,* novels coauthored with Dave Hoing, music plays a large role. Not only do singers, pianists, and fiddle players make repeated appearances, the authors weave musicality into the tale itself, employing lyrical dialogue and a well-cadenced story.

Roger gigs around Iowa with a jazz band and a British-style brass band, and directs a brass choir. He began his writing career as a playwright and screenwriter, but turned to prose when writing with Dave. Roger also enjoys history, especially the family kind, so his ancestors frequently become fodder for his fiction.

In his nonfiction world, Roger works at the University of Iowa College of Public Health. He lives with his wife lu in Iowa City, near most of their three daughters and four grandchildren. He claims to have no pets, but he plays a bass trombone he named Eddie.

If You Enjoyed This Book
Visit

PENMORE PRESS
www.penmorepress.com

All Penmore Press books are available directly through
our website

Dave Hoing & Roger Hileman

Dakota Territory in the 1880s

A KILLING SNOW

by **Dave Hoing & Roger Hileman**

When aspiring journalist Mariel Erickson leaves the civilized comforts of Chicago for Goss Valley, a small town on the Dakota prairie, she isn't prepared for the turmoil she and her husband encounter. As if hostile homesteaders, harsh weather, impoverished Indians, and shady frontier politics aren't bad enough, Mariel soon finds herself embroiled in Goss Valley's first murder case.

The facts of the case appear straightforward. In full view of five witnesses, wagon driver Clyde Hartwig beat an Irish immigrant to death with a baseball bat. The victim was known as a decent and hardworking family man. But Mariel hears rumors of his involvement with homemade bombs and Fenian terrorism. Could that have been Hartwig's motive? On assignment for the town's fledgling newspaper, Mariel must get the killer's side of the story before he's silenced by the hangman's rope.

Hartwig's trial, set for early January, promises to be the biggest event to ever happen in the short history of Goss Valley, and the residents eagerly anticipate a fine spectacle. Little does anyone know that a much larger force is about to descend on the town, revealing how capricious life on the prairie can be.

Order Now: www.PenmorePress.com

"Dave Hoing and Roger Hileman write historical fiction so believable, you'd swear the authors have been alive since before the Civil War...."

— **Carol Kean**, Reviewer, *Perihelion*

Penmore Press

WHAT HAMLET SAID
BY
TERRY MORT

Hollywood in the Thirties: Nazi saboteurs, gangsters running gambling ships, British spies and diplomats, FBI agents, starlets looking for the big break, cheap hustlers on the fringes of the law, local cops – some are friends and some are adversaries, but all are involved somehow with Riley Fitzhugh, a private eye who's wondering whether the death of an English aristocrat really was an accident.

PENMORE PRESS
www.penmorepress.com

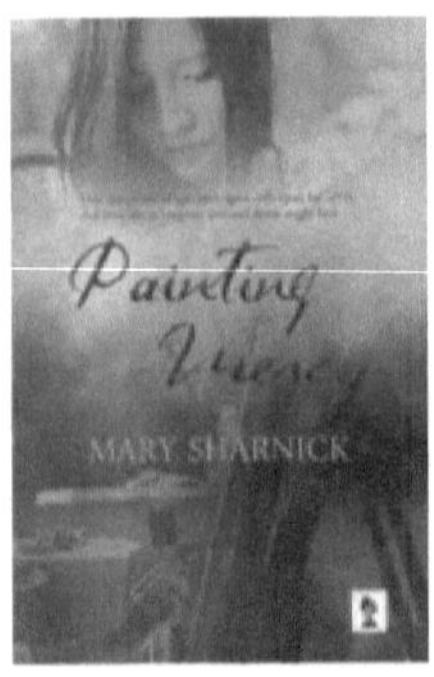

Painting Mercy

By

Mary Sharnick

In Painting Mercy, the sequel to prize-winning Orla's Canvas, Orla, now twenty-four, has been studying and painting in New York City. It is 1975. Saigon has fallen to the Communists, and Vietnamese refugees have been invited to settle in New Orleans by Archbishop Hannan, a former paratrooper and military chaplain in WW II. Orla's childhood friend and forever confidant, Tad Charbonneau, is practicing immigration law in New Orleans, where he mitigates challenging adoption cases involving children, many of them bi-racial, recently airlifted from Saigon and in need of new families. On her way back home for Katie Cowles' wedding and a summer painting in misspelled St. Suplice, Orla reconnects with Tad and contemplates her future. While she anticipates marriage and family with her undisputed soul mate, she discovers upsetting news about Tad's sexuality and learns that her forty-three-year-old mother is pregnant. Adding to her troubling personal revelations, Orla becomes involved in the devastating costs of war for former GI and Katie's brother Denny Cowles and Mercy Cleveland, a Vietnamese orphan who eventually becomes as essential to Orla as her art. Orla once again calls upon her art to make sense of loss and gain. Through her craft she reimagines how Love and Home might look, finally charting a future for herself she had not previously considered possible.

PENMORE PRESS
www.penmorepress.com

Royal Blood

by

Bruce Woods

Historical and fictional characters come together and change the future of Africa forever. Renowned actress Lady Ellen Terry, detective Sherlock Holmes, financier Cecil Rhodes, hunter/naturalist Frederick Courtney Selous, King Lobengula, and a mysterious, undead adventuress named Paulette Monot become chess pieces in the Great Game, which takes the form of Africa's First Matabele War.

"It is unlikely that anyone will ever read this. In fact, if you are perusing these pages, and you're not one of the Kin ("vampires" to the uninitiated), it is almost certain that there's either been some sort of terrible mistake or that I (Miss Paulette Monot) have decided to take a mortal lover. The latter is perhaps more likely. Lucky you."

penmorepress.com

9 781950 586455